A Liberated Woman

A Liberated Woman

Kate Loveday

Book 2 of the "Redwood Series"

1st Edition   published in Australia in 2011 by Scribe's Ink Publishers, SA, Australia.

2nd Edition published in Australia in 2018 by Scribes Ink Publishers, South Australia

National Library of Australia Catalogue-in-Publication entry

A823.4

Loveday, Kate

A Liberated Woman/Kate Loveday

2nd. Edition 2018

ISBN: 978 0 646 55492 1 (pbk)

Typeset in 12/16 Garamond

Scribe's Ink Publishers

Also by Kate Loveday

Inheritance

Black Mountain

The Trophy Wife

Reflections

The Redwood Series

An Independent Woman

A Liberated Woman

An Ambitious Woman

Acknowledgements

I'd like to thank Jacqui Winn for her critiques, editorial suggestions and encouragement, to say nothing of her time spent over numerous cups of coffee.

Thanks to Janice and Roger, Kay and Melissa for their supportive assessments, and to Leonie Bell for loaning me her copy of 'The letters of Rachel Henning' which first sparked my interest in the early days of Bulahdelah.

I thank my publishers for help in getting it all right.

I must also thank Peter for all his listening, support and encouragement.

And last but not least to all my readers and particularly those who have told me they are eagerly awaiting my next book, thank you all.

For Adam & Sophie

Chapter One

Bulahdelah 1893

As Kitty Barron hovered near the front door at Redwoods, she chided herself for feeling like a young girl awaiting the arrival of a new beau. She tried to tell herself she was nervous only because she looked forward to having her daughter home from school. It had nothing to do with the fact that Joy was bringing her friend Lily with her for the holidays. And Lily's father, Rufe Cavanagh. Of course not.

Sixteen years ago Kitty and Rufe shared a passionate love. But sixteen years was a long time. She was now a mature woman in her thirties, with an almost grownup daughter, and the responsibilities of a business that she had run successfully since the loss of her husband, before Joy was born. She was a different woman now, and it was foolish to think Rufe would be the same man she had loved to distraction so long ago. It was lunacy to entertain romantic ideas about him after all these years. Her mood swung from elation to anxiety and back again, as she imagined them spending time together.

As she flitted from room to room, rearranging ornaments and plumping up cushions, she heard wheels crunching up the path, and her heartbeat quickened. Kitty called her mother, Bella, and Mary, who'd been her housekeeper for so long she was now a friend, and hurried to the door and down the steps to greet the arrivals.

'Welcome to Redwoods once again Mr. Cavanagh.'

Rufe held Kitty's hand a fraction longer than necessary as he smiled down at her, his eyes warm. 'Thank you for inviting us, Mrs. Barron.'

Kitty turned to Lily. 'And welcome to you too, Lily. I'm so glad you've come to visit us.'

'Thank you Mrs. Barron. I've been looking forward to coming.'

Rufe looked up towards Bella and Mary, waiting on the verandah. He bounded up the steps. 'Mrs. Morgan, how wonderful to see you again.' Taking Bella's hands, he kissed her on both cheeks.

'Mr. Cavanagh, I am happy to see you again. It's been a long time.'

'It has indeed. Too long.' He turned to Mary. 'You still look the same as ever,' he told her as he took her hand. 'And I hear you and Patrick are married, too. I have so much to catch up on.'

'Yes, a lot's happened since we last saw you, Mr. Cavanagh. Now come inside and I'll show you to your rooms.'

Dinner that night was a cheerful event. The conversation between Rufe and Jack turned to the night they'd been involved in the ambush and capture of an outlaw gang, so many years before.

'How exciting,' Lily exclaimed. 'How did it all happen?'

'And how is it I've never heard about it before?' Joy added. 'Was I here too?'

'No, it was just before you were born,' Bella told her.

'Then I wasn't here either, was I?' Lily asked.

Rufe shook his head. 'No, you hadn't been born, either.'

'Were you living here then?'

'No, Lily, I never lived here.'

'Then how was it you were involved?'

'Mrs. Barron allowed us to use Redwoods as a decoy for the gang, so we were able to catch them red-handed.'

Between them Rufe and Jack recounted the story of how the fake diamond mine had been 'salted' and they had helped the police to round up the gang.

'Was my father here when all this happened?' Joy asked.

Kitty shook her head. 'No. It was after he drowned.'

'Was my mother here?' Lily wanted to know.

'No, it was before we were married,' Rufe told her.

'How did you know Mrs. Barron then?'

'Mrs. Barron and I met when she and Mrs. Morgan first arrived in Australia. And Mr. Barron, too. We all met then.'

Lily frowned. 'But if you were all friends then why haven't you been here since, Father? It's not too far away from Morpeth.'

Kitty felt her cheeks turn pink. They were treading on dangerous ground.

'I'm afraid I've let the pressure of business keep me away,' Rufe said.

Bella fluttered her hands. 'So many questions from you girls! It's now way past bedtime for you, Joy, and I'm sure Lily must be tired after the journey. I'm sure you can be excused if you want to go to your room.'

'Yes Grandma, thank you.'

The girls slid from their chairs, said their good nights, and left the room.

When they had gone, Rufe turned to Kitty. 'What do you plan on doing with your cleared land?'

'I'm not sure. The usual alternative around here is cattle, and that's one solution. But I'm interested to hear about your venture into horses.'

'Certainly. My brother Edward and I started our breeding programme after we bought Riverside, and it's proved very successful. The market for strong, reliable mounts is enormous, both from Cobb & Co and the Army, as well as for stock horses. We can't keep up with the demand; we're getting more orders than we can fill, and I believe Cobb & Co will continue growing.'

'And needing more horses.'

'Exactly.'

'That sounds like an excellent business. Unfortunately I know nothing about breeding horses.'

'I'm happy to help in any way I could, if you decide it's what you want to do. I could help you choose breeding stock, for a start.'

'That's very generous of you. But I'd need to have people who know something about caring for horses, wouldn't I? Do you have any ideas on that, Jack?'

'Patrick worked in a stable as a lad. I don't know how much he knows, but you could talk to him and find out, before making any decisions.'

'That's a good idea. I'll do that.' She turned to Rufe. 'Will you come with me and talk to him? You know what he needs to know.'

'Certainly. And perhaps we can have a look around the property as well. I'd like to see how much cleared land you have.'

'An excellent idea. Perhaps we can make it tomorrow morning?'

Rufe smiled. 'I'm at your service.'

Kitty noticed how his eyes crinkled at the corners in a most attractive way when he smiled. 'Thank you. And now I must let you call it a night. You must be tired after your journey.'

Chapter Two

'What do you want to do first?' Joy asked Lily the next morning.

'Can we go to the horses?'

'Of course. I'm dying to see Dancer again. Come on.'

Joy called out as she ran toward the paddock, and Dancer's head appeared over the gate. She whinnied and tossed her head as she saw Joy coming, and when Joy went in and threw her arms around Dancer's neck, the horse turned her head and nuzzled her.

'Oh Dancer, I've missed you so much,' Joy told her, kissing her on the nose. 'Now come on out and meet Lily. You're going to be good friends.'

Lily patted the horse's neck. 'Yes, she's a beauty all right. I can see why you love her so much.'

Joy's heart swelled with love and pride. 'Let's walk Dancer around for a bit now, shall we? We could go down to the river, and then we'll go for a ride.'

Lily nodded. 'All right.'

They walked side by side toward the river, with Joy leading Dancer.

'Have you always lived at Redwoods?'Lily asked.

'Yes, I was born here. But I love Sydney better. There always seems to be so much happening there, not that we get to see much of it, shut away in school. But I really want to travel and see the rest of the world.'

'It'd be exciting to travel all over the world, wouldn't it? I'd like to do that, too. '

'I'd like to go to England and meet my father's family.' Joy sighed. 'But I don't know when that's ever likely to happen.'

'Why not?'

'I once overheard Mother and Grandma talking. Grandma asked if she had considered sending me somewhere else to school, perhaps to England, and Mother said if Father was still here, he'd have different ideas, but she'd decided I should stay at the local school for the first few years.'

Lily's eyes widened. 'What happened to your father?'

'He drowned, before I was born.'

'How awful. I don't know what I'd do if I ever lost Father.' She paused. 'But then I haven't got a mother, and that must be good too. Well, I do have a mother somewhere, but I don't remember her. I was only three when she left.'

'Do you wish she'd come back?'

'I did when I was younger. But now I don't really care.'

'Perhaps your father will marry again, and then you'd have a new mother.'

Lily shook her head. 'She wouldn't be my real mother, would she? And Father won't marry again. He says he's content with just the two of us. He says we're happy the way we are.' Lily leant over and patted Dancer. 'Come on; let's give Dancer a bit of a run down to the river. Last one there's a rotten egg!' Away she sprinted.

Kitty rose early, and after breakfast she decided to take a walk. Going down to the river she stood on the bank, looking out over the water. The early mist was lifting. A faint breeze stirred its white wisps, coaxing them to melt away, revealing the smooth surface of the water below. On this side it reflected the blue sky and a few white clouds, while on the other side it mirrored the deep green of the trees lining the riverbank.

On this side of the river the property around her was still well timbered, in contrast to much of the rest of the estate, where the trees had fallen prey to the building industry's insatiable lust for the cedar and hardwoods that had been so plentiful when she first arrived at Redwoods, as a bride. Now, as Kitty looked around at the tall trees, she pondered the next direction Redwoods must take. The saleable timber was fast becoming depleted. The time had come to make a decision on its future. Was horse breeding the way to go?

And what of Rufe? She wondered, for what seemed like the hundredth time, if she and Rufe had changed too much to be able to resume the relationship begun so many years ago. He still had the power to quicken her pulses when they were together, but was it the same for him? And was that enough? Life was about more than passion. How did he feel? His manner toward her so far had been friendly, but no more so than with the others. Had seeing her here at Redwoods, surrounded by her family, and with Joy and Lily here, made him realise she was no longer the young woman he had fallen in love with all those years ago?

Kitty looked up to see Rufe striding down the path toward her.

'Good morning, Kitty,' he called out. 'I hope you slept well.'

Kitty was transported back to that other morning, sixteen years ago, when he had asked her the same question. That had been after their night of lovemaking, and she felt awkward. Was he remembering it too?

'Quite well, thank you. I hope you did too.'

'Not as well as I would have liked, but we won't go into that now. You promised me an extended tour today, so let's go saddle our horses and be about it, shall we?'

Taking her arm he turned her around and marched her back along the path.

'So what are our children up to today? Or are they still in bed?'

'No, they finished breakfast early, and they've left to go riding.'

'Then we have the morning to ourselves, so let's go.'

They spent he rest of the morning riding around Redwoods, looking at how much land had been cleared. Along the way they visited the mill, and talked to the timber cutters. Rufe resumed his acquaintance with Patrick, saying it felt like old times again.

After lunch Lily demanded that Rufe accompany her and Joy on a trip into Bulahdelah town. He agreed readily enough, and Kitty understood that Lily was the most important thing in his life. It seemed as if he would always put his daughter first, and Kitty couldn't argue with that. As the day wore on she became even surer he no longer felt the way he used to feel about her. They would remain friends, but no more. She had been a fool to think it might be otherwise. Her dreaming had been for nothing.

After dinner that night Bella excused herself early, confessing to a headache, and Jack retired with her, leaving Kitty and Rufe alone.

'There's a bright moon tonight, do you feel like a stroll in the garden before bed?' Rufe asked.

'Yes, I'd like that.'

Outside, Rufe moved close beside her as they stood on the verandah looking out across the garden, which was bathed in the silvery light from the full moon hanging in the clear, starry sky. Kitty's heart beat a little faster at the feel of Rufe so close.

'What a wonderful night. It's so clear you can see right down to the river. Do you feel like walking down there?'

'Yes.'

As they walked along the path in silence, Rufe felt for Kitty's hand and took it in his own. His touch roused a longing in her as she remembered how his hands caressed her, all those years ago.

'It's been a long time since we parted and yet, now we're here together, I feel as if it's only days ago,' Rufe told her, his voice husky.

Kitty's heart thudded. 'I know what you mean, it all comes flooding back. I was so stupid then, I…'

'No.' Rufe shook his head. 'We were both at fault, but we paid dearly for our mistakes. At least, I know I did.'

'So did I. Very dearly.'

He stopped and turned her toward him. The next moment his arms were around her, and his lips found hers. Tenderly at first, then with a mounting passion that caused the blood to pulse through her veins. She wrapped her arms around his neck and pulled him closer, and there they stayed, locked in embrace, until, panting, he lifted his head.

'Oh, my love, the magic hasn't gone,' Rufe whispered. 'I hope it hasn't for you.'

'No, quite the opposite.'

'Then let's go back to the house,' he said urgently, holding her tight against him.

He released his hold on her just enough to turn her around, and with his arm around her waist he guided her back along the path and up the steps to the verandah.

As they reached the door it opened and Lily burst out with Joy close behind her. Lily stopped short when she saw them and looked from one to the other, and then back to back to Rufe.

Rufe dropped his arm from around Kitty's waist.

Kitty took a step away from him, and her hand flew to her mouth as she felt a rush of blood to her cheeks.

'What are you doing, Lily?' Rufe asked. 'Where are you going at this time of night?'

'It's not late, and we're just going for a walk.' Lily frowned, staring at Kitty. 'What are you and Mrs. Barron doing out here?'

Rufe answered calmly. 'We've been enjoying a walk, so I suppose I must say that you can do the same as it's such a lovely night. But don't go beyond sight of the house. He stood aside to let them pass. 'Off you go then. But don't be too long. Mrs. Barron and I are going to have a nightcap. Come in to the drawing room to say goodnight when you come back.'

Lily scowled at Kitty, who put out her hand and touched Joy briefly on the arm as she passed. 'Don't take Lily far, it's getting late. I'll see you when you come back.'

'Yes, Mother.'

The girls swept down the steps and raced off along the path. Rufe held the door open for Kitty and followed her into the drawing room.

'Oh dear,' Kitty turned to him. 'I'm afraid we've upset Lily.'

'Nonsense. She saw nothing to upset her. I simply escorted you up the steps.'

'Do you think she believed that?'

Rufe crossed the room and splashed brandy into two glasses. 'If it comes up, which I doubt, I'll make sure she understands it.' He handed her one of the drinks with a smile. 'Now sit down, and we'll have our nightcap very circumspectly, until our children are safely in bed.'

As Kitty sipped her drink, she worried that Lily had seen Rufe's arm around her, and that it had upset her. Whatever would Lily think if she found out about their previous relationship? Or if they were to resume it? From the look on Lily's face, Kitty didn't believe she'd be happy about it. For that matter, how would Joy feel? Oh dear, it was all so difficult. Twisting the glass in her fingers, she watched the light reflecting from the crystal goblet.

'Kitty. What's the matter?'

'I'm concerned at what the girls must be thinking.'

'We don't have to worry about what they're thinking. We're their parents, and we don't need their approval for our actions.'

'That's all very well, but I don't want either of them to be upset.'

'There's nothing for them to be upset about.'

'But if they hadn't come out just then…'

'If they hadn't come out just then you and I would now be discussing our feelings for each other, instead of our children's feelings, and I would be much happier.'

'But...'

He reached across and touched her hand. 'No buts. When they've gone to bed we can talk. For now we just drink our nightcap.'

'Very well.'

They had only minutes to wait before the front door opened and closed, and the girls entered the room.

'Did you enjoy your moonlight walk?' Rufe asked.

'Yes,' Joy replied, 'we went down to the river. It looks beautiful at night. All silvery.'

'You looked as if you'd enjoyed *your* walk,' Lily added. 'Did you go as far as the river?'

'Not quite,' Rufe answered. 'And now it's time you were in bed, young lady.'

'Would you like a glass of milk first?' Kitty asked.

'Yes please,' Joy replied. 'And some cake, too. How about you Lily?'

Lily hesitated before nodding. 'Yes please.'

'No, don't you bother, Mother,' Joy added, as Kitty started to rise. 'We'll go down to the kitchen and I'll get it. Then we'll go to bed. Come on Lily.'

When they had gone, Kitty and Rufe sipped their drinks until they heard them go into Joy's bedroom.

After listening for a few minutes Rufe stood and came to stand in front of Kitty. Smiling down at her, he reached out his hands.

'Come with me.'

Kitty shook her head. 'No Rufe, I can't.'

His smile faded. 'You don't want to?'

'It's not that. It's the girls. Lily looked daggers at me when she saw you had your arm around me.'

'Lily is safely in bed by now, and Joy too.'

'But what if they come out for something? What if they were to discover us together?'

'Kitty darling, we can't have our lives dictated to by our children.'

'It would be too sudden for them – they're still so young – they wouldn't understand.'

Rufe dropped her hands and took a step back. His lips twisted wryly. 'I see the magic hasn't come back for you.'

'It's not that.' She hesitated. How to make him understand? 'When we were outside I felt all the old feelings, but now I'm too concerned about how the girls would feel. They'd both be shocked. We need to take more time.'

'And what about how I feel?' He frowned down at her. 'Doesn't that count?'

'Of course it counts.' She bit her lip. 'But we need to let them get used to the idea first, to accept that we both care for each other. Surely you can see that.'

'I can see that you put their feelings before mine.' His voice hardened. 'If we were together, is that how it would always be?'

Kitty shook her head, a ball of misery forming inside her. 'No, of course not. But we have to let them become accustomed to the idea first. We need to let them see, gradually, that we care for each other.'

Rufe narrowed his eyes as he looked down at her. 'So you want me to woo you, do you? To court you like some lovesick young swain. Don't you think we're a bit old to be playing such games?'

'Is that what love is to you? A game?'

'You're twisting my words, Kitty. That's not what I meant.' He turned toward the door. 'All right. I'll play it your way. I'll woo you. But don't try my patience too far.'

With that he turned and strode to the door. And slammed it behind him as he left.

Chapter Three

Rufe greeted them all with a smile when he joined them for breakfast.

'And what do you girls have planned for today?' he asked, as he sat at the table with his plate.

'We're going riding,' Lily replied.

'Again? You'll be wearing your horses out,' he joked. 'Do you have anything left to see?'

'Oh yes. Heaps,' replied Joy.

'In that case, perhaps you'd like to stay another two or three days. Mrs. Barron and I have some business to attend to that will take a while longer. Don't we, Mrs. Barron?'

Kitty swallowed her surprise. 'Yes, we do.'

'Does that mean you've decided to go ahead with the horses?' Bella asked.

'It sounds like a good business,' Kitty told her, 'but I need to satisfy myself that it will be as profitable as it seems. Mr. Cavanagh has a wealth of information that he's willing to share with us.'

'That's all right with us, isn't it Lily?' Joy asked her friend, as she folded her napkin and placed it on the table.

'Yes, if we can ride every day.'

'We can. May we be excused, Mother?'

'Yes, run along. Have a good day.'

Bella turned to Kitty. 'I didn't realise you had made a decision about horses already. You must have had quite a long discussion last night.'

'Not as long as I would have liked, but we covered enough ground to realise there's much more to discuss,' Rufe told her. 'That's correct, isn't it Kitty?'

'Yes, that's so.'

Bella pushed back her chair. 'Well, I have some things to discuss with Mary, so I'll leave you to continue with your planning.'

When Bella left, Rufe smiled at Kitty. 'So now we have time to continue where we left off last night. Time for me to woo you.'

Kitty bit her lip. 'Rufe, I didn't mean....'

'It's all right. I'm happy to take the time for us to become re-acquainted.' He held his hand out to her, his gaze searching her face. 'After all, it has been a long time.'

'Yes, it has.' As she placed her hand in his she knew without doubt that she still loved him, but she remained resolute. 'But as the girls are in the house, I think we must observe the proprieties.'

Rufe shook his head, a wry smile twisting his lips. 'All right, my love. We'll do it your way. For these three days.'

Two days later Rufe opened the door into the drawing room, lured by the sound of the piano.

Lily sat at the piano, playing. She stopped as he entered and dropped her hands in her lap, but didn't turn around

'Hello, Lily. I thought you'd still be out riding with Joy. Don't tell me you came back early to keep up your piano practice?'

'Not really. I just wanted to be alone for a while.'

'Then I'm sorry to intrude. I'll leave you…'

'No, don't go,' she said quickly. She still faced the piano, her back stiff and straight. 'I suppose you came in early hoping to find Mrs. Barron here alone.'

'What do you mean by that?'

Lily swung around to face him, her face flushed and her lips set in a straight line.

'You can't see enough of her, can you? And I suppose you thought she'd be here alone at this time of the day.'

Rufe's eyes narrowed. 'What are you getting at, Lily?'

'I've seen the way you run after her. Paying her attention, always opening doors for her and holding out her chair, and helping her up onto her horse. Always seeing she's got everything she wants.'

'What are you saying Lily. That I shouldn't be courteous to our hostess?'

'It's more than courteous, isn't it?' Her voice rose. 'Always running after her, you're acting like some stupid schoolboy with her.'

Even through his anger Rufe felt his stomach knot as he remembered Kitty's worries. 'Mrs. Barron and I are old friends,' he replied in a quiet voice, 'and you and I are staying in her home. At your request, I might remind you.'

'I didn't ask you to come too. You and Mrs. Barron arranged that bit.'

'I didn't hear you make any complaints about me accompanying you, before we came. In fact, I seem to remember you expressing your delight about it.'

Lily twisted her hands together. 'I hadn't seen you together then. Now I see the way you look at each other. I think you must've been more than friends before.' She glared at him. 'Were you in love with her then?'

'Don't be ridiculous.'

'You knew her when you were married to my mother, didn't you? Maybe that's why she left us. Maybe it was because she knew you didn't love her, because you loved somebody else.'

'Now you *are* being ridiculous. I never saw Mrs. Barron after your mother and I married.'

'Are you sure?'

'I give you my word I hadn't seen Mrs. Barron after your mother and I married, until I saw her again at your school.'

'Are you going to marry her now?'

Rufe turned sharply and walked to the window. He stood for a moment before taking a deep breath and turning around. 'What I decide to do in my life is not your business, Lily. However, should Mrs. Barron and I ever decide to take such a step, you'll be the first person I tell, believe me.'

Lily's eyes narrowed. 'That means you're thinking about it.' She slid from the piano stool. 'You don't care about *me* anymore,' she flung at him over her shoulder as she crossed the room. She slammed the door behind her.

Kitty closed the door as she entered the room seconds later.

'Whatever's the matter with Lily? She just rushed past me in the hall, crying. I tried to ask her what was wrong, but she just said, 'don't talk to me.'

Rufe's face wore a worried frown. 'I'm sorry about that. I'm afraid she's a bit upset.'

'I'd say she's very upset. What is it about?'

'She asked...that is...she wanted to know...'

'It's about us, isn't it? She's guessed we have feelings for each other, and she's upset about it. I'm right, aren't I?'

'Well...yes. She's probably a bit fearful of any change in relations between us, but she'll get over it.'

Kitty felt a jolt of dismay. 'What happened?'

'She wanted to know if we're more than just friends.' He paused, grimacing. 'In fact, she asked if I'm going to marry you.'

Kitty's stomach clenched. Over the last few days she had relaxed, as she believed Rufe wasn't acting in an overly attentive manner, but now all her worries flooded back. Lily sensed there was something between them, and the shock of believing Rufe cared too much for Kitty distressed her. It was just too much for Lily to accept a woman in Rufe's life.

'Oh Rufe,' Kitty shook her head, 'I don't want to upset her. If she doesn't accept me now, it could well be the cause of a major problem for us in the future. That is – if we have a future together.'

Rufe narrowed his eyes. 'Don't you believe we have?'

'I don't know what to believe any more. I thought so, but if it's to be at the expense of your relationship with your daughter – and I don't know how Joy will take it either – then I just don't know if it's right or not.'

'We can't let our children dictate our lives.'

'I think we need to give them more time to become accustomed to the idea. After all, Lily's had you to herself for almost as long as she can remember. She needs time to accept the idea of another woman in your life. We have to give her time to accept me. At the moment she blames me for stealing your affections. That's how she sees it, and she probably hates me. It's no way to start a family relationship.'

Rufe ran his fingers through his hair. 'I'd like to stay here longer, but I really can't. I have a meeting with George Reid, the Premier, down in Sydney next week. It's very important. I can't cancel it.'

'I understand. Perhaps it's for the best. The girls will be returning to school soon. Let's give them a bit of breathing space.'

'But I might be in Sydney for some time, for meetings. It'll be several weeks, at least, before I can come here again. I'd hoped we could settle our future before I leave.'

'If we rush Lily now, she may well hate me forever.'

'Very well. We'll leave tomorrow, as planned, with our future still unsettled. It's not what I want, but I suppose I must accept it.' With that Rufe, his face bleak, strode to the door and left the room without another word.

Kitty stared at the door, feeling shattered.

That night Kitty toyed with her dinner, trying to pretend nothing was wrong, and she was relieved when Jack began to question Rufe about the push for Federation.

'You spend a lot of time in Sydney, so you must be privy to more information than we are up here. So, what's your opinion of the political situation at the moment?'

'Change is coming, there's no doubt about it,' Rufe replied. 'The question is, which way are we to jump?'

'There's so much talking about one great national government for all of Australia, as Sir Henry Parkes proposed. It's all we read about in the papers,' Bella said. 'Do you think we'll become a Federation?'

'I'm certain of it. The query is, when?'

'Will it be a good thing for us, do you think?' Jack asked.

'Yes, I do. At the moment each of the colonies has its own set of laws, of rules and regulations, even different rail gauges. For one thing, it makes trade between the colonies difficult and expensive.'

'But how would it work?' asked Bella. 'Would there be just one government? I thought I read that each colony would still have its own government.'

'Ah, there's the uncertainty. Parkes proposed that each colony keep its own separate government, parliament, and Governor, with one Federal government overseeing it all. And that's what was favoured at the National Convention in 1891. But what's being proposed now is one Federal government with small local governments.'

'But not everyone's in favour of Federation, are they?' asked Jack.

'No. Definitely not. Some of the colonies see it as annexing their territory, although in reality it would be a partnership between the colonies. In each colony there are people who want things left as they are, and others who don't.'

Jack nodded. 'You'll never get everyone to agree. Everyone sees things from their own point of view.'

'There must be so many things to consider, apart from trade,' Kitty said.

'There are countless political, financial and commercial questions to be examined, and satisfactory answers found, before a final Bill can even be considered.'

'And how long do you think all this is going to take?'

Rufe shook his head. 'God only knows. There's so much bickering, it's hard to imagine it ever being decided. But we have a strong leader in Reid. If he and Turner in Victoria can come to an agreement, it'll be a good start and we'll have a chance of unity.'

'Do you think they will?'

'I should have a better idea in the next few weeks. Reid has arranged a series of meetings with several of the different groups, and I'll be sitting with him.'

'So that's why you have to be in Sydney next week?'

'Yes. I said I have a meeting, but, in fact, there'll be many meetings, spread over several weeks.'

'Yes. I see.'

As Kitty sat digesting this information she felt that the question of their relationship must seem trivial, in comparison to the momentous events in other areas of Rufe's life at the moment.

Chapter Four

Kitty's heart was heavy as she waved goodbye to Rufe and Lily. There had been no chance of a private word with him. Lily rose before anyone else in the house, and never let her father out of her sight since breakfast.

After they had gone, Kitty kept busy at her desk, trying to overcome feeling letdown. Rufe had come and gone, and her life remained the same. It seemed she was destined not to find happiness with Rufe.

A few days later Mary handed Kitty a letter post marked from England.

'And there's one here for Joy, too,' she said.

Kitty recognised the handwriting, and her lips tightened. 'It's from Lady Barron. And it's not Joy's birthday, so I think I know what this will be about. Joy was less than a year old when I received the first letter from Lady Barron. She told me that, as Joy is William's daughter, and part of the Barron family, she should be brought to England. *"So she could be brought up in a manner befitting a family member."* I replied then that I had no intention of sending my daughter to England. However, I knew then I that hadn't heard the last of Lady Barron and her demands, and I've had several letters since. One even offered me a home in England as well.' She laughed grimly. 'That would have been hard for her.' Her face softened. 'However, I did receive a very warm letter from William's father offering me the same, or any help I might need. His would have been genuine concern.'

'He was always a gentleman.'

'Yes, he was. But this will be more harassment to send Joy to England. Well, she's not going. I've made that plain to the old dragon before, and I haven't changed my mind. You'd better take Joy's letter in to her,' she added, as she tore open her envelope.

No sooner had she finished reading, and put the letter down on her desk, than Joy bounded into the room, letter in hand.

'Oh Mother, how exciting! Grandmother Barron is going to arrange for me to be presented at Court. Just imagine. Me. Being presented to Queen Victoria. Can you imagine it? And to have a season in London. Oh Mother, it's like a dream come true. I can hardly believe it.'

'Then don't, because it's not going to happen.'

Joy's face fell. 'What do you mean? It's here in the letter. Grandmother's arranging it all. I'm to go to Bournbridge Hall first, to meet all the family, and to learn all about the proper procedure and how to act at Court and…'

'Joy, you're not going. You're too young and you're going back to school to finish your education.'

'But Mother…'

'No. It's quite out of the question. Besides, you'd hate being in England. You've no idea what life is like there.'

'I would not hate it. I wouldn't. I want to go.'

'I'm afraid you can't. You have to trust me in this, Joy. You don't belong in England, you belong here at Redwoods. It's your home, your heritage.'

'I don't want to stay at Redwoods.' Joy stamped her foot, tears in her eyes. 'I want to go to England. *That's* my heritage. It was my father's home. It's *his* family. *My* family. I want to meet them. I want to go!'

Kitty was dismayed. 'Joy, I'm sorry, but it's quite out of the question.'

'I'm going to go.' Joy's body shook. 'You can't stop me. I'm going.' With that she spun around and raced from the room, slamming the door behind her.

Kitty sat back in her chair, her heart pumping. She took several deep breaths and clasped her hands tightly, trying to still their trembling. Never had she seen Joy behave in such a manner. As she sat there trying to regain her composure the door opened, and Bella came into the room, concern on her normally calm face.

'Whatever was that all about?'

Kitty held back threatening tears as she shook her head. 'It's Lady Barron again. She's written directly to Joy this time as well, filling her head with ideas of grandeur. She wants to present her at Court and give her a London Season.'

'I see. And she wants to go, I presume?'

'Oh yes. She's all full of it.'

'Kitty,' her mother responded gently, 'you had your season.'

'Yes, and a lot of pomposity it was, with everyone trying to outdo everyone else.'

'You must remember that the Barrons are an old family. It's their tradition. And she is William's daughter.'

'But she's an Australian, as we all are now, and it's not our tradition. This is where she belongs, here at Redwoods. It's what I've strived for all these years, to keep Redwoods safe for her, so she'll always be secure and happy, so she never has to suffer as we did. This is her home. She doesn't need all their false grandeur.'

'I believe you should give it a lot of thought. Try to see their point of view. She is their grandchild. It's only natural they want to get to know her. And to introduce her into Society, so she can have the opportunities her position as a Barron can give her.'

'And what opportunities are they? To meet a lot of upper crust snobs who look down on everyone else. They'll try to turn her into one of them.'

'Are you afraid they'll succeed?' Bella twisted the beads at her throat. 'Don't you think that her upbringing here will win out? Oh, she may be taken by all the fashion and glamour for a while, but I think that, in the end, she'll be able to separate what's false from what's genuine. I think you'll find that she'll make her own assessments, and decide what's right for her.'

Kitty bit her lip. 'So you think I should let her go?'

'It is for you to decide. You and Joy. But I do believe you should consider all aspects. And look at it from her point of view as well. If she wants to meet her father's family then she'll do so sometime. You won't be able to prevent it. And the prospect of being presented at Court is exciting to her.'

'But she's too young.'

'At the moment, yes. But if she were to finish her year at school, perhaps if she went even to half-year, and then go, she'd be seventeen. Not too young then.'

'But she'd be away for over a year.'

'Would you consider going with her?'

'No.' Kitty shook her head. 'I have no desire to see England again. And as for Lady Barron...' Her voice trailed off as she remembered the day she married William. Remembered how his mother made it plain she would not be welcome in their home, because her father had taken his own life.

'She didn't think I was good enough for William, because of Father's misfortune. She made it plain on our wedding day that she wouldn't welcome me at Bournbridge Hall, and I told her then that I'd never set foot there, and I won't. She's a domineering woman, and I believe she was the cause of many of William's faults. I hate to think of Joy being under her influence.'

'That was a long time ago, Kitty. She may have mellowed. And you always liked Sir Alexander.'

'Yes, William's father is a fine man. But I still don't want Joy to go. Why can't she be content to stay here, where she belongs? How can she want to leave this? This is her home.' Kitty clenched her fists. 'If she only knew what it cost me to keep it safe for her…' her voice trailed off as she remembered the morning she rejected Rufe's marriage proposal, because of her fears for Joy's future security.

Bella rose from her chair. 'You can't expect her to be grateful for what you did to keep Redwoods secure for her. That was a decision you made when she was a baby. This is for you to decide now. But I do think you should consider carefully before making a final decision.'

Joy lay face down on her bed, tears starting every time she thought about the letter from her grandmother. She'd never wanted anything as much as she wanted to go to England. Not even when she was waiting for her first horse. She sniffed as she heard a tap on the door, and rolled over. 'Who is it?' she called, her voice quavering.

'It's Grandma. Can I come in?'

'Yes.' She sat up and swung her legs to the floor, sitting on the edge of the bed and wiping her eyes.

Grandma came in and sat beside her. She reached over and stroked her hair. 'Poor Joy, I hear you've had an upset with your mother. Do you want to talk about it?'

Joy couldn't hold back the tears. 'Oh Grandma, it's so unfair. My grandmother wants me to go to England. She's arranging for me to be presented at Court, and to have a Season in London. And I'd get to meet her and Grandfather, and all my English cousins, and to see London and…and everything.' She gulped. 'And Mother says I can't go.' Joy tried to stop her tears, but they kept coming. 'How can Mother be so cruel?'

Grandma put her arms around her. 'There, there, don't cry. She's not trying to hurt you, you know. She's only doing what she believes is best for you.'

'But it's not best for me. I want to go so much. I want to see London. I want to meet my father's family. After all, they're my family too, aren't they? And they live in a big house in Buckinghamshire, and it'd be so exciting to be presented to Queen Victoria and…'she sniffed, 'I want to go.' She groped for her handkerchief and blew her nose.

'Of course you want to go, my dear. It's only natural for you to want it. But Mother's worried about you going to the other side of the world without her.'

'She could come too.'

'There are reasons why she won't do that.'

'Then that's no reason for her to stop me. She's just being mean.'

'No, dear, she's not. I know you don't want to hear this, but you're still very young to be away from home for so long. After all, you wouldn't be presented until you are eighteen.'

'But Grandmother said I'd need to be over there beforehand, to learn how to curtsey, and walk properly, and to learn how to behave in polite society.'

Grandma smiled at her as she sat back. 'Do you think she really believes you're a little savage, growing up here in the colonies?'

Joy managed a smile. 'It almost sounds like it when you put it that way, doesn't it? But I suppose she means there's a lot to learn about deportment, and clothes and things. I suppose they dress and act a bit differently over there.'

'Oh yes. Everything is much more formal. You'd find it vastly different to life here.'

'That's what I want to *see*. There's a whole big world out there, and I want to see it. I'm sick of living here. I want to see other places, exciting places. It's so boring here.'

'And do you find Sydney boring, when you're at school?'

'No, I love Sydney. But I don't get to see it very much when I'm at school. We have excursions and things, and we're taken to the galleries and places, but it's not enough. We always have one of the mistresses with us, and we don't have the chance to go places and see things we want to see.'

Grandma's eyebrows rose. 'And do you think you'd be unchaperoned in England?'

'Well...no...I don't suppose so.'

'Believe me, Joy, your grandparents would make sure you were supervised very carefully. As your mother was.'

'Yes, I suppose so, but I wouldn't care, it would be so exciting just to be there, to see England. And to actually have a Season there. Can you imagine it?'

Grandma nodded. 'Oh yes. Remember, I grew up there, as your mother did. I remember my Season well. It can be quite stifling at times, believe me.'

'Things would have been different when you were a girl. But we're in modern times now, Grandma. It wouldn't be as strict now as it was when you were a girl, or even when Mother was young.'

'I'm not so sure about that.' Bella stood up and smoothed her skirts. 'Try not to take it too hard. Perhaps if you wait a few days, and then talk to Mother again, calmly, and in a grown up manner, with no tears or tantrums,' she warned, 'you could discuss it with her again. Who knows, you may be able to reach a compromise.'

Joy sighed as Grandma left her alone. She did feel better, but the longing was still there. Grandma was right. She shouldn't have behaved as she did. She felt ashamed when she remembered how she shouted at her mother. But she did want to go so much. She had never wanted anything in her life as badly. Not even when she wanted Dancer for her own. There must be some way she could make her mother change her mind. But Grandma was right, she needed to keep quiet about it for a while, and then speak to Mother again.

Chapter Five

Lily was angry with her father. She blamed him for spoiling her holiday with Joy. All the way back to Morpeth she'd thought about him and Mrs. Barron together. She simmered with resentment at the woman who was coming between them. Father always said they were happy the way they were, but once he met up with *her* again, he'd ignored her, and spent all his time with her. Just how close had the two of them been before? Perhaps he'd been in love with her then. She clenched her hands as anger and jealousy flooded through her. That woman was a threat to her own relationship with Father, whom she loved more than anyone else in the world.

The more she brooded about it, the more Lily became convinced that her mother, Irene, had left them because of Mrs. Barron. Oh yes, he'd told her he hadn't seen her after he married Irene, but was that true? Lily decided Mrs. Barron was the cause of making her mother unhappy, and that was why she'd left them. It added fuel to the fire of animosity growing within her.

Realising Father became cross with her whenever she mentioned anything bad about Mrs. Barron. She kept it all shut up inside, and pretended she'd forgotten her anger.

She stood by Rufe's bed, watching as he packed his bag to leave for Sydney. 'How long do you think you'll be gone this time?' she asked.

'I'm afraid it's going to be several weeks, I've a lot of meetings to attend. You'll be back at school by then, but I'll see you at school before I come back here, and we'll have a day together. Think about what you'd like to do on a Sunday in Sydney. Maybe lunch somewhere nice? Or perhaps we could go out on the water. What do you think?'

'I'll think about it,' she told him, pleased at the idea of having him all to herself.

'Perhaps you'd like Joy to come too?'

'Oh, no. Just the two of us.'

'I'm ready to go now.' He closed his bag, turned and put his arms around her, and hugged her. 'You take care while I'm away. I love you very much, you know.'

Lily swallowed a lump in her throat as she hugged him fiercely. 'I know,' she whispered, 'and I'll miss you.'

'I'll miss you too. Now come and wave me goodbye.'

Lily followed him to the front door and out onto the verandah. Uncle Edward already sat on the driver's seat of the trap, ready to take him to the wharf, where he would board the steamer to Sydney. As Father climbed up into the passenger seat Aunt Erin and her cousin David came out, and they all stood waving as the trap set off down the driveway.

As Lily turned to go inside David touched her arm. 'Hey, tadpole, want to come and help me with the horses?' he asked.

His dark eyes twinkled as he gazed down at her, and Lily thought again how much David looked like a younger version of her father, lean, tanned, clean shaven, with dark curly hair that he said was the bane of his life, and eyes that seemed always close to laughter. When he left boarding school in Sydney, at sixteen, he chose to work here with his father and uncle, learning all about breeding horses. They were his passion.

Normally Lily loved to help him. He was fun to be with, he laughed a lot and enjoyed life, and she liked being with the horses. But today she didn't want his cheery company.

'No thanks, I have some things to do.'

'Okay, see you later.' He bounded down the steps.

Lily went to her room and shut the door. She had to try and think how to come between Father and Mrs. Barron.

Kitty slit the envelope with trembling fingers. She recognised the handwriting. The last letter she received from Rufe had been after they quarrelled so long ago, and he rushed away. It delivered the crushing blow that he had married Irene. What would this one say? It began, 'My dearest Kitty'. She dropped her gaze to the end. It was signed, 'affectionately yours, Rufe Cavanagh.'

She let go the breath she was holding. Dropping into a chair, she read the letter. Rufe told her he was caught up in a whirlwind of meetings that, he regretted, prevented him from taking the time necessary to come and visit her, as he wished to do. She read on with a sinking heart.

'However', it occurs to me that in two weeks time our daughters will be returning to their school, and I am wondering if you plan to escort Joy back to Sydney yourself? If so, could you see your way clear to spending a few days here in Sydney? There is an important matter that I wish to discuss with you, and I think that, free from the interruptions and distractions of our children, we would have the chance to resolve some important issues.

I sincerely hope you will be able to make this trip, as I believe it is important to both of us to continue the discussion of these important matters as soon as possible.

I remain,
Affectionately yours,
Rufe Cavanagh

Kitty folded the letter and dropped it on the desk. Going to the window she stared out. What to do, what to do? Impulsively she turned and left the room. Walking down to the river, she sat on the stump where she went whenever she had a big problem to mull over. She loved to sit there, gazing out over the water, so still today that it reflected the trees on the bank opposite. She remembered the day William drowned. Then it had been wild and turbulent, and it had dragged him to his death when he had been foolish enough to enter the water while trying to save a load of cedar on the punt tied up there.

Kitty sighed as a patchwork of memories floated through her mind. Joy's birth, Bella and Jack's marriage. Her decision to manage Redwoods herself with Jack's help in spite of opposition from the bank manager and many of the men hereabouts. The building of the mill, and the eventual success of the business. The wonderful, passionate night of love she spent with Rufe. And her refusal of his marriage proposal because she feared losing control of Redwoods, which was Joy's inheritance.

Yes, everything she had done since William died had been to keep Redwoods secure for Joy. She had bypassed love and happiness because of it. And now it seemed she was to have another chance at love with Rufe.

But she sensed Lily would not welcome her coming into Rufe's life after having him to herself for so long. It was all very well for Rufe to say Lily would accept it, but would she? Perhaps, given time. But Rufe didn't want to wait; he didn't want to give her that time.

Kitty knew that it would weigh on her conscience if she took her own happiness with disregard for Lily's feelings without trying to win her over. After all, Lily might well hate her for it, and what trouble and unhappiness would that bring to their future? Could the friction sour their love?

Rufe's letter lay on her desk and she must answer it. Should she stay in Sydney after leaving Joy at school, as he wished? She longed to be with him, but concern over Lily made her hesitate.

And what of Joy? How would Joy feel about a relationship between her and Rufe, after having such a short time to get to know him? Joy was already annoyed with her for her refusal to allow her to go to England. Might not this add to her dissatisfaction, and cause more trouble? Kitty hated to think of a rift between her and her daughter. Might not this inflame matters even more?

Why did everything have to be so difficult? Sighing, she stood and walked to the edge of the water. Today, its tranquillity had not helped her. She still did not know what to do.

The next morning Kitty's mind kept turning to Rufe's letter lying unanswered on her desk. She really must make a decision on whether to stay in Sydney or not. Her thoughts were interrupted by a knock on the door and Joy opened it and came in to the room.

'Are you busy, Mother?'

'Not too busy to talk to you. Come in and sit down.'

'Mother, I'm sorry for my bad behaviour the other day. It was really bad of me to make such a scene.'

Kitty's heart leapt at Joy's apology. 'I understand you were upset, and I know it's hard for you to accept my decision, so we'll say no more about it. But I really do believe that you're too young to think of going to England yet.'

Joy bit her lip. 'Oh Mother, if you could only know how badly I want to go. To see London, to actually have a Season, and to be presented at Court. It's like a dream come true.'

Kitty saw the longing in her daughter's face, heard it in her voice, and felt a pang of dismay.

'Perhaps when you're older we'll talk about you going for a visit.'

'But then I'll be too old for a Season.'

'Having a Season is to introduce a young lady into English Society, with the main object being to find her a suitable husband. An English husband. That's not for you. Your life is here. Redwoods is your home, where you belong, where you'll always have security.'

Joy screwed up her face, shaking her head. 'But I don't want to always live here. There's an interesting, exciting world out there. I want to see it. I want to know what it's like.'

Kitty lifted her brows. 'Don't you find your life here interesting enough, with the people who love you, your friends, your horse, everything you've grown up with?'

Joy shook her head. 'Not interesting, no. Of course I love you all, and I'd miss you. But I don't care that much about Redwoods. It's your home. You're the one who loves it. I don't.'

Kitty's heart plummeted. She took a deep breath. 'It's taken many years of hard work to make Redwoods what it is today. I've always believed I was working so you could be safe all your life, no matter what happened. Redwoods is your security.'

'I don't care. Life here's boring. I want to go and meet my father's family, see what they're like, what it's like over there. And to meet the Queen.' Her eyes widened. 'Can you imagine that?'

'Oh yes, I've met the Queen. When you get past her gowns and jewels she's just an ordinary lady, no different to us.'

'I don't care! If you've met her why can't I?'

'I lived in England; I didn't have to go across the world to meet her.'

'You just don't understand.' Tears sprang to Joy's eyes. 'I don't suppose you've ever wanted to do anything as much as I want to do this.'

Kitty picked up the envelope containing Rufe's letter, and turned it over idly as she considered Joy's words. Joy was so young, she had no understanding of the dilemmas in life, but she was growing up. Much as Kitty wanted to, she couldn't keep her here forever. She couldn't protect her from life.

But if she let her go, perhaps she would be so seduced by the glamour of that other lifestyle that she would never return. Kitty cringed inside at the thought. But perhaps she had to let her go in order to keep her. She dropped the envelope and took a deep breath.

'You're wrong about that, Joy, but we're talking about you, not me. Believe me, I do understand how you feel. But even if I agreed, you couldn't be presented at Court until you're eighteen. You are still too young to go so far away for so long.'

A flicker of hope lit up Joy's face. 'Perhaps I wouldn't need two years to get ready. Do you think one year would be enough?'

'Yes, I'm sure one year would be enough.'

'So if I waited another year, could I go then?' Her voice pleaded.

Kitty sighed. 'I can see you've set your mind on being presented, and meeting your father's family.' With a sinking feeling, she capitulated. 'Very well, if you finish your next year at school, and if I can make arrangements for someone to accompany you on the voyage, you may go then.'

Joy jumped up and rushed around the desk. Throwing her arms around her mother, she hugged her.

'Oh thank you, Mother, thank you. You're absolutely the best mother in the whole world.'

Kitty laughed as she hugged her back.

'I hope you think so once you're over there. You'll find life more restrictive there than here, believe me. But I see you'll never be happy until you find out for yourself.'

'I know I'll love it. It'll be so exciting. I can't wait for this year to pass. Can I write to Grandmother and tell her I'll be coming?'

'Yes. I'll write to her myself as well, of course.'

'When will you make the arrangements? You'll have to book the passage soon, won't you?'

'Not just yet, but I need to find out about ships sailing at that time, and also about a companion for you. When you go back to school, and I come with you to Sydney, I'll make enquiries.'

Chapter Six

Kitty hurried along George Street, through the fading light, on her way to meet Rufe. Her mind flew ahead to their meeting. He would ask her again to marry him and, while she ached to be with him, she still worried about the situation with Lily.

As the crowd thinned, she stopped. She'd been warned of the 'Rocks Push' and it seemed as if she was about to meet some of its members face on. Pushing and jostling each other, a noisy group of young men and women approached.

The girls were as bright as native birds in their gaudy colours, with feathers in their straw hats, and high lace-up boots reaching up to their short skirts, well above their ankles. Their voices chirruped high above the strident tones of their male companions, who couldn't match them for colour except for the kerchiefs tied around their necks. The men's trousers hugged their legs beneath loose flapping shirts, and their hats perched jauntily on the backs of their heads.

As the rowdy group came closer, Kitty regretted her decision to refuse Rufe's offer to come and meet her after she left Joy at St Catherine's. She'd wanted to visit a shipping agent, and arranged to meet Rufe in the foyer of her hotel. It all took longer than she expected, and when she left the shipping agent's office she was unable to find a cab, so she'd decided to walk.

She moved across to the edge of the footpath to avoid the approaching group. At that moment a carriage swung around the corner at breakneck speed. The rear of the swaying carriage struck her on the shoulder, sending her sprawling into the gutter.

As she lay there, winded, she heard voices chattering around her, and when she opened her eyes, one of the youths was bending over her.

'Gee, missus, are yer orright?'

Kitty struggled to sit up, and immediately two strong pairs of hands were under her armpits, as two of the lads helped her to sit and slid her back on to the footpath.

''Ere now missus, don't try and move yet. Are yer orright? Is anyfink broken?' asked one of the lads, who seemed to be the leader.

''Ere, Billy, wothcha want t'elp 'er for? She aint one o' us.' The angry question came from a tall, black-haired girl.

'Cause 'e fancies a bit o' quality skirt, that's why,' sniggered one of the other girls.

'Shut yer gobs,' Billy ordered, then turned back to Kitty. 'D'yer fink summat's broken?'

'I…I don't think so.' Kitty moved her legs gingerly, then clutched at her right shoulder as pain shot through it as she attempted to move. 'Ooh. My shoulder.'

'That's where yer got biffed,' said the other lad who had helped lift her. 'No wonder it's sore. Yer better go see a doctor.'

Suddenly all the group started talking at once, offering advice.

'Yeah, that's right, missus. That's what yer gotta do.' Billy nodded. 'I dunno where we can find one round 'ere though.'

Kitty attempted to stand, and once again strong hands helped her. Once upright she took a careful step, supported on both sides by her anxious rescuers.

'Maybe yer should wait while we try an' find a doc,' suggested another girl.

Kitty had her breath back by now. She felt shaky and her shoulder hurt badly, but she didn't feel as if anything was broken.

'No, if I can get back to my hotel I'll be all right. I can call one then if I need to.'

The two lads removed their hands from her arms. 'Well, if yer sure, then, I'll find yer a cab,' Billy offered.

'Thank you. That would be wonderful.'

He moved out onto the road and let out a piercing whistle, and within seconds a passing cab pulled in to the kerb.

''Ere's yer bag, missus, and yer 'at.' The lad thrust them at her. 'They both went flyin' when yer fell.'

Kitty took them and extracted a pound note from her purse. 'Thank you all so much,' she said as she handed it to Billy. 'I don't know what I'd have done if it hadn't been for you.'

'Gee ta, missus. We'll drink t'yer good 'ealth wiv it.'

Rufe's smile of welcome changed to a worried frown as he saw her white face and dishevelled appearance.

'Kitty, what's the matter. Whatever's happened to you?' He grasped her free hand in his own. 'Here, come and sit down.' He led her to a couch, sat her down and sat beside her, turning toward her and gently rubbing her hands. 'Now tell me what happened?'

Kitty tried to smile but her mouth trembled. 'It was probably my own fault. I moved too close to the road and a carriage swung round the corner and caught my shoulder, and knocked me over. It was going very fast.'

'What imbecile of a coachman would drive like that through the city streets? It's lucky you weren't killed.' Removing her hat, he stroked her hair, tucking the straggly wisps back. 'My poor darling. We must call a doctor, you're probably injured.'

'I think I'm just a bit bruised, I don't think anything's broken.'

'We need to be sure. Look, I'd planned for us to go to dinner but you're in no fit state for that. I think you should come home with me, and I'll call a doctor. He can check you over and make sure you're all right. You could have bones broken and not know it.' He shook his head, and smiled wryly as he saw her about to protest. 'Don't worry, you won't be compromised. My housekeeper is there and a couple of maids. Mrs. Barnes can put you to bed while I call the doctor.'

Kitty still felt weak and the idea of having someone take over was appealing. She attempted to smooth her skirt. 'I can't go like this. I'm a mess, I need to change.'

Rufe stood up. 'You stay here,' he told her. 'I'll arrange something.' He walked over and spoke to the receptionist behind the counter. 'Mrs. Barron has had an accident; she was knocked down by a coach. I'd like you to find a maid to go with her to her room and pack some things for overnight for her, please. She needs medical attention.'

'Oh dear. Poor Mrs. Barron. It's a disgrace the way some of those coaches tear through the streets. It's no wonder there are so many accidents.'

'Quite. Now, if you'll find a maid to escort her to her room and help her, please, I'll wait down here for her.'

'Certainly, sir. I'll get someone straight away.'

'It's all arranged. A maid will take you to your room and she'll pack whatever you need. Don't bother to change now, Mrs. Barnes will have a maid draw a bath and attend to you. Just relax now until someone comes.'

Kitty leant back and let her eyes fall shut, still feeling quite shaky. It seemed only seconds until a middle aged woman came over to them.

'Good evening. I'm the housekeeper. You've had a nasty experience, Mrs. Barron. I'll look after you myself. Do you feel able to walk to your room?'

'Yes, thank you.'

Rufe helped her to her feet and held her arm as far as the stairs.

'Thank you, sir. I'll attend to Mrs. Barron now,' the housekeeper told him. 'We won't be long, sir.' She took Kitty's arm. 'Now then, are you sure you can manage the stairs? Hold on to the banister now, that's right, and I'll help you on this side.'

She led Kitty to her room and opened the door for her. 'Now, you just sit down, and tell me what you want. I'll have it all packed in no time.'

When they came downstairs Rufe took Kitty's arm. 'I have a cab waiting. We'll soon have you home and I'll send for the doctor.' He squeezed her arm gently as he escorted her outside. 'I need to know you've suffered no harm, my love,' he added, as she started to protest.

Once inside the cab, Kitty let her head rest against the back of the seat and closed her eyes. She had a headache, her shoulder ached, and she felt as if she had been beaten all over. She would probably have a fine crop of bruises tomorrow. For now, it was a relief to let Rufe take charge, and the promise of a hot bath sounded like heaven. In what seemed like no time at all, the cab stoped and the coachman opened the door for them.

Kitty saw they had stopped in front of a large Italianate style house, with a garden enclosed by an iron railing fence. Rufe led her through the gate and up the path to shallow steps leading to a verandah, where he opened the heavy, carved wooden door. Ushering her inside, he set her bag down on the floor of the entrance hall.

'Mrs. Barnes,' he called.

A door opened at the back of the hall and a large, bosomy woman with dark hair, smoothed back into a bun, came bustling out.

'Why, Mr. Cavanagh, I wasn't expecting you back yet.'

'No, I know I told you I'd be late, and I'm sorry to upset your plans, but we have a guest. Mrs. Barron has had an accident and she'll be staying the night. I want you to show her to her room and have Milly draw a bath and help her. And send Tom to fetch Dr Ramsay.'

Mrs. Barnes hurried forward, concern on her face. 'Mrs. Barron, what happened to you?'

'I was struck by a carriage, and my shoulder feels bruised.'

'How terrible. You certainly need to have Dr Ramsay see to you. Now come along and we'll get you bathed and into bed. Then I'll bring you a nice hot cup of tea. By then the doctor should be here.'

Kitty let herself be led upstairs, where she was fussed over by Mrs. Barnes and a young dark haired girl, whom she learned was Milly.

After soaking in a hot bath she put on fresh night garments, brushed out her hair, and climbed into bed with a sigh, allowing herself to be tucked in. Then she relaxed against the pile of pillows Milly put behind her.

She was sitting up sipping a cup of tea when Rufe knocked and entered the room a short while later.

'How are you feeling?' he asked anxiously.

'Much better, thank you. A hot bath does wonders.'

'After Dr Ramsay has been in I'll have a tray brought up. I believe Mrs. Barnes has prepared soup and roast beef. I hope that appeals to you.'

'I'm not very hungry, but that sounds tempting. I'm sorry to have spoiled your plans for dinner tonight.'

A glimmer of a smile banished the worried look from his face. 'There'll be other nights. I just want to be sure you've taken no serious harm, from what could have been a tragedy. It doesn't bear thinking about. If I found you again, only to lose you...' He frowned and shook his head.

'That didn't happen, so don't even think about it. I'm sure I'll be fit and well after a good night's sleep.'

A knock came at the door, and when Rufe opened it, Mrs. Barnes stood there with a tall, gaunt grey haired man carrying a black bag.

'Ah, Dr Ramsay, please come in.' Rufe opened the door wide and gestured to the bed. 'Mrs. Barron is your patient. She was knocked down by a tearaway carriage. She needs to be fully checked over.'

The doctor moved to the bed and placed his bag on a chair.

'I'll leave you to it, doctor. I'll see you when you come downstairs.' Rufe left the room, closing the door behind him.

Kitty related the story of the accident, and when she finished the doctor drew back the bed clothes.

'Fortunately there's nothing broken,' he told her after he finished examining her and closed his bag. 'You have quite a lot of incipient bruising and, you'll be stiff and sore for several days, I'm afraid. And you have had a bad shock. I'm going to prescribe a potion for you that will help, but you need to rest in bed for a few days.'

'Oh really doctor, is that necessary? I have things to do here in Sydney, and then I must go home. I live in Bulahdelah, and I'm expected back there by the end of the week.'

He shook his head. 'Out of the question, I'm afraid, dear lady. I doubt you'll be well enough to travel for at least a week. I'll call again tomorrow, but if you feel worse before then, have Mrs. Barnes call me and I'll come straight away. Do you understand?'

'Yes.' Kitty nodded. She didn't feel up to arguing with the doctor.

'Good. Then I'll give this prescription to Mr. Cavanagh on my way out, and he can have it filled. I want you to take it three times a day. It will help to make you sleep. Understand?'

'Yes.'

'Then I'll bid you good day.'

Minutes later, Rufe came into the room, a worried look on his face.

'How are you feeling?' he asked, as he pulled a chair up to the bed and sat down, taking her hand in his own. 'Dr Ramsay tells me you're in shock and must rest in bed for the next week.'

'Oh, I'm sure he's being over cautious. I feel a little sore, but I can't believe I need to be laid up so long. At any rate, I must go back to the hotel tomorrow.'

Rufe shook his head. 'Absolutely not, you must stay here. I'll send someone for your things tomorrow.'

'But Rufe, I can't stay here.'

'Why not?'

'Because I can't stay here. In your house.'

'Of course you can. Unfortunately I have meetings to attend during the day, which I can't cancel, but Mrs. Barnes will take care of you, and I'll sit with you in the evenings. Don't worry; it will all be quite proper.'

'But I'm expected back home in a few days.'

'I'll send a message to your mother. I'll tell her what's happened, and that she doesn't need to worry, that you just need rest. Leave it to me; I'll take care of everything. You just rest and recover.'

Kitty was tempted. But she worried that if she stayed here, in his home, she would be under more pressure to make a decision regarding marriage, and she would be at a disadvantage, being confined to bed.

Rufe squeezed her hand. "You're very precious to me, Kitty. I just want you to get better, I want to see some colour back in your face."

Kitty felt a warm glow at his words. Smiling, she returned the pressure of his fingers.

'When you put it like that, how can I argue with you?'

The tension left his face. 'That's my girl. Now you just relax. I'll tell Mrs. Barnes you're ready for a tray now, shall I?'

'Yes, I think I can eat a little.'

'Good.' He stood, leaning over to kiss her gently on the cheek. 'I'll look in and see you later, before you go to sleep.

When Rufe entered the room later, Kitty was fast asleep. He stood looking down. Her golden hair was spread over the pillow and her face was relaxed in sleep. Age had been kind to her, she looked little older now than the young woman he remembered when she first arrived in Australia.

Although he would never have wanted Kitty to be hurt, he blessed the accident that meant she would be under his roof for the next week. It seemed as if fate had given him a second chance. He would use the time well. Without pushing her, he would try to have a firm commitment from her before she left his home.

Chapter Seven

When Kitty woke the next morning her right shoulder throbbed. She felt stiff all over, and her left leg ached. After rubbing it, she stretched first one leg, then the other, and then the rest of her body. When she pushed back the bedclothes she found her hip and thigh beginning to discolour. She turned her attention to her sore left elbow. The skin was broken. Her left side must have taken her weight when she fell, and she was lucky nothing was broken.

She drank the glass of physick Milly brought her with a cup of tea, and laid back against the pillows. At that moment there came another knock, and Rufe's voice called out, 'Can I come in?'

When Milly opened the door Rufe crossed the room and stood beside the bed.

Kitty was struck by how handsome he looked, clad in a dark city suit and starched white shirt. He had retained the slim figure of his youth, and no middle age paunch marred the elegance of the gold fob watch chain gleaming against his waistcoat.

'Good morning Kitty. How are you feeling this morning?' She heard concern in his voice.

'A little achy, but that's only to be expected. I'm lucky there's no real damage.'

'You must do as the doctor said, and stay in bed and rest. I've arranged for your luggage to be brought here this morning, and Mrs. Barnes will make sure you have everything you need. If there's anything you want just ask her or Milly.'

'You're all being very kind to me.'

'I'm not being kind at all. I want you to be well so I can enjoy the pleasure of your company.'

'In that case, I promise to be up and about quickly.'

'That's my girl. But you're not to get up until you're well enough.' He leant down and planted a light kiss on the cheek. 'I'm sorry I must go and leave you, but, unfortunately, I have meetings I can't put off. However, I'll be home as early as I can. Now, promise me you'll spend the day resting.'

Kitty felt the aches in her limbs, and realised she felt like doing exactly that. 'Yes, I promise.'

For the rest of the day she drifted in and out of sleep.

When she opened her eyes Rufe was sitting by the bed, holding her hand. She had no idea if she had been asleep for just a few moments or much longer, but she saw relief on his face as Rufe leant over and kissed her gently on the lips.

'You need to sleep,' he told her, 'so I'm going to leave you now.'

Kitty put up her hand and touched his cheek, and then her eyes closed again. Rufe left the room, closing the door gently.

The next morning Kitty felt much better and, after drinking her morning cup of tea, she put her feet to the floor, and was relieved to find that, apart from a little stiffness and a few sore spots, she felt fine. When Mrs. Barnes knocked and came in a few moments later she was dressed and sitting in front of the mirror, pinning up her hair.

'Mrs. Barron.' She gasped. 'What are you doing out of bed. Dr Ramsay said you must stay in bed for another two days.'

'Dr Ramsay can say what he likes, I'm up, and I'm staying up. I feel perfectly well. I have a few bruises and I'm a little stiff, that's all. I'm not an invalid and I don't intend to be treated like one. And I'm not taking any more of that physick he ordered for me. It makes me dopey.'

'I see. I take it you'll be downstairs for lunch then.'

'I will indeed. And seeing I've been eating very little, I'm looking forward to it.'

Mrs. Barnes beamed. 'Would a cold collation with smoked ham and freshly baked bread suit you?'

Kitty smiled. 'It sounds like just what I need, Mrs. Barnes.'

Kitty looked up as Rufe entered the drawing room in the late afternoon and smiled at him. 'Why Rufe, you're home much earlier than I expected.'

In two strides he crossed the room. He took the book from her hands, and laid it on the small table next to her, then bent over and took her hands in his own. Raising one to his lips he kissed it.

'Kitty, you're up and dressed, and you look well again.' Emotion thickened his voice. 'I've been so worried; you seemed so weak last night. I made excuses and left early, before the meeting ended. I dreaded finding you still prostrate and exhausted, and, instead, here you are, looking as if you've never been ill.'

'I feel so much better, quite well again in fact, apart from a little stiffness.'

Rufe took a deep breath as he let go of her hands, and seated himself alongside her.

'So what's brought about this miraculous transformation?'

'Oh, I simply felt bright when I woke this morning, and I had no need to stay in bed. I feel wonderful, apart from a little stiffness. But I agree, I should wait until the end of the week before I travel home.'

Rufe saw a sparkle in her eyes, and was certain she was looking forward to staying a few more days. Elated, he decided to make sure to show her how good their life together could be.

'So, we have three more days. Three whole days with no one to tell us what we should do.' He smiled. 'We must make the most of them. How fortunate I told George Reid I might not be available for the rest of the week.'

'Oh. Why did you do that?'

'I want to spend the time with you, and now I find you recovered, we'll be able to do whatever you want.'

Kitty smiled. 'That sounds like a holiday.'

'Let's make it one.' He seized her by the hand. 'Let's have a little secret holiday, just three days all to ourselves, to do with as we please.'

Kitty's eyes shone. 'What a self-indulgent idea.'

'Do you like it?'

'I love it.'

'Then what would you like to do tonight, the first night of our holiday?'

'Mrs. Barnes is cooking dinner for us, so I'd like to have dinner here, and then perhaps we could take a stroll.'

'And tomorrow?'

'Hmm' She cocked her head. 'This may sound silly, but I've never been to the Zoo, and I'd really like to see it. Would you mind?'

'I'd enjoy it. And perhaps, tomorrow night, we can go to the theatre. Nellie Stewart is singing the role of Yum-Yum in Gilbert and Sullivan's *Mikado*. I've heard it's very entertaining. Would you like that?'

'Yes, I would indeed.'

'Perfect. That's tomorrow planned, then. And now we have time for a drink before dinner. I think a glass of champagne to celebrate your recovery is in order.'

Over dinner Rufe kept the conversation light, avoiding any discussion of their future. He recounted some of the lighter moments that came up during the endless political meetings being held in the effort to reach a consensus regarding the unification of the colonies. For her part, Kitty told him of Lady Barron's letters, and Joy's desire to go to England, and the compromise they had reached.

After dinner Rufe tucked her arm in his and they took a short walk. When they returned he gave Kitty a sedate kiss on the cheek and bade her goodnight.

The next day dawned bright and sunny, and Kitty professed herself quite well again, so they headed to the Zoo. Here they exclaimed over the lions and tigers, laughed at the antics of the monkeys as they fed them peanuts, and admired the peacocks strutting around their enclosure. Then they ate the picnic lunch Mrs. Barnes packed for them by one of the lakes in Moore Park. They talked a lot – about politics and the coming Federation, and discussed possibilities for Redwoods' future.

When they returned to the house, Kitty was pleased to go to her room and rest before dressing for their outing that night.

After a light meal they headed to the theatre. They had not been seated long when the lights went down, and Rufe reached over to take Kitty's hand in his own. There it stayed until the lights went up again.

'What a wonderful day it's been,' Kitty told Rufe when they arrived back at the house. 'Thank you for it.'

'It's been one of the most enjoyable days I can remember. But it's been a very full day, and you need a good night's sleep. So I'll say goodnight and let you go to bed.'

With that he leant across and kissed her gently on the cheek.

As she undressed for bed Kitty felt baffled. There had been plenty of opportunities, but Rufe had made no attempt to discuss their personal issues, or even to kiss her, since she had been here. Did he no longer care for her? Her mind went back to his letter — it said *'there is an important matter I wish to discuss with you'*.

Kitty interpreted that as meaning he wished to discuss their future, but had she been wrong? She remembered how impassioned he had been in Moore Park when talking about the plight of the poor. Had he realised that he needed to devote all his energies to politics, and he now had no time for anything else — including her? Is that what he wanted to tell her? Or, because she had rebuffed him at Redwoods yet again because of her concern for Lily, did he feel she was unreliable, and he wanted to tell her he no longer wished to see her anymore?

But if so, why had he insisted on her coming here and staying until she was fully recovered? Was it mere chivalry on his part? Was he secretly wishing her to go?

And even if he did wish to discuss a future together for them, she knew he would insist on marriage, and, after all, nothing had really changed regarding the situation with Lily. If he were to ask her again, what would she say?

Tired though she was, it took Kitty a long time to fall asleep.

45

Chapter Eight

At breakfast the next morning Rufe was as attentive to her as he had ever been, and Kitty was at a loss to know what to make of him, and his feelings for her. She decided to put her concerns aside, and concentrate on enjoying the day.

After breakfast they set out again in the trap and headed through the city towards the ferry wharf. They passed the Haymarket, busy with shoppers, and headed down Pitt Street. Pedestrians bustled along the footpaths, and the roadway teemed with wagons, trams, cabs, carriages, and riders on horseback.

Kitty turned to Rufe. 'You know, this reminds me of when we first arrived here in Sydney on the *Osprey*. Do you remember that very first day?'

'I remember it very well.'

'Mother and I were surprised to see the streets so busy, and everything looking so up-to-date. I suppose we expected the city to be rather outlandish in some way. And I'll never forget my first sight of Sydney, how beautiful it looked in the early morning as we sailed in through the Harbour. I fell in love with Sydney then, and I looked forward to living here. But, of course, that never happened.' She fell silent then, remembering the days after her arrival, the days leading up to her decision to marry William and leave Sydney and go with him to Bulahdelah. She felt a stab of pain remembering her anguish at the death of her brother, Robert, and the worry that her past in England would catch up with her.

'So much has happened since then.' She sighed. 'Ah well, one can never go back. Today is another day.'

Rufe gave her a sharp sideways look. 'Do you still love Sydney?'

'Yes I do. I'm sorry I never got to spend more time here, but that's life, isn't it? Things don't always work out as we expect, and I've been lucky to visit here over the years.' She smiled at him. 'And this visit is one of the best. I mustn't let past memories spoil it. Today, I'm looking forward to going on the Harbour again. It will be a pleasant memory when I'm home in Bulahdelah.'

'I hope it won't be the only pleasant memory you take back.'

'Oh no. I'll often think of yesterday, and how much I enjoyed it. Both our day at Moore Park, and seeing *Mikado* last night.'

They spoke no more as they arrived at the ferry wharf, and Rufe needed to concentrate all his skill on guiding the horse and trap onto the wharf amongst the other vehicles, and to get them safely on board the ferry. Here they joined the other carriages, wagons and horses waiting to cross, and in a few moments they were under way.

On board the ferry they were close to the water. Kitty looked back at the wake streaming out behind them, and the small boats and yachts zigzagging about. A stiff breeze whipped up whitecaps on the water and caused the ferry to toss a little. The water held no terrors for her; she loved the feel of the ocean, the motion of the boat, and the frisky breeze teasing her hat. It was all so exciting.

When the ferry started to roll and dip as it met the swell coming in from the ocean as they passed the Heads she laughed, clutching her hat to stop it being whipped away by the wind.

After a day spent sightseeing and a quiet dinner in a small restaurant, they returned home. All was quiet in the house.

'Are you tired?' Rufe asked Kitty, as he led her into the drawing room.

'No, not at all.' She turned to him with a smile. 'I have so enjoyed today. Thank you for indulging me.'

He smiled down at her. 'That's what our little holiday is for, for you to do the things you want to do.'

'Oh, but it should be for you to enjoy, too.'

His gaze was intense as he looked down at her. 'As long as I'm with you I'm happy, no matter what we do.'

Kitty's heart fluttered as she looked up at him. How handsome he was, maturity suited him. She noticed a streak of silver at his temple and reached up a finger to smooth it.

'I do believe I see a grey hair.'

He caught her hand, and raised it to his lips. 'I have plenty of those.' A shadow crossed his face. 'Time is passing, Kitty. For both of us.' His voice became husky. 'We need to make some decisions.'

All at once his arms were around her, and he pulled her to him. His lips sought hers and he kissed her, hungrily, passionately.

Kitty felt the blood pound through her body as she returned his kiss. Her passion flared to match his. As their bodies pressed close together desire surged through her, hot and strong. His hand moved to the back of her neck and tilted her head back. He kissed her upturned face. Then his lips moved down her neck and on to the uncovered tops of her breasts, dropping little kisses, lingering there, as if savouring her loveliness. She felt she must dissolve with longing. He raised his head and his gaze searched her face, as his fingers traced its outlines.

'All those long years since we parted I've dreamt about you. Dreamt about your beautiful face, dreamt of holding you, loving you.' His voice wavered. 'I thought I'd lost you forever. I thought I'd never hold you again, never kiss you again.'

Their lips came together once more and Kitty clung to him, kissing him, wanting him. Their embrace lasted a long time, and then he pulled away from her and guided her across to the sofa.

'Let's sit for a moment.'

He eased her down and sat beside her, then placed his hands on her shoulders and turned her toward him.

'I love you, Kitty. I've never truly loved anyone but you.' His voice was deep with emotion. 'Now that I've found you again I couldn't bear to lose you. I want to be with you always. I want to share your life. I want us to spend the rest of our lives together.'

His words wiped away all of Kitty's doubts. Whatever the problems, they would overcome them. Her voice was sure as she answered him. 'I love you too, and I want to be with you forever.'

'I've waited so long to hear those words.' He pulled her to him and kissed her again, long and hard, and his hand slipped down to caress her breast.

Kitty felt as if she was on fire.

Rufe stood then, and held out his hand to her. 'Come with me.'

Taking his hand she stood and walked with him, out of the room, down the hall and into her bedroom. Rufe closed the door firmly behind them.

It was several hours later when Kitty woke, in a state of dreamy euphoria. She turned languidly in bed and felt Rufe alongside her in the darkness. Her stirring caused him to move, pulling her gently into his arms.

'Are you awake, my love?' he whispered.

'Mmmm, yes.'

'I have a question for you. I'm almost afraid to ask it.'

'Hmmm, what is it?'

'Will you marry me?'

'Mmmmm. Yes darling.'

'You will?' He propped himself up on an elbow.

'Mmm, yes.'

'We have to talk sometime.'

'Mm.' She snuggled against him, and he slid down beside her.

'But not right now, perhaps.' His hands began caressing her body. 'We have more important things to do at the moment. That is, if you're not too tired.'

Kitty was suddenly awake. 'I'm not a bit tired.'

There was a tap on the door, waking Kitty from a deep sleep. She turned and stretched sleepily as Milly entered carrying her morning tea tray. As she placed it on the bedside table Kitty realised she was alone in the bed. Rufe must have slipped out before daylight to spare her from embarrassment.

"Good morning, Mrs. Barron.' Milly was her usual cheerful self as she crossed to the window and drew back the curtains, letting in a flood of sunlight. 'I hope you slept well.'

'Very well, thank you Milly.' Kitty sat up, breathing deeply as she stretched again. 'What a lovely morning.' She reached across and picked up her teacup. 'I'll have a bath as soon as I've finished my tea this morning,' she told Milly, as she sipped the hot brew.

'Right-o, I'll run it for you. Going out somewhere early, are you?'

'I'm not sure, but it's too lovely a morning to lie in bed.'

'It certainly is a beautiful day, might as well make the most of it.' She paused at the door. 'Can I get you anything else?'

'No thank you.'

As Kitty drank her tea she relived the night before. Her spirits soared like a bluebird in flight. How had she ever thought that she was content to spend the rest of her life alone at Redwoods? The only cloud in her bright sky was Lily. How would she take the news? She felt she would be very upset. She wouldn't let it spoil their happiness now, but the problem would have to be dealt with before long.

When Kitty entered the dining room for breakfast Rufe jumped up from his chair and hurried to her, smiling as he kissed her.

'And how is my beautiful wife-to-be this morning?'

Kitty returned his smile, happiness singing through her. 'I can't remember having ever felt better.'

He raised an eyebrow. 'No regrets?'

She shook her head. 'None whatsoever.' She reached up and kissed him on the cheek.

At that moment Mrs. Barnes entered the room carrying a fresh pot of tea, and placed it on the sideboard. Rufe turned to his housekeeper with a broad smile, his arm still around Kitty.

'Mrs. Barnes, you're the first to know. Mrs. Barron has consented to become my wife.'

Mrs. Barnes beamed. 'Why, Mr. Cavanagh, that's wonderful news. Congratulations. I wish you both every happiness.'

'Thank you. I'm sure we'll be very happy. And now to more mundane matters, we won't be in for lunch. We have some shopping to do.'

'Very well.' She nodded, and with that she left them alone.

Kitty raised her brows. 'Shopping?'

'Yes. Today we must find a ring for you. And then we must make some decisions.'

After breakfast Rufe called a cab and they headed into the city, to George Street, where they pulled up outside a jeweller's shop.

After paying off the cab, Rufe ushered Kitty inside. A silver haired, aristocratic-looking man came forward to meet them. His rather austere face broke into a smile as he recognised Rufe.

After they greeted each other Rufe introduced Kitty, and Rufe told him they wished to see some rings.

Armand smiled. 'Certainly. Only the finest will do for you, I know. Please come with me.'

They followed him into a hallway leading from the shop, and into a small room furnished as a sitting room, where he waved them to seats.

A few moments later a young woman entered with coffee, closely followed by Armand carrying a display tray glittering with diamond rings.

He set the tray in front of Kitty.

'Take your time now, madame. See if anything here pleases you.'

Kitty looked at the dazzling array of rings set before her. After regarding them for a moment she picked up one after another, turning each to catch the light, then placed it back in the tray. Finally she selected a solitaire diamond set in a circlet of smaller diamonds, and slipped it on her finger. She held her hand out in front of her, turning it this way and that, admiring the ring as it gleamed and flashed in the light.

'This is beautiful.' She looked at Rufe. 'What do you think?'

'I think it was made with you in mind.'

Armand beamed. 'Ah madame, you choose well. This is truly a beautiful work of art.'

He glanced at Rufe, who nodded his head.

'This one? You're sure?' he asked Kitty.

'Absolutely sure.' She took the ring from her finger and handed it to Armand.

He bowed slightly as he took it. 'It will bring you much happiness, madame. Of that I am sure.'

'Finish your coffee while I go with Armand.' Rufe rose from his chair. 'I won't be long.'

He was back within minutes, and Kitty stood up to join him.

'Business concluded,' he said lightly. 'Now do you feel like a stroll? I thought we might wander around the gardens for a while, enjoy the sunshine, and catch sight of the harbour again.'

'Yes, I'd like that.'

After they had taken their leave of Armand Rufe led Kitty outside. A short walk brought them to the Botanic Gardens. Once inside, he tucked Kitty's arm in his, and they strolled along a pathway until they came to a seat in a secluded spot, screened by a shrubbery, and here they sat.

'This is the happiest day of my life,' Rufe told Kitty, as he reached into his pocket and withdrew a small box. 'I can't wait for you to wear this, my love.' He removed the ring, picked up her hand and placed the ring on her finger. He raised her hand to his lips. 'This is just the outward token of my love. I intend to spend the rest of my life showing you how much I love you. We've wasted so much time. I don't want to waste any more, so let's set our wedding date. And let's make it soon.' He studied her face. 'I hope you feel the same. Do you?'

As she saw the happiness in his face and the adoration in his eyes, Kitty's heart swelled with love for this man who had come back into her life after so long, to bring her such bliss. She smiled. 'I do. I want us to be together, and I see no reason to wait too long.' She paused, reaching her hand up to touch his cheek. 'But there are things we need to discuss that might affect the timing.'

'Yes, of course. I'm afraid I have to spend a good deal of time down here in Sydney now, so I was happy to hear you say how much you enjoy Sydney. I hope that living here most of the time won't be a problem for you?'

'No, not at all. I'll look forward to it.'

'Good.' He frowned. 'I know how much you love Redwoods. We'll still be able to spend some time there, but I hope you won't miss it too much.'

'Oh no.' She shook her head. 'My attachment to Redwoods has always been for Joy. I've always wanted to know she'll be independent, to have a home and a living, no matter what happens. It was never for me. Redwoods is for Joy, although I have come to love it.'

His face cleared. 'Then you won't mind not living there all the time. I'm relieved, I want your happiness above all else, and I was afraid it might be a problem for you.' He paused and smiled down at her. 'Then there's nothing to stand in the way of us marrying immediately.'

Kitty bit her lip. 'Nothing except our daughters.'

'Do you think Joy will be upset?'

'No, I don't think so. I think she'll be happy for me. Besides, at the moment she's so excited at the thought of going to England that I doubt anything would upset her. But I worry about Lily. I think she'll feel she's losing you, and she will be extremely upset.'

'I hope not, but she'll just have to be sensible and realise I can't live my life to please her.' He thought for a moment. 'I think we should take them both out for lunch tomorrow. We'll tell them our plans then.' He paused, nodding. 'Yes. A small celebration lunch so they don't feel left out. Do you think that will work?'

Inwardly Kitty sighed. She felt sure Lily would not be happy, but she knew they must break the news to her. Best to get it over with.

'I hope so.'

But she felt far from sure.

Chapter Nine

Lily sat in the classroom, but her mind was not on the book open in front of her, it was on Joy. She was sick of hearing Joy prattling on about her forthcoming visit to England. Although it was still a year away, she'd talked of nothing else since they returned to school. She supposed she shouldn't be jealous, Joy was her best friend, but Lily would love to go to England too.

It wasn't fair, why should Joy get to go while *she* had to stay home. Joy was going to be presented at Court, and have a Season in London. She would have heaps of new clothes, and get to meet all sorts of people, including the Queen. And lots of eligible young men, too; how exciting *that* would be! It just wasn't fair.

The bell interrupted her thoughts. Classes were over. As she walked out of the classroom one of the prefects came up to her.

'Miss Darling wants to see you in her office. You and Joy Barron. What have you two been up to?'

'Nothing. I wonder why she wants to see us?'

The prefect shrugged. 'You'll soon find out. Hurry along now. Don't keep her waiting.'

'Ah, Lily,' the principal looked up as she entered the office. 'I have a message from your father. He will be coming tomorrow to take you out to lunch with Mrs. Barron and Joy. So you are both excused from classes tomorrow. I know Mr. Cavanagh is a busy man, so make sure you're ready when he calls for you at noon.'

'Yes, Miss Darling I'll be ready,' she replied, wondering why Joy and her mother were coming too.

'Good. Then you may go now.'

'Thank you Miss Darling.'

As Lily walked out she was puzzling what it was all about. Suddenly a flash of excitement hit her. Could they be going to tell her that she was going to England with Joy?

That night, the two girls talked about the reason for the lunch, but Joy was as much in the dark as Lily.

'I know Mother had things to do in Sydney when she left me, but that was nearly two weeks ago. I thought she'd be back home again by now.'

'Do you think it's something to do with your trip?'

'I don't know. If it is, why would your father come too?'

Lily felt a thrill of elation. It must be something to do with both of them, and she could think of nothing else except the trip. But she kept her thoughts to herself.

'I don't know. I suppose we'll just have to wait and see.'

They were both ready when Rufe arrived, and after a short cab ride they walked into the dining room in Petty's Hotel. The waiter escorted them to a table, and a few moments later Kitty joined them, all smiles as she took her seat.

Rufe beamed at them all. 'Well now, isn't this nice. All together like one big family.'

Lily felt a stab of irritation. What was the matter with her father? No way were they a family. 'But Mrs. Barron and Joy aren't our family, Father.'

Mrs. Barron bit her lip, and shot a warning glance across the table at Father as she removed her gloves. The movement drew Lily's attention to her hands, and she saw that the plain gold band she always wore was gone, and replaced by a diamond ring, flashing in the light cast by the overhead lamps.

In that instant she knew her father had given her the ring, which meant he was going to marry her. Jealousy seared through her. How could he do this to her? He was pushing her into the background. She was no longer the most important person in his life. A knot of anger tightened her stomach.

Her father's voice cut through her fury.

'That's why we're here today, to tell you the good news. It won't be long before we *are* one family. We want you both to know that Mrs. Barron and I are to be married. We want you to join us in celebrating.'

Joy was all smiles. 'That's wonderful.' She turned to Lily. 'Isn't it? Now we won't be just best friends, we'll be almost sisters.'

Lily bit back the angry retort that rose to her lips, as she remembered how much she wanted to go to England. Could she possibly turn this situation to her advantage? Taking a deep breath she forced herself to speak calmly.

'Does it mean we'll all be living together now?'

'After we're married, yes, of course. We'll spend all the holidays together, because we'll be living here in Sydney much of the time. Won't that be good? You'll enjoy being with Joy all the time, won't you?'

'Of course, we like doing things together.' Lily paused, weighing up her next words. 'But Joy's going to be in England for a whole year or more.' She put on her most innocent expression. 'Does this mean I'm going with her now?'

Mrs. Barron's face paled, and Father looked stunned. It took him a moment to answer her.

'I'm afraid not. Joy's going to stay with her father's family. They'll be taking care of her while she's there. You're a total stranger to them; they couldn't do the same for you.'

'I don't see why not. If we're almost sisters. It's not as if I'm a baby or anything, I wouldn't be any trouble, I'd just do whatever Joy does.'

Her father shook his head. "No Lily, I'm afraid it's quite out of the question.'

Her throat tightened with anger and disappointment. 'So while Joy's in England I'll be here on my own with you, both of you.' She glared at her father. 'And all you care about is *her*, you don't care about me any longer. Ever since you met Mrs. Barron again you've been different. You've pushed me aside. I wish you'd never met her. We used to be happy before.'

She felt tears of frustration pricking her eyes. Let them see her cry. Perhaps it would make them change their minds. She let a tear roll down her cheek, and managed a small sob.

'Oh Lily, don't cry.' Mrs. Barron pulled a handkerchief from her purse and handed it to her. 'Here, wipe your eyes.' Her face looked stricken. 'I don't want you to be unhappy because your father and I are going to be married. I don't intend to take him away from you. I'm hoping you and I can become friends. Believe me, I'll do everything I can to see that both you and Joy are happy.'

Lily wiped her eyes and sniffed. 'How can I be happy when Joy will be away for so long? You'll be together, and I'll be feeling as if I'm in the way?'

'You'll never be in the way,' Father said.

'Yes I will, and it'll be awful. I'll be lonely.'

Mrs. Barron leant toward her. 'Perhaps there's something else you'd like to do after you finish school, until Joy comes back?'

Lily started crying again. 'There's nothing I want to do except go to England with Joy.'

Father and Mrs. Barron sat back in their chairs and exchanged glances.

'Do you want to go so very much?' Mrs. Barron asked, frowning.

A quiver of hope ran through Lily. 'Oh yes. I won't feel so bad if I know that Joy and I will be going away together. Then we'd both have something to look forward to.'

Mrs. Barron was silent, looking at her. After a moment she patted Lily's arm. 'I can't promise anything, but I'll see what I can do. Perhaps we may be able to arrange something.'

Lily gave one last sniff and dried her eyes. 'Do you think you could? That would be wonderful.'

'I'll try.'

The words almost stuck in her throat but she managed to say, 'Thank you Mrs. Barron.'

'That's better,' her father told her, beckoning the waiter who had been hovering nearby. 'Now then, let's look at the menu, and decide what you want to eat. Remember we're here for a celebration.'

Lily felt a thrill of triumph. Maybe things weren't going to be too bad after all.

On the way back to St Catherine's Joy was troubled. If she went to England and Lily couldn't come too, her friend would be unhappy. How was Mother going to find anyone for Lily to stay with? And wouldn't she be happier if they could stay together? She resolved to write to her grandmother.

'Kitty, my love,' Rufe said, as they sat in the drawing room after they had delivered the girls back to school, 'however do you think you're going to be able to arrange things so Lily can go to England with Joy?'

'I don't really know. I suppose I was a bit rash in saying I'd try, but she was so unhappy.' Kitty bit her lip. 'It was all my worst fears come true. She thinks I'm trying to take you away from her.'

Rufe frowned. 'That's stupid; she'll just have to get over it.'

'It's not as easy as that. I don't want her to resent me for the rest of our lives. If I can do his for her, perhaps she'll see that I care about her, and she'll feel friendlier toward me.'

'But where could she stay? You're not thinking she could go to the Barron's, are you?'

'No, but we have relatives in England that Mother still corresponds with. I'll talk to her about it when I go home, see if she can think of someone.'

'But who would supervise her while she's there? I couldn't expect strangers to do that.'

'No, of course not. But I have to find a travelling companion for Joy, so perhaps it might be possible to engage someone trustworthy who would supervise them both on the trip, and then stay on as a chaperone to Lily while she's there.'

Rufe raised his brows. 'For a whole year or more? What would she do all that time? What will Joy be doing?'

'Joy will be learning all about Court etiquette. She's going to be presented to the Queen, and have a season in London. She'll have a lot to learn. And then there'll be her wardrobe to buy, so many things to decide.'

'None of which Lily would be doing.'

'Oh, I think she would enjoy shopping in London. Joy will be able to arrange for her to receive invitations to most of the balls and functions during the Season, I'm sure, and she'll need to dress in the latest fashions for those.'

'I suppose the first thing to do is to speak to your mother.'

'Yes, you're right.'

'And in the meantime, my love, we have something more important to do.' He took Kitty's hand in his. 'We have a wedding to arrange.'

Kitty smiled. 'Yes, we do. There's a lot to think about. When is it to be, and where? We must decide.'

'When? As soon as possible. Where? That's up to you. And what sort of wedding do you want?'

'Oh I don't think we need to make too big a fuss, do you? It's not as if it's a first marriage for either of us.'

'I agree. The important thing is to be together all the time, and as we can't do that with propriety until we're married I'd like it to be as soon as possible, and I don't care if there's no one else present except the necessary witnesses.'

'I think we need to have family present, they'd all be hurt if we left them out, but I'm happy with just that.'

'Yes, we need to include your mother and Jack, and my brother and his wife, and young David, and perhaps a few old friends. I think I'll advise the Premier I won't be available for a couple of weeks, and I'll come with you back to Redwoods. On the way we'll stay a couple of days at Riverside. I want you to meet Edward and Erin, and David.'

'I'm looking forward to meeting them. Then we can arrange the details of the wedding.'

'That's settled then. I need to spend another three days with the Premier, and then we can leave, if that suits you.'

'It suits me very well.'

Chapter Ten

Kitty and Rufe travelled by steamer from Sydney to Morpeth, where Rufe collected his horse and trap from the livery stable, and they headed out of town.

'Here we are,' he told Kitty, as they came to the gates of the property he owned with his brother Edward. 'This is Riverside.'

As they drove through the gates Rufe slowed down. Kitty looked around at the gentle rolling hills, carpeted with lush green pasture and ringed by sheltering ramparts in the distance. Horses grazed in the paddocks, or lazed under the clumps of sheltering trees dotted around. A curving driveway led to the homestead. A little way beyond were timber horse stalls. She was spellbound by the idyllic picture of harmony between man and nature.

'It's magnificent.' She turned and put her hand on Rufe's arm. 'Do you think Redwoods could ever be made as good as this?'

'Close to it. Mind you, it'd take a lot of work. But you have the basics. You have sloping paddocks, and enough room to be able to rest the paddocks regularly. You still have clumps of trees left for shelter, and you have the river. Yes, it would work well.'

'Then we must talk about it properly.' She sat back with a determined air. 'But later. For now, I'm looking forward to meeting the rest of your family. How do you think they'll feel about you marrying again?'

'They'll be delighted. Erin has told me more than once that it's high time I settled down. You'll like her, she's a dear girl, and Edward's easy to get along with. I'm sure you'll be right at home with them.'

'And your nephew, David?'

'He's developed into a fine young man. He's twenty four now, and horses are his passion. He's always been keen to learn all he can about them. I swear he's now as knowledgeable as both Edward. His ambition is to breed thoroughbreds for racing.'

Kitty's interest was piqued. 'Is that a feasible ambition? Is there a future in that?'

'Yes, racing is big business now.'

Kitty gazed around as they drove towards the homestead. Horses grazed contentedly, or lifted their heads to watch as they passed.

'Are any of these thoroughbreds?'

'No, so far we've stuck to our bread and butter. But the time will come when we'll branch out.'

'Hello, Rufe,' called the red-haired woman who came through the door as Rufe pulled up outside the house. 'I've been waiting for you.'

'I have a surprise for you, Erin,' Rufe said. He led Kitty up the steps, smiling broadly. 'I'd like you to meet my future wife, Kitty.' He turned to Kitty. 'Kitty, this is my sister-in-law, Erin.'

The surprise on Erin's face turned to pleasure, and she hurried to take the hand Kitty proffered.

Kitty was relieved to see that she was happy at the news. 'I'm so pleased to meet you, Erin.'

'And I'm delighted to meet you.' Erin put her arms around Kitty and kissed her cheek. 'Welcome to Riverside.' She turned to Rufe. 'You certainly know how to surprise us, you tight-lip. Why didn't you let us know? We'd have prepared a proper welcome.'

'We didn't want any fuss.'

Erin shook her head. 'Why ever not, it's momentous news. I'm so happy for you both, and Edward will be too. Now, come inside, and I'll have David bring in your bags and take care of your horse.'

The next moment Kitty was enveloped in hugs as introductions were made. It seemed that Rufe's family was happy to meet her, and to have her join the family. All except Lily, she thought wryly.

But it was Erin who brought Lily into the conversation, turning to Rufe as they sat talking over their tea and cakes.

'And how does Lily feel about you marrying again?' she asked him.

Rufe shrugged. 'Initially she was a little put out, but she seems happy enough now. She and Joy are close friends, so there's no problem there.' He paused and looked at Kitty. 'Right now the problem is that she wants to go to England with Joy next year, and we're not sure how to arrange it. Joy will be staying with her father's family, but, of course, we can't expect them to welcome Lily as well.'

'No, of course not.' Erin looked thoughtful. 'Are you happy for her to go to England?

'Yes, if we can find someone for her to stay with.'

'Yes, I can see that's a problem.'

Rufe sighed. 'We'll just have to try and sort it out, I'm afraid. At least we have time on our side. '

After two pleasant days spent at Riverside, they headed up to Bulahdelah.

Bella met them at the front door of Redwoods. 'Why, Mr. Cavanagh. What a pleasant surprise,' she greeted them. 'Kitty didn't let us know you were coming with her.'

Rufe kissed her on the cheek. 'I hope you'll be seeing much more of me in the future.'

'That would be most welcome, but may I ask why?'

Kitty laughed. 'We have a surprise for you, Mother.' She held out her hand, displaying the ring.

Bella gasped. 'Oh Kitty, does this mean what I think it means?'

'It does. Rufe and I are engaged to be married.'

Bella's joy was unmistakable. She threw her arms around Kitty, and then Rufe, in a most uncharacteristic display of emotion.

'Oh my dears, what wonderful news. I am so happy for you. And when is the happy day to be?'

'We haven't decided yet.'

'Soon,' Rufe told her.

'As it should be. You've wasted too much time already.' She ushered them toward the open door. 'Now, come inside, we have much to talk about.'

As she walked down the hall, Bella called out to Mary, who bustled out from the kitchen, all smiles as she saw Kitty and Rufe.

'Hello, Mrs. B. And Mr. Cavanagh, too. It's good to see you again. Is your daughter with you?'

'No Mary, she's safely in school. So I can have a peaceful visit this time.'

Bella interrupted, excitement in her voice. 'They have news, Mary, good news.'

'Really, what...'

She broke off as Kitty held out her hand, and her face lit up. 'Why Mr. Cavanagh, you've finally been and done it. I thought you were never going to get around to it.'

Rufe laughed. 'Yes, I'm afraid I've been a bit slow, haven't I?'

'Well, you've done it now, that's all that matters. And I know you'll both be very happy.' She caught hold of Kitty's hand. 'Oh, Mrs. B, what a beautiful ring.'

'It is magnificent,' Bella added. 'And I think this calls for a celebration, I think we need something a little stronger than tea, Mary. Would you get a message to Patrick and ask him to come in, and to fetch Jack as well? And then bring us champagne into the drawing room, please, and come in yourself. Shall we meet in the drawing room in, say, half an hour?'

When they were all assembled, and the greetings over, Jack opened the champagne, and Mary handed the glasses around.

'I can't tell you how much pleasure this gives me.' Jack looked across at Kitty and Rufe as they sat alongside each other on the sofa. 'I wish you both all the happiness in the world, and I know that goes for all of us.' He raised his glass. 'I'd like to propose a toast to Kitty and Rufe.'

Kitty reached for Rufe's hand, and held it for the toast. There was no doubting that all those at Redwoods, the people Kitty loved, were glad of their betrothal, and Kitty's happiness almost overwhelmed her.

'Now,' asked Bella, as the glasses were refilled, 'when is the wedding to be, and where?'

'It must be at a time and place when our daughters can be part of it, so that means during school holidays.'

'And as I refuse to wait any longer than necessary,' Rufe added, 'we've settled on Easter, and as they only have one week's holiday then, there won't be time to come up here, so Sydney it is.'

Bella clasped her hands together. 'An Easter wedding in Sydney. How perfect.'

Lady Barron put down the letter as she finished reading, and looked across the breakfast table at her husband, who was immersed in The Times.

'Really, Alexander, that child has no sense of propriety. But what can you expect, being raised in some obscure colonial backwater as she has been? And schooling in Sydney instead of here, as she should be.'

Sir Alexander Barron put his paper aside. 'I presume you are speaking of William's daughter, our grand-daughter, Joy?'

'Of course. Who else would it be?'

'And what has she done to deserve your displeasure?'

Lady Barron pressed her lips together. 'I have a letter from her telling me how pleased she is that she's finally to be allowed to visit, although her mother won't allow it until she's seventeen. So ridiculous, when you consider it gives us only a year to prepare her for her Season, and goodness knows how much grooming she will need, being brought up…'

'I am sure William's wife is competent enough to have brought her up in a civilised manner. And I have made enquiries about St. Catherine's School, and it has an excellent reputation. So I don't think you need concern yourself too much about that.' He reached for his paper. 'Is that all, my dear?'

'No. It is not! She has the temerity to ask me if there's any possibility of another young woman, a school friend who is also the daughter of the man her mother is about to marry, coming with her to stay. Really!'

Alexander raised his brows. 'Ah. So Kitty is to marry again. I'm surprised she has not chosen to do so before. She's an attractive and intelligent woman, I'm sure it wouldn't have been due to lack of offers. I wonder who she is marrying?'

Lady Barron consulted the letter. 'Someone by the name of Cavanagh. He has something to do with the government, according to Joy, as an adviser.'

'I shall make enquiries from Henry Brand.'

'You mean Brand, Viscount Hampden?'

'Yes. He's currently serving as Governor of New South Wales.'

'I see, well, yes, he's bound to know. At any rate, she wants to bring this person with her, *'if it would not inconvenience you,'* she says.'

'I can't see that it would inconvenience us. It's not as if we don't have room, either here or in the Town house.'

'That is not the point. Who knows what she would be like, or who her family are? It will be hard enough to ensure Joy understands etiquette, without another possible hoyden to educate.'

'But you wouldn't need to present her at Court.'

Lady Barron bristled. 'I most certainly would not. But are you telling me that you think I should seriously consider this request?'

'I see no reason why not. After all, it will all be strange to Joy, and she would feel more comfortable with a familiar companion, a friend. And I do want her to be happy here with us. I'm sorry her mother won't be accompanying her.'

'Really, Alexander! William should never have married her in the first place, after the disgrace of her father's death.'

'As to that, my dear, it was revealed at George Arnold's trial that Charles Morland had been swindled by him, by a man he believed to be his friend. I sympathise with him.'

'There can never be an excuse for suicide.'

'He knew he would be destitute and, in his despair, he took what he saw as the only way out. I'm not saying I condone it, but I do understand it. And it was all over twenty years ago. As far as I'm concerned Kitty is welcome in my home, and I would expect you to extend the same courtesy to her, should the occasion arise.'

'Harrumph. That's not the question.' Lady Barron pursed her lips. 'The question is, how am I expected to answer this letter?'

'You shall answer Joy by saying that her friend is welcome.' He picked up *The Times* again. 'And now I wish to finish my paper.'

Lady Barron glowered. 'Very well. If you insist. But she must bring her own chaperone with her. I will not be held responsible for her behaviour.'

Chapter Eleven

Joy received a letter from her mother telling her that she and Mr. Cavanagh were to be married at Easter in St James Church here in Sydney, and she wished Lily and Joy to be part of the bridal party. How exciting! Mr. Cavanagh's brother Edward, and his nephew David, would be best man and groomsman.

Lily had heard from the same details from her father too, but she didn't seem pleased about the wedding. This puzzled Joy. When she asked Lily if she wasn't happy for her father, Lily shrugged, and told her he'd been quite happy, before her mother had come back into his life. She glared so fiercely when she said this that Joy said no more. Lily was in a bad mood for days.

Chapter Twelve

The bride's carriage pulled up outside the brick and stone Church of St James, whose spire had been a landmark for ships in the harbour for the last seventy years. The two bridesmaids stepped down first, Lily in a dress of lemon silk, to suit her dark colouring, and Joy in pale green. Wearing matching satin slippers, and with their hair up for the special day, they both looked quite grown-up in their finery.

Kitty stood for a moment, lifting her face to the autumn sun, and then smoothed down her dress – a simple, stylish gown of soft oyster-pink silk. A tiny matching hat, with upturned brim and a curling feather, perched on her head, and she carried a small bouquet of deep pink roses. She turned to Jack with a smile. 'Here we are. Time for the big occasion.'

Jack bent and gave her a swift kiss on the cheek. 'No one deserves happiness more than you, my dear girl. And I'm proud to be the one giving you away.'

'There was never any question of it being anyone else.'

The music swelled, coming out to greet them, and Jack proffered his arm. 'Let's go.'

As they stepped through the door Kitty hesitated, and took a deep breath. Sunlight streamed through the stained glass windows, highlighting the bronze chrysanthemums, arranged around the church, that glowed against the red cedar panelling.

Smiling faces turned to see the bride arrive, but Kitty's gaze was drawn to Rufe. He stood with his back to her as he waited at the altar with Edward, his best man, and David, his groomsman.

He turned his head and their eyes met, and she stepped forward on Jack's arm, down the long the white marble aisle, to embrace their future.

When the ceremony was over, and the groom had kissed his bride, the small bridal party followed them and watched while they signed the register. They all signed below as witnesses, and Kitty was now Mrs. Cavanagh.

As Joy moved away from the register she caught David watching her. As he saw her looking at him, he winked at her and, embarrassed, Joy turned away.

As they prepared to walk down the aisle behind the bride and groom David positioned himself alongside her, and took her arm.

'My father can escort Lily,' he told her. 'I'll look after you.'

'I don't need looking after, thank you, but you may escort me.'

'Point taken.' He laughed. 'I shall be delighted to escort you.'

Looking up at him, Joy saw his dark brown eyes twinkling down at her. She had little experience of the opposite sex, but she felt something stir inside, and her heart gave a little flutter. What could she say so he wouldn't consider her a baby? She remembered Lily had told her he was good fun to be with, and that he was obsessed with horses, but you couldn't start a conversation about horses during a wedding, could you?

She was saved from the dilemma by David squeezing her arm and whispering, 'Lovely wedding, isn't it? Your mother looks beautiful, and Uncle Rufe is suave and handsome, as always. They make a striking couple. '

Joy smiled up at him, her moment of unease gone.

'Yes, don't they? And they both look so happy.'

He nodded. 'Mother's so pleased. She's been trying to find a wife for him for years.'

As they proceeded down the aisle behind the happy couple Joy was well aware of the young man at her side, holding her arm firmly.

As they made their way down the aisle, Kitty was surprised to see such a large congregation. Many of Rufe's friends and colleagues had come to see him tie the knot, and, on Kitty's side, she had her family, Mary and Patrick, and a few friends from Bulahdelah who made the trip to Sydney. She was surprised, and a little hurt, that Harry Osborne was not with them, as she knew he came to Sydney often. He had not even acknowledged receiving the invitation, or sent a reply.

Although Kitty did not know it, Harry Osborne was in Sydney. In fact, at that moment, he was loitering outside the Hyde Park Barracks, opposite the church. With his hat pulled down low, and his coat collar turned up, he wasn't noticeable among the small groups of women who had stopped to watch. He saw the bride's carriage pull up and watched the bridal party enter the church. His face twisted with jealousy. He stayed there until they all emerged after the ceremony, then he spat on the ground and hurried away.

The reception was a lively affair held at Rufe's house in Summer Hill. From the quiet gathering first contemplated it had grown. After the wedding breakfast the rugs were rolled up in the drawing room, and Erin played the piano while they all danced.

When David first asked Joy to waltz with him she felt shy. Although they learned to dance at school, she wasn't used to dancing with the opposite sex. When his arm went around her waist she felt quite breathless, and little tingles ran down her spine. When the dance was over she realised she'd found the experience exhilarating.

After Kitty and Rufe left on the first stage of their honeymoon trip, to the Imperial Hotel at Mt Victoria in the Blue Mountains, the dancing continued among the guests until well into the night. And if anyone noticed that David Cavanagh danced more often with Joy Barron than with anyone else, no one remarked on it to Joy.

When her grandparents announced it was time to go home, David thanked Joy for being such a charming companion, and gave her a chaste kiss on the cheek – and Joy felt her heart go flip-flop.

When Joy received a letter with an English post mark she knew it must be a reply from her grandmother. When she finished reading it she let out a whoop, and rushed from the room in search of her friend. She bumped into her in the passageway as she turned a corner in haste, and caused Lily to stumble.

'Lily, wait till you hear my news.' She waved the letter, hardly able to contain her excitement.

'It better be good. You almost knocked me over, you ninny.'

'Never mind that. Just listen. I've had a letter from my grandmother in England. I didn't tell you before, but I wrote to her, and asked if you could come with me to England, and stay with them.'

Lily's jaw dropped. 'What? You really did that?'

Her face was a picture of fear and hope as Joy nodded, laughing.

'Yes. And guess what? She said yes!'

Lily blinked. 'You're sure?'

Joy nodded. 'Yes, really!'

Lily's face split into a wide grin. 'Yippee!' She executed a quick jig on the spot, at the same moment as the headmistress turned the corner

'Lily Cavanagh, what are you doing? That is no way for a young lady to behave.'

Lily stopped, but she couldn't remove the smile from her face. 'I'm sorry, Miss Darling, but I'm so excited. Joy just told me I can go to England with her. Can you imagine that? We're both going to England.'

'That is good news. I'm happy for you. But perhaps you should save your dancing for a more appropriate time and place.' A smile quivered at her mouth. 'Now, off you go, don't loiter in the halls.'

As they entered their room, Lily grabbed Joy's arm, her face alight with excitement. 'So what does she say exactly?'

'She says you can come with me and stay at Bournbridge Hall, and then come when we go to the Townhouse in London, and stay for the whole Season.'

Lily's eyes sparkled. 'Wonderful. So when do we go?'

'Grandmother says we're to be there in August next year.'

'Not till then?'

'No. She says they'll all be back at Bournbridge Hall in August, in time for the hunting. It'll give you and me time to learn 'the rules of social behaviour,' as she calls it, before we go to London in the following February.'

'So when do you think we'll be leaving here?'

'Probably in May or June, I suppose.'

'Oh.' Lily's teeth caught her bottom lip. 'Then we'll have about six months after we finish school at the end of the year until we go. What are we going to do then?'

'I suppose we'll just stay home.'

'But – where? Where is home now?'

Joy frowned. 'I suppose it's at the house in Summer Hill, with your father and my mother. After all, they want us to be a family now. Don't you want to stay there, with them?'

'No.' Lily's voice was fierce. 'They'll be busy, they won't want us.' She paused. 'I think I want to go back to Riverside. And I want you to come with me.' She caught Joy by the hand. 'You will come, won't you? We'll have all the horses there. Please say you'll come.'

Joy was surprised and disconcerted by Lily's intensity. She would sooner stay in Sydney, but Lily sounded desperate. After hesitating, she replied.

'All right,' she told her friend. 'I'll come.'

Chapter Thirteen

Finally school ended for Joy and Lily. As they stepped up onto the dais to receive their graduation certificates from Miss Darling, Joy saw her mother and Rufe sitting in the front row, clapping. When the speeches were over they all returned to the house in Summer Hill, where they sat in the drawing room.

'Congratulations,' Rufe told the girls, beaming as he handed them both a glass of champagne. 'I'm proud of you. You've both done well.'

'Yes, indeed you have,' Kitty added, raising her glass. 'And I'd like to drink a toast to your futures, to both of you.'

'I'll second that. To the two cleverest and prettiest girls from St Catherine's.'

'How you do exaggerate, Father,' Lily said, but she joined in the laughter as they drank.

'Now, we need to talk about your futures. Your immediate futures, that is, seeing that you're both going to England next year. And what to do in the time until you leave, which you'll be spending here at home.'

Joy felt a flutter of butterflies inside her as the subject she had been dreading came up. 'Don't you mean at Riverside?' Lily asked Rufe.

He frowned. 'Of course not. This is home now. We'll still spend some time at both Riverside and Redwoods, of course, but I want you to regard this as home.' He turned to Kitty. 'That's what we both want, isn't it?'

Kitty nodded. 'Yes it is. We hope you'll both be happy here in Sydney. There are so many things for you do, and so many places to go. It'll be fun for us all. We're looking forward to showing you places, doing things together.'

'I do love being in Sydney,' Joy said hesitantly.

Lily looked mutinous. 'Joy and I have decided we want to go to Riverside until we leave for England.'

'What nonsense is this?' Rufe asked, looking angry. 'When did you decide this?'

'When Joy received the letter from Lady Barron and we knew we wouldn't be going for about six months. Didn't we, Joy?'

Joy nodded. 'Yes.' She was now regretting her promise to Lily, but a promise was a promise. Was there perhaps some way they could compromise? 'Um – perhaps we could go to Riverside for a bit, and then to Redwoods, and then back here before we leave. Would that be all right?'

Lily glared at her. 'You promised, you said...'

'You will need to spend time here,' Kitty interrupted. 'Now that you've left school you need new clothes, and fittings take time. We can't have you arriving in England looking like country cousins, can we? And I can understand that you both want to spend some time in your old homes before you go.'

'Would that suit you, Lily?' Rufe asked tersely.

Lily glowered at Joy, but she answered her father quietly. 'Yes, Father.'

'Good. Now there are some things we need to discuss. As you know, Lily, I had a letter from Lady Barron and in it she spelt out certain requirements for you, for your visit to her home. It's exceedingly gracious of her to invite you to stay when she hasn't met either you or myself. I'm sure you realise that, don't you?'

'Yes Father, I do.'

'Good. Now, we must find someone to accompany you, someone who will act as a chaperone for you for the whole time you're there, and I've found a woman whom I think will be ideal. Her name is Mrs. Frobisher. She's a widow, about thirty years old, and she seems very pleasant. I've arranged that she'll sail with you and Joy on the trip over, and she'll go with you to Bournbridge Hall, and then to London.'

'I see. Joy says everything is very formal in England, and it's customary for young women to be chaperoned. You've been to England, do you think so?'

'Yes. You'll find there are many more rules about what you can and cannot do over there.'

'Will this Mrs. Frobisher have to go with me when we go out?'

'That will be for Lady Barron to arrange. You'll do exactly as she says while you're there.'

'Yes, of course.'

'I'll make financial arrangements so you can have an allowance while you're there. And Lady Baron informs me I'm to see you have an adequate dress allowance. It seems young ladies of fashion need abundant amounts of clothing for a Season in London.'

Kitty nodded. 'Oh yes. They certainly do. I remember it well. You can't wear the same clothes all the time.'

Joy hadn't thought of this. 'Does that mean I'll have one too?'

'You will indeed.'

'And I've been wondering, how will we get from the ship to Bournbridge Hall?'

'Sir Alexander will send a coach to meet you.'

'It all sounds wonderful.'

Lily clapped her hands then, smiling, and Joy was pleased to see her bad mood had passed.

The first morning after Joy and Lily arrived at Riverside dawned fine and sunny. Joy jumped from her bed and pulled back the curtains to breathe the pure, fresh air wafting through the open window. A few fleecy clouds gave the sky a third dimension, and the sun's rays slanting across the lush green pasture revealed horses in the nearest paddock, heads down as they grazed.

After breakfast Erin shooed the girls outside. 'Go and enjoy yourselves,' she told them. 'I don't need any help today. Lily, I'm sure Joy wants to have a look around, and David will find a horse for her. Go on, off you go.'

They needed no more urging, but before they had time to do more than reach the top of the verandah steps, a voice hailed them.

'Hey, tadpole, I need a hand.'

Looking over the verandah rail Joy saw David brandishing a halter.

'Come and help me, both of you,' he called out.

'Do you want to?' Lily asked Joy.

'Sure. Come on.'

Bounding down the steps they ran to join him.

'We have a prospective buyer coming today, and I have to groom three horses,' David told them. 'Can you groom a horse?' he asked Joy.

'Of course I can. I have my own horse at home.'

'Some of the girls from those posh schools are useless. I hope you're not one of them, are you?'

Joy bristled. 'No, I'm certainly not.'

David eyed her up and down, lifting his brows, while a smile played around his lips.

'Hmm. There's not much of you, is there? You're even smaller than tadpole over there.' He indicated Lily. 'You're just a shrimp. Are you sure you can handle a horse?'

Joy tightened her lips. 'I'm sure I can groom a horse as well as you.'

'We'll see. I'm a hard taskmaster, you know. I've had to train tadpole here, and now she's not too bad. If you both help me, we'll be done in no time.'

'Don't call me tadpole,' Lily told him. 'I'll be seventeen soon.'

'Yes, I know. I saw you both at the wedding, with your hair up pretending to be ladies and all grown up.'

'I am seventeen, and next year I'm going to be presented to the Queen,' Joy told him. 'So I am grown up, thank you!'

He laughed down at her, his eyes dancing. 'Well, now, shrimp, that's something, isn't it? But do you reckon you can forget that long enough to race over to the stalls with tadpole, and bring back another couple of halters, so I can catch these horses? I'd be obligated if you could. I'll be in this first paddock. Just bring them to the gate.'

Lily pulled at Joy's arm. 'Come on. He's hopeless. He never stops teasing.'

Joy turned then, and joined her in a sprint to the stalls.

'Last one back's a rotten egg,' David shouted after them. Then he turned and strode toward the gate to the first paddock, whistling cheerfully.

By the time the girls returned with the halters, David had caught his first horse. He handed the leading rope to Lily. 'You hold this while I catch the next one,' he said, taking the halter from her.

'I can catch one,' Joy told him.

'No. They don't know you, best I do it.'

She shrugged, and watched as he approached a good looking bay with a white blaze down his nose. The horse stood quietly while David put the halter on him and led him back. He handed the rope to Joy, and went back into the paddock.

Joy stood by the horse's head while she stroked his neck and spoke softly to him, giving him time to become accustomed to her. Ears pricked, he turned his head to watch her.

'What's his name?' she asked Lily.

'Blaze.'

'Good boy, Blaze.'

Blaze tossed his head and whinnied. She rubbed his ears, talking softly to him.

The last horse took a little longer to catch, but at last all three horses were tied to a rail. Lily showed Joy where the grooming tools were kept, and she collected the gear and moved back to Blaze.

'Good boy, Blaze,' Joy repeated. She picked up the curry comb and massaged him with it, before taking a stiff brush and working all over his coat. So engrossed did she become in her job that she did not notice David watching intently as she went about her task.

Joy talked to the horse while she worked, and Blaze stood calmly, shifting his position occasionally.

'There, my bonny boy, you're starting to look like a champion,' she told him as she went to work with the soft finishing brush.

When she had finished she stood and stretched, aware of an ache in her back and across the shoulders.

'Ooh, I'm out of practice,' she muttered, wiping the sheen of perspiration from her face. Looking around she saw that Lily had gone, and David was standing nearby watching her. She straightened as he sauntered towards her.

'Well done, shrimp. I couldn't have done a better job myself.'

Her aches forgotten, Joy flushed at his praise. She even overlooked him calling her 'shrimp'.

Later that day the buyer came and chose the two that had been groomed by David and Lily.

'I wonder why he didn't choose Blaze,' Joy mused, when David told her.

He shrugged. 'People choose horses for a lot of different reasons. He decided he only wanted two horses, and he chose those he thought best suited his requirements.' He paused for a moment, eyeing her seriously. 'You really like Blaze, don't you?'

'Oh yes, I really do.'

'Seeing you did such a good job of grooming him, would you like to have him to ride and look after while you're here?'

'Oh yes please.' Joy was elated. 'I'll take good care of him.'

David smiled at her. 'I'm sure you will.'

Over the next few weeks the two girls spent their time riding, or helping David with his work in caring for the horses. Their mutual love of horses forged a bond between them, but when they were together Joy sometimes noticed David watching her with a look on his face that caused her heart to flutter. What did it mean? She wished she was more experienced in worldly matters.

On the day they were leaving Riverside, Joy went to the horse stalls alone to say goodbye to Blaze. 'I'm going to miss you, Blaze.' Her arms went around the horse's neck and she hugged him. 'I suppose you'll be sold by the time I come back, but I'll never forget you. Next to Dancer, you're the best horse ever.'

She realised David had followed her to the stall and was watching her.

'Well, shrimp, I can see you're going to miss Blaze,' he said, 'but what about the rest of us? I don't suppose you'll miss any of us, including me.'

Joy dropped her arms and turned. 'Of course I will. I've loved being here and I'll miss you all. I'll especially miss you David. I'll always remember how good it's been working with you, with the horses. And the fun we've had together.'

'I'd like you to remember me for more than that.' Covering the ground between them in quick strides, he pulled her gently to him. 'Joy, I know you're only a baby yet. I wish you weren't going away. I wish I had time to help you grow up, to find out what it's like to have a woman's feelings for a man. To know what it's like to be kissed. Like this.'

Joy felt a jolt of surprise as his arms went around her. Then he bent his head and his lips found hers. His lips were soft, and he kissed her gently. Her heart began to beat faster. Her arms stole around his neck and she kissed him back, tentatively. Then she felt a wave of heat flash through her, and suddenly she was kissing him fiercely. His arms went around her and he pulled her close to him. She felt his body pressed to hers. It made her legs go weak.

He stepped back from her, breathing heavily. His colour was high, and his eyes glittered.

'Is that the way you kiss a baby?' she asked him.

'Not all babies – just you. That was something for you to remember me by. Will you remember me?'

'Yes, I will.'

He laughed shakily. 'I'll hold you to that. And now we'd better go back to the others, before I forget myself completely.'

She put her hand up and touched his cheek. 'I won't forget you. That's a promise.'

Chapter Fourteen

'Do you want to go to the Guy Fawkes bonfire in Bulahdelah tonight?' Joy asked Lily.

They were sitting under a tree in the garden at Redwoods, deciding what to do for the rest of the day.

'Yes, it might be fun and we're not doing anything else.'

'Then we need to go in and buy some firecrackers for it. Do you want to walk in, or ride?'

'Let's ride.'

'All right.'

Jumping up they made their way across to the paddock where the horses were grazing, and a short while later they rode into Bulahdelah and tied up their horses outside the General Store.

'Gee, it's busy in here today,' Joy remarked as they selected their fireworks from the large display in the store.

'Yes, all the kids are buying their crackers for tonight. What have you got so far?'

'Catherine wheels and sky rockets and sparklers. And a string of small crackers. I'm not getting any of those big penny bungers, they're too loud, I hate them. What about you?'

'Yes, same as you. And I'm taking some jumping jacks too.'

'I think I have plenty here.'

'Yes, me too.'

They paid for their purchases and walked outside. At that moment there was a loud bang from a short distance down the street. Their horses shied and tugged at the halters tying them to the rail. Their eyes rolled and their nostrils flared as they reared.

'You little buggers,' shouted a passerby as a knot of lads scattered and fled. 'I'll have the police on to you, for tossing crackers around like that and frightening the horses,' ' he bellowed.

Joy and Lily ran to calm their horses.

'Here, Dancer, here, it's all right. It's all right, I'm here now. It's all right, girl.' Joy held her horse's head and stroked the shivering mare's neck as she soothed her. When Dancer settled Joy looked around, and saw Lily had managed to calm her mount too.

'Let's get out of here before those little hooligans do any more damage,' Joy said angrily. Stuffing her parcel into the saddlebag and untying the halter, she swung herself up into the saddle. There she sat for a moment, stroking Dancer some more before turning her around and out on to the road, with Lily following them.

They rode out of town, and were inside the gate at Redwoods, on their way down the driveway, when an explosion right alongside Joy caused the horses to rear and plunge, neighing with terror.

Joy screamed as Dancer bolted. She tried to hang on but it was no use, and she hit the ground heavily with all the wind knocked from her body.

She heard Lily screaming and tried to sit up, but her limbs refused to move. She lay there gasping for air, and when she was finally able to raise her head she saw Lily running back up the track towards her. Lily was shouting something, but Joy couldn't understand her.

Propping herself up on one elbow, her breath coming in gasps, she tried to make out what she was saying. She caught the word 'Dancer' and looked around frantically for her horse. When she saw her she screamed. Dancer lay beside a fence with one leg caught in it, writhing on the ground. Pulling herself to her feet, unaware of the pain, Joy hobbled toward her as fast as she could.

'No Dancer. No, no,' she screamed, fear making her voice shrill. When she came nearer she saw the near side front hoof had become caught under the fence, and the foreleg had snapped. It was still caught in the fence, with the bone sticking through the skin. She stared in horror. Time stood still while the enormity of it sank in.

Looking up, she saw Lily had stopped, and was staring at her with terror on her face.

'Go and get Grandpa,' Joy shouted. Lily stood there mutely. 'Go on,' she screamed, 'get him. Run. Run.'

Lily turned and bolted down the track. Joy dropped to the ground beside Dancer, great sobs racking her body, and lifted the horse's head onto her knees, cradling it against her chest. As the tears poured down onto Dancer's face she cradled her in her arms and kissed her over and over, feeling her pain.

'Dancer, Dancer, I love you. Don't die, don't leave me.' But even as she said it she knew it was futile. Nothing could save her. Dancer was still now, her painful breathing filling the air. Joy nursed her head, trying not to look at the leg, and crooned softly to her.

'Remember all the good times we've had, all the things we've done together. I'll never forget you, never.' Gently she stroked Dancer's face and rubbed her ears, talking to her all the while, as her tears fell on the beloved face.

Joy was not aware anyone else was there until she felt a hand on her shoulder and she looked up to see Grandma standing beside her with Grandpa, grim faced and with his rifle in hand.

'Come on now, dear,' Grandma said, 'come with me. Grandpa will take care of Dancer now.'

With Grandma helping her, Joy stood up and turned, sobs shaking her body and her heart almost bursting with pain. Grandma's arms came around her, pulling her close.

'There, there, my lovely,' she soothed, 'come with me. You can't do any more for Dancer. We'll go home now. Come along.'

Joy let herself be led away, and they walked together toward the house. They had not gone far when Joy heard the shot, and she tore herself free. She ran to the house, into her room, slammed the door shut, and threw herself down onto the bed. Burying her face in the pillow she clutched it with both hands and gave way to the storm of sobbing that racked her body.

Later Bella went in and sat with Joy, cradling her in her arms, speaking soothingly to her. But nothing she said could stem the outpouring of grief. She sat with her for a long time, and when the tears lessened, she covered her with a rug and left her alone. After she came out of the room she refused to allow anyone else to go in.

'She needs time to herself to cry it out. We'll leave her be for tonight. Lily, I hope you won't mind sleeping in the spare room tonight?'

'No, of course not.'

Mary made up the bed, and it was a very sombre household that retired early for the night.

When Joy came out of her room next morning, her eyes were swollen and her face was blotchy.

Bella was waiting nearby. She went to her and put her arms around her.

'Joy, my dear, we are all so very, very sorry for what happened. There's nothing I can say to make you feel better.'

Joy leant her head against Bella. 'Poor Dancer, I hate to think of her in pain like that, she...' her voice trailed off as she gulped.

'I know, it's dreadful, but you helped her by comforting her. You calmed her. It stilled her and the pain wouldn't have been so bad for her then.'

'Do you really think so?'

'I'm sure of it.'

'Where....is she...' Her voice faltered.

'Grandpa and Patrick have buried her under a tree in the horse paddock. When you feel up to it we'll go there. But now you'd better come and have a cup of tea.'

'I'm not hungry.'

'No, but a cup of tea will be good for you.' She took Joy's arm. 'Come on.'

Joy let her lead her into the dining room.

Lily was waiting there, staring out of the window. She turned when they came in and bit her lip as she stood looking at Joy. She seemed on the verge of tears.

'It was one of those hooligans from town, you know. I caught a glimpse of him as he ran away, but I couldn't see him clearly.'

'Would you be able to recognise him if you saw him again?' asked Bella.

'No, I didn't see his face.'

'Then nothing can be done about it, I'm afraid. He'll go scot-free.'

'It's not fair,' Lily said fiercely, brushing tears from her eyes.

'No, it's not. But there's nothing we can do, I'm afraid. The police will want to know what you saw, but unless someone else saw him too, nothing will happen.'

'If I ever caught him, I'd kill him myself,' Joy said violently.

Bella was pleased to hear the anger in her voice. It would help to dissipate the grief.

Just then Jack came in, carrying a wooden cross in his hands.

'Ah, there you are, Joy.' He walked over to her and bent, kissing her gently. 'I made this for you, dear,' he said. He offered the cross to Joy. 'I think she deserves it.'

Joy took it from him, swallowing the lump in her throat. On the cross bar, burnt into the timber, was the word, 'DANCER'. She stared at it for a minute, then ran a finger across the word.

'Did you make this, Grandpa?' she asked, her voice shaking.

'Yes.'

'Thank you.' She reached up and kissed his cheek. 'I think I'd like to go and see her now.'

Mary and Patrick joined them as they walked over to the horse paddock. In a corner, in the shade of a tall red-flowering gum, was a patch of freshly dug earth. The horses already in the paddock ambled over to them and stood nearby, watching curiously, as Jack and Patrick helped Joy to erect the cross at the head of the grave.

When they finished Joy stood back and surveyed their work, then looked around at the horses.

'Dancer won't be lonely here. They'll keep her company.' Joy took a deep breath. 'Thank you. I think I'd like to be alone with her now to say goodbye, if you don't mind.'

When they arrived back in Sydney later that month Joy found a letter waiting for her. It was from David, telling her how sorry he was to hear of her loss. It was a short letter, expressing his sympathy, and in it he wrote *'I know how much you loved Dancer, and no other horse can ever take her place, but I know you became attached to Blaze while you were here, and I am writing to tell you that I am not going to sell him. When you return from England he will be here and if you want him, he is yours. I am sure he missed you when you left and you both fitted so well together, you made a good pair, and I know he would be happy to belong to you.*

Blaze is not the only one to miss you, and I look forward to seeing you again when you return.

Affectionately yours,

David Cavanagh.'

The letter brought a smile to Joy's face, and a feeling of lightness to her heart that had been missing since the accident. She read it through several times before sitting down and penning a reply. She thanked David, and told him she would be so happy to have Blaze when she returned.

On the day before they were due to sail Joy received a telegraph. It contained only three words. *Bon Voyage. David.*

She tucked it into a bag that was going with her to England.

Chapter Fifteen

It finally happened. Joy, Lily and Mrs. Frobisher boarded the *Miranda,* bound for England. The excitement of finally being under way, and the long shipboard journey, which passed pleasantly enough, helped to push Joy's grief into the background.

Joy and Lily were happy to find Mrs. Frobisher agreeable company on the voyage. Aged about thirty, she had brown hair, pale blue eyes and a pleasant face with a rather pert nose. She arranged their hair for them and saw to their clothes, but apart from the time she took attending to that, and meal times, she spent most of the voyage sitting in the saloon or on deck reading romance novels, of which she seemed to have an endless supply.

By the time they reached England Joy was able to think of Dancer, if not without pain, at least without tears. And it was helped by remembering that when she returned Blaze would be waiting for her. And David. When she remembered him kissing her she tingled all over. But then she reminded herself that he considered her a baby. He was just being friendly – or more likely, she decided, he'd been teasing her. Yes, that was probably it. He was a terrible teaser. That was all it had been.

When the ship berthed they were met by Sir Alexander's steward, James Bennett, and a footman, and whisked away with their luggage in Sir Alexander's carriage.

They arrived at the luxurious Claridges Hotel in Mayfair, and gazed around in awe as Mr. Bennett escorted them across the black and white tiles of the elegant foyer and attended to their reception. When the formalities were completed he handed Joy a note.

'Sir Alexander asked me to give you this, Miss Barron.'

'Thank you, Mr. Bennett. And for all you've done for us.'

'Not at all. You'll be quite safe now. You'll be shown to your rooms and Sir Alexander will see you shortly.' He nodded to a bellboy standing nearby. 'You may show the ladies to their rooms now.' He turned back to Joy. 'I'll see you later, Miss Barron.'

With a nod he left them, and the bellboy led them up the wide curved staircase and opened the door to a suite on the first floor.

'Your luggage will be up in a moment,' he told them as he led them inside to a large sitting room. He opened the doors to the adjoining bed rooms before leaving.

'Well now, this is very nice,' observed Mrs. Frobisher.

She and Lily examined the sitting room, then went into each of the bedrooms and the bathroom, while Joy opened the envelope and extracted the note.

'Which bedroom do you want?' Lily called out to her.

'I don't mind,' she called back. 'You pick.'

Her heart beat faster as she read the communication from her grandfather. *My dear Joy, welcome to England. I have waited many years for the pleasure of meeting you. I would welcome your company at 4pm if you are rested enough by then. My suite is 157, next to yours. I look forward to our meeting.'* It was signed, simply, 'Grandfather.'

Joy felt a lump in her throat as she put the note down, and tears blurred her eyes. After all the years of wondering about her father's family she was finally about to meet them. She had never known her father, who drowned before she was born, but now she was going to meet his father. What would he be like? He must be very old by now. Her musing was interrupted by the arrival of their luggage.

Mrs. Frobisher bustled around and directed the cases to the appropriate rooms, and began unpacking.

'Mrs. Frobisher, I'm going to meet my grandfather in two hours time. I want to have a bath first, and I think I'd like to wear my blue dress.'

'That's all right. I'll make sure it's ironed.'

'Thank you, and would you mind fixing my hair for me please?'

'Of course. You need to look your best for such an important meeting.'

Lily came back into the room. 'Are you nervous, Joy?'

Joy drew a deep breath. 'Yes. A little. I've thought about this, and imagined it so many times, but now it's actually happening, well, it is a bit scary.'

'Your grandfather must be very wealthy, to put us all up here,' Mrs. Frobisher said. 'Claridges is very exclusive. Why, Queen Victoria and Prince Albert have stayed here.'

Lily's eyes opened wide. 'Really. Are you sure?'

'Yes, I read about it in the paper. It was when they came to visit Empress Eugenie of France. She always stays here, too.'

Joy left them to their discussion of Royalty and, going into the bathroom, ran herself a bath in the enormous claw-foot bath. She sniffed at the scented bath salts that stood in glass jars on the wash stand, and added some that smelled of roses.

As she enjoyed a long soak she let her mind drift. What would her grandparents be like? She knew Mother liked her grandfather but, from what she had overheard, she knew she didn't like Lady Barron. 'An autocratic lady', that was all she would say when Joy asked about her. And Grandma told her she would make up her own mind when she met her. That didn't sound promising. Would there be other family members at Bournbridge Hall? She supposed so, but she didn't know.

And what of the etiquette Grandmother had told her she must learn? She sighed. There would be so much to find out – would she be able to live up to their expectations? When she thought about it she felt nervous, but then her normal optimism returned, and she knew it would all be a great adventure, and she couldn't wait for it to begin.

After she bathed and dressed, and Mrs. Frobisher put her hair up, she still had half an hour left before meeting Grandfather. She joined Lily and Mrs. Frobisher in the sitting room, and seated herself in one of the armchairs. They were both engrossed in reading.

'What are you reading?' she asked Lily.

'*La Gazette du Bon Ton*. It's marvellous. It's got all the latest fashions in it from Paris. Here,' she picked up another magazine and handed it to Joy. 'This is Harper's Bazaar. Have a look at all the fashion pages. Now we'll know all about the latest designs when we buy our new clothes.'

'Thanks.' Joy flicked through the pages. 'This is good. Now we won't appear ignorant. We don't want everyone to think Australia is behind the times.'

Joy hesitated a moment and stared at the door, trying to still the butterflies fluttering inside her. Taking a deep breath, she raised her hand and knocked on the door. It opened within seconds. A tall, distinguished-looking man with snow white hair and strong features stood there. He regarded her with piercing blue eyes.

'Joy.' He opened the door wide and stood back. 'My dear child, come in.'

Joy walked past him, then stopped and turned as he closed the door behind her.

'Let me look at you, my dear.' He reached his two hands out to her, and she placed hers in them.

'Grandfather,' she said shakily.

'My dear child,' he repeated, studying her face intently. 'Yes, you look like your mother, but there's a semblance of William too. Something in your demeanor.'

He dropped her hands then and put his arms around her, holding her gently. Returning his embrace, Joy felt him take a deep breath as he released her. 'I've waited many years for this. I've always hoped you would want to come and meet us.'

'I've wanted to come for a long time, but…' her voice trailed away. She didn't want to say her mother wouldn't let her.

'But it's such a long way. I know. It's the tyranny of distance that has prevented me from visiting you.' He smiled. 'Old bones don't take kindly to long voyages, I am afraid.' He paused. 'But I forget my manners, come and sit down.' He guided Joy to an armchair. 'I've ordered tea for us.'

He pulled on a bell-pull. 'So how is your mother?' he asked, as he sat next to her, leaning back in his chair.

'She's very well, thank you, and she asked to be remembered to you.'

'That's kind of her. A charming lady, Kitty, and I regret we never had the time to become more closely acquainted.'

'She told me you were kind to her after she and Father were married.'

'We knew each other for only a short while, but I saw from the start that she was strong, as well as beautiful. A fact that was borne out by her decision to stay in Australia and raise you on your own, after your father's unfortunate accident. It can't have been easy for her.' He shook his head, smiling. 'She's a very independent woman, your mother.'

Joy smiled back at him. 'Yes, she is. She's recently remarried, you know.'

Sir Alexander nodded. 'Yes, I know.'

They were interrupted by a knock at the door, and a waiter entered with a tea trolley.

'Ah yes, we will have it here,' he motioned for the waiter to place it alongside them. 'We'll help ourselves. Thank you.'

'Very good, sir.' The waiter bowed and left.

'I know that you have companions here,' he told Joy, 'but I've been very selfish and ordered just for the two of us. I want to have you all to myself this afternoon. Tonight we'll dine together downstairs, but this afternoon is for us, to get to know each other. I hope you don't mind?'

Joy looked at his kindly face. She relaxed as she smiled at him, and reached across and touched his hand. 'I think it's just perfect. We need to do that. And I want to know all about the family, about what to expect here in England. Maybe you can help me be prepared.'

His eyes twinkled at her. 'I'll warn you about all the family members, and in return you can tell me about your life in Australia. How's that?'

'Wonderful.'

He leant back in his chair. 'Then perhaps you'd care to pour, my dear.'

91

Chapter Sixteen

The next day they all drove in the carriage to Bournbridge Hall. When they arrived Grandfather left them after directing Denman, the butler, to escort them to Lady Barron's sitting room, where she awaited them.

Lady Barron rose from her chair as they entered the room and studied the three women standing before her.

'So you're William's daughter,' she said to Joy. 'Come here, child.'

Joy swallowed and obeyed the imperious demand. Lady Barron raised her lorgnette and peered through it, then she reached over and took hold of Joy's chin, turning her head first one way, then the other.

'Yes,' she said finally, 'I see the likeness.' She lowered her lorgnette, letting it fall onto her ample bosom. 'So, you're finally here with us, which is where you should always have been. It would have happened much sooner if your mother hadn't been so stubborn.'

In spite of her unease Joy felt compelled to defend her mother. 'I don't believe she was stubborn, she just wanted me to be with her, Lady Barron.'

'You may call me Grandmother.' Moving across the room Lady Barron tugged on a bell-pull before turning and directing her gaze at Lily. 'I suppose you're Miss Cavanagh.'

'Yes, that's right, Lady Barron.'

'And who is this with you?'

'This is Mrs. Frobisher.'

'Hmm. Frobisher. I presume Mr. Cavanagh has told you of your duties?'

'I'm to act as chaperone to Miss Lily.'

'Yes. That means that unless Miss Cavanagh is accompanied by me or Mrs. Rupert Barron, you will accompany her at all times. In particular, she must never be alone in the company of a gentleman, even here at home. Is that understood?'

'Yes, Lady Barron.'

'While you're here you will take orders from me. You will also act as Miss Cavanagh's maid.'

'I wasn't told that.'

'Nevertheless, that's what you'll do while you're here.' She turned her head as a severe looking woman, dressed all in black except for a white cap over her dark hair, entered the room. 'Ah, there you are, Davis. Show Miss Cavanagh to her room and take Frobisher to the staff quarters. Make sure Frobisher knows how to do hair properly, and anything else she needs to know. And see they both know how to address people in the correct manner.'

'Yes, milady,' replied Davis.

'They're from the colonies. That means considerable work for us all. I'll hold you responsible for Frobisher.'

'Yes, milady.' Davis bobbed her head, then turned to Lily and Mrs. Frobisher. 'If you come with me, I'll show you to your quarters.'

Mrs. Frobisher opened her mouth to say something, but closed it without a word. She turned and walked out behind Lily, her back stiff and straight.

Lady Barron turned her attention to Joy. 'Now then, we have much to discuss.' She seated herself in an armchair. 'Come, sit here.' She indicated the seat next to her.

'Now that you're to take your rightful position in the family you must never forget that you are a Barron. You must acquire poise, and you need to learn proper etiquette. You've much to learn in the next few months and I'll oversee your training myself, with assistance from my son's wife.'

'Do you mean Margaret, Rupert's wife?'

Lady Barron raised her eyebrows, and seemed to unbend a little. 'Ah, so you have some knowledge of the members of the family?'

'Yes. Grandfather told me a little about the household yesterday. I know that I have two uncles, your eldest son Rupert, who lives here with his wife and family, and your other son Hector, who's in India with his regiment.'

'Yes. Rupert's daughter Felicity is at home but his two sons, Walter and Harold, are away at school now.'

'And Uncle Rupert helps Grandfather run the estate. And then there's Aunt Anne, who spent some time in Australia with her husband, but is now back here.'

'Yes. Anne wished to return, so they're now farming sheep in Scotland. They don't visit very often.'

'So Margaret, Rupert's wife, will be the one to help me?'

'That's correct. Margaret is not as strong as she could be, but she'll assist me with your training. You have a lot to learn before we go to London in February. Added to which we must assemble an appropriate wardrobe for you.' She sniffed. 'And for your companion, Miss Cavanagh. If she's to accompany you to events she must be suitably attired. And her manners must be beyond reproach, or it will reflect on you. So she may accompany you when you're receiving instruction.'

'Thank you, Grandmother. Lily and I are good friends, and I'm very grateful that you were kind enough to invite her to stay here with me.'

'Yes, and I expect her to give me no cause to regret my invitation.'

'Oh, I'm quite sure she won't.'

'Good. Now, to get back to your wardrobe, I'll prepare a list of garments you need, and I'll have samples of material sent from my drapers in London. A seamstress will attend us, and I'll decide on styles and colours.'

It sounded to Joy as if she was to have little say in her choice of clothing, but she decided now was not the time to raise any objections.

'There's a lot to do in a short time. It's now the end of August, and come December we'll have Hector home on leave, and the boys home from Eton, and Christmas festivities will begin. I won't have time to spend with you then. While your garments are being made you'll spend your time learning etiquette and proper manners. In the afternoons, we'll often entertain friends and neighbours, and sometimes we'll visit them. You'll take notice of how we all act. That's how you'll learn to act in polite Society. I'll correct you when you make mistakes. Is that clear?'

'Yes, Grandmother. Will Lily accompany us?'

'Yes. Her manners must also be beyond reproach. I shall correct her also.'

'I'm sure she'll appreciate it.'

'In the mornings you'll have lessons in deportment. Including how to curtsey.'

'Oh yes, I must get that right. I'm so excited that I'm to be presented to Queen Victoria. It's like a dream come true.'

'You must be prepared to work hard. I won't allow the Barron name to be embarrassed. If you're not ready, I'll not present you next Season.'

'I'll work hard, I promise you.'

Over the next few months Joy was to remember those words often.

After showing Lily to her room, Davis led Mrs. Frobisher up another flight of stairs and opened the door to a small room containing a bed, a wardrobe, and a wash stand with jug and basin sitting on it.

'This is your room, Frobisher.'

'It's Mrs. Frobisher, thank you.'

'Not while you're here, it's not. It's Frobisher, same as most of us senior staff. Only the housekeeper and the butler get Mr. and Mrs., and the young ones, tweenies and the like, are called by their Christian names.'

'Oh, I see.' She moderated her voice. 'I was employed as a chaperone, but I don't mind acting as a maid to Lily. I've been doing their hair, for both of them. I suppose someone here will act for Joy, will they?'

'Yes, I'm acting for her. And while you're here you'll have to call her Miss Joy.'

'Oh, all right, and I suppose it's Miss Lily too.'

'No, she's Miss Cavanagh, because she isn't family.'

'Really. Looks like I've got a bit to learn. You're all very formal here, aren't you?'

'I suppose it must seem that way to you, coming from Australia like you do.' She paused. 'I've been there, you know.'

'To Australia? Have you really?'

'Yes, I travelled with their lordships when they went out there all those years ago.' She looked wistful. 'I enjoyed it. Everything's so free and easy.' She sighed. 'Look, just put your things down, and we'll pop along and have a cup of tea. Her ladyship expects me to fill you in on our ways, and we might as well do it in comfort.'

When they were seated in a small sitting room with their tea and a slice of Madeira cake each she continued.

'I wouldn't have minded staying in Australia, but of course I couldn't. I envied Mr. William. But then he had his Papa to see him right, while I had no money, of course.'

Mrs. Frobisher was interested. 'So you knew Joy's father. When he was young, before he met Joy's mother, did you?'

'Of course. I've been with the family since I was a girl. Quite a to-do there was, when he met the young lady on board the ship and wanted to stay over there and marry her. But although her ladyship was very put out, his lordship had the final say, as always, and he thought it'd be good for the lad. I believe he thought it'd make him stand on his own two feet, and behave better.'

'Behave better, why was that? Had he been misbehaving?'

Davis lowered her voice. 'I'm not the one to gossip, but it was all so long ago, it doesn't matter now. Yes, he was a bit wild. That's why they took him with them on their trip.'

Mrs. Frobisher was fascinated. 'Wild? Really? In what way?'

'Oh, you know. Gambling. Chasing after dancers and chorus girls, and the like.'

'Really! It's hard to imagine. Sir Alexander's such a stately gentleman you wouldn't expect him to have a son like that.'

'You don't know the half of it. Can you keep things to yourself?'

'Whatever you tell me will go no further, I promise.'

'Well, in the end he ran off, not with some little piece from the one of the burlesques, but with one of our own housemaids. Cora was her name, and pretty as a picture. I suppose that's why he fell for her in such a big way. They went to Gretna Green and got married. What do you think of that?' Davis sat back in triumph.

'But – if he got married then, how could he have married Joy's mother in Australia?'

'Sir Alex went after them and caught them the next day. He brought them back to London and managed to have the marriage annulled.'

'But – if they'd been together...'

'Ah, it's not what you know, it's who you know. Oh yes.' She nodded. 'It cost him a pretty penny, so we heard.'

'Well, I never!' Mrs. Frobisher could see that Davis enjoyed shocking her.

'There was even a rumour at one time that there was a child, a boy they said, but we never knew for sure.'

Mrs. Frobisher gasped. 'A child! Do you think it's true?'

'There are some who swear it is. Mind you, no one ever talks about it. It'd be more than our job's worth.' She looked around guiltily. 'There, I've let my tongue run away with me. But it was all a long time ago, wasn't it, and now, well, Mr. William's dead, isn't he? But don't tell anyone I told you, will you?'

'No, of course not.'

'Good. Now, let's get on with some of the things you need to know.'

Chapter Seventeen

Lady Barron decided Felicity could be included in the tuition whenever she liked, as it was never too young to begin training for the all-important event of Court presentation.

So they assembled in the schoolroom after breakfast. Accompanying Lady Barron was Margaret, a slim, fair woman with a pale face and a nervous manner, and Felicity.

Joy regarded her young cousin with interest. She had met the rest of the family at dinner the previous night, but Felicity had eaten earlier in the schoolroom, and so had not been present. She saw a fair haired girl with similar features to her mother, but, whereas Margaret seemed weary, Felicity was full of life and energy.

She bounced up to Joy without a trace of shyness.

'Hello, I'm Felicity Barron. You're my cousin from Australia. And I was cross because I couldn't stay up for dinner last night to meet you.'

Joy smiled at her. 'It's very nice to meet you now. I'm Joy, and this is my friend Lily Cavanagh. I hope we'll all be friends.'

'I hope so too. I don't have many friends here.'

Lady Barron clapped her hands. 'We're here for a lesson. You may chatter later. Now we must get down to work. When you are presented to Her Majesty you will walk gracefully across the room to meet her. It takes practice. Firstly, I want to see you walk.' She motioned to the three students. 'All of you. Walk across the room.'

She watched them. 'You are supposed to glide, not clump. Margaret, show them how.'

'Yes Mother.' Margaret crossed the room. Her feet seemed to slide over the floor without leaving it, and her willowy figure swayed gracefully.

'That is how you walk,' Lady Barron told them. She gestured to a table. 'Pick up a book each from that pile.'

She waited until they each held a book. 'Now, balance them on your heads, and walk.'

With both hands at the ready to steady the books, Joy and Lily each took a tentative step. Felicity's book fell off immediately she moved, and she burst out laughing as she bent to pick it up.

Joy tried to suppress a giggle as she had to clutch her book to prevent it falling, and when she saw Lily having the same problem she could hold it in no longer.

Lady Barron frowned. 'It's no laughing matter,' she admonished them. 'If you can't walk properly, you'll never be presented at Court.'

Felicity looked at her mother and, seeing her frown, adopted a serious look. 'Yes, Grandmama.'

'I'll leave you now. You will all continue to practice until you can walk properly.' She turned to her daughter-in-law. 'Margaret, I leave them in your charge. Keep them walking until lunch, and then every morning until they can walk properly.'

'Very well.'

'When they can walk correctly, you may add the train.'

'Yes, Mother.'

When she left the room there was silence for a moment. Joy drew a deep breath. She recalled that Mother had referred to her mother-in-law as domineering. No wonder.

Felicity stared at the door and pulled a face. 'Grandmama is having one of her horrid days.'

'Now then Felicity, you mustn't say that,' Margaret admonished her.

'But Mama, she is.'

'You mean she's not always like this?' Lily asked Margaret.

'Some days she does seem a little stern,' Margaret replied, sighing.

'Mama says she's a dragon sometimes,' Felicity told them.

Margaret gave the girls a worried look. 'Felicity imagines things sometimes. If Mother heard...'

Joy cut her off. 'She won't hear from us. What a martinet she is, I don't know how you stand it, if she's like this very often.'

Margaret hesitated, biting her lip. 'If she thought that I criticised her...'

'Don't worry,' Lily chimed in. 'We won't say anything.

Margaret's face cleared. 'I have been looking forward to you girls coming to stay. I hoped that you might make things...well...that you might be pleasant company. Mother can be a little wearying at times.'

'That's putting it very tactfully. I wonder you stay if that's how she is all the time.'

Margaret grimaced. 'Rupert can't leave here, he's the eldest son. And besides, I'm very fond of Sir Alexander, and Felicity adores him.'

'Grandpapa calls me his little princess, and he gave me my own pony last year and sometimes we go riding together. When I'm older he says I can go hunting with him.'

Margaret smiled. 'Well now, that's all very good, but I think we'd better get on with our walking.'

'Were you presented at Court?' Joy asked.

'Yes, of course.'

'Then can you tell us what happens? Neither of us know, do we Lily?'

'No. I can't be presented, but I'm still interested. I'll be there to see Joy.'

'It's all very strict. It takes months to organise. Everything must be done according to strict protocol.'

'So what happens on the big day?'

Margaret rolled her eyes. 'I can never forget. You want to hear?'

They all nodded. 'Every detail,' Joy added.

'There are always a whole throng of girls, each one accompanied by her sponsor. For you , Joy, your grandmother. Once you're in St. James Palace you wait to be called. Then you wait in St. James Gallery to be summoned. Finally you join the line, and you're ushered into the Queen's presence in order of precedence, lined up according to importance.' Margaret paused. 'I'm not boring you?'

'No, no, go on.'

'When you eventually step into the drawing room where the Queen is, Lord Chamberlain announces your name. Then you walk across this huge room, watched by all the on-lookers, and approach the Queen's throne. You make a full curtsy to the Queen, hoping you don't lose your balance and fall over, and then you bow and kiss the Queen's hand.'

'You did all this?'

'Oh yes, but that's not all. At this point, you rise and curtsy again to the other royals present, and then you make one last curtsy to the Queen. Then comes the real trick – backing out of the room with a ten-foot train. To do this, you have to bend back and reach for your train, remember everyone is watching you, and drape it over your arm to get it out of the way. Then, step-by-step, you back out of the room without tripping on your gown or losing your sense of direction.'

Joy felt a sinking sensation, something akin to panic. 'You can't just turn around and walk out?'

Margaret looked shocked. 'Oh no, it's against all the rules of etiquette to ever turn your back on a royal person. Never, ever do that.'

Lily shook her head. 'I think I'm rather glad I won't be doing it. Do you think it's worth it, Joy?'

Joy thought back to when the invitation to come to England had arrived, and how excited she had been at the thought of being presented at Court. And how she had pleaded and argued with her mother to persuade her to allow it. It was the dream of her lifetime. Was she going to turn her back on it all now, just because it all sounded too hard?

'Yes, it's worth it.' She picked up the book and placed it on her head. 'Let's get on with it.'

For the rest of the morning, and every morning that followed, Joy walked back and forth across the schoolroom floor with the book on her head. Lily and Felicity gave up after the second day and left her alone with Margaret, but Joy was determined to master it.

One morning, after a week of practising, Margaret clapped her hands. 'Yes,' she exclaimed. 'Yes, yes, yes! I thought yesterday you had it, but I had to be sure. There's not a wobble. Take that wretched book off your head, and show me.'

'Thank God.' Joy threw the book across the room. 'I'll never look at a book in the same way again. I've never thought of them as instruments of torture before, but I do now.' She glided across the room before turning back to Margaret. 'You're sure?'

'Quite sure. Now all you have to do is learn to do it with a train. And backwards. And to curtsy.'

Joy groaned, but having mastered walking correctly, she found that doing it backwards, even with a tablecloth trailing behind her as a train, took only a few more days. The curtsy was much more difficult and was going to require a lot of practice.

They spent their afternoons visiting other ladies who lived nearby, or in entertaining them. Or with the seamstress, who took measurements for both Joy and Lily.

For Joy, the best part of the day was often the time between tea and dinner. At that time Sir Alexander was usually alone in his study, and he sought her company. Sometimes they sat and talked, at other times they just sat reading, occasionally discussing some interesting point or other. And their affection and respect for each other grew.

Joy wrote regularly to her mother and her grandmother, telling them all about her life here in England, and all the preparations for her presentation at Court, making light of the hours she spent practising, and telling them how much she was enjoying her visit. She looked forward to receiving their letters in return, but when their replies came with news of their life back in Australia it all seemed so far away.

When a letter arrived from David one day she opened it eagerly. It was to tell her that he was riding Blaze regularly while she was away, so that he would have plenty of exercise, and would be fit when she returned. He then went on to tell her the latest happenings at Riverside, including how his mother was raising a young wombat whose mother had been found dead. He described its antics, making it all sound light-hearted and amusing, and ended by telling her to make sure she ate all her vegetables so she could continue growing up. His letter made her laugh, but as she put it down she thought that he had said nothing to make her believe he did not still regard her as a baby. Even if he did sign it, as before, *'Affectionately Yours, David Cavanagh'*.

Life was very different to what the two girls had known in Australia. Their days were strictly regimented.

While Joy spent her mornings practising deportment, particularly the curtsy, which was proving difficult, Lily found herself at a loose end.

If the weather was fine she went walking or riding, always accompanied, albeit often unwillingly, by Mrs. Frobisher, and sometimes by Felicity as well. If it rained, she was expected to sit with Lady Barron doing needlework or reading, or to join Joy and Margaret in the schoolroom. She longed for the time when they would go to London.

She would much rather be back at Riverside with the horses, or passing her time with Aunt Erin. Was it for this that she had been so anxious to come to England? Now, the only excitement in her life seemed to be in the preparation of the gowns and things she would need for the Season. As well as the seamstress, the shoemaker came to take patterns of their feet for slippers to match their gowns, and there were gloves and fans to be chosen.

Lily enjoyed that as much as Joy, but even in that she chafed at having to allow Lady Barron to make the decisions as to what she would need, and what was suitable for her.

The time passed slowly for Lily until December, which held the promise of Christmas festivities, but still another two months to go before London.

Lady Barron viewed Joy's progress in deportment and professed herself satisfied. 'I'm pleased to see the Barron fortitude coming to the fore in you,' she told her. 'You're now ready to take your place in Society.'

The house buzzed with activity as Christmas preparations got under way. Cook seemed to be constantly consulting Lady Barron with menus, and the maids hurried to and fro under the housekeeper's direction as bedrooms were aired and prepared for the arrival of guests.

'Oh dear. What a dilemma. Rufe, listen to this.' Kitty held a letter that had arrived in the post that morning.

Rufe stopped spreading marmalade on his toast. 'Yes?'

'It's from Sir Alexander. He says it's been a delight for him to get to know Joy, and that she's been working very hard in preparation for her presentation at Court.

He goes on to say, '*I feel sure Joy would be pleased to have you with her at this important occasion in her life, and that you may well wish to be present. If this is so, then I would be delighted for you and Mr. Cavanagh to be my guests in my townhouse in London, for whatever time you may wish to stay during next year. It has been a cause of sorrow to me that we have never been able to further our acquaintance, and I will be delighted if you accept my invitation. However, should you feel that to share my household may renew painful memories for you, I would be happy to arrange accommodation for you, or to be of assistance in any way I am able, should you decide to come*'.

She put down the letter. 'What do you think of that?'

'What do you think of it? Do you want to go to?'

'I must admit I do miss Joy, and, much as I pooh-pooh being presented at Court, it is a big event for Joy. I confess I would be happy to be there.' She paused, taking a sip of tea. 'But,' she added, 'I told Lady Barron I'd never set foot in her home, and l meant it. I still do. Besides, although I'm sure she'd acquiesce with Sir Alexander's wishes, it would be uncomfortable for both of us to be in the same house together.'

'If you'd like to go we could rent a house for the Season, or we could stay in a hotel.'

'Can you take time away?'

'Yes, now that the referendum is over and Federation is a certainty, I can arrange it. And we could also look at horses while we're there. It's something David and I have been discussing. Maybe we'd go across to Ireland where the horse breeding is excellent. We could see a bit of the country, and possibly pick up some breeding stock.'

Kitty's face lit up. 'Then let's go.'

It was two weeks before Christmas, and Joy and Sir Alexander were enjoying one of their quiet times together. Both sat reading in companionable silence when Joy's grandfather put down his book.

'May I interrupt your reading for a moment, my dear?' he asked.

'Of course.'

'I wish to tell you about a letter I received today.'

'What is it?'

'It's from your mother, and is in reply to an invitation I issued to her. I felt sure she'd wish to be here when you're presented to Her Majesty, and that you would wish her support at that time, therefore I invited her and Mr. Cavanagh to be my guests for the Season.'

Joy felt a rush of gratitude. 'Thank you, Grandfather. That was most thoughtful of you.'

He leant back in his chair and regarded her, then tapped his fingers on the arm of his chair. 'Your mother and I didn't have much time to become acquainted during our short stay in Australia, which has always been a cause of sorrow to me. I don't know how much you know of the history of that time?' He paused, awaiting her reply.

'Very little. Mother doesn't talk much about it.'

'We had gone to visit my daughter Anne and her husband George, who were sheep farming out there at the time. Your mother, a very beautiful and charming young woman, may I add, and your father, my son William, met on board the ship carrying us all to Australia.'

'Yes, I know that.'

'William was immediately enamoured of your mother and she, I presume, returned his affection. Being headstrong, as all young people are, he decided to stay in Australia and wished to marry immediately, before we left to return home. Unfortunately, Lady Barron objected to the match and, being outspoken as she can be at times, it caused friction between your mother and herself.'

'I see.' Joy sighed. 'How sad.'

'It was indeed. And so Kitty has written to me to thank me for the invitation, but has declined to accept the offer to stay in our home.'

Joy bit her lip, embarrassed and disappointed. 'Oh dear, I am sorry. She...'

'No, don't be upset.' He picked up a letter lying on the small table beside him, and tapped it on the table top as he spoke. 'I quite understand her feelings. I would feel the same myself.' He smiled at her. 'But she has asked me to arrange accommodation for herself and Mr. Cavanagh for the Season, and I'm sure that will please you.'

'Oh yes. How wonderful that they're coming. When will they arrive?'

'Sometime in February.'

'I must tell Lily.'

'Both you and Lily will receive letters yourselves, and I've told you all this only so you'll understand why they won't be staying with us. I hasten to add that there has always been only the most cordial feelings between your mother and myself, and she stresses this in her letter. I'm looking forward immensely to seeing her again, and also to making the acquaintance of Mr. Cavanagh.'

'He's very nice.'

'If your mother has chosen to marry him then I quite believe this must be so.'

A Liberated Woman

Chapter Eighteen

Lily was not pleased when she learnt that her father and stepmother were coming. After all, one of the reasons she had wanted to come to England had been to get away from *her*. But she was looking forward to going to London.

It was all right for Joy to be here – she had the excitement of her presentation to look forward to, and that had been enough to keep her interested in the lessons and other preparations, but all Lily had to be interested in was the arrival of her new clothes, and even that had not been much fun when the only places to wear them had been on visits to Lady Barron's tedious friends.

Lily pulled viciously at a knot in the thread as she sat sewing, and swore to herself as she pricked her finger with the needle. How she hated needlework. And how she hated sitting here with Joy and Margaret under the old dragon's watchful eyes. She felt she would die of boredom.

Suddenly there was a flurry of excitement as a carriage pulled up before the house. Lady Barron put down her work and looked expectantly at the door, which was flung open a moment later as a stranger entered. Ruddy-complexioned, with dark hair and a commanding presence, he looked to be in his mid thirties, and was dressed in a resplendent scarlet tunic, the uniform of an army officer. Behind him followed two younger men, similarly attired.

'Mama, here we are.' He crossed the room in two strides.

Lady Barron stood and held out her hands, a rare smile illuminating her face. 'Hector, how pleased I am to see you. I wasn't expecting you until next week.'

'I know. Our ship arrived a week early and we came straight here.' Taking her hands in his, he kissed her on both cheeks. Then he dropped her hands and turned.

'Allow me to present my t fellow officers, Captain Thomas Hastings and Captain James Pierce.'

Captain Hastings, a lanky, red haired man in his thirties, with a face splotched with freckles, stepped forward and bowed over Lady Barron's hand. 'I'm honoured to meet you, Lady Barron.'

Captain Pierce, a confident looking young man with a tanned face and a thin black moustache, followed suit. 'How kind of you to invite us into your home, Lady Barron.'

'I'm pleased to welcome you, gentlemen. Allow me to introduce my daughter-in-law, Mrs. Barron,' she nodded at Margaret, 'my grand-daughter, Miss Barron, and her friend, Miss Cavanagh.'

Lily caught her breath as her gaze flicked over the officers. How handsome Captain Pierce was.

Captain Barron addressed his brother's wife. 'Margaret, how nice to see you. I trust you're well?'

'Quite well, thank you, Hector.'

He moved along to stand in front of Joy. 'So you're William's daughter. How very nice to meet you at last.'

'It's my pleasure to be here and to meet you all, Captain Barron.'

'No, no, not so formal. It's nice to have another niece, so you must call me Uncle Hector, dear girl.'

Joy smiled at him. 'I never had any uncles before.'

'Then we must make up for lost time, eh?' He turned toward Lily. 'And Miss Cavanagh. I take it you're from Australia also?' he asked, taking her hand and bowing.

'Yes. I came over with Joy.'

'Splendid. We'll all have a jolly time over Christmas, I'm sure.'

His two fellow officers followed behind him, bowing briefly over each outstretched hand. When Captain Pierce reached Lily, he held her hand just a fraction longer than necessary as he bowed.

She dropped her eyes. How fortunate she'd worn one of her new gowns today. When she raised her gaze she saw he was still regarding her, and when his eyes caught hers, she saw an interested gleam in them.

Over the next few days the mood in the house seemed to change. A sense of cheerfulness prevailed. Walter and Harold arrived home from Eton for the week of the Christmas holiday, and the young people filled the house with laughter. Even Lady Barron lost her usual stern expression. The servants bustled about, seemingly happy to make sure family and guests wanted for nothing. Dinner became a lively affair, their numbers often swelled by visiting neighbours, so that there were often up to twenty people seated at the large table in the formal dining room. After dinner, small tables were set up, so that those who wished could play cards or other games.

The days were filled with activities, with all members of the family and guests taking part. If the weather was not conducive to walking or riding, indoor games were played at the tables, such as chess, backgammon or checkers. When these palled, hours were spent playing charades or blind man's bluff, always the cause of much merriment. A few days before Christmas Joy received a Christmas card from David, and as she read it she felt a glow inside that he had not forgotten her. He put a little note on the bottom saying, *Blaze sends you greetings too!*

When Joy woke three days before Christmas and looked out of the window she saw a mantle of dazzling white covering everything within sight. It had snowed during the night. Excitedly she hurried into Lily's room. 'Lily, wake up, wake up. Take a look outside.'

Lily turned sleepily in her bed. 'Mm, what's happening?'

'Snow. It snowed last night. Come and take a look.'

Wide awake now, Lily jumped from her bed and threw back the curtains. 'Oh, just look at that. It's like the postcards of Christmas.'

'We were hoping for a white Christmas, and now we're going to have one. Hurry up and dress, the day's too good to waste.'

They went down to breakfast together, and found the three officers had already finished their meal and were about to leave the dining room.

Hector turned to Joy. 'We're going for a walk to look for a suitable Christmas tree. Felicity is coming with us, and we hope you young ladies will join us as well.'

'I'd love to come,' Joy replied, 'I can't wait to go out in the snow. How about you, Lily? Do you feel like a walk?'

While they had been talking, Captain Pierce was standing a little behind the other two men watching Lily, and now he raised his eyebrows and gave an almost imperceptible nod as he caught her eye.

'Yes, I do,' Lily replied.

'Good, good,' Hector rubbed his hands together. 'Then you ladies must have your breakfast first. Rug up well, and we'll all meet in the hall in half an hour.'

After breakfast Joy and Lily gathered their coats, hats, gloves and scarves. With Mrs. Frobisher and Felicity they met the men in the Hall.

They all trooped outside in high spirits, to find a silent, white world. The day was crisp and cold, with wintry sunshine filtering through the trees.

Felicity laughed as she came out into the cold air and her breath turned to white vapour. She formed her lips into a circle and forced the air out in little puffs.

'Look, I'm smoking,' she called out, and they all laughed at her.

The snow crunched beneath their boots, and Joy looked back to see their footprints in the fresh snow. She gazed in wonder to see how the snowfall transformed everyday objects into things of beauty, whilst the bare branches of the trees formed white lacy patterns against the blue sky.

As they walked along the snow covered path toward the forest there wasn't room for them to all walk abreast, so Joy and Felicity fell into step alongside Hector, and Lily and Mrs. Frobisher followed with Captain Pierce and Captain Hastings.

Lily was pleased when Captain Pierce positioned himself alongside her, and fell back a little so Captain Hastings and Mrs. Frobisher were in front of them.

Lily bent and scooped up a handful of snow from the ground in her gloved hand, and formed it into a ball. 'A snowball,' she said, as she showed it to her companion. 'It's the first one I've ever seen.'

'Really? Don't you see snow in winter where you live?'

'We don't have snow in Australia. Or at any rate, not in Sydney, although it does snow sometimes high in the mountains. But I've never seen it.'

Captain Pierce looked down at her, and Lily felt her heart flutter as she gazed into his dark eyes with their attention focused intently on her. 'I know practically nothing about Australia, I'm afraid, but I would like to learn about it. Perhaps you could give me some lessons while we're here.'

Lily knew he was flirting with her, and that she shouldn't encourage him. But she didn't care. She could hear Mrs. Frobisher talking to Captain Hastings, and Felicity was chattering away to Joy and her uncle. No one was taking any interest in them, and it was exciting to have such a handsome man paying attention to her. She smiled up at him. 'It would be a pleasure.'

He looked at her with knowing eyes as he gave her a slow, warm smile. He moved closer to her, so that his arm was brushing against hers, and his gloved fingers sought hers. He gave them a brief squeeze. 'I'll look forward to it with the greatest pleasure.'

Lily's heart leapt, but she dropped her eyes demurely. 'I hope you won't be disappointed,' she told him softly.

They reached the forest, and as they entered they were joined by one of the gardeners carrying an axe. He positioned himself behind them, at the rear of the group, and Captain Pierce put more distance between them. Lily fumed. Why did the wretched man have to come along and spoil things just as they were getting on so nicely? They walked on in silence, but Lily was acutely aware of the man at her side.

When Hector found a tree that satisfied him he called to the gardener. 'Here we are, Barnes, this one will do nicely.'

The man swung his axe and began chopping..

'Stand back,' Hector called after a few minutes, 'it's ready to fall.'

Stepping back to a safe distance, they watched as the tree toppled to the ground amidst shouts of approval.

'Jolly good show, Barron,' Captain Hastings called.

He stepped forward to help Hector and the gardener to drag it back along the path. When they reached the edge of the trees he left Hector and the gardener to drag the heavy tree across to the house. It scraped through the snow, leaving a deep gash behind that showed the ground beneath.

'Oh look,' cried Felicity, 'it's spoilt the snow. We'll have to put it all back.'

As the two men and the tree disappeared inside the house she bent over and started trying to scrape the snow back over the black earth. The snow mixed with the earth to form mud, and Felicity looked as if she was about to cry.

'It was so pretty and now it's all spoilt,' she wailed.

'Never mind,' Joy consoled her. 'When it snows again it'll be all covered up again. And you want to have a Christmas tree in the house, don't you?'

'Yes, but...'

'Why don't we build a snowman? Would you like that?'

Felicity's face lit up. 'Oh yes.'

'Then let's find a good spot for it.'

They walked a short distance away from the others before Felicity stopped beside a sun dial, crusted now with snow.

'This is a good spot. Let's build him here.'

'Yes, this is an excellent spot.'

Joy started scooping up the snow, and Felicity followed her example, chattering excitedly.

Captain Pierce watched them from where he stood with the others on the path. 'Well now, that's going to keep them occupied for quite some time. What shall we do now? I must say that I'd welcome continuing our walk. I don't feel like going inside yet.'

'Nor do I,' Captain Hastings agreed. 'Barron was telling me there's a summerhouse nearby. Perhaps we could walk as far as that.'

Lily clapped her hands. 'Yes, let's.'

Mrs. Frobisher looked uncertain. 'Well, I'm not sure that we should...'

Lily cut in. 'It's quite all right, there are four of us, and we'll stay all together. I do want to see the summerhouse. I'm sure it will look pretty with snow on it.'

'Come on, Mrs. Frobisher,' Captain Hastings urged. 'It's such a super morning for a walk. We become so tired of the heat in India, you know. It's a real treat to breathe this cold, fresh air.'

'Yes, I used to dream about our English winters,' added Captain Pierce. 'You don't know how wonderful snow is, until you have to put up with the broiling sun day after day.'

Lily frowned. 'Oh, do come along. We're wasting a beautiful morning.'

Mrs. Frobisher pursed her lips. 'Well – I suppose it's all right, as long as we don't go too far from the house.'

'We won't,' Lily assured her.

'Just where is the summerhouse?' Mrs. Frobisher asked.

'Barron said it's down this way.' Captain Hastings gestured toward the trees at the edge of the garden. 'Close to the lake, he told me. We'll lead the way.'

He and Captain Pierce moved off across the open snow that covered the grassed area, and the two women followed. As soon as Joy and Felicity could see them no longer, and they were out of sight of the house, the two men stopped, and waited until Lily and Mrs. Frobisher drew level with them.

'It could be a bit slippery underfoot from here on,' Captain Hastings said. 'If you would permit me to escort you, Mrs. Frobisher, I'll make certain you don't fall.' He moved alongside her and took her hand, tucking it inside the crook of his arm. He smiled down at her. 'There, now I can look after you.'

Mrs. Frobisher bit her lip as she looked up at him.

'You mustn't worry,' he told her. 'You're quite safe with me.'

'But – what if Lady Barron should find out...'

'I doubt she will be out walking today. Just relax and enjoy yourself.'

Mrs. Frobisher smiled up at him. 'You're probably right.'

Captain Hastings put his hand over hers. 'You know, you look very pretty when you smile. You should do it more often.'

Blushing, she made no reply, but she continued to smile.

Captain Pierce took hold of Lily's hand. 'Hold tight to me, I don't want you to slip.' He pulled her close to his side, and his arm circled her waist.

Lily's heart beat fast as they walked close together. It was many minutes before the summerhouse came into view. A hexagonal shaped structure with a shingled roof powdered in snow, it was a set a short distance from a lake, and was surrounded by trees.

The door was shut but Captain Hastings, releasing Mrs. Frobisher's arm, pulled a key from his pocket, unlocked the door, and went inside.

'I say, this is quite cosy. Come and have a look.'

Captain Pierce took his arm from around Lily's waist, and the three of them followed him in. They were in a good sized room with timber walls and ceiling, furnished with a table against one wall, an upright dresser, and a large chintz covered sofa against the opposite wall. Several chairs were arranged around the room, and a potbellied stove, cold now, stood in a corner. A window, with its curtains drawn, obviously looked out on to the lake.

'Top-hole,' said Captain Pierce, looking around appreciatively.

'It is a lovely little place,' exclaimed Mrs. Frobisher. 'I'm glad we've seen, it but I think we should be getting back.'

Lily was walking around the room looking at everything. Suddenly she put her hand up to her chest. Removing her gloves and tossing them on the table she felt around some more.

'Oh, my locket,' she cried. 'I've lost my locket. I must find it, it's gold and it's very special. It belonged to my mother. It must have fallen off while we were on our way here.'

'Oh dear. Are you sure you put it on this morning? I don't remember seeing it.' Mrs. Frobisher looked worried.

'Yes, yes, I did. We'll have to look for it. I can't bear to lose it. Could you go back and see if it's lying in the snow? Please! I'll look around here.'

'Yes, come on, I'll come with you,' Captain Hastings said. He took Mrs. Frobisher's arm and led her out.

Captain Pierce raised an eyebrow as he looked at Lily. 'So you've lost your locket? You must be very upset.'

'I am.'

'Then perhaps I should try and console you, I hate to see you upset. Come and sit over here.' Taking her hand he led her across to the sofa.

Dropping to the seat she looked up at him. He was smiling down at her, crinkling his eyes at the corners. Her heart began to pump with excitement, but she kept her face calm.

He sat beside her and removed her hat gently, and suddenly she was in his arms. His lips were on hers, and she opened her lips just enough to put out the tip of her tongue so she could taste him. She heard his sharp intake of breath, and then he was crushing her to him, kissing her. She loved it, loved the throbbing of her pulses it caused.

'Lily, Lily. You're so beautiful. I've wanted to do this since the first time I saw you. It's been driving me mad. Put your arms around me, Lily. Kiss me properly.'

She wound her arms around his neck and kissed him, parting her lips, and his tongue touched hers. It sent little quivers down her spine, but when his hand slid down to caress her breast, she pushed it away. 'No,' she murmured. He took his hand away.

His kisses grew more ardent, and Lily loved the warm feeling inside her as she responded. After several minutes he pushed her away from him.

'This is driving me mad,' he panted. He stood up and pulled her up with him, holding her tightly against him. 'Do you know what you do to me, Lily? Or are you too young to know.'

As he pressed his body to hers she felt him hard against her. It caused a wave of heat to start deep inside and rise through her like a tide. She clung to him, her breathing fast.

'This is not the time,' he told her, pushing her away. 'The others will be back soon. I need to cool down. We must go outside.' He put up his hand to tuck a strand of her hair back that had come awry, and then he picked up her hat and placed it on her head carefully, moving it around until it sat just right. He picked up her gloves. 'Come with me.'

In the cold air Lily felt her breathing return to normal. She bent down and ran her hands across the snow, then put them to her cheeks to cool them.

'Good girl.' He handed her the gloves.

'Thank you, Captain Pierce,' she said demurely.

He smiled at her. 'When we're alone you must call me James.'

'James Pierce. It's a nice name.'

'It's actually James Benjamin Pierce. A few of my close friends call me Benjy. You can call me that, if you like.'

'Benjy.' She savoured the name. 'I like that. It's what I'll call you. That means I'm a close friend then, doesn't it?'

'A very close friend, my sweet one. Now then, let's go and find the others.'

They met them coming back toward them moments later.

'Did you find your locket?' Captain Hastings called out as they approached.

'No, I'm afraid it's gone for good.'

Lily thought Mrs. Frobisher looked flustered, and her face was flushed. It amused her to think that maybe they had been kissing too, hiding in the bushes. It couldn't have been anything like what had happened between her and Benjy. Nothing could be.

When she lay in her bed that night Lily relived the experience. She knew she had stirred Benjy's passions. She had been around horses long enough to know what his hard body pressed against her meant and it gave her a sense of power to think she could do that to a man. It thrilled her.

She remembered how her pulses raced when they kissed, and the feelings that had started inside her when his hand touched her breast. But she had been right to stop him then. It wouldn't do to let him take liberties with her. Not yet. Maybe later. She hugged the thought to her, and wondered what it would be like to be loved properly. For the first time in her life she could imagine that it would be wonderful, and she tried to imagine just how it would be with Benjy.

As she drifted off to sleep she had one thought in her mind. She must never let him know she had not been wearing a locket today.

Chapter Nineteen

On Christmas day family and guests feasted. The footmen waited on everyone, filling their plates from the sideboard, which groaned beneath the numerous platters of quail, roast beef, stuffed goose, vegetables, fancy cakes and plum pudding, and they ensured the glasses were kept constantly filled with wine to wash it all down.

After the meal was over the guests retired to their rooms to rest for the remainder of the afternoon. The servants went to their dining room to enjoy their own festive meal, safe in the knowledge they wouldn't be required until teatime.

Lily waited in her room until she was sure the house was still. Then she crept from her room, tiptoed downstairs, and slipped out of the house and headed for the summerhouse, pulling her coat around her to ward off the cold. Benjy was there waiting for her. He pulled her inside and locked the door behind her.

'Lily my sweet, I've been thinking of nothing else but you. I was afraid you wouldn't come.' He gathered her into his arms and smothered her face with kisses.

'I told you I'd come.' She wrapped her arms around him.

'Yes I know, but I was desperate. It's torture to see you all the time, and not be able to be alone with you.'

'We're alone now.'

He released his hold on her. 'Yes, and we must make the most of it.' He guided her to the sofa. 'Look, I've found a rug for us, so we won't be cold. Let me take off your coat.'

Lily stood still while he peeled off her coat, pushed her gently down on to the sofa and sat beside her, pulling the rug over them both.

'There, now, that's better. Are you warm enough?'

'Yes, quite warm.' She snuggled closer to him.

Next moment his arms were around her, holding her to him, and he was kissing her, murmuring her name.

'Lily, you're so beautiful. I think about you all the time when we're apart. I want to be with you every moment of the day.'

He turned his head to nibble gently on her ear, and then kissed her throat.

Lily's heart beat faster. His kisses became more passionate, and when his hand moved down to caress her breasts she responded by running her hands up the back of his neck and through his hair. But when he tried to slip his hand inside her bodice she pushed his hand aside, and pulled back from him.

'No.' She gasped.

Benjy removed his hand. 'I'm sorry, Lily darling. Please forgive me. It's just – I forget myself when I'm with you. I can't help it. It's what you do to me. Say you forgive me.'

His handsome face looked so contrite, and she wasn't angry with him. Besides, she wanted his kisses. 'I forgive you.'

He scooped her into his arms again and kissed her even more passionately than before. 'Thank you, my darling. I'll try not to forget myself again.'

For the rest of their time together Benjy restrained himself to kissing and fondling her. Finally he sat up and disentangled their arms. 'It's time to go, I'm afraid, my sweet.'

Lily sat up and smoothed her skirt. 'Yes, I must be back before everyone wakes up. We mustn't let the old dragon suspect anything.'

Benjy shuddered. 'No, indeed. But you will come again, won't you? I'll die if I can't be with you.'

'Yes, I'll come. Whenever I can get away. It may have to be at night, when everyone's asleep. What with both the old dragon and Mrs. Frobisher around, it's like being in prison.'

They walked back together, and Benjy stayed behind the bushes until Lily was safely inside. He waited until she had time to be back in her room before he sidled into the house, making sure to lock the door behind him.

The summerhouse was unused at this time of year. It was always kept locked but the key hung on a hook with the other outdoor keys, and it was no trouble for Benjy to slip it from its hook at night, and all through January they met there once or twice a week while the household was asleep.

It was a night late in January when Joy turned restlessly from side to side as sleep refused to come. Excited thoughts of her future life in London, and feelings of impatience at still being in this quiet backwater, chased each other around in her mind like mice on a treadmill, making sleep impossible. She had been tossing in her bed for an hour or more when she heard a noise. Someone walked past her room. Who could be up and about at this hour? Was it Lily?

Sliding from her bed she opened the door and looked out, just in time to see Uncle Hector heading toward the stairs. Thinking that probably he'd been unable to sleep and was going down for a nightcap she closed the door and headed back to her bed. As she was about to climb between the sheets a feeling of unease stopped her. Without knowing why, she turned back and opened the door again, and stood there listening. The house was silent.

Tiptoeing to Lily's door she turned the handle and pushed the door slightly open. In the faint light from the hall she saw that the bed was empty. Entering the room she saw it hadn't been slept in and Lily was certainly not in the room.

Joy shivered in the cold. Returning to her room she sat on the bed. Where was Lily? Could she possibly be with Hector? The thought sent a chill of fear through her. Climbing back into bed she lay listening for footsteps for what seemed like hours. She checked Lily's room again. She was still not back. Finally she drifted off to sleep.

When Joy woke next morning she dressed and went to Lily's door, knocked and entered. Lily was sitting at her dressing table, humming a little tune as she brushed her hair.

'You certainly sound in a good mood this morning,' Joy greeted her coolly.

Lily stopped brushing and turned around, a smile on her lips.

'Yes, I am. Why not? It's a lovely day. I'm looking forward to it.'

'I thought you'd be tired – seeing you were away from your bed for a good part of the night.'

The smile disappeared from Lily's face. 'What do you mean?'

'I know you weren't in bed for hours. Where were you?'

Lily swallowed. 'I couldn't sleep, so I went down to the library and sat down there reading.'

'I don't believe you.' Joy paused, looking at her through half narrowed eyes. 'Were you with Hector?'

'Hector? Good God, no!' Such a look of incredulity came over Lily's face that Joy believed her.

'Then who were you with?'

'No one. I told you, I was in the library.'

'If you were, I'm sure someone else was with you. You wouldn't sit up all that time on your own.'

Lily tossed her head. 'If I was it's none of your business. It's so boring here, day after day. You've got your stupid lessons to keep you busy, I've got nothing. You don't know what it's like.'

'Oh Lily, I'm frustrated too. I want to be in London as much as you. But it's no use compromising yourself with one of the officers, there'll be plenty of eligible young men when we reach London.' A sudden thought struck her. 'Is it one of the officers, or is it one of the staff? A couple of the footmen are rather nice-looking. Is it one of them?'

'None of your business. It's no one. No one. How many times do I have to tell you? I was in the library. On my own.' She swung around to face the mirror again, slamming the brush down on the dressing table. 'Now go away and leave me alone. I want to finish dressing.'

Silently Joy left the room, knowing she would learn no more, but not totally believing her friend's story.

Benjy was always at the summerhouse before Lily arrived, with a candle lit and a rug for them to snuggle under. Lily thought of it as their special sanctuary.

She had never been so happy. She loved the excitement of their secret meetings, and the danger of discovery added spice to their trysts. Most of all she loved the wonderful feelings Benjy caused inside her as he kissed and caressed her. She longed to let him touch her more intimately as he tried to slide his hand inside her gown but she always stopped him. That was for when you had a ring on your finger.

As the month drew to a close preparations began for the household to move to London in time for the opening of

Parliament, when Sir Alexander must take his seat in the House of Lords.

Lily was filled with dread. What would happen to her and Benjy? Were the officers coming to London with them? When she asked Benjy he told her they were going to London too. But, he warned her, it wouldn't be so easy for them to meet then.

'We won't have anywhere like the summerhouse to meet. I'll have to spend time at the Barracks, and you'll be strictly chaperoned in London. We'll never be alone together. Protocol does not permit unmarried ladies to be alone with a gentleman unless he's of the same family, you know that.'

Lily's heart plummeted. 'What are we to do?' she wailed, pulling him closer.

'I'll try to think of something, my darling. In the meantime, we must make the most of our remaining time here.'

'We might only be able to meet here once more,' she told him miserably. 'I heard the dragon giving orders to repaint the summerhouse. The workmen are starting in two days time to move everything out in preparation.'

'And we leave next week for London. It won't be finished before then. Lily darling, you must meet me tomorrow night. It may be our last chance to decide what we're going to do.'

She clung to him, holding back tears with difficulty. 'I'll be here, and you must decide what we're to do.'

'I will, my darling, I will.' He kissed her passionately, then drew back and looked at her as if considering something. 'Perhaps...' he paused.

'Yes?' she prompted him.

'I was just wondering...perhaps this is the right time...'

'For what?' she asked impatiently.

'I've been thinking – I want to take you to meet my parents. Perhaps we could go up there after we return to London.'

Lily drew in her breath sharply as elation filled her. To meet his parents! That could mean only one thing. Mrs. James Benjamin Pierce! It had a nice ring to it.

'Oh Benjy, I would love to meet them. I'm sure they must be as wonderful as you.'

He laughed. 'My darling, you mean you think I'm wonderful?'

'Of course I do.'

'I hardly think you're an unbiased judge, but I love you for it.' He bent his head to kiss her again and she responded even more enthusiastically than usual.

As she lay in her bed later she couldn't sleep for excitement. Benjy was going to take her to meet his parents. It meant he wanted to marry her. He hadn't exactly asked her yet, but, of course, he would want his parents to meet her first. It was a shame he couldn't meet Father just yet, not until he arrived in London. But when she was married to Benjy, she reflected smugly, she wouldn't have to put up with her odious stepmother all the time. She'd be living with Benjy, in their home.

She wondered where they would live. Probably in London. Of course, he was a soldier. Would he go back to India one day, and expect her to go with him? That would be interesting. She'd heard that army wives had a great life out there with big bungalows and coloured servants to cater to their every whim. Yes, that would be exciting.

The next night when Lily arrived at the summerhouse she found Benjy had lit a fire in the little potbellied stove in the corner.

'I want you to be warm and cosy,' he told her as he removed her coat. 'It may be our last night together for a while.'

'Please don't remind me.' She put her arms around his neck and rested her head on his chest.

'I hate to think about it, my darling.' He held her tightly. 'But we'll be together again. After all, we have the rest of our lives.'

Her heart leaped at his words and she raised her head. 'Oh Benjy, if only I could be sure about that.'

He bent his head and kissed her lightly on the tip of her nose. 'You let me worry about that. Right now I want you to come over by the fire and warm up, your nose is cold.' He laughed. 'I can't have you catching cold. Come on.' He led her across the room to the two chairs he had pulled up in front of the fire. 'Sit here, you'll soon be warm.'

He sat next to her he leant across, took her hands in his own and rubbed them gently. 'That's better; you'll be warm in no time.'

Lily really wanted to be on the sofa where they could be close together. Tonight's kisses might be their last for a while. They were wasting time.

'I'm quite warm now, thank you. In fact, it's quite hot so close to the fire.'

Benjy sprang from his chair. 'I'm sorry darling. Come over and sit on the sofa. It's more comfortable there anyway.'

'Yes, it is.' Lily smiled up at him. 'And I like sitting next to you.'

'My lovely little Lily, I'm glad to hear that.'

As they sat down on the sofa Benjy turned her toward him. He twined his arms around her and began kissing her. Her heart began to beat erratically as she returned his kisses. After a few moments he drew back. Leaning over, he swung her legs up on to the sofa and pushed her back tenderly so she was lying down.

'My darling, I just want to lie next to you for a while. I want to feel what it's like to hold you properly in my arms.' He lay alongside her, stretched out so they were pressed closely together. 'This is better. This is how it should be.'

He ran his hands down over her body, kissing her all the while, and when his hand slid inside her bodice she didn't stop him. When his fingers caressed her breasts she gasped in delight.

He undid some buttons and slipped the gown off her shoulders and kissed her breasts. Lily felt as if her body was on fire.

Benjy stood up and pulled her up with him. He held her pressed against him as he undid the rest of the buttons with his free hand, and eased her gown to the floor. As he began to remove the rest of her clothes she offered no resistance. After all, they would be engaged before long.

'You're so beautiful,' he told her, running his fingers lightly over her body. 'I needed to see you like this so I can remember it until we're together all the time.'

When he lifted her back onto the sofa she lay there watching as he took off his own clothes. The sight of him inflamed her passions even more. Then he was on the sofa with her, kissing her, his lean, muscular body pressed to hers. As his hands began caressing her body she felt the blood bubbling through her veins. When his fingers felt her nipple it sprang erect to meet him. His lips slid down the length of her neck and he kissed the nipple, ran his tongue around it, slowly, and then sucked gently, setting a pulse throbbing between her legs. Never had Lily dreamed of such sensations. The throbbing increased as his hand moved down and slid between her legs. His fingers explored her, stroking, gently. As the stroking became more urgent she felt a wave building inside her, taking her higher, higher, until all other thoughts disappeared and she was aware only of him and the pulsing longing inside her. Lily offered no resistance as he moved on top of her and parted her legs. She gasped as he entered her, slowly at first. His thrusting became more urgent, and she cried out as she felt a sharp pain. Then she gave herself over to the ecstasy of being fully loved as her passion rose again to meet his.

Lily was in a state of euphoria the next morning. She couldn't wait to see Benjy. They met on the stairs as she was going down and he was coming up. He had obviously breakfasted early. She stopped and smiled, her heart lifting at the sight of him. 'Good morning, Benjy,' she said softly, 'how are you this morning?'

He looked around hurriedly. 'Fine Lily, just fine.' He went up another step.

Lily put out her hand and touched his arm. 'Don't hurry off, darling. We can have just a few words.'

He frowned and shook off her hand. 'For God's sake, Lily, not here. We mustn't be seen alone together, you know that.'

Her body stiffened. 'There's no harm in just a few words.'

'We'll be seen, and that won't do.'

'But I want to talk to you.'

'I can't talk to you right now.'

His words hit her like a slap in the face, and she stood dumbfounded as he continued on up the stairs.

After a few steps he stopped and, after scanning the hall below and seeing no one, he came back down.

'Look, we mustn't be seen alone together, it would compromise you.' His tone was conciliatory. 'I have to go into the village with Barron and Hastings today, and I want to write a letter first. Meet me outside the summerhouse before dinner tonight and we can talk then.'

'Outside it?'

'Yes, I can't get the key any more. One of the workmen has taken it.'

'All right. I'll see you then.'

With a troubled mind she continued down the stairs as he turned and bounded up. Of course, he was only thinking of her reputation. That's what it was. And surely the letter he was going to write was to his parents, to arrange their visit. That was it, he was protecting her. It wouldn't do to have any scandal before she met his parents.

Joy looked up from her breakfast as Lily entered the dining room. 'Hello. You look a little tired,' she said. 'Didn't you sleep well last night?'

How scandalised she would be if only she knew, Lily thought. 'No, not all that well.' Wandering over to the sideboard she poured herself a cup of tea, placed a biscuit on the saucer, and brought it back to the table and sat down.

Joy raised her eyebrows. 'Is that all you're having for breakfast?'

'Yes. I'm not really hungry this morning.'

'You look as if you need cheering up. Aren't you excited to be going to London at last?'

'Of course I am.'

'Davis has nearly finished my packing. Has Mrs. Frobisher done yours yet?'

'No.'

'She'll have to do it today then. Some of the staff left yesterday to get the Town house ready, and most of the luggage is going tomorrow.' She paused. 'You do know that we're all leaving the day after tomorrow, don't you?'

Lily was startled. 'No, I thought we had a few more days yet.'

'Haven't you been listening to anything that's been said the last couple of days? It's been decided to go early to avoid all the traffic going into the city at the beginning of February.'

Lily frowned. She hadn't been paying much attention to anything lately. All her thoughts had been centred on Benjy. 'I didn't know.'

'Well, you know now. I thought you'd be as excited as me to be going to London at last.'

'Yes, of course I am. I'm just a bit tired this morning, that's all.'

'You'd better have a bit of a rest today. You won't want to be tired for the journey to London.'

'You're right. I might just sit somewhere with a book.'

Lily didn't feel like being with the others today, but she would have loved to tell Joy about Benjy. Well, all except last night, that would always have to remain a secret. But she couldn't tell her anything yet. Wouldn't she be surprised when she learnt they were to be married?

Lily spent the day in the drawing room with a book, pretending to read but daydreaming about their future, hers and Benjy's. About an hour before dinnertime she put on a coat and hat, and pulled on her gloves.

Slipping outside she made her way down to the summerhouse. Benjy wasn't there yet, and the door was locked, so she couldn't go inside to wait. Thank goodness it wasn't snowing. But it was cold. Alternately sitting on the summerhouse steps and walking around, stamping her feet against the cold, she waited. And waited.

Tears started to fall as she began to fear Benjy wasn't coming. What could have happened? Had he had an accident? Or was he just late getting back? Perhaps he was waiting near the house for her now. She made her way back to the house, but he was nowhere to be seen. She just had time to change for dinner and take her seat at the dining table. None of the officers showed up for dinner, and she didn't dare enquire about them. Excusing herself after dinner, pleading a headache, she went up to her room.

Mrs. Frobisher was in there attending to the last of her packing. When Lily sat in front of the dressing table and started to remove the pins from her hair she left the packing and crossed the room, standing behind Lily.

'I'll do that for you, I've nearly finished the packing.' Removing the last of the pins from Lily's hair, she picked up the brush and started to brush it.

A sigh escaped her lips. 'I must say it won't be the same around here without the officers in the house. They really livened things up, didn't they? Even her ladyship unbent a bit while they were here.'

Lily spun around on her stool. 'What do you mean? Where have they gone? I thought they were just going into the village for the day.'

'Oh no, they went to London. Their ship leaves the day after tomorrow.'

'Their ship? What ship?'

'Why, the ship that's taking them back to India.'

'Back to India? Why are they going to India?'

'Why, to rejoin their regiment, of course.'

Lily moistened her lips. 'They must have been called back suddenly, I suppose.'

'No. Their leave was up. It was their time to go.'

'You mean they knew all along they had to go back today?'

'Oh yes. They were only here on leave.'

A wave of fury swept through Lily. Fighting to stop her hand from trembling she took the brush from Mrs. Frobisher and put it down on the dressing table.

'That's enough.' She stood up. 'I'm going to the bathroom. You finish the packing.' She managed to speak calmly, but she felt like screaming.

The blood thundered in her ears she stood in the middle of the bathroom, clenching and unclenching her fists. She wanted to pick up the china jug with the roses painted on it and smash it on the floor. She wanted to scream at the top of her voice and tell everyone what a lying, cheating, conniving scoundrel Captain James Benjamin Pierce was. Pressing her knuckles against her mouth to hold back the sound she paced back and forth until she finally collapsed, to sit on the edge of the bath. Here she sat while the bitter bile of betrayal gnawed her insides.

Finally, waiting until she thought Mrs. Frobisher would be gone, she went back into her room. The chaperone was still there, folding clothes. She looked at Lily with narrowed eyes as she came back into the room.

'You're upset, aren't you?' she asked.

Lily felt a dart of fear at the thought of discovery. 'What do you mean? Why should I be upset?'

'You're upset because they've gone, aren't you?'

She tossed her head. 'Why should I be upset?'

'Because they're gone, or at least because one of them is gone.'

'I don't know what you mean.'

'Oh yes you do. I know the signs. You're sweet on one of them, aren't you? Which one?'

Suddenly Lily remembered how flustered Mrs. Frobisher had been when she and Captain Hastings had come back from looking for her locket.

'Well, it wouldn't be Captain Hastings, would it? Because you've been carrying on with him, haven't you?' She narrowed her eyes. 'Instead of concentrating on chaperoning me, you've been playing fast and loose with him.'

Two red spots appeared on Mrs. Frobisher's cheeks. 'I don't know what you're talking about.'

Lily felt a thrill of triumph. She was right, they had been carrying on. Now she had the upper hand.

'I saw you,' she lied. 'I saw you sneaking out to meet him. I suppose you've been lovers. How will it be if I tell her ladyship what you've been up to? I wonder what she'd do. Fire you, I suppose. Without a reference so you'd find it hard to get another job. And she'd tell my father, so it wouldn't be any use you going home, either.'

Mrs. Frobisher bit back. 'And it'd be nothing compared to what she'd do to you if she thought you'd been up to no good with one of them.'

Lily shuddered at the thought. She must make sure Mrs. Frobisher held her tongue, so she spoke calmly now.

'I don't want to make trouble for you. If you don't tell anyone about what you think – not that it's true, of course – then I won't say anything about you and Captain Hastings.'

'You're a sly one, aren't you? All right, I won't say anything. But you want to be careful, girl, or you'll get yourself into trouble.' She paused, her head on one side as she scrutinised Lily. 'I wonder which one it was, Captain Pierce or Captain Barron. Well, I don't suppose you'll tell me, but you'd better be careful in future. I'll be watching you like a hawk from now on.' She turned and walked from the room.

Lily climbed into bed, relieved she had taken care of the chaperone's suspicions. She wouldn't dare say anything now. But her mind went back to Benjy and his deception. He had lied to her all the time. He had never intended to introduce her to his parents.

He'd known he was leaving today and he set out to seduce her. He sweet talked her into thinking he was in love with her, and led her to believe he wanted to marry her — even if he hadn't actually asked her.

What a fool she'd been to believe him.

Chapter Twenty

Joy crossed to the window on the second floor landing of the Town house in Curzon Street, in Mayfair, and looked out.

'Look Lily, from this high up we can see across into Hyde Park. After all this time we're finally here in London. I can hardly believe it.' She looked at her friend and frowned. 'Aren't you excited? You've been very quiet for the last couple of days. What's the matter?'

Lily shrugged. 'Oh, nothing really. I've had a bit of a headache, that's all.'

Joy was concerned. 'It's not like you to have a headache, especially one that's lasted for two or three days. Perhaps you should see a doctor.'

'No, no, I don't need a doctor. I've just been a bit down. I thought I had a cold coming on but it seems to be all right now.' She moved away from the window. 'Come on, let's go and see if our new gowns are unpacked yet. That'll cheer me up.'

They went along the hallway to Lily's room. Opening the doors to the large wardrobe that dominated the room Lily looked inside. Mrs. Frobisher had placed all her gowns on hangers inside. The evening gowns in exotic silks and satins hung at one end, with the light, floaty day wear next to it, and coats and capes and shawls at the other end. On the shelf above was a selection of hats.

'Here's your riding habit,' Joy exclaimed, touching a black costume hanging at the end of the day clothes. 'Bring it out and let's have a proper look.'

Lily removed it from the wardrobe and spread it out on her bed.

'It is smart, isn't it?' She picked up the fitted jacket and held it against herself, moving across so she could look in the mirror.

'How do I look?'

'Wonderful, you'll have all the men wanting to ride alongside you when we go riding in Rotten Row.'

'Do you think so?' she asked, sounding much brighter.

'I'm sure of it. Now let's have a look at some of your other things.'

By the time they had gone through her wardrobe Joy was pleased to see Lily looking cheerful again.

The next day Lady Barron summoned Joy and Lily to her sitting room and bade them be seated. 'Now that we are here in London, life will be much busier than you are used to in the country, and your days will be fully occupied,' she told them.

'We understand, Grandmother,' Joy replied, and Lily nodded.

'Very well.' She turned her attention to Lily. 'Now, your parents will be arriving in London this month but as they will be travelling much of the time, it has been arranged that you will stay here until further notice. Is that clear?'

Lily nodded. 'Yes, perfectly clear, thank you.'

'Good. Tomorrow you will both commence riding in Hyde Park. Margaret will accompany you and you will ride for one hour. The Park will not be overcrowded at this time of year but she will doubtless meet acquaintances to whom she will introduce you. You will not acknowledge any overtures from anyone to whom you have not been introduced. Is that clear?'

Joy and Lily both nodded. 'Yes.'

'Good. In the afternoon we shall visit an exhibition at the Art Gallery, and at five o'clock Lady Asplin will be taking tea with us. Dinner will be a quiet family meal tomorrow, as Sir Alexander has some preparations to attend to for the opening of Parliament next week. Is that all clear?'

Once again both girls nodded. 'Yes.'

Her manner softened somewhat. 'Now, as you have not been in London before, you will wish to see some of the city's attractions and do some shopping. Up until Easter will be a good time to do so, as the city is not so busy then. Margaret or Frobisher will supervise you when you go out, if I do not wish to accompany you. You may ask either myself or Margaret for information on where it is suitable for you to go.'

Joy smiled. At last they were going to see something of London. 'Thank you, Grandmother.'

'That is all then. You may go now.'

The next morning, just before nine o'clock, Joy, Lily and Margaret, dressed in their riding habits, were astride their horses and trotting along the wide bridle path in Hyde Park that was known as Rotten Row. They had not gone far when an immaculately garbed gentleman, with deep blue eyes and golden brown hair, tipped his hat as he reined in his horse alongside them. 'Good morning, Mrs. Barron,' he greeted Margaret.

'Good morning, Mr. Quincy,' Margaret responded as they all halted. 'What a lovely morning it is for a ride.'

'Indeed it is.'

'Mr. Quincy, I would like to present you to my niece, Miss Barron, and her friend, Miss Cavanagh. They are our guests for the Season.'

A smile creased his finely chiselled features. 'Miss Barron, it's a pleasure to meet you. And you too, Miss Cavanagh.'

He gave a slight bow in their direction before turning back to Margaret. 'My mother is holding a soiree on Friday evening. I believe she has sent an invitation to Lady Barron and yourself. She will be delighted to meet your guests, and I sincerely hope you will all be free to join us.'

'That is most kind of you, Mr. Quincy,' Margaret replied graciously.

'I look forward to our next meeting.' Although he spoke to Margaret, his gaze was on Joy and Lily. 'Good morning, ladies.' He tipped his hat again before riding away.

During the next hour Joy and Lily were introduced to many of Margaret's friends and acquaintances, both men and women.

As they dismounted after their ride, Margaret was all smiles. 'Well, my dear young ladies, that was a most satisfactory introduction to your Season. The invitations will now pour in as those eligible young men ask their Mamas to include you on their guest lists.'

'It's exciting to be able to show off our new clothes at last,' Lily said as they dressed for the visit to the Art gallery..

'Yes, it is. This morning was a start. I thought we both looked elegant in our riding habits.' Joy gave a little giggle as she remembered the parade of young men who had stopped to speak to Margaret, and to be introduced to them. 'And I think some of the young men thought so too, don't you?'

Lily laughed. 'We certainly met a lot of them on our first morning out. I wonder how often they all go riding.'

'Every day, I hope.' Joy paused. 'I must say I think Mr. Quincy handsome, don't you?'

'Mmm, yes, I suppose so. I wonder if there'll be any young men at the Art Gallery.'

'If we were back in Australia I don't think the Art Gallery would attract many, but here, well, who knows?'

'And I believe there's always a big crowd for the Sunday Church Parade in Hyde Park, and we'll be there.'

'Maybe we'll have English beaus before much longer.'

Laughing together they went downstairs to join Lady Barron for the visit to the Art Gallery.

The atmosphere in the Gallery was hushed as visitors moved slowly from room to room viewing the art hanging on the walls, and stopping here and there to discuss a particular painting. Most of the visitors had come as couples or in small groups, but occasionally a lone figure could be seen wandering around.

After the first hour Joy was bored, and she sensed Lily was too. They had accompanied Lady Barron from room to room and, thanks to those school visits to Sydney's galleries, had been able to comment knowledgeably on many of the paintings.

Long wooden seats stood in the centre of the largest rooms, their slatted seats and curved backs offering rest for weary feet or just a spot for friends to sit, with the ladies languidly waving their fans back and forth as they chatted. Catching sight of two of her friends occupying one of the seats Lady Barron moved across to join them, waving Joy and Lily on to continue their promenade.

'Don't go further than the next room without me,' she told them. 'I'll join you in a short while.'

'Good to be rid of the old dragon for a bit,' Lily muttered.

They moved through an open archway into the adjoining room. As they turned the corner and started to move slowly along the first wall, they saw a young man on his own examining the next painting.

'Excuse me ladies,' he said. He turned to them, politely doffing his hat. His blue eyes peered earnestly at them from a rather babyish face with a soft mouth, and thick blond hair with sideburns. 'I hope you don't mind me speaking to you, but I'm visiting on my own and you two young ladies seem to know about these here pictures, and I was wondering if you could tell me if this one is by a well known artist.' He indicated the portrait of a cavalier he had been examining. His accent proclaimed him an American.

Joy knew Grandmother would expect them to snub the young man and walk away, but he seemed respectable and she could see no harm in at least replying. She looked at the name of the artist on the brass plate beneath the painting.

'George Romney,' she read. 'He's not as well known as, perhaps, Gainsborough or someone like that.'

'But he's still a good artist,' Lily added, smiling at the young man.

'Yes, I can see that. It's a very fine portrait.' He paused for a moment. 'Do you young ladies come here often?'

'No, this is our first time,' Joy told him.

'Mine too. In fact it's my first time in London. I'm not English, you know. Allow me to introduce myself. My name is Winston Paget-Smythe and I come from Lexington, Kentucky, in the United States of America. I'm visiting here and staying with friends of my parents. I'm trying to pick up a bit of your English culture.'

While Joy was wondering whether to continue the conversation or excuse themselves Lily replied, smiling sweetly at him.

'It's our first time in London too. We're from Sydney, in Australia. I'm Lily Cavanagh and this is my friend Joy Barron.'

'I am sure pleased to meet you, I don't know. . .'

As he was speaking Lady Barron sailed around the corner. She took one look at the threesome and her face became a storm cloud. Drawing herself up to her full height she interposed herself between them.

'Come.' She barked the word in a voice that would not have disgraced a sergeant-major. She grabbed each girl by the arm.

'I say, I am sorry if I...'

The flustered man halted in mid sentence as she turned her icy glare on him. He tried again. 'I...I didn't mean...' he stammered, then gave up as she turned her back on him and marched them both away.

Joy threw him a hopeless look, and Lily grimaced back at him as they followed her out of the Gallery and down the steps, to where a footman waited.

'My carriage,' she snapped.

Joy's heart was like a lead weight as they waited in silence for the carriage.

Once inside, Lady Barron sat ramrod straight, glowering at them as they sat opposite her.

'I am most displeased. I've impressed upon you many times that you do not speak to strangers, especially of the opposite sex.' She glared at Joy. 'I expected better of you. If you have been observed your reputation will suffer.'

Joy was mortified. 'But we were only...'

A gloved hand was raised to silence her.

'I want no excuses.'

No further words were spoken for the rest of the journey.

'I hate her! I hate her, the old dragon.' They were in Joy's room, and Lily was pacing back and forth. 'What harm were we doing? We were only trying to be friendly, and he seemed so nice.'

'I know. It's not as if we arranged to meet him, or anything like that.'

'And now we have to go down and have tea with one of her boring friends.' She stamped her foot. 'I wish I'd never come here.'

Joy felt bad, and after spending the teatime hour listening to Lady Asplin hold forth with an account of each of her ailments, which seemed innumerable, Joy couldn't wait for the day to end, and was beginning to wish she had never come, either.

The next morning they again went riding in Rotten Row with Margaret, and it wasn't long before Mr. Quincy, followed by another horseman, rode up and stopped to talk with them. After exchanging greetings he turned to the man who reined in beside him. At the sight of the newcomer Joy raised her hand to stifle a gasp.

'Mrs. Barron, may I present my friend, Mr. Winston Paget-Smythe, who is visiting from America.'

Mr. Paget-Smythe raised his hat and bowed to Margaret. 'What a pleasure to meet you, Mrs. Barron.'

'How nice to make your acquaintance. Allow me to present my niece Miss Barron, and her friend Miss Cavanagh.'

The young man bowed again, betraying no hint of recognition. 'I'm surely pleased to meet you young ladies.'

As they continued their ride Lily whispered to Joy. 'Fancy him being a friend of Mr. Quincy's. I do like him. I hope we meet him again.'

Joy and Lily accompanied Lady Barron and Margaret to Mrs. Quincy's soiree later in the week. Having never attended a soiree before, neither girl knew what to expect.

Mr. Quincy greeted them on arrival and when he introduced his friend Mr. Paget-Smythe to Lady Barron Joy held her breath. However, if Grandmother recognised him, she gave no indication. Mr. Quincy then ushered them to chairs set up in the salon, and the two gentlemen took seats alongside them.

For the next hour both Joy and Lily tried to look as if they were enjoying themselves as Mrs. Quincy's daughter, Mildred, entertained them with her renditions of old English folk tunes. She sang in a high, fluting voice, enlivened with fluttering movements of her fan, and finished the recital with a spirited version of the aria *'l'amour est on oiseau rebelle'* from the opera *'Carmen'*.

'I hope you'll allow me to escort you in to partake of refreshments,' Mr. Quincy asked Joy, offering her his arm the end of her performance.

'Thank you.' She placed her hand on his arm and they went into the next room, followed by Lily with Mr. Paget-Smythe, while Lady Barron and Margaret remained in conversation with friends nearby.

After they were escorted to chairs and the gentlemen left them in search of champagne, the two friends looked at each other, and Lily rolled her eyes.

'Boring,' she whispered.

Joy had to raise her fan to hide the twitch of her lips at the sight of Lily's pained face.

'Look on the bright side,' Joy giggled. 'We have two men dancing attendance on us, which is more than some of the women here can say.'

Lily looked around and smiled then. 'Yes, that's true, and the two most handsome ones here, I do believe.'

Chapter Twenty One

After watching the pageantry of one of the most important days in London, the opening of Parliament, Joy and Lily accompanied the family to a ball given in honour of the occasion in the evening. It was a dazzling affair, with the ballroom lit by crystal chandeliers and the walls hung with silk tapestries, beneath which stood silk covered *chaise longue* and chairs. At one end of the room a small bevy of musicians played, in an area enclosed by lavish palms in enormous pots.

The women shone too, dressed in their décolleté gowns, with jewels sparkling at their throats and ears, and anywhere else that could be adorned. Joy's fingers strayed to her throat to finger the strand of pearls Mother gave her as a parting gift before leaving Sydney, and the matching earbobs from her stepfather.

'I'm glad we chose our most elegant gowns tonight,' Lily whispered, as they followed at the rear of the family party.

'So am I, but I'm afraid we're outshone tonight with all the jewels on show here. I hope we're not wallflowers.'

'Oh, how mortifying it would be if nobody asked us to dance. We'd never get over the shame.'

Margaret laughed at their remarks.

'You both look lovely; you have no need to worry. I can see many of the gentlemen we met while out riding. I'm sure your dance cards will be filled.' She paused. 'In fact, I can see Mr. Quincy and Mr. Paget-Smythe making their way over here now.'

Margaret was right. Their cards were soon filled, and the only time either of them stopped dancing throughout the night was when refreshments were served.

Over the next few weeks their days and nights became a whirl of engagements as the city filled with ladies and gentlemen all with one aim in mind – to meet as many members of the opposite sex as possible. And having done so, to enjoy their company. Joy and Lily found themselves much in demand. During the day it was riding or shopping or taking tea. The evenings were filled with balls or parties, and visits to the theatre.

Joy was caught up in the whole, frenetic pace of the Season, the excitement, the colour, the glamour. She basked in the admiration of the young men who gravitated to her side wherever she went. This was the thrilling life she'd longed for back in Bulahdelah, and if it meant her days were regimented, with everything arranged for her, and that she had little choice in her life, well, that was the price of being in the centre of this exhilarating existence.

It was made all the more stimulating by the attention Mr. Quincy was bestowing on her, and Joy found herself looking for him, feeling a slight breathlessness when he joined her, or disappointed if he wasn't present.

He often materialised alongside her when riding in Rotten Row, always finding her among the throng of riders who now rode daily, and he accompanied her as if it was the natural thing to do. They attended the same parties and balls, and he was always the first to take her dance card, usually claiming as many dances as propriety allowed.

Easter came and went and the Social Calendar became even more demanding. The weather was warmer now, and London became more crowded from week to week. The bridle path in Rotten Row was packed each morning and afternoon with members of both sexes, all eager to see and be seen. It was still a must-do for both Joy and Lily who, accompanied by either Margaret or Mrs. Frobisher, often arrived early in order have a short gallop before it became too crowded. And Mr. Quincy and Mr. Paget-Smythe were often present to accompany them.

Early one morning Mrs. Frobisher entered Lily's room to waken her as usual, only to find her huddled beneath the bedclothes with her head covered, and the sound of sobs coming from beneath the blankets. Startled, she stood by the bed and reached her hand out to pull back the covers.

'Here, Lily, whatever's the matter?'

Lily's response was to grab hold of the bedclothes, and cover herself again. 'Go away.'

'Here, come on now, are you sick?'

'Go away. Leave me alone.'

'I'm not going anywhere until I know what's the matter with you. Come out from under there and talk to me.'

'No.'

'Just tell me what it is. If you're sick, I'll fetch the doctor.'

A fresh outburst of crying was the only response.

Mrs. Frobisher was becoming alarmed. With a sudden tug on the blankets, she managed to pull them back far enough to see Lily's face, blotched and puffy from crying. Lily made a desperate attempt to cover herself up again, but the chaperone was too quick for her.

'No you don't.' She pulled the covers back even further. Lily turned on her side and put her head under the pillow.

Mrs. Frobisher took a deep breath. 'If you won't tell me, there's nothing else for it. I'll have to call her ladyship. Maybe you'll tell her what the matter is.'

This brought Lily's head out from under the pillow. 'No. Don't you dare tell her.' Sitting up, she wiped her face with the sleeve of her nightgown.

'Then tell me what's the matter with you.'

Lily gave a loud sniff and hiccupped. 'I'm all right. It's nothing for you to worry about.'

'Aren't you feeling well? Have you got a pain somewhere?'

Lily shook her head.

'I'm not going away until I know what's the matter, so you might as well tell me.'

'It's nothing.'

'Doesn't sound like nothing to me.' She thought for a moment. 'Have you had a tiff with one of those young men that's always hanging round?'

Tears sprang to Lily's eyes. She swallowed. 'I wish that's all it was,' she muttered.

Mrs. Frobisher gasped. 'Dear God...don't tell me...no, it couldn't be. Could it?'

She stood silent for a moment, her hand covering her mouth. 'You haven't been up to anything, have you?' she asked sharply. Then she shook her head. 'No, you couldn't have. You've both been under someone's eyes every moment since we've been here.'

'I don't know what you're talking about,' Lily replied sullenly.

Mrs. Frobisher looked at her with narrowed eyes.

'Have you been getting sick in the mornings?'

'No.'

'Not even feeling a bit queasy sometimes?'

Lily shrugged, turning her head away. 'Well, what if I have?'

'And your monthlies? Stopped, I suppose.'

Lily's silence was enough answer.

'Oh my God, you stupid girl! Was it one of those military gents?'

No answer.

'Well, I suppose his lordship will make it his business to find out.'

At that Lily sat up in the bed and slapped her across the face. 'Don't you dare,' she shrieked. 'Don't you dare mention this to anyone.'

Mrs. Frobisher reeled back, clutching her face.

'You little bitch. I'll tell them all right.'

Lily was panting now. 'It doesn't matter who it was, but if you do then I'll tell them how you were carrying on with Captain Hastings. I'll tell them you encouraged me, and that we made up foursomes so I wouldn't say anything. So you could go out in the night and meet him.'

'So that's what you did, is it? Slipped out at night to meet him?'

'Only because you encouraged me. Who do you think they'll believe? Me, an innocent young girl, or you, who's been married, and knows the ways of the world? I'll put up a good story, believe me.'

Mrs. Frobisher bit her lip. 'You are a sly one, aren't you? Yes, I can see you'd put up a good story. But even if I don't say anything, you're going to be found out. It's not going to go away, you know. How far are you? When did it first happen?'

Deflated, Lily sank back on the bed. 'There was only once, just before we left.'

'Only once? You were unlucky then. But that's how it happens. You should've had more sense.'

'I didn't know...'she paused, and bit her lip. 'He let me think we'd be married.'

Ms Frobisher snorted. 'That's the oldest trick in the book.' She sighed. 'Ah dear, what to do? Let's see. It was late January when we left, wasn't it?' She counted on her fingers. 'February, March,

April and now we're into May. So you're over three months. Too late to do anything about it.'

Lily started to cry again.

'No use blubbering. That won't help.'

At that moment there was a knock on the door, and Joy's voice called out. 'Lily. Lily are you awake? We'll be late if you don't hurry.'

Mrs. Frobisher raised her eyebrows. 'Do you want me to let her in?'

Lily drew a shuddering breath and nodded. 'Yes.'

When the door was opened Joy came in and looked from Lily's tearstained face to Mrs. Frobisher's, stern and unsmiling, and felt a stab of apprehension.

'What's the matter? Are you sick, Lily?'

'Not sick,' Mrs. Frobisher answered. 'But she's not feeling the best. I don't think she'll be going riding this morning.'

Joy frowned. 'What is it Lily? What's the matter with you?'

Lily moistened her lips. 'I...I'm...'she started to cry.

Worried now, Joy sat beside her and put an arm around her shoulders. 'There now. Tell me what's the matter.'

Lily cried even harder.

Mrs. Frobisher shook her head. 'Looks like she can't bring herself to tell you, but you need to know, so I'd better do it for her. She's gone and got herself in the family way.'

Joy's blood froze. She dropped her arm and leant back so she could look into Lily's face. 'What? You don't mean...you can't mean ...?'

Lily dropped her gaze, then threw herself back on the bed, sobbing.

'Oh yes, she means just that.' Mrs. Frobisher spoke over Lily's sobs. 'And you'd better shut that noise or you'll have the rest of the household in here to see what's the matter.'

Lily quietened her sobs.

Joy shook her head, her mind swimming. 'But...when...how could it have happened?'

'In the usual way. I don't know of any other.' Mrs. Frobisher's voice was grim.

Joy frowned, unwilling to believe what she was hearing. 'But she hasn't been out anywhere on her own. We've always been with someone.'

'It was before you came to London, when you were in the country.'

Suddenly the memory of Lily's empty bed one night sprang into her mind – and of her uncle going downstairs that same night. Lily had denied meeting anyone, but had she been telling the truth? Joy felt sick in the pit of her stomach, but she tried to think calmly. She frowned, and touched Lily. 'Do stop crying, try and pull yourself together. Who was it?'

Lily stopped crying and sat up, wiping her eyes.

Mrs. Frobisher opened her mouth to say something, but caught a warning look from Lily.

'She's not saying.'

'Now look Lily, don't be silly.' Joy took a deep breath. 'Whoever it is, have you told him?'

'No, and I can't.'

'What do you mean, you can't? You have to. He has to marry you.'

'I can't. I tell you, I can't.'

'Look, try and be sensible. You have to get married, what else can you do? And the first step to that, is to tell him. You must see that. Is it someone who's here in London now?'

'No.'

'Then you'll have to write him a letter.'

'It's no use.' She drew a shuddering breath. 'He wouldn't marry me.'

'What makes you think that?'

'Because he made me think he wanted to marry me, and then – afterwards – he wouldn't even speak to me, hardly.'

Joy felt a wave of pity and put her arms around her friend. 'Oh Lily, what are we going to do?'

Lily looked up at her, her eyes pleading.

'Don't tell anyone, will you?'

'But they'll have to know.'

Her tears welled up again. 'I don't know what to do.'

Joy suddenly knew what she had to do right now. She turned to Mrs. Frobisher. 'It's lucky you were coming riding with us this morning, not Margaret. If anyone asks you, you're to tell them Lily has a headache and, as we're both a bit tired this morning, we're not going riding. We'll go shopping this afternoon; we want to find a gift for our parents, who'll be here next week. You'll come with us, no need for Margaret to come.' She turned to Lily. 'This will give you time to pull yourself together.'

Mrs. Frobisher looked at her with respect. 'Well, I'm pleased one of you has a head on her shoulders.'

'And not a word to anyone, remember.'

'Right.' Mrs. Frobisher nodded, and left the room.

'Now Lily, you have to behave normally if you don't want anyone to think you're sick, or something worse. Are you actually feeling sick?'

'No, not really. Just scared.'

Joy wanted to sympathise with Lily but she knew it would cause her to break down again, so she kept her voice neutral. 'Do you think you'll be able to go riding tomorrow?'

Lily swallowed. 'Yes, I'll be all right. I just felt so overwhelmed this morning that I couldn't face anyone. And so alone, not knowing what to do.'

'Now that I know, you won't need to feel so lonely. But you're going to have to tell your Father when he comes.'

Lily gnawed at a nail, and Joy noticed they were all bitten. She caught at her hand and pulled it away from her mouth.

'Don't do that, people will notice.'

'What does it matter? No one will want to know me soon, anyway.' She turned troubled eyes on Joy. 'What am I to do? What will happen to me?'

Joy felt a knot of tension building inside her, but she mustn't let Lily know how desperate she felt.

'When your Father comes you'll have to tell him. He'll decide what's for the best. And in the meantime, you must try to act as if nothing's wrong. I'll do what I can to help you.'

Chapter Twenty Two

Edward Craddock sat sipping his coffee in the coffee salon of the Savoy Hotel in London, taking his time over it and watching the passing parade in the elegant lobby beyond the doors of the salon.

His prison pallor had gone after spending the last year with his sister down in Somerset, recovering from fifteen years in the hellhole that was Her Majesty's prison, but his determination for revenge on those who put him there still blazed as fiercely as ever. It was the only thing that had kept him sane during his incarceration.

Leniency. His lip curled. They promised him leniency if he turned Queen's evidence and incriminated his former employer, George Arnold. They'd brought him from Australia back to London to do so. It saved him from the hangman's noose, to be sure, but he didn't consider a sentence of fifteen long years as lenient.

He'd been George Arnold's right hand man ever since coming into his service as a youth, learning to enjoy the good life while living in his mansion in Knightsbridge. He'd been well paid, and when Arnold asked him to go to Australia to help his cousin, Thomas, set up a similar operation, he agreed, seeing it as an adventure.

At first everything went well, and they had rich pickings. In addition to diamonds, which Arnold had been '*appropriating*', as he preferred to call it, rather than '*stealing*', on an international scale for years, Australia provided them with gold from the newly discovered mines. Then a group of his men fell into a trap set at a bogus diamond mine. The troopers were waiting for them, and, to save their own skins, they spewed forth all the information they could. It led to his ultimate downfall.

Craddock blamed three people for his demise; Jan van Mayen, a South African diamond merchant who had hounded the gang on three continents, Rufe Cavanagh, an Australian business man and adventurer, and that bitch, Kitty Barron, who provided Redwoods, her estate, as the site for the decoy mine. It was this that led to their capture, and his imprisonment.

Jan van Mayen was beyond his reach, he'd died three years ago, but he was determined the other two would pay for their part in his suffering.

The time had come to settle old scores. And he didn't just want to make trouble for them. There had to be a way to hurt them and, at the same time, turn a profit for himself. This meant finding some way to cost them money, plenty of money.

So he was now trying to recoup some of what it had cost him in prison to ensure he was treated better than those who had nothing. Then he would plan a trip to Australia. A man of his talents could always make a killing from the unsuspecting tourists who flooded London for the Season each year, and the Savoy Hotel was a Mecca for the well-heeled.

As he sat musing he saw a sight that almost made him choke on his coffee. Crossing the lobby and heading toward the reception desk he saw a man who looked like Rufe Cavanagh, accompanied by the Barron bitch.

As they reached the desk Craddock left his coffee and sidled out into the lobby, positioning himself behind a palm, gazing around as if looking for someone.

'Yes sir,' he heard the clerk say, 'Mr. and Mrs. Cavanagh. I have your booking here.'

He took a key from a rack behind him, and handed it over. 'Here you are. Room 408. Your luggage will be up in a few moments.'

So it really was them.

Cavanagh took the key and handed the clerk two envelopes. 'Could you please have these notes delivered for me?'

'Certainly sir.'

'Do you have someone available to take them immediately? I'd like them delivered as soon as possible.'

'Right away, Mr. Cavanagh.'

Cavanagh nodded his thanks, and as he and his wife moved to the escalators, the clerk called a boy over.

'These notes are to be delivered immediately.' He looked at the first address as he handed them over. 'This is to Miss Cavanagh, 7 Curzon Street. Do you know where that is?'

'Yes sir.'

'And this one is to Miss Barron at – oh, it's the same address. Off you go.'

The boy took the letters and sped away.

Craddock's face was thoughtful as he memorised the address and made his way outside, where the commissionaire signalled a cab for him.

Arriving at the end of Curzon Street he paid off the cab and sauntered along the street until he reached number 7. It was one of several townhouses, similar to its neighbours. Walking slowly by, he continued along the street for another hundred yards or so, then turned and walked back. As he reached number 7 a young woman, dressed in maid's black, came out of the door and hurried down the steps.

Craddock stopped, pulled a slip of paper from his pocket, and appeared to study it.

'Excuse me.' He tipped his hat. 'I wonder if you could help me find an address. I'm looking for Sir Thomas Willoughby. Am I correct in thinking this is his home?' He indicated No7.

'Oh no, this is Sir Alexander Barron's house. I've never heard of Sir Thomas Willoughby. You must have the wrong address.'

'I'm so sorry to have bothered you. I'll have to check further.' He tipped his hat again. 'Thank you for your help.'

'No bother.' She hurried away, and he continued walking.

On his return to the hotel he chose a seat that offered him a good view of both the entrance and the reception desk. There he settled himself to read The Times.

From behind his paper he observed every person who came and went from the Savoy for the next two hours. He was beginning to think he was wasting his time when three women came through the door, and the sight of one of them made him catch his breath. He was looking straight into the face of Kitty Barron of twenty years ago. Folding his paper he stood up and strolled behind them toward the desk, where he bent over and retied his shoe lace.

'We're here to see Mr. and Mrs. Cavanagh', he heard the older woman say.

'Yes, they're expecting you. Room 408, you may go straight up.'

She turned back to the two girls, who hovered just behind her. One of them, the dark one, was looking agitated.

'I can't do it,' she said.

The older woman frowned at her. 'Don't you make a scene, Lily.' Her voice came out as a hiss as she took her by the arm and lead her away from the desk. 'Come on, Joy. We'll go into the coffee salon and sort this out.'

Craddock straightened. He followed them, seated himself at the next table, and pretended to read his paper while he eavesdropped on their conversation.

'I can't do it. I can't tell them. I can't face them.' Lily said in a choked voice.

'Now look here, my girl ...'

'Don't, Mrs. Frobisher, don't upset her any more, or she'll be in tears.'

Mrs. Frobisher sat back. 'Well then, what do you suggest we do?'

'I think it best if I go up first. I'll tell them.'

'Would you do that? Will you break it to them for me?'

'Yes. Once they know, I'll come down and get you. You have a cup of coffee while you're waiting. It'll help to steady your nerves.'

Joy stood and left the table as the waitress came to take their orders.

After his order was taken, Craddock continued to feign an interest in the paper as he sipped, with his ears alert for any further revelations, but the two women remained silent.

While Mrs. Frobisher drank her coffee, Lily sat staring into space.

As Joy knocked on the door, her stomach was turning nervous somersaults. She had no idea how she was going to break the news; her mind seemed to go blank every time she tried to frame the right words.

Kitty opened the door and her face lit up. 'Joy! Darling, come in.'

She pulled her inside and threw her arms around her, hugging her. Joy returned the hug, pleasure and terror flooding through her in equal amounts.

'Let me look at you.' Her mother held her away from her, studying her intently, her face aglow. 'My, but haven't you blossomed into a young lady. You look wonderful, London must agree with you.' A faint crease showed between her brows. 'But you don't look happy to see me.' The crease deepened. 'Didn't you want me to come?' Her delight faded.

Joy hurried to reassure her. 'Of course I wanted you to be here, it's not that...it's...it's Lily.' She swallowed, her throat seeming to close up.

'Lily!' Kitty looked alarmed. 'Where is she? Didn't she come with you?'

'Yes, she's downstairs. With Mrs. Frobisher.' Joy felt desperate. 'Look, we'd better sit down. Is Uncle Rufe here?'

At that moment Rufe opened the door from the bedroom, and came into the room. He beamed at the sight of her.

'Joy, how lovely to see you.' He stopped short at the sight of their faces, his welcoming smile fading. 'Is something the matter?'

'Yes, sort of.'

'It's Lily, she's downstairs,' Kitty told him. She turned to Joy. 'What's the matter? Is she sick?'

'No, not really.' Joy felt worse with every minute. 'Look, please sit down.'

As they sat, silent and waiting, she forced herself to be calm. 'Lily's not sick, she's waiting downstairs. But there's something you must know. Something she wants me to tell you.'

They were both watching her apprehensively. Kitty reached out and took Rufe's hand, clasping it tightly, while he sat very still.

'Yes?'

Joy bit her lip. There was no easy way to do this. 'I'm afraid that Lily has been rather foolish, if that's what you can call it. It seems that she was rather led on and she's...well... she's in trouble.'

The colour drained from Rufe's face.

Kitty's eyes grew large as she sucked in her breath. 'Dear God,' she whispered, her hand going up to cover her mouth.

'You mean she's with child?' Rufe's voice was harsh.

'Yes, I'm afraid so.'

'And who is the father?'

Joy shook her head. 'I don't know. Lily hasn't said.'

Rufe sprang from his seat. 'By God, I'll find out and when I do...'

Kitty interrupted him. 'Rufe, steady now, let's talk to Lily. And Mrs. Frobisher.'

'Mrs. Frobisher. Yes. Some chaperone she's turned out to be. Where was she while this was happening?'

'Rufe, try to be calm.' Kitty put her hand on his arm. 'I know this is a shock, but let's talk to Lily and see if we can find out some more. We need to try and see what's to be done for the best. For Lily and...and everyone concerned. It's no use losing control.'

Rufe ran a hand across his forehead. 'Yes, of course, you're right. Give me a few minutes, and then we'll talk to her.' He stood up and crossed the room to a drinks cabinet in the corner, and picked up a decanter. 'Would you like a drink, darling?'

Kitty shook her head. 'No thanks.'

'I hope you don't mind if I do?'

'No, go ahead.'

With that he poured some whisky into a glass, tossed back half of it, and then came back and sat beside Kitty with the glass.

When he spoke again his voice was steady. 'Do you know anything about it, Joy? Has Lily told you anything? Anything at all?'

Joy shook her head, feeling helpless. 'No, nothing. Only that she expected to be married.'

'Poor Lily.' Kitty shook her head. 'She's not the first girl to be taken in by an unscrupulous man.'

Rufe took another gulp of his drink. 'Huh. Little fool. I thought she'd have more sense. Besides, she's only a child herself.'

Kitty shook her head. 'Girls marry younger than her.'

Rufe's lips twisted. 'All right. You'd better bring her up. But tell Mrs. Frobisher to wait down there. I don't want to see her yet.'

'All right. I'll tell her to wait.' Joy rose and left the room, thankful her duty was done.

While Mrs. Frobisher and Lily waited in silence for Joy to return, Craddock continued his perusal of *The Times*, lingering over his coffee. When Joy returned he didn't raise his head as he heard her speak.

'Come on Lily. They want to see you now.'

'How are they?' He heard fear in Lily's voice.

'Well, you know, upset, of course. Come on.'

'What about me? Does Mr. Cavanagh want to see me too?' Mrs. Frobisher asked.

'Not just yet. He told me to ask you to wait here for now.'

After the other two departed Mrs. Frobisher sat muttering to herself.

Craddock waited a few minutes before putting the paper down with an exaggerated sigh. Glancing across, he caught her eye, and allowed the glimmer of a discreet smile to appear as he bowed slightly in her direction.

'Ah, it seems there's little else but bad news in the world these days,' he said, indicating the paper.

'The bad news isn't all in the papers either. There's plenty of it as never reaches the papers.'

'Really?' His voice was solicitous. 'Have you had bad news recently?'

'I've got it right now, if you must know.'

'Is that so?' He shook his head. 'There are times when life becomes very hard, I'm afraid. And often through the fault of others, sadly.'

Mrs. Frobisher tightened her lips. 'You can say that again. Especially when they're young and stupid, like the one I'm in charge of.'

'Young people can be very difficult. It seems the old values count for nothing these days. I noticed a couple of young ladies with you earlier. Are they causing you problems?'

'Hah, one of them is. And now I've got to sit here and cool my heels, while I wait for them to summon me.'

'I am sorry to hear that.' He hesitated. 'Is that an Australian accent I hear?'

Mrs. Frobisher looked startled. 'Yes. How did you know?'

'I spent a lot of time out there, oh, quite a few years ago now. I say, would you think me too forward if I asked if I could buy you a cup of coffee? Perhaps we could have a bit of a chat, while you're waiting. I don't know many people here, I'm from Somerset, you see. Just up for a few weeks on business.'

Mrs. Frobisher hesitated. 'Well...'

'Please allow me to introduce myself. My name is Brown, George Brown. I own a drapery store, and I'm up here to select new stock.'

'Are you now? Well, I'm Mrs. Frobisher. I'm chaperoning one of the girls, Lily, while she's on holiday here. Staying with Sir Alexander Barron in Mayfair, we are. And Joy, the other one that's with me, is his granddaughter, and she's to be presented to Queen Victoria.'

'You don't say? Well, isn't that something. And you live in Mayfair? Very nice. I always stay here at the Savoy when I'm in London, but it's a bit lonely on your own.'

'Your wife doesn't come with you, then?'

He shook his head. 'Sadly, she passed away three years ago.'

'I'm sorry to hear that. I'm a widow myself, so I know what it's like.'

'But you have a good job with the aristocracy now. That must be very agreeable for you.'

'Hmph, the aristocracy! They're not all that high quality, believe me. Why, the stories I could tell you...' She stopped. 'But then, I'm not one to gossip.'

'I'm quite sure you're not. Now, shall I order that coffee for you?'

'I'm expecting Mr. Cavanagh, that's Lily's father, to send down for me any minute, so p'raps I'd better not, thanks all the same. But we can talk until then.'

Craddock looked disappointed. 'I'm so enjoying our little chat, I don't suppose you'd consider meeting me some time when you're free, so we could talk about Australia. Such a wonderful country, and I never have a chance to reminisce about it.'

'I do have Sundays off. I suppose I could meet you then, if you like.'

'Splendid. What say we make it next Sunday then, say at the Corner House just down the road from here? We can have a cup of tea, and see then if there's anything you fancy doing. What time would suit you?'

'Shall we say eleven o'clock?'

'Eleven o'clock it is then. I'll be looking forward to it.'

'Right. So shall I.'

Chapter Twenty Three

By the time Joy returned to Room 408 with Lily, Rufe seemed to have regained his usual equanimity.

'Hullo Lily,' he greeted her, then put his arms around her and held her close. As he let go of her he shook his head and looked into her face, sighing. 'Ah Lily, what have you done?'

Tears sprang into Lily's eyes. 'Oh Father, I didn't mean...'

'No, I don't suppose you did. Well, no use crying about it. It's a bit late for that. Come and sit down.'

Joy admired his control; she could tell it was costing him a great effort.

'There's not a lot for me to say at this stage. It's no use me telling you how foolish you've been, I'm sure you realise that yourself. As Kitty has just been telling me, we now have to think about what's best to do.' A shadow crossed his face. 'I've asked Kitty and Joy to stay while we talk about this, because I believe it's a family matter. You're going to need a lot of family support in the next few months, perhaps for some years.'

Lily sat with her head down, twisting her hands together.

'Now Lily,' Rufe continued, 'I want you to tell me, who is responsible for this?'

Lily shook her head.

'Come now, be sensible. You're going to have a child and we need to know who the father is.'

'I can't tell you.' She sniffed, and dabbed at her eyes with a handkerchief.

Rufe's face darkened. 'Why not?'

'It wouldn't do any good.' She looked up now, a determined look on her face, the handkerchief clutched in her hand. 'He wouldn't want to marry me, and even if he agreed, which he wouldn't, I wouldn't want to marry a man who didn't want to marry me.'

Rufe stood up and looked down at her, clenching his fists at his sides.

'That may be what you think now, but when you're trying to bring up a child on your own you'll feel differently. Besides, what about the child?' His voice rose. 'How will he feel when he knows he has no father? Or doesn't know who it is. Do you think that's fair? No, of course it's not. Now, tell me, who is it?'

Lily was crying in earnest now, with big sobs shaking her.

Kitty stood up and put a hand on Rufe's arm. 'Perhaps we should leave that for a while. Perhaps we should concentrate on the immediate future. What to do right now.'

Rufe took deep breaths, and cleared his throat. 'Yes, you're right. We're getting nowhere here.' After a moment he resumed in a quieter voice. 'I have to call on Sir Alexander in the next few days, I'll ...'

Lily's hand shot out and grabbed his arm. 'You're not to tell him,' she said fiercely. 'I don't want anyone to know.'

'My dear girl, everyone's going to know soon. It's not something you can hide for long, you know.'

'But not yet, I don't want anyone to know, not while I'm living here.'

Joy heard the desperation in her friend's voice, and her heart contracted with concern. 'I don't want to intrude, but do you mind if I say something?'

'Of course not. That's why I asked you to stay. This is a family matter.'

'Well, it seems to me that Lily still has a few weeks before it becomes obvious.' She turned to Kitty. 'Isn't that right, Mother?'

Kitty nodded. 'Yes.'

'Then perhaps nobody here needs to know. I can't leave just yet, but once I've been presented, Lily and I can go home. Or it might even be better if we go somewhere here in England where nobody knows us, until...until it's all over.'

Kitty turned and put a hand on her arm. 'You don't have to do that. There's no need for you to give up your Season. Before Lily's condition is obvious we'll decide what to do for the best. In the meantime, Lily can act as normal. No one needs to know.'

Joy had a sudden thought. 'What about Mrs. Frobisher? Do you think she'll keep it to herself?'

'I'll make quite sure she does.' Rufe's tone was grim.

Kitty spoke now in a firm voice. 'Then I suggest we all leave it at that for the moment. It's been a very emotional day. Let's wait until we've had time to think things over before we make any firm decisions about the next few months.' She turned to Lily. 'Do you agree?'

Lily nodded. 'Yes. No one can tell yet, and I want to stay as long as I can. It's not as if I'm sick or anything. I want to see Joy presented, and I want to be part of as much of the Season as I can. I don't suppose I'll ever have another chance.'

Rufe sighed. 'Very well, let's leave it at that for the moment. Do you have any engagements for tomorrow afternoon?'

'No.'

'Then I'd like to see you again then. Perhaps it would be best if you call here. Shall we say two o'clock?'

Lily looked as if she would rather say no, but she nodded her head. 'Very well, Father. We'll see you then.'

'You may send Mrs. Frobisher up now, if you will.'

The next morning as they returned from their morning ride Joy received a summons to attend her grandmother in her sitting room. Lady Barron was waiting for her and, waving Joy to a seat, she picked up a gold edged card from the table beside her.

'I have received confirmation of your Court Presentation,' she told Joy, 'and the date. It is to be in two weeks' time. Are you prepared?'

Joy's stomach flipped with excitement. 'Oh yes, Grandmother, I'm ready.'

'Perhaps it will be as well for you to practice the curtsey again, and to make certain that you understand the procedure. I'll inform Margaret.'

'Yes, I would like to go through it all again.'

Lady Barron's face softened. 'You're a good child, Joy. I hope you'll decide to stay with us after the Season is over.' She paused. 'I have noticed Mr. Quincy paying you much attention. Has he given you any reason to believe he may have serious intentions toward you?'

'No. He's always exceedingly polite and solicitous, but that's all.'

'He's from a good family. You could do worse, if he should declare his intentions.'

'He's said nothing to indicate he has that in mind.'

'We shall see. I notice these things. Just remember that such a match would meet with my approval.'

'If it should happen, I'll remember.'

'Good.' She paused for a moment. 'I have also noticed that Mr. Paget-Smythe seems to be enamoured of Miss Cavanagh.'

Joy was startled. 'Oh. Oh...oh...I don't think she's...' she stammered, giving a small shake of her head.

Grandmother shrugged. 'It's of no account, but it is as well her father is here. That's all, you may go now, make sure you're well prepared for your presentation.'

'I will, Grandmother. Thank you.'

As Joy left the room she turned the conversation over in her mind. Mr. Quincy was certainly a pleasant man, and she wondered if she should think of him as a serious suitor, although he'd really given her no reason to think of him in such a way. However, he certainly sought her out whenever they were at the same functions, and he flirted mildly with her, in a playful fashion. It was like a game they played. She wondered what it would be like to be kissed by him. She tingled at the thought.

She had only been kissed once, by David, and she enjoyed that. Sometimes she thought of David, and she always enjoyed his occasional light hearted letters, and wrote back telling him all about what she was doing. But he was so far away, almost as if it had been another life back there, and her thoughts were always taken up with each day's happenings.

But coming back to Grandmother's words, what would she say if Mr. Quincy proposed marriage? She wasn't sure she wanted to marry anyone yet; she was having far too much fun. But she did like Mr. Quincy. Quite a lot, actually.

Fancy Grandmother thinking Mr. Paget-Smythe might be interested in Lily. She wouldn't be interested in him, not now.

Her mind turned to the exciting prospect of her presentation, and all other thoughts were forgotten.

'What good news,' Lily said when Joy told her. 'I'm pleased it's going to be so soon, I'll still be able to fit into that red dress I bought specially for the big event. How exciting it'll be to go to the Palace and see the Queen. Are you nervous?'

'A little,' Joy admitted. 'I'm going to go over everything again with Margaret. I'm lucky to have her to coach me. She's so patient.'

'Just imagine how terrible it'd be if you had the old dragon coaching you.' Lily shuddered. 'It would be worse than me having to listen to Mrs. Frobisher lecturing me about how stupid I am.' She screwed up her face. 'I do hope Father doesn't go on at me again this afternoon.'

'Are you worried about seeing him again?'

'A bit. I suppose he'll try again to find out who I was with, but I'm not going to tell him. I'll never tell anyone.'

'Perhaps the man would want to know that he's going to be a father.'

'Well, he's not going to know. He's never going to have anything to do with my baby.'

Joy refrained from pointing out that it was his baby too. But she couldn't help worrying about what would happen, to both Lily and the baby.

Lady Barron composed a note and sent it to Charles Quincy, requesting him to call on her at a time when she knew Joy would be otherwise occupied.

When he was shown in to her presence, she wasted little time in coming to the point.

'I've noticed you taking an interest in my granddaughter, Joy,' she said, once the pleasantries were out of the way. 'I'll tell you now that I wish to see her remain here in England, and the best way of ensuring this, is to make sure she marries someone who will always remain here. I am, of course, cognisant of your station in life, and that you'll be expected to make an advantageous marriage. Forgive my curiosity, but I'm wondering if you have any intention of marrying in the near future.'

Mr. Quincy narrowed his eyes as he considered her remarks.

'Of course, it's expected of me that I will marry some time, however, I haven't contemplated doing so in the immediate future.

Miss Barron is indeed a most charming young lady, but I have done nothing to cause her to believe I am considering suggesting marriage to her.'

'No, she's not given me reason to believe this is so. Quite the contrary, in fact. However, will you allow me to speak freely? Whatever we discuss here will go no further from me, and I ask that you give me the same undertaking.'

'Of course. You may be assured of my discretion.'

'Good. You come from a highly respected family, one that I should be happy to see associated with the Barron name. However, times have been hard recently, and in addition, it has come to my attention that you have incurred large gambling debts recently.'

She held up her hand as he made to interrupt her. 'No, hear me out, please. I'm not concerned about this. I'm sure that once you settle down, and take over the running of your estate, you will mend your ways. In the meantime, I believe you would benefit from an injection of funds. I can tell you now, in confidence, that Joy will one day be a wealthy woman. Sir Alexander has made generous provision for her in his will, as well as the fact that she will one day inherit the timber cutting property that my son William established in Australia. But in the meantime, I would be willing to grant you an immediate amount of ten thousand pounds upon your marriage, if you have such feelings toward my grand-daughter. In strict confidence, of course. I wouldn't wish anyone else to know of this.'

Mr. Quincy regarded her steadily for a moment.

'That's quite a large sum of money.'

'I'm sure you could make good use of it.'

He strode to the window and looked out for a moment, then turned back into the room.

'Miss Barron is a most exemplary young lady, and I am exceedingly attracted to her. On consideration, I believe she'd make me an excellent wife.'

Joy felt a little apprehensive when Rufe opened the door for them, but he was smiling as he ushered them in to the sitting room where Kitty was waiting.

'Well girls, how was your ride this morning?' he asked.

'Very good, thank you Father,' Lily replied. 'And Joy has some news for you.'

'Good news, I hope?'

'Yes. The date has been set for my presentation. It's to be in two weeks time.'

'Oh darling, that's great news,' Kitty said, jumping up to hug her daughter. 'Are you ready for it?'

'I think so, but I'm going to practice again with Margaret.'

'I'm sure you'll be perfect,' Rufe told her. 'It's a big day for you, and I'm glad we'll be here to see it.'

Joy felt a rush of affection for her stepfather. He was so supportive, the sort of man she admired. She thought of Mr. Quincy. Would he be like that? She really knew little about him. Perhaps she should observe him more keenly. A picture of David flashed into her mind. Would he be like his uncle? His offer of Blaze and his letters to her suggested he might be. Before she could give this anymore thought she had to bring herself back to what Rufe was saying.

'As it so happens,' he was continuing, 'the timing fits in well with our plans. We're staying for Ascot, but we have planned to spend time looking at horses, with a view to buying something, so that will bring us to about the end of June.' He looked over at Kitty. 'And you think that will be as long as Lily will want to remain here, don't you?'

Kitty nodded. 'Yes, Lily, by then I don't think you'll be able to hide your condition for much longer. So we think, if you're agreeable, that it would be wise for you to come with us. How do you feel about that?'

Lily shrugged. 'I don't have much choice, do I?'

'Yes Lily,' Rufe told her. 'You can return home. You can go and stay at Riverside. Aunt Erin will look after you.'

'And stay there where everyone knows me, and will talk about me. No thank you.'

'Then you'll come with us?'

'Yes. But what will happen once...once it's born?'

'You and your baby will have a home with us for as long as you wish.'

'That's something to look forward to.'

'Then what do you want to happen?'

'I don't know.'

'Haven't you thought about it?'

'No.' Lily screwed up her face, frowning. 'Oh, I wish Aunt Erin was here. She'd know what to do about it, she knows about herbs and everything.'

Kitty paled. 'I take it, by that, you mean how to abort the child?'

'Yes, of course.'

'I'm afraid it's too late for that, even with a great knowledge of herbs.'

'Are you sure there's nothing that can be done?'

'Not now, it's too late to do anything.'

Lily's face crumpled. 'Then I suppose I'm going to have my life spoilt by it. No one will want me now.' Out came her handkerchief as tears welled in her eyes.

Joy had the feeling she was thinking of Mr. Paget-Smythe.

'Don't cry. Tears won't do any good.' Rufe spoke sharply.

Lily sniffed and dried her eyes.

'Would you ever consider giving the baby away?' Kitty spoke slowly, as if considering her words carefully.

Lily looked up quickly. 'Giving it away? What do you mean? Who would want a baby that someone else doesn't want?'

'There are people who are looking for babies to adopt.'

'Are there? Well, they can have this one. I don't want it.'

'Think about what you're saying. This is a big decision.'

'I tell you I don't want it. If we can find someone else who wants it, I'd be stupid to keep it.'

Rufe's face looked like thunder. 'You're taking this very lightly, Lily. This is your child you're talking about. It isn't asking to be brought into the world. It's because of your actions it exists. Doesn't that mean anything to you?'

Lily started to cry again.

Kitty raised her hand. 'Rufe, don't. Don't say things you might regret later.'

He turned to Lily angrily. 'This is a human life we're talking about. A person. Not some article that can be disposed of at will.' He paused, shaken. 'This is my grandchild we're talking about.'

There was silence in the room. Even Lily's sniffles stopped.

In that void Kitty's voice sounded loud. 'Let's just stop here. Something has come to me. Something that might help the situation. If you're sure you don't want to keep the baby, Lily, I might have a solution. But are you sure? Think about it carefully. It's a very big decision – to relinquish all rights to a child you bring into the world. Are you sure?'

'Yes. Quite sure.'

'What do you have in mind, Kitty?'

'We're in a country where we're not known, apart from here in London. I propose that Lily comes with us and we'll do what we set out to do, look at horses. For the last couple of months of her pregnancy, Lily and I will go somewhere out of the way, somewhere isolated. After the baby is born, and we leave there, I'll claim it as my own. The child will be our child, Rufe. When we go home, no one will suspect anything else.'

Joy held her breath. She felt as if time was suspended as she looked around the room. No one spoke. No one moved.

The spell was broken as Rufe drew a deep breath. He crossed to the window and looked out for a few seconds, then whirled around.

'Well?' he barked. 'What do you say to that, Lily? Would that suit you?'

'Yes,' she whispered.

'You would give up all claims to your child. You realise if we do this, you'll never be able to change your mind, no matter what happens.'

'Yes.'

'And you're happy with that?'

'Yes.'

'Then that is what will happen.'

Chapter Twenty Four

The next two weeks were a time of excitement for the household in Curzon Street. It seemed as if everyone from the butler down to the scullery maid was excited by Joy's forthcoming presentation at Court.

Lily acted as if the meeting at the Savoy Hotel had never happened. Neither she nor Joy ever referred to it.

For Joy it was a time of rehearsing for the big event until she felt she was perfect. Over and over she curtseyed, until she could be sure she had not the faintest wobble. Her clothes were pressed and hanging ready, together with her gloves, her slippers, the feathers for her hair, and her fan.

At last the great day arrived and, dressed in her finery, Joy accompanied Lady Barron in the carriage to St James Palace. Here they joined a line of carriages awaiting their turn. She was excited, but so relentlessly had she practiced, so often had she gone over every detail with Margaret that she felt she was as ready as it was possible to be.

As they came to a halt at the front of the Palace the door of the carriage was opened by a footman, who helped them down. When she stepped onto the ground Joy turned and retrieved her train from behind, draping it over her arm as she had practiced so many times. They were ushered into the long St. James Gallery, where they waited with a crowd of other young women and their sponsors.

'Now we must wait for your name to be called,' Lady Barron told Joy as she settled herself on a chair. 'We must be prepared for a goodly wait, I fear.'

Each time an usher entered the room Joy, along with all the ladies present, watched hopefully, hoping to hear her name called. Finally it happened, and she joined a seemingly endless line moving slowly into the room where Queen Victoria awaited them.

Joy's heart beat faster when her turn came and she handed her card to the Lord Chamberlain.

'Miss Joy Barron,' he announced.

Focused only on the Queen she barely noticed the group of royals, dressed in their richly coloured gowns and uniforms, grouped on one side of the room. As she approached the Queen she prayed she wouldn't trip or disgrace herself. Finally, she found herself standing before the Queen. With a beating heart she looked into her Sovereign's lined face. Why, she's an old woman, just like anyone else, except she's the Queen.

'Miss Barron,' Queen Victoria said with a faint nod, extending her hand.

Inwardly shaking, Joy made a full curtsy until she was almost kneeling on the floor, then she bowed, and kissed the Queen's hand. When she rose she remembered to curtsy to the other Royals, and then finished with one last brief curtsy to the Queen, as she had been taught.

Relief flooded through her as she realised she had come through without disgracing herself. But she still had to leave the Royal presence without turning her back on her, with a ten foot train trailing behind her. Her heart beat a mighty tattoo. A footman came forward at this crucial moment and, deftly scooping up the long train from behind her, draped it across her arm, all in a few seconds, and then stepped back.

Carefully, step-by-step, she backed out of the room, hoping she was heading in the right direction. Almost there, she faltered, unsure if she was on track for the exit door. By then another young lady was approaching the Queen and all eyes were on her. A footman came forward to guide Joy's last steps, and she passed through the open door into the blessed obscurity of an anteroom.

Joy's mouth was so dry she was barely able to thank the footman as he whispered 'Well done.'

She found herself in a small room lined with chairs and sank on to one of them. Gratefully she accepted a glass of water from the young woman in attendance, but shook her head at an offer of smelling salts.

'I'm quite all right,' she told her. 'Just a bit flustered.'

'You've done very well. I've had young ladies faint after that ordeal.'

After a moment Joy's heartbeat slowed to normal, and she made her way out into a large reception room, where she found her family awaiting her. Her ordeal finally over, she began to enjoy the congratulations that were showered on her.

Back at Curzon Street, the servants had prepared a feast for the crowd of guests Lady Barron had invited, including many of the young men and women whom she had met over the last few months. Joy became the centre of an admiring group of young men.

Mr. Quincy eased his way to her side, holding a glass of champagne. He handed it to her with a flourish.

'You were magnificent, Miss Barron, all the other young ladies were green with envy. And now I'm sure you're in need of refreshment.'

'Thank you, Mr. Quincy.' As Joy accepted the glass she remembered her Grandmother's words. Was the interest in his eyes more than mere friendliness? The thought brought a tingle of anticipation. He was really quite fine-looking. After taking a sip, she handed him the glass. 'Do you mind taking care of my glass for me while I go upstairs to remove my headdress? All these feathers are weighing me down.'

Mr. Quincy smiled down at her. 'Certainly.' He took it from her. 'I shall consider it a privilege to drink from where your lips have touched it.' With that he raised the glass and drank, his gaze never leaving her face.

Joy's heart missed a beat, and she felt the colour rise in her face.

When she came back downstairs Sir Alexander was standing talking with Kitty and Rufe. Her grandfather beckoned her over, and smiled as he put his arm around her shoulders.

'You did very well today, my dear, I'm proud of you. And I must add you outshone all the other society belles there.' He looked across at Kitty. 'I admire you for bringing Joy up to be such a charming young lady, my dear.'

'Thank you.

'Joy and I have had many interesting talks. She has taught me much about Australia, but there is more I'd like to know, particularly about the political scene.' He removed his arm from Joy's shoulder and turned to Rufe. 'I wonder if you would give me some of your time while you're here to enlighten me on that subject, Mr. Cavanagh.'

'I would be delighted.'

'Thank you, we'll arrange a time to suit. And I'd be delighted if you'll join our party for the racing at Ascot week. I believe you're interested in thoroughbreds, in a business sense, as well as pleasure. Am I right?'

'Yes, I am. I hope to find something to take back to Australia with me. Thank you for your kind offer, we'll be delighted to accept.'

'Excellent. I'm sure you'll find it interesting.'

When the time for came for dinner, Sir Alexander offered Joy his arm and led her into the dining room, where the long table was set for forty people. Joy was flattered to think that this was all in honour of her presentation at Court.

And when she took her seat she was pleased to see that Mr. Quincy was seated next to her. Looking down the table, she saw Mr. Paget-Smythe sitting beside Lily.

The morning of the first day of the Ascot Races dawned bright and sunny. Joy dressed carefully, having been warned that all the ladies wore their most elegant and finest gowns today, and morning dress was *de riguer* for the gentlemen.

Joy looked around her with interest as their party passed through the gate into the Royal Enclosure at Ascot racecourse. She had never attended a race meeting before, although she knew they were held regularly in Sydney.

They were in an enclosed area of the racecourse that already, two hours before the start of the first race, was packed with a large crowd of both men and women.

'That's the Royal box,' Grandfather indicated the largest of a series of boxes, bearing the Royal Coat of Arms. Then he pointed out the grandstand with its rows of seats, many of which were already occupied, as well as his own box, the track itself, and the saddling ring in front of the Royal enclosure where the horses would parade before each race.

'Where are the horses?' Joy asked.

'They're in their stalls, which are a little way from here. As each race is announced, the strappers lead the horses engaged in that race into the paddock where they parade so we can see them.'

Joy was excited. 'Oh, I'm going to enjoy this, I know. I love to watch horses, and it'll be something new for me to see them race like this.'

'I hope you do enjoy it, my dear. Now we'll go to our box.'

The box was quite commodious, with chairs placed so they had a clear view of the track.

'Please make yourselves comfortable,' Sir Alexander told them. 'An attendant will come to see if you wish refreshments, please feel free to order anything you wish. But if you're not ready to be seated just yet, you may wander anywhere you wish.'

'Could Lily and I go to see the horses?' Joy asked.

'Yes. I'll have someone show you where to go.' He called an attendant, and Joy and Lily were escorted to the horse stalls.

This was a long row of open fronted boxes, with a horse and attendants in each, and the name of each horse on its box. Joy and Lily moved along in front of the stalls.

Some of the horses stood quietly, while others moved restlessly about, or stamped their feet, while still others were being rubbed down, or saddled up.

Watching them reminded Joy of Dancer, and brought a lump to her throat. How she missed her. Although she had left Dancer behind when she was away from home before, like when she was at school, she always knew she would be there waiting for her when she returned. Now she was gone forever. Biting her lip, Joy tried to push the thoughts away, and started talking.

'They all look fit. I wonder, how do you manage to pick the ones that are going to win?'

'Well, I can see one that looks as if he's going to sleep. I wouldn't want to back him.'

Joy looked along the row. 'Oh yes, I can see him.' She moved closer to look at the name above the stall. Trumpeter. Yes, he looks tired. He doesn't look as if he'll run very well.'

A young lad standing by the horse winked at them. 'Don't you be taken in by 'is looks, young ladies, 'e's jest savin' 'is energy. Yer can put yer shirt on 'im, yer can. Once 'e starts ter race, 'e'll go like the wind, I'm tellin' yer. Yer c'n take me word fer it, yer can.'

'I like the look of this one,' Lily said, as they stopped in front of a horse called Speedy Bill. A chestnut with a shining coat, he pawed the ground and tossed his head. 'I think I'll back him.'

'He's certainly alert, but I think I'll back this black one, Dark Avenger.'

When they reached the last stall, they retraced their steps back to Sir Alexander's box, where they read the list of horses entered in the first race from their race cards.

'Oh look, Speedy Bill is in it,' Lily exclaimed.

'So is Dark Avenger, we'd better have our bets.'

'Just tell the attendant which horses you want, and give him the money,' Margaret told them. 'He'll place your bets for you.'

No sooner had he returned with their betting tickets than a bugle sounded.

'The horses are coming out. You can see them parading from up here, but if you want to see them up close you may go down to watch,' Grandfather told them.

Joy jumped up. 'Yes, come on Lily, let's go down.'

Hurrying down they stood pressed against the fence watching the horses come into the ring one by one, each wearing a saddle cloth with a number on it and led by a strapper.

'Good morning ladies.' They turned around to see Mr. Quincy standing close behind Joy. 'I see you are giving the choice of runners some serious consideration.'

'Oh, hullo Mr. Quincy, yes, isn't this exciting?' Joy said. 'I've backed Dark Avenger. There he is, isn't he beautiful? He looks very strong.'

'Yes he does, but can he beat Trumpeter?'

'Trumpeter? He looks as if he can hardly hold his head up, he looks tired already.'

'Just look at Speedy Bill, Lily chimed in. 'He's so fit he's pulling on his lead. It's all the lad can do to hold him, he's so lively. I've backed him, and I'm sure he'll win.'

'I beg to differ,' Mr. Quincy told her, 'but we'll see.'

At that moment Mr. Paget-Smythe joined them. After greeting them, he turned to his friend with a pleased look on his face.

'I say, I managed to get five to one on Trumpeter.'

Mr. Quincy pursed his lips. 'Hmm, good work. I only managed fours.'

'Have you backed that tired looking horse?' asked Lily.

'I have indeed.'

'Here come the jockeys and trainers.' Mr. Paget-Smythe pointed to where the jockeys, clad in their colourful riding silks, were entering the paddock.

After a few words with the trainers who accompanied them, the jockeys were legged up on to their mounts. They paraded around the ring once, and then made their way out through the gate and on to the track.

Mr. Quincy raised his binoculars and watched as they cantered around to the starting gate, then lowered his glasses.

'Time to go and watch the race,' he told them, as a bell rang and the crowd started to move. 'The Barron's have kindly asked us to join you in their box.'

He took Joy's arm to guide her through the throng back into the enclosure, and Joy felt a thrill run through her as his side pressed against hers. Looking back she saw Mr. Paget-Smythe escorting Lily, who was holding his arm and smiling up at him.

There was an air of anticipation in the crowd, and then they were off. With a mighty surge the horses leaped forward, packed together at the start, but jockeying for the best positions as they settled down. Around the first bend they raced, those at the rear strung out behind the leaders.

When they were at the back of the course Joy found it difficult to separate the horses, so she wasn't sure of Dark Avenger's position. Then they swept around the home turn and her excitement mounted as they flew down the straight, the sound of their hoofs loud in her ears.

As they thundered down the track Joy's heart beat a furious tattoo. The sight of these magnificent animals stretched to their fullest, their powerful muscles rippling under their glistening coats as they gave their all in the battle to win, brought her to her feet, oblivious of all else.

Her eyes searched for Dark Avenger. He was back behind the leading bunch but racing swiftly down the outside, gaining ground with every stride. Her pulses began to hammer. She gripped her hands together. 'Come on Dark Avenger.' She was hardly aware she cried aloud. 'Come on,' she urged.

As they flashed past the winning post Dark Avenger, for all his trying, could manage only second place

As her heartbeat slowed she turned to her grandfather.

'Wasn't that exciting? I think it's the most wonderful thing I've ever seen.'

He smiled down at her. 'Spoken like a true racegoer already. Aren't you disappointed your horse didn't win?'

'Oh no, he tried his hardest.'

'You're quite right. Another few strides and he may well have beaten the winner.'

'I was so excited watching Dark Avenger that I didn't really see who won. Who was it?'

'Trumpeter.'

'Really? He looked half asleep before the race; he didn't look as if he wanted to race at all.'

'That's what makes racing the interesting sport it is. You can never tell.'

'It must be wonderful to see your own horse win a race.'

'Oh yes. That is very exciting.'

'You should have followed me, I told you Trumpeter would win,' Mr. Quincy told her.

'Well I don't know how you knew,' Lily said crossly. 'Speedy Bill looked as if he was sure to win. I suppose this is no good now?' She held up her betting ticket.

Mr. Paget-Smythe shook his head. 'He didn't get a place, I'm afraid. You can tear that up. But that was only the first race,' he added consolingly. 'Plenty of time to back a winner yet.'

They all studied their race cards then and the discussion centred around the runners in the next race. It seemed as if everyone had a different opinion, and Joy found her head spinning as she tried to assimilate it all.

'I'm going to go down to the ring and watch them all go around before the next race, and I'll pick the one I think looks the best, and that's the one I'll back,' she declared.

When the horses came out for the next race, Joy turned to Rufe. 'You're an expert on horses. Will you come with me and give me some pointers?'

'I don't know about an expert, Joy, but I'll happily pass on what I know, for what it's worth.'

As the horses began to enter the ring Joy studied each one, and then turned to Rufe.

'What can you tell me to look for?'

'It's important to have big hindquarters for power, and strong straight legs, but other things count. For example, a light front can't support heavy hindquarters. A long neck's a good sign, too. Ideally, you're looking for good balance.'

'Yes, I see.' Joy nodded thoughtfully. 'What about temperament? Does that play a part?'

'Yes, excitable horses use up a lot of energy getting stirred up before a race, while the calm ones are saving their energy.'

'I suppose that was the difference between Trumpeter and Speedy Bill?'

'It was a big factor, certainly.' Rufe smiled down at her. 'But what you must realise is there's no set formula for picking winners, and even the best horses lose more races than they ever win.'

'I see the race card always gives the names of the sire and the dam. I suppose breeding counts too, does it?'

'Of course. A sire who's a proven winner is far more likely to produce winning offspring than one who's never won, especially if he's mated with a mare who's also won races.'

'What a great thrill it must be to breed a winner.'

'Indeed. And even more if you could manage to breed a champion who goes on to win big races, like the Gold Cup here, or the Melbourne Cup back home.'

Just the thought of ever achieving such an ambition quite took Joy's breath away.

A Liberated Woman

Chapter Twenty Five

Later that afternoon Mr. Quincy and Mr. Paget-Smythe invited Joy and Lily to accompany them for tea.

Once seated at a table in the crowded tearoom, the talk centred on the merits of the horses still to run that day, until the waitress served their tea.

As Mr. Paget-Smythe reached for a cream cake his arm brushed the milk jug and sent the milk spilling across the table. It splashed over the edge onto Lily, who sat next to him, and ran onto her skirt. He grabbed a napkin, his face flushing crimson.

'Oh dear, I am sorry. Here, let me...'

As he spoke he leant across and bent to dab at the offending patch on her skirt. At the same moment Lily also bent to inspect it. Their heads bumped together and they both jerked upright.

'Oh!' Lily's hand flew to her temple.

'Oh my, Lily, now I've hurt you. Oh dear! Let me see.'

Looking more confused than ever, Mr. Paget-Smythe inspected her forehead. A pink spot showed where their foreheads collided. He rubbed the mark with one finger.

'My poor dear Lily, look what I've done to you. I'm so sorry.'

Lily took his hand. 'It's all right, Winston. You haven't hurt me.'

'Are you sure?'

'Yes, quite sure.'

As Joy watched them sitting there, holding hands and gazing soulfully into each other's eyes, her nerves jangled. Whatever was Lily doing, leading him on like that, when she was in no condition to encourage any man? And for how long had they been on first name terms?

The waitress came bustling up with a cloth, and the two moved apart as the waitress soaked up the milk, and dabbed at Lily's dress.

'Tsk, tsk, it's only a little bit, but I hope it doesn't stain.'

Lily smiled sweetly. 'It's quite all right, accidents will happen. Mr. Paget-Smythe is not to blame. The jug was too close to the edge.' She smoothed the skirt. 'This is only an old thing anyhow, it's of no importance. Leave it now.'

The waitress moved away, and Mr. Paget-Smythe turned an adoring gaze on Lily.

'It's so kind of you not to make a fuss.'

'I wouldn't do that. I'd hate to embarrass you.' Lily gave him a melting look before she turned back to the others. 'Now, what were we talking about? Oh yes, the horses for the next race.'

Joy didn't see Lily alone until they returned home that night when they went to their rooms to change for dinner. After dressing she went along to Lily's room, where she found Lily laying on her bed in a wrapper.

'Are you all right?' she asked her.

'Yes, just resting a bit, but I suppose I'd better dress now.'

She slid from the bed and removed her wrapper, then picked up the clothes Mrs. Frobisher had put out for her and began dressing.

Seeing her in her undergarments Joy realised for the first time that Lily's waistline was thickening. It was still not enough to show up when fully dressed, but soon it would be plainly visible.

'I suppose you'll think it's none of my business, but I was surprised to see you encouraging Mr. Paget-Smythe today.'

'What do you mean, encouraging him?'

'You know quite well what I mean, making eyes at him and leading him on.'

'I was not.'

'Yes you were, and you know it. I could see today that he's smitten with you, and it's not fair to him when you're going away soon, and you know you can never marry him.'

Lily smiled a satisfied smile. 'So you think he's smitten with me?'

'It was pretty obvious from the way he looked at you when he spilt the milk.'

'Good. That's just what I wanted.'

'But why? You're going away and....let's face it, you're going to have a baby. Another man's baby,' she emphasised.

'So what?' Lily tossed her head. 'I'm not going to keep it. Once it's born I'll be free to do what I like. And if I can marry Winston, then that's what I'm going to do.'

'Have you thought that when he knows you've had a baby he may not want to marry you?'

'He won't know I've had a baby, will he?'

'Lily, you're mad. You can't possibly keep it from him.'

'Why not? We're going away somewhere no one will know us, and everyone will think it's your mother's baby. How is he going to know, unless someone tells him?'

'But you couldn't marry him and not tell him, not something like that. It's too important.'

Lily turned on her fiercely. 'There's no reason for him to know. I'm sure he's building up to ask me to marry him, and I mean to have him. Do you think I want to go back to Australia, where you'll all be thinking how terrible I've been?' She picked up a shoe and threw it, hard, across the room. 'Where I'll always have to see it, always be reminded of who it is. No, I want to marry Winston and go back to America with him, where nobody will know. Where I can forget it ever happened.'

Lily was panting as she finished her outburst, and Joy felt as though she had been winded. It seemed as though the baby meant nothing to Lily. Nothing, except something to be rid of, and never to think about again.

'How will you explain your absence for the next months?'

'I'll think of something, don't worry.'

'I suppose you will. But what if he finds out?'

'He won't find out unless someone tells him.' She looked piercingly at Joy. 'Will you tell him?'

'No, I won't tell him,' Joy said slowly. 'But I think you'd be taking a risk in marrying him without telling him. Besides, I'm not sure you could hide it from him, after...'

'After we're married? Leave that to me, I'll be able to manage it. He's not the brightest person in the world, you know.'

'That's not a very flattering thing to say about a man you want to marry.'

'It doesn't mean I think less of him. I'm just stating a fact. It'll make things easier for me, though.'

Joy's lips tightened. 'Well, if that's what you want, I wish you luck.'

Lily came over and threw her arms around Joy's unresponsive figure. 'I knew you'd stand by me. After all, we're friends, aren't we? Almost sisters.'

'I suppose so. And now I'd better go and finish dressing.'

As she turned to leave the room, Lily called after her. 'I'll be a good wife to him. You needn't worry about that.'

Although Joy was tempted to discuss Lily with her mother, she decided against it. She tried to put the matter out of her mind and concentrate on horses and the rest of the week's racing.

The activities of the Season reached fever pitch in Ascot week, with dinners and parties every night after the racing. It seemed as if Society was bent on extracting the maximum amount of enjoyment from the time left to them before it was time to return to the tedium of the country.

The young people mingled and flirted discreetly under the watchful gaze of their elders. The seemingly innocent touch of a hand, the provocative glance of a pair of eyes over the top of a fan, the solicitous attention paid by a man toward a young lady, all were duly noted, duly assessed.

Whenever Joy and Lily appeared, be it at the races, a dinner, or a party, Mr. Quincy and Mr. Paget-Smythe materialised to escort them, to bring them refreshments, and to dance with them. Joy could see that this was very much to Lily's taste, and, for herself, she found Mr. Quincy the most interesting of the young men whom she met.

His good looks, impeccable manners and worldly ways impressed her, and his interest in racing and his extensive knowledge of the horses was a common interest between them. She felt sure he was attracted to her. He always put his name by the waltzes on her card, and when they danced he held her as close as discretion would allow, causing her heart to beat faster. Then, when he escorted her back to her seat, he held her hand for as long as he could. She found herself looking forward to his company more and more as the days passed.

Lily was aware that she wouldn't be able to conceal her condition for much longer, and she was becoming anxious. Although Winston gazed at her with adoring eyes he uttered no words of love. Of course, they were almost always under the eyes of those old tabbies, who watched their every move, but he made no attempt to try to see her alone. Father said they would leave at the end of the month, so she had only two weeks to get a commitment from Winston. She must see him alone.

As they walked back to the enclosure after watching the horses parading in the paddock on the last day of Ascot, she squeezed his arm to make him look down at her. With a pensive look on her face, and her eyes bright with unshed tears, easily induced when she thought of how badly life had treated her, she gazed up at him.

'Oh Winston, I feel so sad when I think that we will only see each other a few more times before I go away.'

He stopped walking. 'What do you mean?'

'I have to go away at the end of the month, and then we'll never see each other again.'

'But...but where are you going?' he stammered. 'Why you are going away? Is it because of me?'

'No, of course not. It hurts me to be leaving you, but I must.'

'But why?'

Lily glanced around nervously. 'I can't tell you here,' she whispered, 'someone might hear.'

'Then I must see you alone.'

'That wouldn't be proper, you know it wouldn't.'

'But I must talk to you.' His voice was desperate.

'Well...,' she put on the appearance of thinking. 'Are you going to Mrs. Howatch's party tonight?'

'Yes.'

'Then I'll try to slip away unnoticed and go outside into the garden. After a few minutes you can follow me.'

'How can we do it?'

'Let me see.' She paused. 'At the end of a dance when we are partners, I won't go back to where I was, I'll go down the passage as if I'm going to the ladies' room. But instead I'll slip out through the door to the garden. When you see me go, you wait a few minutes and then follow me.'

'All right.'

All went as Lily planned, and when she was outside she waited behind a bush until she saw Winston coming down the path.

'Over here,' she called as she moved out from the shadows. He came swiftly toward her and she took hold of his arm.

'Let's move away to where we can't be seen if anyone comes out.' Leading him away from the path, she stopped when they were in the shadows under the trees, well away from sight.

'Now tell me,' Winston begged, 'where are you going, and why must you go?'

'My father and Mrs. Cavanagh need to go away at the end of the month, and I have to go with them.'

'Where are they going?'

'At first they'll be visiting horse studs, but then they're going somewhere quiet for two or three months.'

'Why do you have to go?'

'Well, you see, she needs to have a woman with her, and she wants one of her own family.'

'I don't understand.'

'It's because of...of her delicate condition.'

'You...you mean...'

'Yes, she's with child.'

'I see.' He took a deep breath. 'I think it should be her daughter to accompany her, surely, rather than you.'

'Oh no. You see, this is Joy's big year, what with her being presented to the Queen, you know. I want her to have her Season. I don't mind, or I didn't, until I met you.' She gazed up at him sorrowfully, tears welling in her eyes.

He swallowed. 'Does that mean...dare I hope it means...that you care for me?'

'Oh yes I do. I care dreadfully, and I don't want to go away and leave you, but I promised, and I can't go back on my promise, can I?' She sniffed gently.

He grasped her shoulders. 'But Lily, I love you. I love you and I want you to be my wife. That is, if you'll have me. Will you?'

Wide eyed, she tilted her head back and looked into his face. 'Oh yes, darling Winston. I'll be glad to be your wife.'

'Oh my sweet, wonderful Lily, you've made me the happiest man in the world.' He moved closer. 'May I kiss you?'

She looked away bashfully, and then turned her head back. 'If we're engaged then it's all right, isn't it? Are we engaged?'

'Yes, we are. That is, if your father agrees. I should have asked him first, really.'

'Oh no. Let's not bother him right now; he has so much on his mind. With Kitty in her condition, you know, and she's not young any more, he's quite worried. Let's leave that until after the birth. Let's keep it our secret for now. As long as we know, that's what matters, isn't it?'

'Yes, I suppose so.'

'Oh it is. And Winston ...'

'Yes?'

'I'd like you to kiss me now,' she said shyly. 'If you want to, that is.'

'I do.'

With that he leant and kissed her tentatively. Lily let her body melt toward him as she opened her lips under his, ever so slightly, and suddenly he took her quite masterfully into his arms and kissed her for a long time. As her arms stole around his neck she whispered to him. 'Oh Winston. I can't wait to be your wife. I wish it could be straight away.'

He lifted his head. 'We could tell them now,' he said hopefully.

'No. I promised I'd be with Kitty, and I won't go back on my word. Promise me you won't tell anyone yet. I don't want them to feel they're holding me back.'

'All right, I won't say anything.'

'Until I say it's all right? Promise?'

'Yes, I promise.'

Chapter Twenty Six

Craddock scowled as he looked over the fence into the Royal enclosure. The week was almost over and it had been a total waste of time. The Cavanagh's had attended the races, gone to parties and dinners, and in general relaxed and enjoyed Ascot week. Not once had he seen any sign of business activity or anything to suggest their visit to England was anything but social. It fuelled his anger and his hatred of the pair even more.

His meeting with Mrs. Frobisher in London had been less than illuminating. He wasted a whole afternoon with her only to learn that Cavanagh's daughter was in trouble. So, another stupid girl had got herself up the duff. That information was of little use to him. He needed something significant.

He arranged to meet Mrs. Frobisher again next Sunday, and he could only hope she would have something worthwhile for him then. So far his trip had been a waste of time and money.

'My dear Mrs. Frobisher, how good to see you. I've been looking forward to today.'

'So have I, Mr. Brown. And isn't it a lovely day? The sunshine reminds me of home.'

'Ah, yes, indeed. What I wouldn't give for the sun of Australia again. But we must make the most of what we have here, and I was wondering if you would care for a stroll in the park before we take some refreshments? It seems a shame to waste such a lovely day inside.'

'Oh yes, it does. I was just thinking the same. And it'll be cooler in the park, too.'

Taking her arm he led her across the street and into a nearby park. Here they wandered along, and Craddock listened while Mrs. Frobisher prattled on about the excitement of a day at the Ascot races.

'It was so exciting,' she told him, 'the staff were all given a day off during the week, and I went with my friend Davis, and Molly the parlour maid.'

'Did you back a winner?'

'No such luck, but Molly did. She won three shillings on Trumpeter. You'd have thought she'd won three pounds, she was so excited.'

'I suppose the family all spent the whole week at Ascot, did they?'

'Oh yes, they made a big week of it. All mad about the races, they are.'

'And the girls, your charges, did they go too?'

'Oh yes, and their parents from Australia too.'

At that moment they reached the end of a path where a gate ahead of them led out into a street, and Craddock turned to her.

'I say, I see a pub over the road there,' he pointed to the other side of the street, 'do you fancy something a little stronger than a cup of tea?'

'Well now, I don't mind if I do, Mr. Brown. It'd be welcome on such a warm day.'

He led her through the gate, across the road, and into the pub.

'Well now, isn't this nice,' Craddock said, as he seated her at a table in the timber panelled room. 'What would you like to drink?'

'I'll have Madeira if they have it.'

'I'm sure they will.'

He brought their drinks over, Madeira for her and ale for himself, and sat opposite her.

'Here's hoping you enjoy the rest of your time here.' He raised his glass.

'And here's to good luck with your business.' she replied, raising hers before taking a long draught. 'Very nice indeed.' She settled back in her chair. 'You know, it's too bad. I was hired as a chaperone, which is not a servant, and I expect to be treated as such. But that little bitch Lily, she has me at her beck and call all day long. Treats me like a servant, she does.'

'That's too bad. And what about her sister, what did you say her name is?'

'Joy, but she's not her sister. Joy is Mrs. Cavanagh's daughter, although her name is Barron. And Lily is Mr. Cavanagh's daughter.'

'I see. And who is her mother?'

'I never knew her. She was out of the picture years ago, I believe.'

'It's a bit confusing, isn't it? I thought they were all one family.'

'Well, I suppose they are, sort of, now the parents are married.'

'Yes, I see.' He eyed her empty glass. 'Can I get you another drink?'

'I don't mind if I do. This warm weather makes you thirsty, doesn't it?'

'It certainly does. I'm ready for another ale.'

After returning with the drinks, Craddock resumed their conversation. If he could keep her talking about them he might pick up something useful.

'So who is the Barron girl's father?'

'That was Sir Alex's son William, but he died years ago. Drowned, he was, before Joy was born. Out in Australia.'

'What bad luck. And him from such a good family too. A bit of a comedown for his wife to marry someone who's just a merchant, isn't it?'

She shrugged. 'Oh, I don't know. Mr. Cavanagh's something in the government back in Australia, and he breeds horses. That's why he's here, looking for new blood stock, so I've been told. As well as to see Joy presented at Court, of course.' She took another mouthful of Madeira. 'Mind you, the aristocracy don't always act as good as you'd expect. Take young William, for instance. It seems like his parents were glad to see him stay in Australia.'

Craddock raised his eyebrows. 'Why was that?'

'Well, it seems he had a fancy for young ladies below his own station in life, you might say. Even went so far as to marry one, in fact.'

'Indeed? But I thought he was married to the present Mrs. Cavanagh?'

'Yes, that's right, but he married one of their housemaids first, a pretty little thing by the name of Cora. Took her to Gretna Green, no less.'

'You mean he was a bigamist?'

'Oh no, his father managed to have the first one annulled, but not before they were well and truly married, if you know what I mean.'

'You mean ...?' he left the question hanging.

'Exactly. He didn't catch them until the next day. It cost him plenty, so I'm told, and there's even talk it might have been too late to stop the inevitable results.'

Craddock gasped. 'You don't mean...?'

She nodded triumphantly. 'Yes. Rumour has it there was a child, a boy. All very hush-hush, of course. But it's no wonder they wanted young William out of the way, is it?'

'No wonder at all.'

'It just goes to show that the high and mighty are no better than the rest of us, doesn't it?'

'It does indeed. And does anybody know what happened to the child, or where he is now?'

'Oh, I don't think so. No one ever talks about it, you see. It's all so long ago, I don't suppose anyone's that interested, really. He'd be grown up now, wouldn't he? They wouldn't want him to show up. That'd create a nasty scandal, wouldn't it?'

'I suppose it would, and probably cause a lot of problems, too. Ah well, nothing to do with the likes of us. Shall we wander back now?'

June became a whirl of activities. When Queen Victoria opened the grounds of Buckingham Palace for a garden party it seemed as if most of London was there, so great was the crowd. After that, breakfast parties and garden parties were held almost every day, and the evenings were a dinner, or a ball, or a theatre visit, one after another.

More often than not, Mr. Quincy was at Joy's side, a charming and attentive admirer. She found herself thinking of him more and more often when they weren't together. She enjoyed his company and was flattered by his attention. Was she falling in love with him? Would she like to spend the rest of her life with him? The thought was not entirely unpleasant.

But it was the racing days that still entranced Joy more than anything else. As she thrilled to the superb sight of the glorious thoroughbreds thundering down the track to the finishing post it made her pulses pound, and the blood bubble in her veins. It removed all thoughts, including love, from her mind. Standing outside the winners circle as the horses were led in after a race she longed to be the one out there leading in the winner. She wanted to be the one to utter the words of praise to him as he came back, ears pricked at the applause from the crowd. And when he was unsaddled she wanted to be there, to pat the heaving flanks and sweating coat, and to place the winner's rug on the victorious back.

And one day as she watched a thought insinuated itself into her mind. Could she breed a winning racehorse? At first she pushed the thought away as nonsense, but slowly it took hold. After all, why not? Mother and Rufe had discussed breeding horses. Why not thoroughbreds? And hadn't Mother always said Redwoods was for her? She knew quite a bit about horses, and how to look after them, but could she possibly learn enough to make her dream into a reality?

Joy began studying the race cards carefully. Rufe had said breeding was important, so she took note of the sires and dams of all the winners at each meeting, and a picture began to emerge. Many of the winners were sired by a horse called St Simon. She wondered how much one of his progeny would cost to buy. Probably be a lot of money, and money was something she had very little of.

Nevertheless, each race meeting throughout the Season strengthened her resolve to make it her goal in life to breed a champion racehorse. The more she thought about it, the more she became sure she could do it. But she didn't breathe a word to anyone else. How could she tell any of the family here that this was her secret dream? Grandmother would be scandalised, for a start.

Even back in Australia her idea would be ridiculed. Women didn't breed horses. Oh yes, women helped their husbands, but how could a young girl, as they would call her, ever aspire to breed thoroughbred racehorses? Why, the idea was laughable. They would tell her she should marry and settle down to breeding children. But her mother ran a successful business, so why couldn't she? But for the moment she kept it to herself.

At the end of June England looked set for a heat wave as the summer sizzled. One hot day followed another, and garden parties became the favourite pastimes. While the older ladies sought shade beneath the trees, fluttered their fans and ran the servants ragged fetching cool drinks, the younger ones strolled around in their coolest summer gowns, twirling their parasols and discreetly encouraging their admirers.

'This is no good. These flimsy summer gowns show everything. You'll just have to lace me tighter,' Lily told Mrs. Frobisher, surveying herself in the mirror.

'For Heaven's sakes, you can hardly breathe now, you can't have it any tighter.'

Lily undid the buttons down the front of the bodice, pulled the gown over her head and threw it on the bed. 'I said lace it tighter,' she snapped, grabbing hold of the bedpost with two hands. 'Undo it and pull it in.'

Mrs. Frobisher threw her hands in the air. 'I can't. You'll harm the baby.'

Lily turned her head, her face twisting with anger. 'The bloody baby will just have to take its chances. Pull it tighter, I said.' When there was no response she shouted. 'Do it!'

Reluctantly Mrs. Frobisher undid the laces and wrenched. Lily held on to the bedpost, bracing herself against the pull.

When they were retied she slipped the gown on and, after doing up the buttons, surveyed herself in the mirror again. 'That's better,' she said, patting her now flat stomach.

'It's not right. You'll do your baby some harm. Mark my words, young lady.'

'Rubbish. It's tough. If it died it'd be doing me a favour.'

'That's a wicked thing to say.'

'Shut up and get me my parasol.'

'Where are you off to today?'

'Lady Ashton's garden party with Joy and Margaret. I'll be back in time to have a rest before I have to change for dinner.'

'You better get your corset off and let that baby breathe.'

'Let myself breathe, more like it. Give me that!' Grabbing the parasol she hurried from the room.

Half an hour later she was seated at a table under a tree in Lady Ashton's garden with a group of ladies, all fanning themselves as they complained of the heat. Surveying the array of cakes and sandwiches spread out before her Lily knew she couldn't eat a morsel, so squeezed-in did she feel. Accepting a cool glass of lemon cordial she scrutinised the guests who were still arriving, hoping to see Winston. Knowing she could not hide her condition for much longer she wanted to spend as much time with him as possible before she left.

Suddenly she felt nauseous, and a wave of weakness swept over her. In spite of the heat she was cold and clammy. She took a sip of the drink, but put it down on the table as her head began to swim.

'Are you all right?' she heard Joy ask, her voice sounding as if it came from a distance.

Lily took a deep breath. 'I...I think so, I feel a bit funny...'

'You've gone white, I think you'd better...'

That was all Lily heard as everything went black.

She came to lying on the grass with Margaret waving smelling salts in front of her nose, and with the other women clustered around her. Raising her arm she pushed the bottle away and struggled to sit up.

'Stay there for a moment,' Margaret ordered.

'What...what happened?' Lily looked at the faces staring down at her. 'I felt funny...' her voice trailed off. She felt terrible and she could hardly breathe. She must get away from them; she must take off the corset and lie down.

'It's the heat, that's what it is,' Joy said, leaning over and taking hold of her arm. 'Here, let me help you up.'

One of the other women took her other arm, and they helped her to a chair. She leant back trying to breathe normally, but her breath came in short gasps.

'Margaret, could you send someone for the carriage, please?' Joy asked. 'I'll take Lily home. She needs to cool down.'

Lily saw two of the women whispering together as the watched her. Gossiping bitches, would they believe it was only the heat?

Joy noticed them too, and she picked up a fan and began to fan Lily vigorously. 'I think if you all move back a bit, it might give her more air.'

As they all moved back a maid came hurrying with a damp cloth. Joy took it from her and placed it on Lily's brow, then began fanning again.

'Does that feel better?'

Lily licked her lips and tried to speak normally. 'Yes, that's cooler. I'm feeling better now.' She looked around. To her relief there was no sight of Winston. She must go before he came, and hope he didn't hear about this. If he did she would say she succumbed to the heat, but she must go before she fainted again.

At that moment a footman arrived to say their carriage was waiting. With Joy on one side, the maid on the other, and Margaret hovering alongside, they made their way out and stepped up into the carriage. Lily relaxed against the cushions as she heard Margaret telling Joy she would explain their leaving to Lady Ashton.

As the carriage drove away Joy took Lily's hand. 'How much longer do you think you're going to be able to get away with this? Don't forget, I've seen you without your corset. I don't know how you can bear it.'

Lily felt too unwell to prevaricate. She shook her head weakly. 'I can't do it any longer. I'll have to leave now.' She pressed Joy's hand. 'Thank you for covering up for me. Do you think anyone guessed?'

'I saw a couple of the old pussies looking at you with great interest, but they couldn't prove it wasn't the heat. I think you're safe. For now.'

When Lily walked into her room she found Mrs. Frobisher packing her clothes.

'What are you doing?' she asked.

'As you can see, I'm packing your clothes,' she replied through tight lips. 'Enough is enough. I've been to see your father and we're moving out tomorrow. You can say what you like it won't make any difference.'

'No, it's all right. I'm ready to go,' she acquiesced wearily. 'Help me out of this corset, will you? I'm going to have a lie-down.'

Before she went to bed that night Lily wrote a letter to Winston swearing her undying love for him, and telling him she had to leave as Kitty was unwell and wished to leave the city. She promised to write regularly until they were able to be together again.

A Liberated Woman

Chapter Twenty Seven

Joy was in the garden of the house in Curzon Street, picking roses to fill the vase on the hall table, when Mr. Quincy approached her, hatless, alone, and unannounced.

'Why, Mr. Quincy, what a surprise. Does my Grandmother know you're here?'

He smiled down at her. 'Yes, she told me I'd find you in the garden. I asked her permission to speak to you.'

Joy was startled. 'Alone? How extraordinary. I've never known her to allow that before.'

'Perhaps it's because I told her the reason for my wish to see you alone.' He smiled. 'Miss Barron...Joy. May l call you Joy?'

Joy tensed as she nodded. She wasn't ready for what she sensed he was about to say. Did she love him? Did she want to spend the rest of her life with this man?

'I'm sure you must realise that my feelings for you are more than mere friendship?'

'Why no, Mr. Quincy, I...'

'Please call me Charles. I'm sure we know each other well enough for first names.'

'Yes, I'm sure we do.' As Joy took a deep breath she relaxed. Of course she would accept his proposal. Why wouldn't she? He was good-looking, worldly, sophisticated, and they shared an interest in horses, and racing. He would probably approve of her wish to breed a champion racehorse. Maybe they would do it together?

All this passed through her mind in the few seconds it took for him to remove the basket of roses from her hands and place it on the ground, then take both her hands in his own.

He moved closer and gazed down into her eyes. 'My dear Joy, you must know that your beauty and charm captivated me from the first moment we met. It would make me very happy if you consent to become my wife.'

Excitement rippled through her as she looked up into his face. How handsome he looked. Of course she was in love, and how thrilling to be engaged to one of the most eligible bachelors of the Season. Many of the young women had set their caps at him but he had chosen her, and she'd not even been contemplating marriage.

'Oh Charles, yes, I will marry you. I'm sure we'll be very happy together.'

'Indeed we will. Now we must go and tell your Grandmother the good news. But first we should seal our betrothal with a kiss.' He pulled her into his arms.

As his lips came down on hers and he kissed her she felt a delicious thrill. Her heart beat faster as she enjoyed the feeling, and when a fleeting memory of how her passion had flared so much more fiercely when David kissed her, she pushed the thought away. Besides, David thought of her as a baby, he had told her so often enough. Even his letters were always just friendly, with never a word to suggest he thought of her in any different way. She'd only felt like that because it was the first time a man had ever kissed her. This was different. Charles knew she was a woman, not a baby. She was going to marry a charming man who would adore her forever.

Charles took his arms from around her and stepped back. 'Now, let's go and find Lady Barron, and then I must speak with Sir Alexander and ask for his approval.'

'I suppose it's my mother you should speak to, isn't it?'

'Not at all. In the absence of your father it is Sir Alexander and Lady Barron who must give their approval and your Grandmother already approves of my intentions.'

'I didn't know you'd already spoken to her about us.'

'Yes, we have spoken.' He bent over to pick up the basket of roses and handed it back to her. 'I interrupted you. Have you picked enough flowers?'

Joy took the basket from him. 'Yes, I have more important things to think about now.'

He squeezed her hand. 'I should think so. Now let's go inside and tell her the good news. I'm sure she'll be delighted.'

Grandmother waited for them with an air of expectation. There was no doubt she was delighted when Charles told her their news.

'What a pleasant surprise,' she said, rising from her chair and putting her arms about Joy, who was quite shocked. It was the first time Joy could remember Lady Barron embracing her, or anyone else. 'So you'll be remaining in England now,' she added with satisfaction in her voice.

'Yes. That is unless Charles wishes to go to Australia?' Joy looked at him enquiringly.

He shrugged, spreading his hands. 'Possibly, one day we may visit the colonies.'

'They won't be colonies for much longer. We'll have Federation soon.'

'Your life will be in England from now on.'

'Yes, of course.' She pushed away the slight pang she felt at his words. After all, she loved the life here.

Grandmother rang for Denman, the butler, and asked him to escort Mr. Quincy to his lordship's study. When they had gone, she motioned Joy to a chair.

'Well, my dear, this is a most satisfactory match. The Quincy's are an old family and their estates in Berkshire, which is not too far from here, are extensive. One day you will be mistress of Holsmere Park, which is a fine home.'

'We haven't talked about that, and it didn't occur to me. I don't really know much about his family affairs, except that he's the only son in his family.'

'Yes, and that brings responsibilities with it as well as privileges. But there's time for you to learn all about that. You're a clever and sensible girl. I'll teach you what you need to know.'

The thought of more lessons cast a shadow over her excitement, but she pushed it away and listened to Grandmother speculating about the details of the coming announcement of their engagement.

In a few moments Charles was back again. 'Your grandfather wishes to speak with you,' he told Joy.

She rose and made her way to his study.

'Come in, my dear,' Grandfather said, placing an arm around her shoulder to draw her in. 'Come and sit down here with me.' He escorted her across the room and sat her down before taking the other chair himself. 'So you're contemplating marriage with Charles Quincy, I hear.'

'Yes I am, Grandfather. Isn't it exciting?'

A smile crossed his face. 'If you're quite sure it's what you want, then yes, it is.' He steepled his fingers and looked at her over them. 'Are you quite sure?'

'Oh yes.'

'Have you thought about what it entails? Do you realise you'll have to leave your family and live here permanently, leaving behind all the people and places that have been your life up until now? Have you really thought about that?'

Joy hesitated. 'Mr. Quincy only asked me this morning. We never talked about it before, but, yes, I do realise I'll be living here permanently, although I hope I can go back to Australia sometimes.'

'Australia is a long way away, it's not a place you can reach easily, as you know, so you have to consider the possibility that it might not happen.'

Joy bit her lip. 'I wouldn't like to think I'd never see my family again but I'm sure that won't happen. They would visit here and I would make sure I could visit them.' She brightened. 'Besides I have you here, Grandfather, and I believe Mr. Quincy's estates are not too far away.'

'That's true, and I must say I'd be very happy to have you so close by.'

'So you see, it'll be all right.'

He sighed. 'You are still young, only nineteen; and it's easy to be optimistic. I hope it's the right thing for you. I would hate you to be unhappy.'

'But I'm very happy.'

'Yes, I can see that. I suppose you're in love with him?'

'Oh yes.'

'And he tells me he'll take good care of you, and I have no reason to doubt that, so I suppose I must agree.' He frowned. 'But I will make one proviso. I hope you'll be happy about it.'

'What is it?'

'First I'll ask you a question. Do you truly like the life here in England?'

'Yes I do.'

'But you've only been here for one Season. You had a taste of country life at Bournbridge Hall, but I believe it wasn't enough. I'm going to stipulate that you don't marry for at least another year, to give you time to be really sure it's what you want, and I shall extend an invitation to Quincy to join us for an extended visit, so you may get to know each other properly, away from the false life of a Season here in London.'

Joy considered his words. She knew he had her best interests at heart. Besides it would be fun to have time to enjoy being engaged before settling in to the duties of married life.

She smiled at him as she reached across for his hand. 'I'm happy with that.'

His face brightened. 'Good. Then I'll write to your mother to make sure she approves. I wouldn't go against her wishes.'

'I'm sure Mother will agree. She wants me to be happy.'

'I believe that will be her first concern.' He rose from his chair. 'Now, will you ask Quincy to come back in here, please, my dear?'

Joy stood up and kissed him on the cheek. 'Of course, Grandfather. And thank you.'

Charles returned with a scowl. 'Your grandfather insists we wait a year before marrying,' he informed them, his face like thunder. He turned to Lady Barron. 'Perhaps you can persuade him otherwise.'

'No, if he's made up his mind I can do nothing.'

Joy touched Charles on the arm. 'We haven't talked about the wedding. When did you want it to be?'

'I want it to be by Christmas.'

'That's quite soon. Is there any special reason?'

'No, of course not. What reason could there be?'

'Then why are you so upset?'

He took a deep breath. 'I am not upset. I just want us to be married sooner, that's all. But I suppose I must contain my impatience.'

'Yes, Mr. Quincy, I'm afraid you must wait. But I'll try to make the wait worthwhile for you,' Lady Barron said.

Joy was puzzled by her words, and surprised to see a knowing look pass between Charles and her Grandmother. What could it mean?

The next morning Joy received a newsy letter from her mother, the first since they had left London. They were in Ireland attending the local thoroughbred horse sales. They had seen some magnificent horses and Rufe had decided the time was right to commence their thoroughbred breeding programme. With this in mind he had bought a stallion with excellent bloodlines. '*Riverside will probably be the home for the new venture at first,*' Kitty wrote, '*but we will also use Redwoods in the future. I have bought a mare with a foal at foot. She is the prettiest little filly, I am sure you will love her and, if you do, I plan to give her to you when she can leave her mother. I know you will never forget Dancer, but I hope that she will eventually take her place in your affections. Her bloodlines go back to St. Simon, who is an exceedingly prolific sire of winning racehorses and she will be put to Starlight, Rufe's new stallion, when the time comes. Knowing your love of horses and interest in the breeding programme, I am sure it will be a great interest for you when you return home. Of course, should you decide you don't want another horse at this time, I will use her for breeding myself when she is old enough. But we can talk about that on our way home, and you can also choose a name for her once you have seen her.*'

Joy put the letter down. A filly descended from St. Simon. How she would love to have her. Would the filly be old enough to leave here in England when they went back? But no, they were going as soon as Lily had her baby, and that would be too soon for her to be weaned.

An intense feeling of disappointment filled her. Well, she must talk to Charles about her ambition to breed a champion. Maybe they could go to Ireland together and find another filly just as good.

Picking up the letter again, she learnt that Lily was well, although she complained about her back aching. By the time Joy received this letter they would be installed in a country house on the outskirts of Keswick, in the Lakes District. Kitty would remain there with Lily and Mrs. Frobisher, with a small staff to look after them, until after the baby was born. Rufe planned to spend much of the time visiting horse establishments to gain further insight into the racing industry in the UK, and to see if there was anything else he wished to purchase.

When Joy finished reading the letter, her thoughts turned again to the filly and she resolved to speak to Charles at the first opportunity.

Grandmother had invited Charles to have dinner with them, and he arrived a little early, so she summoned Joy to join them in the drawing room as they waited for Rupert and Grandfather, who had not yet arrived home. While Grandmother and Margaret discussed a forthcoming art exhibition, Charles drew her to the other end of the room to look at the bronze sculpture of a horse and rider that stood on a side table there. Standing close, he took her hand in his, and smiled down at her.

'I didn't really want to look at this; I just wanted to have you to myself for a while. I don't know how I can wait a whole year for us to be married.'

Joy returned the pressure of his hand. 'I know it's a long time, but Grandfather feels it's for the best. And we'll have the rest of our lives together.'

He sighed, and held her hand tighter. 'I hope he's written to your mother today. You don't think she'll object, do you?'

'I don't think so. She'll want me to be happy.'

'Perhaps you should write to her yourself, just to make sure she knows how happy you are, and how much you want us to be married.' He squeezed her hand again. 'You do, don't you?'

'Yes, of course.'

'Then perhaps you should let her know that you don't want to have to wait for a whole year.'

Joy didn't mind waiting but she didn't want to upset him. 'In fact, I had a letter from Mother today, and when I replied to it I told her about us. I'm sure she'll agree to our engagement.'

Letting go of her hand, he patted her arm. 'Good girl. '

'In her letter she told me they've been buying thoroughbreds at the sales to start a breeding programme.' She placed her hand on his arm, and, unable to contain her excitement, gazed up at him, smiling. 'It's so good that we both have an interest in horses, because that's what I want to do. I hope we can do it together.'

He frowned. 'Do what? What are you talking about?'

'Breeding thoroughbreds. I want to breed a champion racehorse. Oh, I know it won't be easy and it'll probably take years to breed a champion, but if we could do it together, wouldn't that be wonderful?'

He stepped back, frowning. 'There is no way I wish to be involved in breeding racehorses. I will have enough to do with the estate.'

The smile slipped from her face. 'Oh. Oh, I see. Yes, of course, you'll be too busy with your other duties. I should have realised.' She brightened. 'But never mind, I can do it alone. It won't be so enjoyable, but...'

Charles cut her off, his face dark. 'You cannot breed horses, I assure you of that. It would not be seemly for my wife. Put all such thoughts out of your head. Good God, I hate to think what my parents would think if you ever suggested such a thing.'

Joy felt as though she had been slapped in the face. Although she had known that Grandmother would object, it had never occurred to her that Charles, with his love of racing, wouldn't support her in her ambition. She stood frozen, unable to utter a word. He must have seen her stricken look, for he took hold of her hand again.

'Be sensible, Joy. To like the races is one thing, but to breed horses for it is not the sort of thing my wife could ever think of doing. I know standards are probably different in the colonies, but here it would be totally unacceptable.' He paused, and squeezed her hand again. 'Besides, you'll have other things to think about once we're married. You'll have to learn about running a household, for when you're mistress of Holsmere Park. Then there will be the children.'

'Children?'

'Of course, we'll have children. Had you not thought of that?'

'Not really, no. But, yes, of course, I suppose we will.'

'Of course.' He patted her hand. 'Now let's join the others. Here are Sir Alexander and your uncle arriving. We'll say no more of this foolish idea of yours, will we?'

Joy looked up into his face as he smiled down at her. Of course she would be busy with her new life when they married. She resolved to put her frustration behind her.

'No, we won't say any more about it.'

Chapter Twenty Eight

Kitty saw that one of the letters in the post was from Joy and she opened that one first, looking forward to hearing her news. As she read it her pleasure turned to dismay, and she struggled to keep back the tears.

'This is terrible. I knew this was bound to happen. Why did I ever agree to allow her to come here? I should have kept her at home, like I wanted.'

Rufe put down his pen and came across the room to put his hand on her shoulder.

'What's the matter? Has something happened to Joy?'

'No. Yes. The very worst thing. Here, read this.' She handed him the letter.

Lily looked up from the magazine she had been reading and Mrs. Frobisher stopped knitting.

Rufe scanned the first few lines and then commenced to read aloud. *I love the sound of the filly you have bought. I did some research and I know that St. Simon is a great sire. How I would love to have her, and I do so thank you for the wonderful offer, but I won't be able to accept. You see, Mr. Quincy has asked for my hand in marriage, and so I will be staying here in England. Grandfather has written to you, for your permission, but I know you want me to be happy. He wants us to wait for a year before we marry, and I don't mind that, although Charles was a bit put out. It is so exciting to be engaged, and one day I shall be mistress of Holsmere Park, his family estate. Just fancy that.'*

Rufe stopped reading and handed the letter back to Kitty. 'I won't read any more, it seems to go on in the same vein.'

'That's quite enough. I suppose becoming mistress of Holsmere Park is so much better than mistress of Redwoods. How I wish I'd followed my instincts and not let her come anywhere near England and the Barron's.'

'You couldn't have stopped her forever. It would have happened sooner or later.'

'I would rather it was later, when she may have had more sense.'

Rufe handed her the other letter. 'Perhaps you should read what Sir Alex has to say.'

Kitty tore open the envelope and read his proposal, that they should wait a year, and that Quincy should spend some time with them at his country house in order that the couple become better acquainted away from the glamour of London in the Season.

'That's a sensible option,' Rufe told her. 'A lot can happen in a year. Joy may change her mind.'

Kitty was filled with dread. If Joy married and stayed here in England she would lose her. They would see each other so rarely they would become strangers. She couldn't bear the thought.

She shook her head. 'No, I can't just leave it like this. I must go down to London at once and talk to Joy and Sir Alex myself.'

'No,' Lily cried, throwing the magazine down on the floor and heaving herself from her chair. 'You can't go to London. You promised you'd stay here with me until the baby is born.'

'But it will only be for a short time. I'll be back here in plenty of time before the baby comes.'

'That's not the point. If you go to London now, everyone will see you. They'll all know you're not having a baby, and they'll guess it's mine.'

'That won't be so terrible; the people I see in London aren't likely to be coming to Australia.'

Lily burst into tears. 'I don't want everyone I've met to know about me. They'll all think I'm bad, and they'll be talking about me. I can't bear the thought of it.'

'You'll never see any of them again, so I can't see it's going to matter.'

'It matters to me.' Lily's tears flowed faster. 'It's not fair. Joy's engaged to a handsome aristocrat and going to become mistress of a big house and what have I got? I'm going to have a squalling brat and no one will ever want me. It's just not fair.'

'Might I remind you,' Rufe told her, frowning, 'that this situation is of your own making?'

Lily's woebegone face screwed up. 'You all hate me. You want to ruin my life.'

Kitty frowned. 'No one back in Australia will know. Everyone will believe the baby is mine.'

'Not if they see you now, with your flat stomach. There are such things as letters, you know. People will find out.'

'You're being completely illogical about this,' Rufe told her, putting his hands on her shoulders. 'And stop that crying, for goodness sake.'

Kitty bit her lip. She hated to see Lily so upset. It wasn't good for the baby, either.

'Yes, stop crying, Lily. If it means so much to you I won't go right now.' She turned to Rufe. 'Will you go and talk to Sir Alex for me? See what his feelings are, really, about the match?'

Rufe took her hand in his. 'Of course I will, if it'll put your mind at rest. And after the baby's born we'll all go back and see them.' He addressed Lily. 'I hope you're happy with that?'

Lily stopped crying. 'Yes. Thank you, Father.'

'You should thank Kitty, not me.'

'Thank you, Kitty.'

That night Lily wrote a letter to Winston telling him how emotionally unstable Kitty was becoming during her pregnancy, how unhappy she was without him, and of her longing to be with him again. And she added that if they could not be together she would die of grief.

Joy enjoyed the delights of being engaged. It was wonderful to be in love, especially with such a handsome beau. True, she'd had some doubts earlier, particularly after her first talk with Grandfather, but when she received permission for the engagement to go ahead, and Charles gave her a beautiful diamond ring, she was ecstatic. She chided herself for having ever doubted that she loved him.

Her grandparents arranged a party to make the announcement. All the family were there, Rupert and Margaret with Felicity, who was allowed to stay up late, and Hector Barron, home on leave from India, as well as several of Charles's friends.

After Sir Alexander made his speech announcing the engagement, and giving them his blessing, they were the centre of attention as everyone crowded around, wishing the happy couple well, and telling Charles how lucky he was.

As the weeks passed they attended the many functions still being held in this latter part of the Season, with Charles escorting Joy in a proprietary manner. Joy basked in the admiration and envy of many of the young ladies and their mothers whom she had met during the Season. To be engaged before the end of the Season, and to such an eligible young man as Charles Quincy, was obviously considered an accomplishment on her part.

One afternoon Joy accompanied Margaret to Harrods, the prestigious department store in Knightsbridge. Here, the latest women's fashions could be bought readymade.

As they browsed in the women's section a saleswoman brought out a gown that was different to most. Not a crinoline, it was straight in the front, and had a bustle at the back.

'This is the very latest fashion and it would suit you *tres bien,*' the little French woman told Joy.

'It's very different, isn't it?' Joy fingered the silky material in a wonderful pale green colour, smoothing it.

'It is the very latest thing, *madame*. Mr. Redfern, the famous couturier in Paris, has created a gown like this for Lily Langtry, so it is the height of fashion, the latest thing from Paris.'

Margaret raised her eyebrows. 'For Lily Langtry? Really?'

'Oh yes, madame. It is very special.'

'It would look beautiful on you, Joy. Do try it on.'

Joy hesitated. 'It is beautiful, isn't it? But I wonder if it's a little too...too modern?'

'Try it on, and see how it looks,' Margaret urged.

'All right. I'll see how it looks on.'

The gown fitted perfectly. It hugged her curves, was cut straight in the front and skimmed smoothly over her hips. The dropped waistline showed off her slender waist and displayed her figure with its simple cut. The skirt was fuller below the hips, and had insertions of lace. The fitted sleeves finished just below the elbow and were edged with fine green piping, which was repeated at the neckline. Joy turned to look at the back of the gown in the mirror. The bustle sat perfectly on her derriere. Joy loved it.

The saleswoman clapped her hands. 'Ah, *madame,* it was made for you. You are more beautiful than Lily Langtry. She would be jealous to see you.'

Joy felt embarrassed by the extravagant compliment, but she knew the gown suited her. She called Margaret to come and look.

'What do you think?' she asked her.

'It's just perfect. It looks wonderful.'

'You don't think it's too daring?'

'It's the latest fashion. All the women will be envious of you, including me. It puts the crinoline to shame.'

'Then I'll take it. I'll wear it to the races on Saturday. I hope Charles likes it.'

'He couldn't fail to like it.'

'Wait, *madame*.' The saleswoman stopped her as she made to take the gown off. 'Wait. I have the very thing to go with it for the races.'

She sped off and returned a moment later with a hat.

Joy gasped. 'What a gorgeous hat.' She took it from the woman and held it up, turning it around, admiring it. It was a cheeky hat, adorned with a huge bow in a green that matched the dress. Tiny pink roses were tucked under the brim at the back, and ribbons trailed down. She put it on and the assistant adjusted it so that it sat at just the right angle.

'There, madame. It is a triumph, *n'est-ce pas?*'

'You look wonderful. You must take both.'

Joy laughed. 'I've never worn anything so stylish. I think I must take them.'

'Of course you must.'

Joy walked out of the store carrying her parcel and happy with her purchases.

As she dressed in her new clothes for the races on Saturday Joy hummed a happy tune. Davis finished doing her hair and sat the hat on her head, adjusted it, and   stood back admiring her handiwork.

'Oh, you do look beautiful, Miss Joy. Now stand up and let me see. That's it, turn around.' She gave a little tug at the back of the skirt. 'There, it sits beautifully. You'll turn some heads today, mark my words.'

Joy smiled her pleasure. 'Thank you, Davis.'

'I hope you enjoy your day, miss.'

'I'm sure I will. I love the races and I'm looking forward to parading in my new gown and hat.'

'And on the arm of such a distinguished beau, too, you'll be the envy of all the other young ladies,' Davis told her in a satisfied voice.

At that moment Margaret opened the door to announce that Mr. Quincy was waiting downstairs for her.

Charles stepped forward to meet them, but instead of the approving smile she expected, Joy saw a frown of annoyance.

'Joy, whatever are you doing wearing a gown like that? Are you shameless, showing you body off like that? I'm surprised at you. Please go and change immediately. Now that you're to become my wife, I expect you to dress appropriately.'

His words hit Joy like a dash of cold water. She stood dumbstruck, her blood running cold.

Margaret stepped forward. 'Mr. Quincy! Whatever do you mean? Joy looks beautiful, and her clothes are the height of fashion.'

'That gown is too...too clinging,' he replied, scowling. 'I've never seen its like.'

'It's the very latest fashion. Mr. Redfern, the famous Parisian couturier who designs gowns for our own Queen, designed one like this for Lily Langtry.'

He raised his eyebrows. 'For Lily Langtry? That's no criterion. What is fitting for an actress is not fitting for my future wife, I can assure you, madam.'

Margaret tightened her lips. 'Lily Langtry is not just an actress, Mr. Quincy, she is a great beauty and...'

'I am quite aware of what Lily Langtry is, thank you. And I can tell you she would never be welcomed into my family.' He looked at Joy. 'And as for that ridiculous hat, it's far too frivolous for you, now that you're about to become my wife.'

With a sob catching her throat Joy turned and ran back up the stairs. Throwing open her door she flopped onto the bed.

Davis stopped tidying the room and stared at her in astonishment. 'Whatever is the matter?' she asked.

Joy bit her lip. Straightening her shoulders she lifted her head and took a deep breath. When she spoke her voice held only the faintest tremor. 'Will you please go down and tell Mr. Quincy I will not be accompanying him to the races this afternoon.'

Davis looked hard at her, but nodded. 'Very well.' She left the room, closing the door behind her.

Joy sat staring at the wall for a moment then removed her hat and placed it on the bed beside her, smoothing its ribbons between her fingers. 'Pig!' she said. 'Superior pig! Who does he think he is?' The blood bubbled in her veins. 'So Lily Langtry wouldn't be good enough for his family, wouldn't she? Well, she's good enough for the Prince of Wales, and he makes no secret of the fact.'

Picking up the hat, she put it on her head again, then got up from the bed and crossed to the mirror, adjusting it. 'I don't care if he thinks you're too frivolous, *for someone about to become his wife,*' she mimicked, tossing her head. 'I think you're beautiful, and I intend to wear you, and my dress, with or without his approval. So there!'

When Davis came back to report that Mr. Quincy had left for the races with her grandparents and Mr. Rupert and his wife, Joy thanked her and added, 'Good riddance.'

The next morning, as Joy was ready to leave with Margaret for the Sunday Church Parade in Hyde Park, Davis came in to tell her that Mr. Quincy was in the drawing room and wished to see her.

Her nerves jangled, but she answered calmly. 'Very well, tell him I shall be down presently. And I'll wear my new dress, thank you.'

When she entered the drawing room Charles rose from his chair and picked up a large bunch of red roses from the small table next to him. A shadow flitted across his face as he looked at her, but he crossed the room with a smile on his lips that did not quite reach his eyes.

He offered her the roses. 'This is to say I'm sorry. I suppose I shouldn't tell you what to wear, but it was such a surprise to see you dressed like that.' His gaze ran down her body and up again, appraising her, and he swallowed. 'I must say you look quite...quite becoming in that, now I see you without the hat.'

'You don't like the hat?' Joy enquired coolly, making no move to take the flowers.

'No, not really, not very much,' he said awkwardly. 'You don't need fancy clothes like that. You're already beautiful without that sort of trashy adornment.'

Joy bristled. Trashy adornment, indeed. What did that say about her taste? And Margaret's, too.

'I mean,' Charles added hastily, seeing her look, 'you look beautiful in anything, and I suppose I prefer simpler clothes on you.'

'It's a shame you don't like the hat because it goes with this gown, and I'll be wearing it whenever I go out in the gown.'

His eyelids flickered, and he took a deep breath. He put the roses down, and moved close to her. Placing his hands on her stiff shoulders he looked into her eyes.

'Joy my darling, I fell under your spell when I first met you. I've been so unhappy since yesterday. I couldn't sleep last night. I love you and I couldn't bear it if anything came between us. I want you for my wife. Please say you forgive me.'

Gazing up into his wide blue eyes, shining with sincerity, Joy felt her heart melt. How could she stay angry with him? She smiled at him. 'Yes, of course I forgive you.'

As he pulled her toward him she didn't see the flash of triumph in his eyes.

Chapter Twenty Nine

As the family, and Charles with them, were all gathered in the drawing room for drinks before dinner a few weeks later Denman entered the room and spoke to Sir Alexander.

'There's a young man here, sir, who wishes to speak to you. I told him you're about to go into dinner but he insists it's urgent. He's most insistent that he must speak to you tonight.'

Then I suppose I must see what he wants. Ask him to wait...'

His words were cut off as the door flew open and a man erupted into the room, brandishing papers in one hand.

Denman turned and put out his hand to stop him, but he pushed past him and addressed himself to Sir Alexander in an aggressive voice.

'I take it you're Alexander Barron?'

'That's correct. And who, may I ask, are you?'

'I'm Alfred Barron. William Barron, your son, was my father. Here's the proof.' He waved the papers in Sir Alexander's face. 'There's no use denying it and I'm here to claim my inheritance.'

The room was silent. Joy stood frozen, mouth agape, as she tried to make sense of what she had just heard. She watched as Grandfather reached out his hand for the papers.

'Show me.' His voice was quiet, but his face paled as he took the papers and began to study them.

His words galvanised the room and everyone began to speak at once as he read first one paper, then the other.

Charles gripped Joy's arm. 'What's this all about?'

Bewildered, Joy shook her head. 'I have no idea. It must be a mistake. My father had no other children except me.'

'Are you sure?'

'Of course I'm sure. There must be some mistake. Everyone knows Father died before I was born, and there were no other children.'

Charles frowned and opened his mouth to speak, but at that moment Lady Barron bustled forward and pushed him aside in her eagerness to confront the intruder.

'What is the meaning of this outrage,' she demanded. 'How dare you burst in here and...'

A touch on the arm from her husband stopped her in full flow.

'Leave it,' he told her, then turned to the man. 'Come with me,' he commanded, turning on his heel and making for the door. 'Carry on, Denman,' he told the butler. 'Make sure everyone has a drink. I'll let you know if I wish you to serve dinner without me.'

Alexander led the way to his study, and seated himself at his desk. He motioned his companion to a chair opposite him.

'Please be seated.'

'Now then, I...'

Alexander held up his hand.

'Wait.'

After spreading the papers on the desk in front of him he picked up one and held it while he studied the individual before him, who shifted in his chair and looked at him with narrowed eyes. He looked to be in his mid twenties. He was tall, with fair hair and pale eyes fringed with almost colourless lashes, and a pallid face. He had similar colouring to William, certainly, and of comparable build, but he could not see any further resemblance. In fact, he found him singularly unattractive.

'Now then, you say you are Alfred Barron?'

'Yes, that's right,' he answered, with a strong Midlands accent.

'And this is your birth certificate?'

'Yes.'

'And Cora Hassell, who is described here as a housemaid, is your mother?'

'She was. She's dead now, died of the influenza, back in the epidemic.'

'I see. This also states that the father of the child, Alfred William, is William Barron, gentleman. You claim that is your father?'

'It's true. It's there in black and white, plain as day.'

'Hmm. This is dated 1875. Do you claim that Cora Hassell and my son William were married at that time?'

'No. I know they were married before but his father, you, that is, put a stop to it.'

Alexander's lips tightened.

'And do you know when this happened?'

'What, the marriage?'

'Yes. And the annulment, because they both happened together.'

'It was more'n a year before I was born.'

'Then how could you have been born more than a year later?'

'Because they still got together after the annulment. He used to come round all the time, and that's how it happened.'

There was the faintest tremor in Alexander's hand as he picked up the other piece of paper.

'You know what this is?'

'Yes. It's William Barron's will, my father's will. And it says he leaves all his estate to his son, Alfred Barron, and that's me. After I was born he still used to come round. Ma told me how he came round to see me lots of times. And then he knew he was going away and he mightn't be back for a long time and that's when he made the will. 'Cause he wanted me to have my birthright in case something happened to him, that's what she said.'

Alexander leant back, his face inscrutable. It all sounded plausible. The timing would be right for when they had left on their trip to Cape Town, and Australia, which was when William had met Kitty on board the *Osprey*. The papers appeared to be genuine. The will was in William's handwriting, or else it was a very good forgery, and the birth certificate looked genuine. That could be verified.

'Well Alfred, if you are indeed Alfred, why have you waited all this time to come here, to make a claim?'

'I'm Alfred all right. It says so there on my birth certificate, all genuine. You can check it out. And I didn't know until just before Ma died. Not about the will, that is. That's when she told me and gave me those,' he nodded his head at the papers on the desk, 'and said I should claim my birthright.'

'She waited a long time. Why didn't she do something before?'

He shrugged. 'She said she didn't want to cause no trouble.'

'But you have no such reservations?'

'I want what's mine, that's all, what my father left me.'

'And what do you think that is?'

He shuffled his feet under the table. 'Well, what it says in the will, all his estate.'

'My son died twenty years ago in Australia. He has no estate here.'

A crafty look came over Alfred's face. 'I understand there's a pretty nice estate over there. A property with loads of timber. Must be worth plenty.'

'What makes you think that?'

'It's what I've heard.'

'Who told you that?'

He shifted in his chair. 'Ma told me. When she gave me the papers.'

'And how would she have known?'

'I don't know. I guess she heard. Anyway, it's true, isn't it?'

'Whether it is or not, William left a wife and child. They would have a claim too.'

Alfred challenged Alexander with his eyes. 'But the will says he left all his estate to me.'

Alexander picked up the papers. 'These will have to be verified. And if they are genuine, then the legal aspects will need to be decided.'

'But the will says...'

'I know what the will says. But I must be sure it's genuine before we go any further.' He pushed back his chair and stood. 'And now you must excuse me. I have guests waiting for dinner. Denman will show you out.'

'I thought you'd be glad to find your grandson. I thought you'd be happy to see me,' he complained. 'And now you're tossing me out.'

'If you come back in a week I'll tell you the results of my enquiries, and if I find you are William's son then I'll welcome you.'

'You'll find they're genuine, all right.'

Alexander pulled the bell-pull.

'Show this young man out, Denman,' Alexander told Denman as Alfred rose reluctantly. 'I'll see you again in one week's time. By then we should be clearer about things.'

When he returned to the drawing room he knew everyone was agog to know what had happened, but he was in no mind to discuss it.

'I'll be looking into certain matters regarding that young man, and that is all I intend to say at the moment,' he told them, then, to Denman. 'We'll have dinner now.'

'Very good, sir.'

No one dared to utter another word on the subject during dinner, but later, after the evening was over, his wife followed him into their room and Alexander sighed wearily. She had been waiting to get him alone.

'So now then,' she started, 'tell me what happened with that scoundrel who had the gall to burst in on us like he did. What did he mean by an inheritance?'

Alexander struggled with the stud in his collar as he undressed.

'He claims to be William's son and wishes to claim his estate.'

'On what does he base his claim to be William's son?'

'On a birth certificate stating he was born to William Barron and Cora Hassell.'

'Cora Hassell! That scheming tart, she promised me she would never make a claim...' her voice trailed away.

Alexander stopped fiddling with the stud and stood very still. 'What do you mean? When did you see Cora Hassell?'

His wife paled. 'Well, I knew her, of course, I saw her all the time, when she worked here.'

'That is not what I am talking about, and you know it. Did you ever see her after the marriage was annulled?'

Lady Barron twisted the rings on her fingers.

'Well, yes, she came to see you one day but you were out, so I saw her instead. There was no harm in that, surely?'

'When did she come here, and why? I want the whole story.'

Biting her lip, she dropped her eyes.

'It was a couple of years after their escapade. Apparently William still saw her sometimes and she came here with a birth certificate and tried to tell me they had a son, and William still wanted to marry her. I knew she was lying, of course, but I didn't want to worry you. So I arranged to meet her and give her some money if she promised me she'd make no further claim on William, and we'd never hear from her again.'

Having worked his stud free, Alexander threw it across the room with all his force. When he spoke his voice shook. 'And you didn't think this important enough to tell me?'

Twisting her hands together, she spoke without meeting his eyes. 'I didn't want to worry you or put you under extra strain. I've always tried to consider your health, you know that.'

'How much did you give her?'

'That doesn't matter, what matters is that she promised...'

Alexander caught her by the arm. 'I said, how much?'

'A thousand pounds.'

'And for that she promised not to make a nuisance of herself?'

'Yes. She promised she'd go away somewhere and never approach us again.'

His eyes narrowed. 'You never considered I had a right to know I had a grandson?'

'I was trying to protect you.'

'It's no wonder you were so insistent that William accompany us on our journey.'

'She was after money, that's all. You wouldn't have wanted William to marry a common housemaid, you know that.'

Alexander sighed. 'That's true, but I should have known about the boy so I could work it out myself. I'd have wished to see him and make arrangements for his future.' He paused, his face bleak. 'Did you see him? The child.'

She hesitated. 'Yes, he was with her when I met her to give her the money.'

'What did he look like?'

'Just some brat, I didn't take too much notice. I knew he probably wasn't William's child.'

'Was he dark or fair?'

'Fair.'

'So it could be the same person. I must try to follow it up somehow, try to find the truth. Do you know where she was living?'

'With her sister, she said. I have no idea where.'

'I see.' Alexander rubbed his hand across his eyes. 'That's enough for tonight, tomorrow I must decide how to find out if he is genuine or not.'

As he contemplated this task, Alexander knew he would need help. He needed someone who was smart and resourceful. Would Rufe help? He had formed an affinity with him in Ascot week, finding him a congenial companion, intelligent and knowledgeable and possessed of sound commonsense, as well as being an excellent judge of horseflesh and bloodlines. Yes, he would write to him in the morning; he felt sure he would help.

Rufe sat with Alexander Barron in his study. He had come to London immediately in answer to the letter telling him of the arrival of a person claiming to be William's son, and Alexander had related the story in its entirety.

'So you believe this person representing himself as Alfred Barron, William Barron's son, is preparing to lay claim to Redwoods?'

'Yes, I believe that's his aim.'

'And you say he wasn't surprised to hear that it's the sole estate of your son William?'

'No, not at all. He also knows it's a timber cutting property and estimates it's worth a great deal.'

'I wonder how he found that out.'

'He says his mother told him, but when I asked how she knew he was evasive. He said she must have heard.'

'And you've had the birth certificate verified?'

'Yes. Thompson, my solicitor, assures me it's genuine. And it seems there's little doubt that the will is in William's handwriting. He's had an expert examine it and compare it with specimens I provided.' Alexander rubbed his forehead, taking a deep breath. 'It is just the damn-fool sort of thing he would have done, I am afraid.'

'At the time he had no estate?'

'None whatsoever.'

'Then perhaps he did it to appease his mistress at the time.'

'Perhaps.' Alexander shrugged 'It doesn't matter now.'

'No.' Rufe frowned. 'What we have to establish is if this person is your grandson, or an impostor.'

'Yes, and this is where I need assistance. I'm hoping you will help me, if you can spare the time before you must return to Australia.'

'I don't intend leaving for two or three months, and I'll be happy to try and help.'

'Thank you. We don't have a lot to go on. All we know is that Cora Hassell was living with her sister at the time the child was born, and for some time after. How long she stayed there I don't know.' He paused, tightening his lips. 'I am ashamed to admit that my wife gave her money, so she might have moved on soon after.'

'Then we'll just have to start with that, and hope it leads us in the right direction.'

Alexander sighed. 'Should it prove that he is genuine, I don't care for the ramifications. As we both know, it's Kitty's business acumen that has made Redwoods the successful enterprise it is today. When my son died it had potential, but that had to be realised. It will be a legal nightmare to untangle. And the consequences for Kitty if she lost Redwoods...' he spread his hands, 'I hate to think about it. And what of Joy? It's her birthright too.' He shook his head. 'What a mess, what a mess.'

'Kitty was certainly upset by the news, and that's even more reason I'm happy to help. Although she now spends much time in Sydney with me Redwoods is still important to her. She built it up so that Joy would always have a home and a livelihood, but she has a love for the place herself.'

'Of course, I understand that. And I realise Joy wishes to marry and remain here, but even so, she should always have the security of knowing Redwoods is there for her. It's her right.' He sighed again. 'I must speak to her and tell her what's happening. I've put it off until I knew if you would be able to help me or not.'

'I'll do my utmost, both for your peace of mind to know the truth, and for Kitty and Joy.'

'Hello, shrimp,' said a voice. 'I see you haven't grown since you've been over here.'

Joy spun around at the words. 'David!' She gasped. 'What are you doing here?'

He grinned down at her, his eyes crinkling at the corners. 'I thought I'd better come over and check up on you.'

Her cheeks grew warm as she glared at him. 'I don't need checking on.'

David laughed. 'Well then, the other reason is that I came to attend the sales and help Rufe choose stock for our breeding programme. While he might not actually need much help I don't see why he should have all the fun on his own.'

'I never expected to see you here. Why didn't you let me know you were coming?'

'Thought I'd surprise you.'

'You certainly have. How did you find me here?'

'I came with Rufe, and he's here with your grandfather. I believe this is the last race meeting before you leave for the country, and Sir Alex kindly invited me. They told me where you'd be.'

Charles Quincy's voice came from beside Joy. 'Perhaps you would care to introduce me to you friend.'

They were standing by the rail at Ascot watching the horses as they paraded for the next race, and Joy turned, embarrassed.

'I'm sorry, Charles. I just got such a shock...'

'That you forgot I was here,' he interrupted her coldly. 'I can see that. You two are obviously old friends.'

Joy felt her cheeks grow even warmer. 'Charles, I'd like you to meet Mr. David Cavanagh, Uncle Rufe's nephew. David, this is Mr. Charles Quincy. We're engaged to be married.'

Charles inclined his head. 'Cavanagh,' he said, extending a hand, his face glacial.

David's eyes narrowed as he took it. 'Quincy,' he responded nonchalantly. 'My pleasure.'

Charles raised his eyebrows. 'I'm acquainted with your uncle, of course. However, I understood he'd left us to attend the sales. Has he completed his purchases then, or will he be continuing with his search?'

'He's bought some, but he's still looking to see what's on offer.'

'And will you accompany him on his search?'

'Yep, that's the plan,' David drawled. 'Providing I can drag myself away from this big city of London and its attractions, of course.'

Joy sensed tension between the two, and why was David acting like a provincial hick?

Looking from one to the other she bit her lip, and turned back to the rail.

'Oh, do look,' she exclaimed, 'the horses are ready to go out on to the track and we haven't been watching. I haven't picked my horse yet.' She watched the horses parading for a few seconds. 'I like the look of number three, let's see, that's Blue Thunder. I'm going to have a bet on him. Are you coming with me?' she asked, looking from one to the other.

Charles offered her his arm.

'Of course, my dear,' he said, and when she placed her hand on his arm he patted it before turning to David. 'Perhaps you would care to accompany us, Cavanagh?'

Chapter Thirty

Charles took Joy's hand in his. They were sharing a seat on the verandah at Bournbridge Hall, overlooking the rose garden.

'There, there, my sweet, don't be so upset. This Alfred will most likely turn out to be an impostor. And if not, if he succeeds in his claim, I'm sure your grandfather will compensate you accordingly. And that will be more use to you than a property in Australia that you may never see again, won't it?'

'But it's not about the money, Charles. My mother has spent most of her life building up that business, and to lose it now would be devastating for her.' Joy swallowed, shaking her head. 'Besides, Redwoods is – well, it's always been my home, even if I never gave it much thought. It's always been there, waiting for me.'

'Be sensible, Joy.' He let go of her hand. 'Once we're married you won't even think about it. Holsmere Park will be your home, and once you're its mistress you may well find there are things there that you wish to change, and if you have the money you can go ahead and do so.'

Joy looked at him in surprise. 'But surely that will be for you to arrange?'

He shrugged. 'Perhaps there will be things you'll wish to do yourself.'

'Oh.' She gave her head a little shake, putting such a trivial matter out of her mind. 'Apart from a claim on Redwoods, I'm finding it hard to come to terms with the fact that I have a brother.'

'You may have, but from what you tell me it's not certain.'

'There's a chance this person may be an impostor, but there's no doubt that my father had a son while he was young, before he came to Australia.'

'You must wait to see what the outcome is before you become too agitated over the matter.'

'But don't you see, whether this is an impostor or not, the fact is that my father had a relationship with a young woman when they were not married. They had a child and then he went off and left them.'

'Well, these young women who carry on in such a fashion have only themselves to blame.'

'Perhaps she loved him very much.'

Charles shrugged. 'Then she should have been more careful.'

Joy felt a jab of anger. 'That's a heartless way to look at it.'

'What do you want me to do? Become all stirred up over some housemaid who was out to try and trap your father into marriage?'

'You don't know that.'

'I can make a very good guess.'

'Be that as it may, I'm disappointed to think that my father would act in such a way. It's not what I expected to hear of him. I've always thought of him as upright and trustworthy.'

Charles raised an eyebrow. 'You shouldn't worry your pretty little head about what happened so long ago. It's of no consequence now.'

'Of course it is.' Joy's body stiffened. 'Surely you can see that?'

'No. What I see is that you should not be deprived of your share of your father's estate, and your grandmother has assured me that you won't.'

'Why were you talking to my grandmother about this?'

He shrugged. 'No reason. We were just talking, that is all.'

'I don't like you discussing my business behind my back'

'Really, Joy,' he frowned, 'you're becoming oversensitive about this matter. Try to look at it sensibly instead of being so emotional.'

Joy sat back and closed her eyes, breathing deeply. Was he right? Was she allowing herself to be swayed by emotion when she should be taking a practical approach? But she couldn't get away from the fact that her father, as a young man, had behaved in a way that made her feel ashamed. Or that somewhere she had a brother she didn't know. That hurt. How she would have loved a brother when she was growing up!

Tears pricked her eyes. She mustn't cry; Charles would think she was overly-emotional then, and she didn't want to argue with him. He'd been so sweet to her since they'd come down here to the country. She didn't want to spoil things.

Swallowing the lump in her throat she turned to him. 'Let's not talk about it anymore at the moment, let's just wait and see what happens.'

He patted her hand. 'That's a good girl. Now let's take a walk before we go inside for tea.' He stood and pulled her to her feet, smiling now.

It was a bright, calm summer's day, the air laced with sunshine and the scent of roses heavy around them. They walked through the garden, hearing the drone of the bees, and a skylark that broke into a melodic song, and Joy though how silly she was to argue with Charles.

This was what mattered. To be arm-in-arm with this handsome man who loved her. Next year she would be his wife, and Redwoods would become but a distant memory, whatever happened. This is where she belonged now. When they reached a secluded spot behind the hedge bordering the orangery he turned and took her in his arms. She melted against him, turning her face up for his kiss. A thrill ran through her. This was the life she'd dreamed of, in a time that seemed so long ago, on the other side of the world.

The next morning Joy woke early, stretching her arms above her head as she watched the early morning sun peeping around the edges of the curtains. It looked like being another beautiful day and she decided she would take an early morning ride. If Charles was up they could go together.

Humming happily to herself, she put on her riding habit. If no one was around, would she dare to ride astride? She giggled at the thought of the shock it would cause if she was seen, and decided best not. Charles would certainly have a fit, and she didn't want to upset him. She smiled as she thought how sweet he'd been to her yesterday. After they had overcome their tiff, that was. Her happiness faded a little as she thought of that. But she pushed the thought away, determined not to let it spoil her day, and as she left the room she hummed a snatch of 'Botany Bay', and was in high spirits at the prospect of riding in the cool of the first light.

A young housemaid was dusting the banisters as she made her way downstairs. She bobbed her head as Joy approached.

'Good morning, Jane. You're up very early.'

'Yes, Miss Joy. I see you be going riding,' she added shyly.

Joy smiled at her, pausing on the stairs. 'Yes. I love to ride in the early morning. Do you ever ride on your day off?'

'Oh, no, miss, not me. I'd be scared stiff o' them big beasts. But I 'ope you enjoy it.'

'Thank you, Jane. I'm sure I will.'

The side door was unlocked, which suggested she wasn't the first one up, but there was no one else to be seen. Letting herself out she headed for the stables. She was half way there when she heard a man's voice, raised and angry, and the shrill squeal of a horse. It sounded as if it was in pain.

Joy stood still for a few seconds trying to decide where the sound came from. It came again. It definitely came from the direction of the stables; one of the horses must be in trouble. She started to run. As she burst around the corner of the hayshed the stables came into full view, and she pulled up short. Her mouth went dry as she felt a shock of disbelief, followed instantly by a wave of fury as her eyes widened in horror at the scene before her.

A horse was tied to a post while a man lashed it viciously with a riding crop. Several angry, red weals stood out along the dark coat on its side, as the assailant continued beating the animal with a furious intensity. The horse tried to rear in order to evade the weapon but a short tether made it impossible. It pulled and tossed its head, its eyes rolling, its hoofs trying to lash out as it screamed in terror. The man wielding the whip was Charles Quincy.

Yelling at him to stop Joy raced across the yard and tore the whip from his grasp. Shouting an oath he turned and tried to snatch it back, but she raised her arm and slashed at his sleeve with it.

'What do you think you're doing?' she yelled, bringing the whip down on his shoulder as he tried to wrest it from her grasp. 'Are you mad? How dare you treat a horse like this?'

Quincy was panting, his face red, and drops of spittle formed on his lips.

'The brute bit me. I'm teaching it manners.' His face contorted with fury. 'It's nothing to do with you. I'll do what I want. Give me that whip.'

He made a wild grab but Joy was too quick for him as she jumped back. 'No way, you cruel bastard!' She stood her ground as he lunged at her, sidestepping just before he reached her. 'I'd like to beat *you*, you miserable coward!'

She slashed at him as he stumbled past, and caught him two blows on his jacket before he regained his footing. He turned, and managed to snatch the whip from her hands.

'Now we'll see who's boss around here.' He brought the whip down across her shoulders, once, twice, three times.

It hurt, even through the layers of her clothing, and it inflamed Joy's rage further as she stepped back.

'You lily-livered, craven apology for a man. Yes, you'd beat me, would you? Or tie up a horse before you savaged it. You're not a man's bootlace. And to think I was going to marry you.' She tore the ring from her finger and threw it at him. 'Here. Keep your ring. Keep your Holsmere Park. And get out! Get out of here! I never want to see you again.'

Quincy picked up the ring and pocketed it. He stood in front of her, his eyes blazing. 'You bitch. Do you think I'd have chosen to marry you, with your crass colonial ideas and tastes, if I hadn't been offered a big enough inducement? Ten thousand pounds is what it took for me to offer for your hand. How do you like that?'

Nausea gripped Joy. 'What do you mean?'

His mouth twisted in a contemptuous sneer. 'Ten thousand pounds is what your grandmother offered me to take you off her hands. Well, it wasn't enough. I'm off. But if you hang around she might find another fool to take you.' With that he turned on his heel and strode away.

Joy stood frozen, feeling her world crumble around her. Surely it couldn't be true? Her grandmother would never have offered money to find a husband for her. Would she?

She crossed to the shivering horse and commenced speaking softly. After a couple of moments she put out a hand to stroke its muzzle. The mare jerked her head back, snorting, but, finally, she allowed Joy to stroke her. When she stopped shivering Joy untied the halter and led her over to the stalls. Finding one empty she coaxed the mare inside it and secured her, then made her way back to the house and up to her room, fighting to keep back the tears.

Once inside her room she flung herself down on the bed and wept. She wept for the loss of her love, and for the treachery of her grandmother. Hurt and humiliation filled her. She didn't know which was worse – the fact that Charles was a fake, or that her grandmother had offered money to induce him to marry her. How could they do this to her?

Joy cringed at the thought of the two of them conspiring to arrange the marriage. Was she really so unattractive and – what had Charles said? – crass, that no one would want to marry her, that he needed a bribe to do so? Crying harder than ever, she remembered how he told her he loved her, how he wanted to marry her. All lies. She pounded her fists into the pillow.

Finally, her tears all spent, she sat up on the bed. Shuddering, she thought of the brutal way Charles had been beating the horse. How could any man do that? The whole scenario played inside her head over and over, and the more she thought about it, the worse she felt.

Suddenly she wanted to get away from here, and a picture of Redwoods popped into her mind. *I want to go home. I want to go to home to Redwoods.*

Then a feeling of panic gripped her. Her brother, if he really was her brother, said Redwoods belonged to him. Mother always said Redwoods was for her, but were they going to lose it?

Joy sat there for a long time, she didn't know how long, before she could bring herself to change from her riding habit and go downstairs again. She sought out her grandmother, who was at her desk, writing.

'May I speak with you, please?' she asked, as calmly she could, although her insides churned.

Grandmother put down her pen. 'Certainly. Take a seat. I've been hoping you'd come to see me,' she continued. 'I believe you and Mr. Quincy have quarrelled?'

'Quarrelled?' Joy felt a quiver of anger. 'I suppose you could call it that. We're no longer engaged. I gave him back his ring, and I never wish to see him again.'

'That was very impetuous of you. It's not unusual to have a disagreement. Surely you had no need to show such a display of temper?'

Joy felt a flush spread up her neck, onto her face. 'I had every need. He's a monster, he...'

Grandmother raised her hand. 'Whatever happened, Quincy was most upset. He wouldn't tell me what transpired between you, but he's left the house. I can only hope you haven't destroyed your chances with him.'

Joy jerked her head back as her anger exploded. 'I wouldn't marry him if he was the last man on earth. He's a sadist, a horse beater, and worse. And even your ten thousand pounds wasn't enough to induce him to marry me.'

Lady Barron paled. 'What are you talking about?'

'He told me all about it. How you offered him ten thousand pounds to marry me. Am I so obnoxious that you had to bribe a man to try and find a husband for me?'

'It was nothing like that. It was...it was more in the form of a dowry.'

Joy gasped. 'A dowry. So I needed a dowry to persuade him to have me?'

'You misunderstand my motives,' she spoke anxiously now. 'I could see that he was interested in you, and that you liked him, and I wanted very much to be sure you would stay here. I don't want you to go back to Australia.'

Joy narrowed her eyes. 'Why not?'

Grandmother's face crumpled. 'Because you mean a great deal to me.' Her voice was low.

Joy could not doubt her sincerity, and the anger left her like air rushing from a balloon. She slumped in her chair, closed her eyes as she took a deep breath and then let it go.

'That wasn't the way to keep me here.'

'It was the only way I knew.'

Joy rose from her chair. 'I've decided to join Mother in Keswick. I'll stay with her until we all leave for home. I'd like to leave immediately, if possible.'

Grandmother sighed. 'I'll have Denman arrange a carriage for you. Davis will help you to pack, and she can travel with you. You can't go alone.'

'Thank you.'

'I'm sorry, Joy. I never meant to hurt you. I thought Mr. Quincy was a good match for you, and I believe you would have been happy with him.'

Sadness made Joy's limbs heavy as she turned to leave her grandmother.

'I'm sure you meant it for the best.'

Chapter Thirty One

Joy and Kitty were sitting alone in the sitting room of the house in Keswick on the morning after Joy arrived. They had come in here to talk alone after breakfasting with Mrs. Frobisher in the small morning room.

'I'm just so heartbroken, Mother. I thought he really loved me.'

Putting her arm around Joy's shoulder Kitty gave her a hug, hating the man who had hurt her daughter so much.

'Well, of course you did, darling. He asked you to be his wife. You would never think it was for any other reason than because he loved you.'

'But all the time, it was just for the money.' Joy sniffed into her handkerchief. 'I wouldn't have believed ten thousand pounds was such a lot of money to him, enough to lure him into marriage. Why, his family must be very wealthy. The way everyone speaks about Holsmere Park, it sounds like a mansion.'

'I'm sure it is, but Charles Quincy is only a son and, while he'd have an allowance, it may not be large, and the Season can be very expensive.'

'But ten thousand would be a lot to spend on amusements.'

'Some young men become addicted to gambling and get into debt. They're usually reluctant to admit it to their parents. It can happen easily because of the clubs they frequent. Perhaps that was his problem.'

Joy shrugged. 'Perhaps. But I would never have believed it of Grandmother.'

Kitty spoke carefully. 'Lady Barron likes to get what she wants, and she can be a trifle....overbearing, shall we say, at times.'

Joy gave a slight laugh. 'You've noticed that too?'

They both laughed together then, and Joy felt a bit happier.

Kitty sobered. 'I think you should write to your grandfather. He's probably feeling hurt that you went off without leaving a message for him. It's up to you, whether you discuss Lady Barron's part in the disastrous affair, or not.'

Joy thought for a moment. 'I don't think I'll mention it. I'll just tell Grandfather we had an argument, and I decided I didn't want to marry Mr. Quincy.'

Kitty nodded. 'I think that's best.'

Joy sighed. 'I'm sure I'll never be able to fall in love again. I'll never trust another man.'

Kitty smiled. 'Oh, I think you will.' She leant across and smoothed Joy's hair. 'One day you'll meet Mr. Right, and you'll forget all about Mr. Quincy, and how he's hurt you.'

Joy twisted her fingers together, dropping her head to look at them. 'Am I so unattractive that he had to be bribed to marry me?' she asked in a low voice.

If Quincy had been nearby Kitty would have gladly throttled him, and Lady Barron as well. She took Joy's chin in her hand and raised it so she could look into her eyes. They glistened with unshed tears, and her heart twisted.

'How can you think that? You're beautiful.'

'I don't think so. He would never have treated me so, if I was.'

'Joy, you caught him in an act of extreme cruelty and cowardice. He knew then that you would never marry him, and he had to try and belittle you, to put himself on top. As for your looks, do you think I am unattractive?'

Joy opened her eyes wide. 'You? Of course not. Everyone says how pretty you are.'

Kitty smiled at her. 'Just as everyone says how much we look alike.'

Joy gave a tremulous smile, and sniffed. 'I suppose that's true, and while I can't see it, maybe I'm not as bad as I've been thinking.'

'Believe me, darling, you're beautiful.'

Joy took a deep breath. 'I'm so glad I came straight here. I couldn't have told anyone else all about this.'

'You can always tell me anything, anything at all.'

'I know.'

Kitty paused a moment, then decided to speak what was in her heart. 'And I hope you won't be upset when I tell you I didn't want you to stay here in England. I would have missed you so. Not that I would have tried to stop you, but I was glad your grandfather insisted on a year's wait.'

'Isn't it lucky he did? Charles wanted us to be married immediately.' She tightened her lips. 'So he could get the money, of course. He told me it was because he loved me so much that he didn't want to wait.'

Kitty felt another stab of hatred. 'Well, it's over now, and we must look ahead. There's Lily to think about, and Redwoods.'

'Yes, Lily.' Joy looked guilty. 'I'm afraid I've been so taken up with my own problems, I haven't thought much about Lily. It was so late when we arrived last night she was ready to go to bed, so we only spoke a few words. How is she?'

'Well enough, but she hasn't changed her mind about the baby. She doesn't want to keep it.'

'Perhaps she'll change her mind when it's born.'

'I doubt it, but we'll know soon.'

'How soon, do you think?'

'Two or three weeks.'

'And how soon after that will she be well enough to travel?'

'It will depend, but probably not for a few weeks more.'

'Hmm.' Joy sat thinking. 'And what about the sea voyage? Will she and the baby be well enough to cope with that?'

'I would think so. But before we can even think so far ahead, let alone plan our return home, there's the problem of Redwoods to be solved.'

Joy bit her lip. 'Yes, I'm worried. What do you think will happen?'

Kitty shook her head. 'I can't answer that. Rufe and David are down in London now, helping your grandfather try to determine if this person is an impostor or not. If he's not, if he is who he says he is, there will be much legal wrangling, I fear.'

Misery clouded Joy's face. 'I couldn't bear it if we lost Redwoods. It would be so unfair. It's our home, and as well, you've worked all these years to build up the timber business. Now someone wants to take it away from us. Oh, I know you and Rufe have a home down in Sydney, but Redwoods is special.'

Kitty gave a half-smile. 'I can remember when you told me you didn't care about it, and that you couldn't wait to leave it.'

'I know. I was so stupid, but I was only a child then. Besides, perhaps I had to come over here to realise how good life is in

Australia. Not that England doesn't have its good points,' she added, 'but I realise now how wonderful Redwoods is.'

Kitty's heart sank. How ironic it would be if Joy should rediscover her love of Redwoods only to have it taken away from her. 'Then let's hope we can hang on to it. I've always meant it for you. That's what I worked for, so you would have security.'

'Yes, I know.' A worried frown crossed Joy's face and when she spoke it was slowly. 'But, no matter what happens, if this person is genuine or not, it doesn't alter the fact that Father had a relationship with this woman, and she had his son and then he went off and left them. That was a terrible thing to do. It makes me feel ashamed of him.'

Poor Joy, what a hard time she'd had lately! On top of Quincy's deceit, she had learnt she may lose Redwoods, and now she had the humiliation of her Father's reprehensible behaviour, and the knowledge she may have a brother. Kitty longed to ease her distress.

'Don't be too hard on him, darling. We all do things that we shouldn't at times, none of us is perfect. Perhaps they were very much in love. He was the youngest son, he would've had no money of his own, and very little say about his life. I remember how much in awe of his parents he was. He was glad to stay in Australia, away from them.'

'But Mother,' again she hesitated, 'it must have hurt you to learn that there was another woman in his life, before he met you.'

'What he did before he met me was his own affair. I doubt it affected our marriage in any way.'

'So you and Father were always happy together?'

The memory of William's heavy hand striking her flashed into Kitty's mind, but when she answered the question, her voice was firm.

'Of course.'

Joy smiled. 'I'm glad.'

The house, with a small garden, stood on its own some distance from the town of Keswick, surrounded by pasture and woodlands, with views to the nearby fells and rolling hills.

The days fell into a pattern, starting with Joy and Kitty taking breakfast in the small morning room, sometimes accompanied by Mrs. Frobisher if she wasn't busy attending to Lily. Lily took her breakfast in bed and she did not come downstairs until mid-morning.

The first morning the two friends sat together before lunch while Joy told Lily her story of Charles Quincy's cruelty to the horse, culminating in her giving him back his ring. On Kitty's advice she made no mention of the money.

Lily obviously felt the discomfort of the last weeks of her pregnancy, and apart from wanting to hear whatever Joy could tell her about Winston, which was little, she showed little interest in anything. She spent her days on a lounge in the conservatory, reading the latest women's magazines, which she had asked Kitty to order to be delivered regularly.

When Joy appeared downstairs on the second day in black breeches, without the skirt from her riding habit, Kitty raised her eyebrows.

'Don't you think that's a bit too daring for England?' she asked.

'Possibly,' Joy replied, 'but who's to see me, way out here?'

'I suppose you're right. There's hardly anyone around at this time of year. Perhaps you should keep away from the town though. We don't want to give us colonials a bad name.'

'Worse than we already have, you mean?'

They both laughed.

'Thank goodness Lady Barron can't see you.'

Joy rolled her eyes and gave a mock shudder.

'She'd have a fit.' She planted a kiss on her mother's cheek. 'Don't worry about me, I'll be home before dark,' she told her, and off she went.

Joy spent much time riding alone around the countryside over the next days. Kitty offered to accompany her, but when Joy said she wanted to be alone for a bit, Kitty understood and didn't press her. Joy relished the lack of restrictions here, so different from her grandmother's constant rules and reprimands.

The surroundings were very different from the structured estate she was used to at Bournbridge with wide, open spaces. Riding astride, and with the wind whipping her hair behind her, Joy could gallop her horse until they were both exhausted.

Exploring nearby woodlands, she marvelled at the autumn tints of reds, russets and browns as the trees prepared to shed their leaves for the winter. One day, as the horse picked her way over a trail littered with fallen leaves, she startled a herd of red deer. They scattered at her approach, melting into the trees and disappearing in seconds. And sometimes she caught sight of a squirrel in a tree as it went about its business of laying in provisions against the coming winter months.

One day she rode as far as the Derwent Water, a large lake with trees lining its placid waters and mountains hovering in the background. She reined in next to a landing that jutted out into the water, and had little boats tied up to it. The only person in sight was an old man, his clothes almost the same colour as the old timbers of the landing, who sat halfway along it. His feet dangled over the side as he sucked on a pipe and focused his attention on his fishing line in the water.

Dismounting, Joy tied her horse to a rail and walked out on to the landing to stand beside him. He took no notice of her.

After watching for a couple of moments she spoke.

'Catching anything?'

'Yep.' Without turning he lifted the lid on a basket beside him. Joy peered in. Three fish, silver scales gleaming, lay inside. One flopped on its side as she watched.

'Nice fish.'

'Yep.'

'Good weather we're having.'

'Yep.'

'Not many people around.'

'Nope.'

'I suppose it's pretty busy here in summer.'

'Yep.'

'It's a beautiful spot.'

'Yep.'

'Do you come here often?'

'Yep.'

'I might see you again sometime; I'm staying not far away.'

'Hrrmph.'

'Well, it's been nice talking to you. Guess I'll be getting along now.' She waited a moment. 'Goodbye.'

'Hrrmph.'

Laughing to herself, Joy walked back along the landing. Halfway she stopped and turned around. The old man still sat in the same position, his eyes never leaving the water. On the distant bank trees came down to the lake, and the mountains loomed in the distance. Water lay on all sides, with the sun casting a silver shawl over a small patch where the breeze riffled the surface into tiny wrinkles, while all around was smooth.

She turned around again, facing the road and the way she had come. She had ridden through pasture land to reach here, and she stood watching the sheep grazing in the autumn sun. Not a sound broke the peace.

Joy threw her arms upwards and tilted her head back, drawing in the pure air. She spun round and round, a dervish in black breeches, arms upraised, and laughed aloud. When she stopped she saw the old man had turned his head, watching her.

'Life's great,' she shouted to him. 'I wouldn't be dead for quids.'

He turned back to watch his line. Joy ran down the landing, untied her horse and jumped on and then, with a whoop, urged her back along the road.

When Joy arrived back at the house Lily was in the sitting room, upright in a chair, her face white and anxious.

'Oh Joy, I'm so pleased you're back, I've been waiting for you.'

'Why, what's the matter?'

'The pains have started.'

Joy swallowed. 'Where's Mother? And Mrs. Frobisher? Do they know?'

'Yes. They're bustling around somewhere with Mrs. Sims, the midwife. They think it's going to be ages yet.'

'How are you feeling?'

Lily's eyes filled. 'I'm frightened.'

Joy crossed the room and took her hand.

'You'll be all right. If the midwife's here already you're in good hands.'

'You can die when you have a baby, it happens all the time. I don't want to die.'

'You're not going to die. Don't even think such a thing. You're young and healthy. You'll have a beautiful baby.'

Lily started to cry. 'I don't want a beautiful baby. I don't want a baby at all.'

'There now, it'll soon be over and...'

'Oh, ow!' Lily almost crushed Joy's hand as she cried out, her body stiffening.

Joy's stomach tied itself into knots as she watched, not knowing what to do to help her friend. As the pain subsided, Lily sagged. 'It hurts so much. I don't think I can stand it.'

At that moment Kitty hurried into the room.

'It's time for you to come up to bed, Lily. The pains are coming faster now.' She turned to Joy. 'I'm glad you're back. Lily's been asking for you. Will you help me get her up to her room?'

'Of course. Come on Lily,' she pulled on her friend's hand. 'Can you stand up?'

Lily nodded, and rose clumsily from the chair.

'We'll take an arm each,' Kitty told Joy. 'We'll need to help her up the stairs, hopefully before the next pain comes.'

With one on either side they helped her slowly up the stairs, and managed to reach Lily's room without mishap. The midwife had prepared the bed, and they assisted her into her night gown and onto the bed, just before the next pain racked her body.

'Now then,' Mrs. Sims told a panting Lily, 'I've fastened a strap here on the top of the bed. When you feel a pain coming on you can pull on that. It makes it easier.'

Lily nodded. 'All right.'

'Now, let's have a look and see what's going on here.' Opening Lily's legs she peered closely before closing them again, and pulling a sheet up over her.

'No, nothing to see yet. We'll have to wait for the water to break. Would you like a cup o' tea, dearie?'

Lily shook her head. 'No.'

'Well, you'll need to drink plenty once the baby's here or you won't have enough milk for it. However, if you're all right, I'll go and get one for myself now.'

'Don't you leave me, Joy,' Lily begged. 'Will you stay with me all the time?'

'Of course I will.'

Kitty went to the door. 'I think I'll have a cup of tea myself. Call me if you need me.'

'I'm so frightened,' Lily said, after Kitty left the room. 'And it hurts so much. No one told me it would be like this.'

Joy felt helpless. 'Oh Lily, I don't know what I can do for you.'

'Could you rub my back for me? I've got a backache.'

'Yes. Roll on your side.'

Joy massaged her back until Lily turned and reached up to grab the leather strap, pulling on it and crying out as another pain seized her.

When she turned over Joy saw a patch of wetness spreading on the bed. She hurried to the door and called out to Mrs. Sims.

'Come quickly. Something's happening.'

When Mrs. Sims came in she took one look. 'Hah. Now we're in business.' She went to the door and called out. 'Mrs. Frobisher, come and help me with these sheets, her water's broken.'

Two hours later, when Joy felt she could not bear to hear Lily screaming any longer, Mrs. Sims pushed her aside, forcing her to relinquish Lily's hand.

'Now then, push, dearie, push. Not much longer now.'

As Lily let out another scream, she shouted. 'PUSH, come on, once more. PUSH.'

Joy watched mesmerised as, with another almighty scream from Lily, and the midwife's assistance, a little bloodied bundle slid out on to the bed.

'Well now, dearie,' Mrs. Sims said in a satisfied voice as she scooped up the baby. 'You've got a boy. Well done.'

The next day, Kitty, Joy and Mrs. Frobisher sat over their morning tea, discussing Lily and the baby.

'I don't know what we're to do. Lily refuses to have anything to do with the baby,' Kitty said with a frown.

'I don't know how she can be so heartless,' Mrs. Frobisher replied. 'She won't even feed it, now the midwife's not here to force her. And she hardly drinks anything. Trying to dry up her milk, she is. She's told Mrs. Sims to send a wet-nurse.'

'I suppose we'll have to agree to that, we can't let the baby suffer for her stubbornness.'

'Is there one available?' Joy asked.

'Yes. There's a girl in Keswick, Alice Preston, whose baby recently died. She's not wed, so she's happy to have a live-in situation. Mrs. Sims is seeing her today.'

'Maybe the father would like to have some say in the matter, if we knew who he was. Has Lily said anything yet about him?' asked Mrs. Frobisher.

Kitty shook her head. 'No. She's still as tight-lipped about that as ever.'

'Do you think she'd take any notice of you about feeding him, if you were to have a word with her?' Mrs. Frobisher asked Joy.

'I don't think so, but I'll try, if you like.'

'Would you, dear?' Kitty frowned. 'She won't listen to me.'

Nodding, Joy left the table and made her way to Lily's room.

'Well, it's all over now, and you didn't die, did you?' she said cheerfully as she went in and took a chair by Lily's bed.

'No, but I'm never going to have any more babies, I can tell you that.'

'They say you always forget the bad time you had, once you're over it.'

Lily shuddered. 'I won't, I can assure you. I'm just pleased it's all over, and I can forget about it and get on with my life.'

'And what about the baby?'

'What about him? Your mother's going to take him. He'll be much better off with her. I'd be a terrible mother.'

Joy thought she probably agreed, but she replied calmly. 'You owe him something. Surely you can at least feed him.'

'No, he's having a wet-nurse. I know you all want me to because you're hoping I'll change my mind about keeping him. But I won't, and that's final.'

Joy sighed. Lily had made up her mind, and nothing would change it. 'What about a name for him? If he's to become part of our family, we have to know what to call him.'

Lily shrugged. 'Call him Benjamin, then. That'll do.'

'Benjamin, I like that.'

'Hmm.' Her mouth set in a hard line. 'Now, would you please help me with something?'

Joy's eyebrows lifted. 'If I can. What is it?'

'Would you help me to tighten these binders Mrs. Sims put on? I intend to regain my figure as soon as possible.' Lily pushed back the bedclothes and raised her nightgown, revealing a flannel binder wound tightly about her stomach. 'She said it helps everything to go back into place, and that's what I want, as quickly as possible.' She undid the pins holding it. 'Here, take this end and pull it as tight as you can.'

Joy did as she asked. 'I suppose you're still hoping to marry Mr. Paget-Smythe. Is that what this is all about?'

Lily lifted her chin. 'No. I just want to get back to normal as quick as I can.'

Alice Preston came to see them, and Kitty liked her at once. Twenty-two years old and with a fresh, pretty face and dark curls, she had a cheerful personality and ready smile. Her baby had died at birth.

'I grieve for him,' she told Kitty, 'but I suppose in some ways it's for the best. His father ran off and left me high and dry when he found out about him. Told me he wasn't the marrying kind, though that's not what he said before. He had a honeyed tongue then, he did.'

'An all too familiar tale, I'm afraid.'

'Yes, so I've been told.' She hesitated, and then seemed to make up her mind. 'Mrs. Sims said you won't be staying here for much longer. My Da has a shop, and he doesn't want me around, and I've no chance of marrying in Keswick now, so I'd be happy to come travelling with you if you want. I've always wanted to see a bit of the world.'

'That would be wonderful, Alice. We'll be leaving for London in a couple of months, once the baby's old enough to travel. I'm not sure how long we'll stay there before we go home to Australia, but I'd make sure you were safely back here before we left.'

Alice's eyes opened wide. 'To Australia. I learnt some things about that place at school. Oh, I'd love to go with you, if you want me.'

Kitty was doubtful. 'Are you sure? It's a long way away, you know. And what would your father say?'

'Oh, he'd be pleased to be rid of me. He says I've disgraced the family.'

'What would you do once the baby has finished feeding? Would you want to come back here straight away?'

'I don't think so. There's nothing here for me.'

Kitty thought for a moment. It would solve some problems if Alice came with them.

'Then if you're sure I'll speak to your father, and if he's agreeable, you'll come with us. If it all works out well, you could stay on as the baby's nursemaid or I could find another position for you. And if you want to come back I'll pay your fare home. How does that sound?'

Alice beamed. 'It sounds like the answer to my prayer.'

Kitty had a satisfactory meeting with Alice's father and Alice became a part of the household.

It was six weeks later when Kitty received a letter from Rufe telling her that he and David had made some progress with regard to establishing Alfred Barron's credentials. '*There is no doubting the papers are genuine, but is he? That is the question. I will return immediately and if Lily and the baby are well enough to travel we will return to London next week, when I hope to be able to settle the matter for once and all. I have booked passages for us all on board the steamship Ophir that leaves Tilbury for Australia next month, whichever way matters go.*'

'Joy, Lily. Look at this,' Kitty waved the letter excitedly, and read it out to them when they came running. 'We must start to pack immediately. How fortunate we are that Alice is able to come with us for little Benjamin, so there's nothing to prevent us leaving. And we'll soon be on our way back home. I can't wait.'

Joy was anxious to know what Rufe had discovered. Would it save Redwoods? However, like her mother, she was anxious to return home, whatever the outcome.

'That's wonderful. I'll start my packing today.'

'Yes, I'll do the same.' Lily turned, and they went up the stairs.

The next morning, Lily was not at breakfast. When she hadn't appeared by ten o'clock, Joy went up and knocked on her door. When there was no answer, she knocked louder.

'Lily, it's me. What are you doing?' she called. When there was still no answer, she turned the knob and put her head around the door. The room was empty and the bed had not been slept in. Two envelopes, one addressed to Joy and the other to Rufe, were propped up on the mantelpiece. Joy tore hers open, read it, and raced down the stairs.

'Mother,' she called. 'Mother, Lily's not here. She's eloped with Mr. Paget-Smythe. They're going to Gretna Green first, and then she's going to America with him.'

A Liberated Woman

Chapter Thirty Two

Rufe paced back and forth, his fists clenched at his sides. 'How could she run off and leave the child? Has she no feelings at all?'

'It seems as if all her feelings are for Mr. Paget-Smythe,' Kitty replied.

'I can't believe it of a daughter of mine, she...' he broke off abruptly and stopped pacing. 'But, of course, she's her mother's daughter as well, isn't she? And Irene ran off and left *her* when she was only three.'

Kitty longed to comfort him but what could she say? Better to let it pass. 'What does she say about the baby in the letter?'

'That he will be better off with us. She wants us to bring him up as our own, and hopes he never learns about her.' He picked up the letter and thrust it at Kitty. 'Here, read it for yourself.'

Taking it, Kitty read. '*I am too young to raise a baby, I would be a terrible mother. Besides I have my whole life ahead of me, and Winston has begged me to come to America with him. He does not know about the baby and I hope he never finds out.*

We have been writing to each other ever since I left London and from his description of life in America, I know I will love it.

By the time you read this we will be married. Please do not try to find me and please try not to think too badly of me. I will write to you after we are settled.'

Kitty looked up. 'She makes it quite clear she doesn't want Benjamin.'

'Yes, and this makes it even clearer.' With a face like thunder he showed Kitty another piece of paper. 'Here she says that she gives up all claims to the baby, Benjamin Cavanagh, of her own free will, and offers him for adoption.'

Sadness filled Kitty, and she put her arms around Rufe. 'Try not to let it hurt you too much. She's young and thoughtless. Look at it this way – instead of a grandson, you now have a son. I believe we should legally adopt him, that way there can never be any doubt about our legal right to him. We'll take him home and bring him up as our own son. He'll never want for love or care. '

Rufe ran his fingers through his hair. 'Are you sure you're willing to take on a baby after all this time? It won't be easy.'

'Yes, I'm quite sure. After all, he's your flesh and blood. I'll love him like our own.'

Rufe sighed heavily. 'But can I?'

A sound from the crib took them both to stand beside it. The baby was awake, and his tiny fists flailed the air. Rufe extended a tentative finger. Benjamin stopped waving his arms, and his fingers curled around Rufe's finger, gripping it. His unblinking gaze stared straight into Rufe's face.

'You see,' Kitty whispered, 'he knows you, he feels the connection.'

'Perhaps that's a little fanciful.'

But Rufe stayed as he was until the baby relaxed his grip. Then, with the strain gone from his face, he turned and wrapped Kitty in his arms. 'My special lady, how did I ever manage all those years without you?'

'Very well.' She laughed.

And then, as his mouth came down on hers, there was no need for further words.

Joy looked out of the window from the room in the Savoy Hotel, and remembered how she had looked from a window of the house in Curzon Street when she first arrived in London.

She turned to Kitty. 'I find it hard to believe that it's less than two years since I arrived in England. I feel like a different person.'

'In many ways you are. So much has happened, it's changed you. You've grown up.'

'Yes, you're right. I was still a child when I arrived here. I remember how I thought I knew all about life, but, in reality, I knew nothing.'

'You've learnt the hard way, I'm afraid.'

'I'm just so happy that I learnt what sort of a man Charles Quincy is before I married him. Whatever could I have done if I hadn't?'

'Very little. You'd have probably put up with him, if you had to.'

'Of course, but people get divorced, don't they?'

'That causes such a scandal, here in England, but also in Australia, that few people are willing to risk the stigma. Better to put up with a bad marriage than be ostracised forever, that's the general belief.'

'But he beat me. How could any woman put up with that?'

'Some women have to. Life is very hard for a woman on her own, unless she has means of her own.'

Joy frowned, and spoke hesitantly. 'Mother, did Father ever beat you?'

Kitty bit her lip, her mind in a whirl. This new Joy, now so much a woman, deserved a truthful answer. Yet she was reluctant to destroy, any further, her cherished illusions of William.

She took a deep breath. 'He did raise his hand in anger to me, on one or two occasions. But, what you must remember is that, in those days, it was considered acceptable, by many, for a husband to, shall we say, discipline his wife, if she angered him.'

'How could that be excused?'

'Before the Act was passed that allowed married women to own property, a woman owned nothing. She was totally dependent on her husband. Whatever she owned at marriage became his property, and she became, in effect, his chattel.'

'That's monstrous.' Joy paused, as she pondered the ramifications of what she heard. 'So that's why you always wanted me to have Redwoods?'

'Yes.'

'I had to come all the way over here to realise how much I care for Redwoods,' Joy said slowly, 'and now it seems as if it might be too late.'

Kitty's heart contracted. 'Yes, it seems that way.'

Several days later Rufe asked Kitty, Joy and Mrs. Frobisher to join him in the sitting room in their suite, for a discussion of future plans.

'Please make yourselves comfortable, as we may be here for some time,' he told them. 'I think a glass of Madeira for you ladies is in order.'

After pouring their drinks and passing them around, he poured a whisky for himself, and was about to take a seat when there was a knock at the door.

'Ah, we have guests.' He crossed to the door and opened it. Two men stood outside. 'Good afternoon, Sir Alex. And you too, Mr. Barron.' He held the door open wide. 'Please come in.'

Joy jumped up from her seat and went quickly to her grandfather, a smile on her lips. 'Grandfather. What a lovely surprise to see you.'

He smiled down at her, and bent to kiss her.

'I'm delighted, Joy. I have missed you.'

'I've missed you too, Grandfather. I've missed our talks.'

'As I have.' He turned toward the young man next to him. 'Allow me to introduce Mr. Alfred Barron.'

Joy held out her hand, but the newcomer ignored it with a surly nod and a muttered, 'How'd you do,' before turning away.

'Please take a seat, gentlemen.' Rufe indicated the chairs. 'Now, can I get you a drink? We may have a few moments to wait until our other guests arrive. What will it be? Whisky, Sir Alex?'

'Thank you.'

'And for you, Mr. Barron? The same?'

'Yes.'

As Rufe busied himself with the drinks, Joy wondered what this was all about. Had Rufe brought them here to explain that Redwoods would pass to this person, who was her half-brother? She felt like crying, but there was no way she would let this loathsome creature see how upset she was.

She looked across at Kitty. Her face was white, and her hands were clenched in her lap.

Rufe passed the drinks, and then took out his watch and checked it.

'Our other guests should be here soon,' he told them, and at that moment another knock at the door had him across the room again, opening it.

Joy was surprised to see David standing outside, accompanied by a woman whom she had not seen before. She was middle-aged, a comfortable-looking woman with plump cheeks and faded good looks.

'David,' Rufe exclaimed. 'And Mrs. Campbell. How good to see you both. Please come in.' He stood back for them to enter. 'Now, before I offer you refreshments, allow me to introduce you. David, I think you've already met everyone, but Mrs. Campbell has not.'

Rufe went around the room, introducing everyone. When he came to Alfred Barron, he paused.

'Mrs. Campbell, perhaps you know Alfred Barron?'

She shook her head. 'No, can't say as I do.'

With the introductions out of the way and drinks handed around, Rufe took the floor. 'Now, some of you are probably wondering what we're all doing here today, and it's because I want you to hear Mrs. Campbell's story. I think you'll all be interested.'

Joy glanced around. Mother and Mrs. Frobisher looked puzzled, Grandfather was relaxed, David looked pleased about something, and Alfred Barron sat up straight, his eyes narrow as he listened.

'Please start, Mrs. Campbell,' Rufe nodded encouragement to her.

She took a sip of Madeira, and cleared her throat.

'Well,' she started, casting a glance at Sir Alex, who sat upright in his chair. 'When I was a girl I went into service with an aristocratic family. Their youngest son was only a couple of years older than me, and after a while he sometimes sought me out and spoke to me. Then he asked to meet me on my day off. I knew I shouldn't agree, but I thought he was lovely, and so I went. We started meeting regularly like, on my day off.' She paused to take another sip of Madeira.

'One thing led to another and soon I was madly in love with him. He started talking about marriage, and I told him he was daft, that it would never be allowed. But he said we could go to Gretna Green and marry, and once we were married there'd be nothing anyone could do about it. But he was wrong. He didn't know that marriages can be annulled. Neither of us thought of such a thing, but that's what happened. His father arranged it. We married, but our marriage was annulled.'

'He was hauled back home and I...well, I didn't have a job anymore, did I? So, I went to stay with my sister. But he searched me out, and started calling to see me, and it was on again. My sister was understanding. She used to leave us alone together, and it wasn't long before I found I was with child.' Mrs. Campbell paused, raising the glass to wet her lips before continuing.

'After our son was born, he started gambling to try and get extra money for me. Then he stopped coming so often. I think it all got too much for him.' She twisted the glass by its stem. 'Anyway, one day we had a barney, and I accused him of not wanting us anymore. He broke down and cried and said he'd still marry me if he could, but he knew they'd never let him, and what was the use? The next day, I went to the house to see his father, to try and persuade him to let us marry once he knew about the babe, or even do something to help us out. But I saw his mother instead. She offered me a thousand pounds if I promised never to see him again, or to bother them, and I accepted.'

Here she looked rather defiantly at Sir Alexander.

'I could see it was no use, you see. So I took the money. It wasn't long after that when he came to see me again, and told me he was going away, maybe for a long time. He gave me a paper he said was his will, and told me he'd left all his estate to our son. That was the last time I ever saw him.'

'Will you tell us what your name was back then,' Rufe asked gently.

'It was Cora Hassell.'

Joy felt the dread that had been building inside her explode into a thousand pieces, each one burning into her soul. She heard a gasp that she knew came from Mother.

'And was your lover William Barron?'

'Yes.'

He gestured to Alfred, sitting impassively in his seat. 'Then this is your son, Alfred Barron?'

Cora looked at him.

'No. I've never seen that man in my life.'

Alfred leapt up from his seat. 'She's lying. That's not Cora Hassell. That's not my mother. It's someone they've planted to do me out of my inheritance.'

Rufe turned to him. 'I think you'd better sit down and listen to the rest.'

He subsided into the chair. 'It's all lies. They don't want me to have what's mine, that's what it is.'

'If this is not your son, then where is he now?' Rufe asked Cora.

'He died when he was three years old, poor little mite.'

Alfred bounded from his chair. 'Lies. All Lies. It's a conspiracy, don't listen to her. They're trying to do me out of my birthright, can't you see?' He rounded on Kitty. 'It's you, isn't it? You don't want to give up your fortune, this Redwoods place in Australia.

Worth a packet it is, I've been told. Well, you won't succeed. I've got friends, I have. My friend'll help me.'

Rufe spun around, his eyebrows raised. 'So who is this friend?' he asked, his voice smooth.

'Never you mind. You'll see.'

Rufe shrugged as he turned back to Cora. 'So your son, yours and William Barron's, died when he was three years old, you say?'

Cora's lips were set in a straight line. 'Yes. And much as it's a long time ago now, it still grieves me. I won't see his passing bantered around now, thank you very much.'

'Mrs. Campbell, I'm sorry. I don't want to cause you further sorrow, but I don't want to see a shyster swindle William's daughter out of her legacy. You have some evidence of your son's death, I believe?'

'Yes.' She fumbled in her reticule and withdrew a paper, which she handed to Rufe. 'Here's his death certificate.'

Kitty leant across then to take Joy's hand and squeeze it, and Joy saw tears in her eyes. Her own heart was beating hard and her throat was choked.

Rufe took the paper from Cora and scanned it. 'This records the death of Alfred William Barron, age three years. Cause of death, smallpox. Mother's name, Cora Hassell. Father's name, William Barron.' He looked up. 'So, what do you have to say to this?' he asked Alfred, who had turned a greenish-white colour. 'I rather think the game's up, don't you? I think you should tell us what it's all about.'

Joy let out a cry as Alfred, showing an amazing turn of speed, leapt from his chair and bolted for the door. But David was faster. As the impostor put his hand to the doorknob, David launched a flying tackle and, grabbing him around the waist, brought him down to the floor. Rolling him over, he straddled his chest.

'What do you want me to do with him?' he asked, looking at Rufe, who had also sprung to his feet.

'Return him to his chair. He has some questions to answer.'

David lifted his hapless victim from the floor and dumped him unceremoniously back in the chair.

Rufe crossed the room to stand alongside Cora. 'Thank you for coming here today, Mrs. Campbell. It's not our business, I know, but I think we'd all like to hear the rest of your story, if you don't mind, just for our peace of mind. What did you do after Alfred died?'

'I met Dougal Campbell not long after. By this time I realised how foolish I'd been to ever think of marriage to William. It could never have happened; our worlds were too far apart. I loved Dougal for his good, steady qualities. We married and returned to his home town, Edinburgh. With the money Her Ladyship gave me...' she stopped and looked at Sir Alexander, inclining her head in his direction before continuing. 'We opened a little drapery and dressmaking business. I've always been good at fine sewing, and we've done all right.'

Joy felt ashamed all over again at the thought of how much unhappiness her father had caused this woman. Thank goodness life seemed to have turned out all right for her in the end.

Rufe placed his hand on Cora's shoulder.

'Mrs. Campbell, I can't tell you how grateful I am to you for coming all the way from Edinburgh to tell us the truth today. You've saved William's daughter from losing her rightful heritage to an unscrupulous impostor.'

'That's all right. I wouldn't want to see that happen.' She held out her hand for the paper in Rufe's hand. 'I'll just take that, and I'll be on my way.'

As she took the paper, Sir Alexander rose to his feet.

'Mrs. Campbell, I would be honoured if you'd stay and join us for tea.'

'Thank you, sir, but I'd best be on my way.'

He crossed to stand looking down at her, and Rufe moved away.

'I never knew—about the child, I mean. My wife never told me. Had I known, I would have offered you both protection.'

She nodded as she rose from the chair. 'I believe you.'

'If there's anything I can do for you now...'

'No thank you sir. The time for that's gone.'

'Yes, I see. Please allow me to escort you outside.'

Taking her by the elbow, he guided her to the door.

As he opened it and they passed through, Joy heard Grandfather say, 'I am sorry...' before the door closed behind them.

Chapter Thirty Three

The room stayed silent after Sir Alexander and Mrs. Campbell left, until he returned and slipped into his seat a few moments later, nodding to Rufe.

Rufe turned his attention to the self-styled Alfred Barron, and stood over him.

'Now, we'll have no more nonsense here.' His tone was menacing. 'First, what's you real name?'

Silence.

'Would you sooner I ask the police to find out?'

'It's Arthur Jones, if you must know.'

'That may be right, or it may not, but it'll do for now. So, Jones, what prompted you to try and carry out this fraud?'

'You'll get nothing from me.'

'If I don't, the police will. I'm going to advise Sir Alexander to press charges if you don't co-operate. You know what that means, don't you? Does Newgate appeal to you?'

Jones slid down in his chair, his face twisting with hate. 'What do you want to know?'

'Where did you get the papers?'

'I found them.'

Rufe looked at David, and gave a slight nod.

In two strides David crossed the room. Reaching down he grabbed Jones and pulled him upright, shaking him like a terrier shaking a rat.

'Don't lie to us.' He thrust his face to within inches of Jones'. 'Do you want me to send the ladies from the room while I thrash the living daylights out of you?' He shook him again. 'Do you?'

Goggle-eyed, Jones screamed. 'Let me go. I'll tell you.'

David tossed him back onto the chair.

'Start talking. And no lies.'

Rufe took over. 'We'll start again. Where did you get the papers?'

'Someone gave 'em to me.'

'Who?'

'His name was Brown, he said.'

'How did it come about?'

'It was in the pub. I was just having a drink, quiet like, when this geezer came up and started talking to me.'

'And?'

'Well, he said he had a plan to make some money, and he needed someone to help him. It was big money, and it'd be a big job he said, but easy, and he'd split the profits with me.'

'What did you have to do?'

'I was to take the papers and pretend I was this Alfred Barron. When I learnt it was to do with a toff like Sir Alexander, I said I'd never get away with it. But I've had some education, and he told me I didn't need to act like a toff, just like myself, 'cause this Alfred's mother, who was dead, wasn't a toff, just a maid.'

'And what was the plan?'

'He told me all about this big estate down in Australia, Redwoods, how it had all these trees that were worth a fortune. It'd belonged to this William, the son, who'd died out there. Worth an absolute fortune, he said. I was to claim it, and when I got it, we'd sell it and split the dosh.'

'What else did he tell you?'

'The whole story, so's I'd know what to say. How William and Cora got together and what happened to them, and all the past history.'

'How did he know all this?'

'I don't know. Said he'd heard the story from someone.'

'From whom?'

Jones shook his head. 'He never said. Though he did say one day that it's interesting the stories you can hear when you're talking in a pub. Something made me think he'd got it from a woman sometime.'

A sudden gasp from Mrs. Frobisher made everyone look at her. She had her hand pressed to her mouth, and her eyes were opened wide.

'What is it Mrs. Frobisher?' Rufe asked her.

'Could I have a word with you in private, sir?'

'Certainly.'

As Mrs. Frobisher left her seat Kitty rose and followed them outside into the next room.

'What is it, Mrs. Frobisher?' Rufe asked again.

'I didn't want to say in there, but I fear I might have been indiscreet. Unintentionally, of course.'

'Go on.'

'I repeated some gossip to a gentleman I've met here. Well, I just started off telling him about Joy being presented at Court, I was so proud of her, you know.'

'Yes, and then what?'

'Well, this gentleman, his name was Brown too, same name as that Jones said. I thought at the time it was funny, but it couldn't be the same one, could it now? There must be hundreds of Browns...'

'Get on with it. In plain words, just as it happened.'

Mrs. Frobisher then related the whole story of how she repeated Davis's tale about William.

'Did he know who you were talking about? Which family?'

'Well, yes. He knew who I worked for and he was interested, you know, to hear a story about how the other half lives. I didn't mean any harm. It was just talking with a friend.'

'Did he ask you questions?'

'Yes, come to think of it, he did.'

Kitty had been listening with growing apprehension.

'Rufe, I have a horrible feeling about this. It started when I heard Jones talk about Redwoods. I wondered how anyone over here would know all about it.' She turned to Mrs. Frobisher. 'You say this man's name was Brown. What do you know about him?'

'His name's George Brown and he's a widower. He's from Somerset. He has a drapery store there, and he was up in London to buy stock.'

'How do you know all this?'

'He told me.'

'What did he look like?'

Mrs. Frobisher shrugged. 'He was just ordinary, tall, had some grey streaks in his hair.'

'Did he ever talk about Australia?'

'Oh yes. He said he'd been out there, spent a lot of time there some years ago. Liked to talk about it.'

'Where did you meet him?'

'In the Savoy Hotel. It was straight after we arrived in London, that awful day when Joy told you about Lily's condition. I was waiting alone downstairs in the coffee salon, and he was at the next table, and he struck up a conversation. He recognised my Australian accent, you see, and he offered to buy me another cup of coffee. I wouldn't allow that, of course. But I was so worried about everything, and it took my mind of it to pass a word or two. After all, he was staying in the Savoy, and you expect anyone staying there to be respectable, don't you? And he said he was lonely, and there seemed no harm in it.'

A knot of fear twisted in Kitty's stomach.

'Rufe, it's Craddock. I'm sure it is.'

'You could be right. Come back in, and

e'll see what we can find out.'

'You won't tell Sir Alex about Davis, will you?' Mrs. Frobisher asked anxiously. 'I don't want to get her into trouble. She was only passing the time of day.'

'I don't know, we'll have to see. I hope this will be a lesson to you not to gossip, Mrs. Frobisher. You see the trouble it can cause?'

'Oh I do, Mr. Cavanagh, I do. In future I'll be tight-lipped as an oyster, I promise.'

'I hope so.'

When they returned to the room David drew Rufe aside. 'I've been trying to find out more about the mysterious Mr. Brown, but it seems he doesn't know much. Not where he lives or how to contact him. They always meet in the Old Bell Hotel, in Fleet Street. He goes in on a day they arrange and waits until Brown shows up. Sometimes he has to wait a couple of hours, but Brown gives him a sovereign if he waits more than an hour.'

Rufe shook his head. 'A wily bird, he's obviously done this sort of thing before. Did you find out when they're due to meet again?'

'Yes. Tomorrow morning.'

'Then I think we'll be there. I don't think we'll find out much more here today. I'll see what's to be done with him.'

A brief conference with Sir Alexander resulted in Jones being sent on his way, with instructions to meet Mr. Brown the next day as arranged, but to say nothing to alert him unless he wished to spend the next twenty years in prison.

The next morning David took a seat at the bar in the Old Bell in Fleet Street. With a pint of lager at his elbow he began scribbling on a paper in front of him, copying the actions of the journalists who frequented the pub.

Across the road Rufe sat at a table in a tearoom, with his collar turned up and cap pulled down. From where he sat he had a clear view of the door opposite, and he, too, wrote industriously.

A little later Jones entered the pub and took his seat at the bar. After ordering a pint of ale he looked over his shoulder nervously then switched his gaze to David, who sat close by, ignoring him.

Soon after, Craddock sauntered down the street, keeping a close watch as he approached the Old Bell. When he reached the doorway he stopped and bent to fiddle with a shoe lace, giving himself time to scan the street in both directions before entering.

Opening the door and going inside he looked around. There were several morning drinkers, including a fair sprinkling of journalists indulging in a morning thirst-quencher as they prepared the copy for their papers. Jones sat with his back to him, but he turned his head at the sound of the opening door, and raised his hand in greeting.

'So how are things coming along,' Craddock asked, sliding onto the seat next to him. 'Ingratiating yourself with the old boy, are you?'

'It's not that easy, you know,' Jones replied, fiddling with a jacket button. 'I don't think he likes me.'

'He doesn't have to like you. He just has to believe you.'

Jones shifted on his seat, throwing a quick glance to one side. 'The papers should be proof enough, shouldn't they?'

'They will be if you play your part, and don't make him suspicious.'

'It's not that easy,' Jones whined, as he stopped twisting the button and picked at a fingernail.

Craddock frowned. 'What's the matter with you today?' he asked sharply.

'Nothing.' Jones shook his head vehemently. 'Why would anything be the matter?'

'You're as edgy as a virgin on her wedding night. If something's happened you'd better tell me, or...'

He broke off as Jones twitched his head, casting a worried look around the bar.

Craddock narrowed his eyes. 'What are you looking for?'

'Nothing.' Jones cringed. 'Nothing, I tell you.'

Craddock scanned the bar, noting each man in turn. As his gaze rested on the young scribe two seats away, the man looked up and turned his head, and for a brief instant their eyes locked, before the other put down his pen.

Craddock's frown deepened.

'What the...'

He broke off and spun around to scrutinise the rest of the room. A serving wench with a tray of glasses was crossing the floor behind him. At that moment the door to the street opened and Rufe entered.

Craddock sprang from his seat and lunged at the waitress, grabbing her and shoving her towards Rufe. With a scream she staggered, the tray and glasses flying in all directions as she clutched Rufe to try and save herself from falling. Craddock ducked around them and bolted for the door.

'Stop him,' Rufe shouted to David, as he tried to disentangle himself. 'It's Craddock. Don't let him get away.'

Wrenching the door open Craddock dashed out into the street, with David only feet behind him. A brewery dray stood outside while the driver unloaded kegs onto the footpath. Craddock tipped one of the kegs onto its side and, as his pursuer charged through the door shouting at him to stop, he pushed with all his might and sent the keg rolling straight at him. It hit David in the legs and knocked him over, just as Rufe came through the door at full pelt.

Craddock sent a second keg crashing after the first, tripping Rufe as he tried to dodge both the keg and David, who scrambled to his feet. David cursed and, as Rufe regained his balance, calling on the lorry driver to grab him, Craddock dashed away.

Their shouts and the curses of the lorry driver followed their quarry up the street, causing passers-by to stare, but no one tried to stop Craddock. He had given himself a few seconds start but Rufe and David were not far behind.

Craddock streaked away, pushing through the pedestrians, until he came to a narrow alleyway between two shops. He ducked down it and raced to the first corner. Here he turned into an even narrower laneway, with Rufe and David close on his heels.

The alley snaked around behind buildings, and Craddock, running furiously, followed it until he reached a gate leading into a stable yard. Opening the gate, he slammed it behind him as he disappeared into the yard. Only seconds behind him, David flung himself against the gate but was brought up short.

'It's locked.'

'Bolted from the other side. Here, I'll boost you up, see if you can unbolt it.'

David climbed onto his clasped hands and leant over the top of the gate. Reaching over he slid the bolt back, then jumped down as Rufe crashed the gate open. But the yard was empty.

Sprinting across to the other side of the yard Rufe wrenched open another gate. It led onto a busy street, packed now with a lunch-time crowd. Craddock was nowhere to be seen.

'The slippery bastard's got away,' David lamented, clenching his fists.

'Yes, he's given us the slip. But at least his brilliant scheme to gain control of Redwoods has come undone. We've beaten him there.'

'Well, let's hope it's the last we see of him.'

'I doubt that.'

Chapter Thirty Four

Later that afternoon Rufe and Kitty were seated together in the sitting room of their suite in the Savoy Hotel. Rufe had just finished relating the details of the morning's events.

'I wish you'd been able to catch Craddock and put him behind bars again, where he belongs.' Kitty twisted her hands together. 'Who knows what else he's going to do to try and harm us?'

'We'll soon be on our way home, well away from him, my love, so don't worry.'

A knock at the door brought Kitty to her feet.

'David, come on in and take a seat. Rufe has just been telling me about this morning.'

David sat, nodding to his uncle. 'It was pretty exciting for a while, but we're mortified we didn't catch Craddock.'

Kitty sighed. 'He's a slippery character. Let's hope it's the last we'll hear of him, although I doubt it, unfortunately.'

Another knock sounded, and Rufe sprang up to open the door to Joy and Sir Alexander. After greetings were over, Rufe produced a bottle of champagne.

'I think we have something to celebrate.'

Joy clapped her hands. 'Yes. Thanks to you, our worry about Redwoods is over. It's safe again. That's definitely worth champagne.'

While Rufe poured the drinks and handed them around, Kitty studied her daughter. The worry had left her face, but there was still a sadness in her eyes that had been there ever since she came to Keswick. The loss of one's first love is always heartbreaking, she reflected, and Joy had the added anguish of betrayal by Quincy and her grandmother. She longed to ease her daughter's pain but knew that only time, or another love, could do that. Thank God she'd not lost Redwoods as well.

She raised her glass. 'Here's to Redwoods. Long may it flourish.'

'Amen,' said Joy, putting the glass to her lips. 'And now I'm bursting to know how you discovered that the supposed Alfred Barron was a fraud. How did you find out that Cora was still alive, and how on earth did you find her?'

'It took a lot of digging, from both David and me. All we had to go on was that Cora had told Lady Barron she was staying with her sister, but we had no idea who her sister was, or where she was. All we had to go on was the address in London of where the baby was born, taken from the birth certificate.'

Rufe paused to drink from his glass before continuing.

'So that's where we started. We went to the address, in Covent Garden, and found it was a corner shop with a residence above. The current owner had been there for ten years, but we were looking back almost twenty-five years, and he had no idea who would have been there then. He remembered that the owner before him, who was called Smith, had been there for about eight years, but we had to go back still further.' He paused. 'Why don't you take over now, David?'

David nodded. 'We decided then that the only thing we could do was to try and find someone who could remember who'd been in the shop in 1875, so we started talking to people, knocking on doors.' He shook his head with a grimace. 'Not easy. It took us three days before we found an old woman who remembered there'd been a couple by the name of Brewster there. She remembered them because she'd been quite friendly with them. She also remembered Mrs. Brewster had a sister, who'd had a baby while she lived with them. So now we had a name, but she couldn't remember where they'd gone when they left, but she thought it was to Brighton, because the husband hadn't been well and his doctor recommended the sea air.'

Rufe took up the story. 'So off we went to Brighton. We figured that they'd probably go into a shop again, so we started digging, and sure enough we struck gold, we found the Brewster's. And we learnt that Cora had met Dougal Campbell and gone to Edinburgh, and the sisters had not met since, although they corresponded occasionally. But,' he paused, 'we also learned that when Cora left, she left behind a packet of personal papers. And that only recently a man came, saying he was a friend of Cora's and that she'd asked him to collect the papers for her, saying she needed them.'

Kitty gasped. 'Craddock.'

'Yes, he must have found her, and bluffed her into thinking he was genuine. She'd have no reason not to believe him, and she handed them over. The next part, to find Cora, was easy, because

Mrs. Brewster gave us her address in Edinburgh. When we called on her, and she heard our story, she was willing to come to London with us.'

'So now we know the full story,' Joy said.

Kitty smiled. 'You've saved Redwoods for us. And Joy and I are both immensely grateful.'

'Yes indeed, I'd have been devastated if we'd lost it,' Joy added. 'You were very clever and resourceful. Thank you both.'

David smiled across at her. 'Think nothing of it, shrimp. Just ask me and I'll slay dragons for you, or fight lions, or anything like that. Any time at all.'

Joy tossed her head. 'Really David, will you please stop calling me shrimp? And can't you ever be serious?'

He grinned, his eyes twinkling. 'Not if I can help it.'

'If you two can stop scrapping for a moment,' Rufe intervened, reaching for the champagne bottle, 'perhaps we can all have another glass of champagne and talk about the arrangements for our return to Australia. Including taking the new horses back home.'

Joy's eyes shone. 'Can I please see the filly before we go?'

'Of course. We can go to the stables tomorrow, if you like. I want to check on the other horses we've bought, as well.'

'Have you thought about the offer I made regarding the filly?' Kitty asked. 'Now that you'll be coming back home with us.'

'Yes I have, and I would love to have the filly. I have a special reason now, you see...' her voice trailed off as she remembered how Charles had received her news. Would they feel the same, or that she was foolish to even think of such a thing? She looked around the room. Everybody seemed to be waiting to hear what she had to say.

'What is it, my dear?' Grandfather asked. 'Please tell us.'

Joy felt her face growing warmer, wondering if they would disapprove.

'Well, you see, we've talked before, Mother and Uncle Rufe and me, about breeding horses at Redwoods, now that the timber is becoming less, and, being here, going the races, has made me realise that's what I want to do. I want to breed thoroughbred racehorses.' Her excitement at actually saying the words overcame her initial diffidence, and she felt a rush of confidence. The words came tumbling out now. 'In fact, I've made up my mind that I want to breed a champion. I know it's a big ambition but I'm determined to do it, even if it takes me the rest of my life. So I want to get started as soon as we go home.' Sitting back, she took a deep breath.

'Well, my dear, if that's what you want to do, then I'm sure you'll do it,' Grandfather said. 'And I understand your eagerness to begin, for it won't be an easy task, nor is it likely to be one that you'll accomplish quickly.'

Joy was grateful for his understanding. 'I know that. I'm prepared to work hard.'

'How do you propose to begin?'

'Well, I'll have the filly, and Mother has always said Redwoods is for me, so I'm sure I can use it, can't I, Mother?'

'You can do more than that. From now on you can have half the income from the timber sales and the mill. There'll be a lot of expenses to start with, but hopefully that will cover them.'

Joy felt her excitement building. 'Thank you, that's wonderful.'

'A most generous offer, Kitty.' Grandfather said.

'William established Redwoods in the first place. I'm sure it's what he would have wished.'

'But your business acumen made it what it is today.' Mother acknowledged the compliment with a nod of her head and a smile, and Grandfather continued. 'I would also like to contribute something to the start of this enterprise, Joy. I would like you to choose, with your stepfather's guidance, a quality mare to add to your initial stock.'

Joy felt her heart would explode with happiness.

'Thank you, thank you.' Jumping from her chair she rushed, first to Grandfather and then to Mother, to throw her arms around them and hug as hard as she could.

'Hey, don't break my bones.' Mother yelped.

Grandfather just sat smiling at her, and she thought his eyes looked quite misty, but perhaps she was wrong.

'So, we'll go to the stables tomorrow,' Rufe told them.

'I would like to come as well, if you're agreeable,' Grandfather said. 'I enjoy looking at good horseflesh, and I'll arrange to have my carriage call for you.'

The head groom met them in the stable yard the next day.

"Ello, Mr. Cavanagh, come to see yer 'orses, 'ave yer?'

'Yes, that's right, Duffy. Doing all right, are they?'

'Sure fing.'

'We'd like to see the filly first, please.'

'I'll 'ave 'er brought out fer yer.' He called to a lad nearby. 'Ere, Alby, bring out Mr. Cavanagh's 'orses. The filly first. Jump to it, lad.'

The boy scampered away and returned a few moments later, leading the filly. She was chestnut in colour, with a lighter mane and a white blaze down her face. Her tail was tipped with white, and she had white socks on her four legs.

She stood quite still as Joy approached her, speaking softly. 'Aren't you a pretty girl? You and I are going to be friends, aren't we? You're coming home to Redwoods with me. You'll love it there.' Standing quietly for a few seconds, Joy looked into the softest brown eyes she had seen in a horse, before reaching out her hand to stroke her. Whinnying, the filly jerked her head back. Joy dropped her hand and took the halter from the lad.

'Don't be frightened, I'm not going to hurt you,' she said, still speaking softly. The filly stood still again, ears pricked and watching Joy as she moved closer. Reaching out her free hand again, Joy stroked her neck. The horse shook her head once, and then stood still. Joy rubbed her ears. 'There now, you like that, don't you?' The horse snickered, and, dipping her head, nuzzled against Joy.

Joy looked into her liquid eyes, and her heart tumbled with love. She led the filly around the yard, twice, speaking to her all the while, before reluctantly relinquishing her to the stable boy to be returned to her stall.

Then Duffy ordered the boy to bring out the other horses. First came the mare that Kitty had bought, a handsome chestnut who had won the prestigious Oaks two years before. Then Starlight, Rufe's magnificent black stallion, followed by a mare with good blood lines that David had bought.

All three looked to be blooming with good health. The prognosis for them to make a safe trip to Australia was reckoned to be excellent, but a long sea voyage was always risky for such highly-strung animals. Rufe had found an experienced and reliable handler, Josh Frazer, to accompany them to Australia, and he was willing to remain and take up employment at Riverside when they arrived.

After Rufe arranged for Josh to spend the remaining time in England at this stable with the horses, he turned to Sir Alexander.

'I believe there's a horse here that you wish to inspect, with a view to purchasing. Am I right, sir?'

'You are. A mare whose blood line goes back to Iambic, I understand.'

'Yes, sir, that'd be Gay Lass,' Duffy said. 'As good a bit o' 'orseflesh as yer ever likely t'see, believe me. 'Ere, Alby, bring out Gay Lass fer 'is lordship. 'Op to it, now, lad.'

When Alby returned with the mare, a handsome bay, Grandfather took Joy's arm.

'Come, my dear, we'll inspect her together.'

The horse stood docilely while they walked around her, and Joy watched as Grandfather ran his hands over the mare's back, and down each of her legs. Straightening up, he nodded.

'Well, she seems sound. What do you think? Is she to your liking?'

'Oh yes.' Joy could hardly contain her excitement. 'We talked about it last night and her bloodlines mean she'd be a perfect mare to put to Starlight, don't they?'

'Yes, they do. With her and your filly, you'll have the nucleus of a family that could give you your champion.'

Joy felt a surge of affection for this man whom she had come to know so late in his life, and who had shown her such warmth and generosity. She gazed up into his face. 'I don't know how to thank you.'

'You can thank me by raising this champion that you want so badly. I hope it will happen in my lifetime, but you must be prepared to wait. There will always be many others striving toward the same goal.'

'I know. But I intend to put every ounce of my energy into it.'

'You'll succeed, I'm sure of that. But you must take care not to focus on your goal to the exclusion of everything else. There are other things in life that are important too.'

'I suppose so.' Joy frowned. 'But I can't imagine anything else as important to me.'

Grandfather smiled down at her. 'People are important too.'

Her brow cleared. 'Of course. And I'm lucky to have Mother and Rufe and my other grandparents.'

'They're all fine people, and you'll always be able to rely on them, but you may need others, to give you a balance in life.' He paused. 'David Cavanagh impresses me. He's a fine young man.'

Before Joy could recover from her surprise sufficiently to ask him what he meant he tucked her hand into his arm. 'Now, let us rejoin the others, and tell them you have an extra horse to take back home.'

As they walked back to the little group Joy looked at David, wondering what to make of Grandfather's remark, and saw he was watching her. As they approached his gaze caught and held hers with such intensity that Joy's step faltered. Why was David regarding her like that? It couldn't be because he had any personal interest in her, he'd always made it quite clear he regarded her as a baby.

Chapter Thirty Five

On the day of their departure Joy stood on the docks at Tilbury with the rest of their party looking at the *SS Ophir*, the ship that was to carry them across the oceans to Australia. In place of sails it had two funnels, already sending forth a trail of smoke as the furnaces were readied for sailing.

Mrs. Frobisher voiced what was in many minds as she turned to Kitty, who stood alongside her.

'I find it hard to believe that ship will be able to sail all the way home safely. It's so huge, and made of steel they say, so it must surely sink before it goes beyond England's shores.' She shook her head. 'Why, it's at least twice the size of the ship we came here on.'

'It is amazing, isn't it?' Kitty replied. 'But Rufe assures me it is safe.' She turned to her husband. 'How big did you say it is?'

'It's just on five hundred feet long. She dwarfs the sailing ships, but she's made several crossing since she was launched four years ago. I promise you, it's quite safe.'

'Well, if you say so...' Mrs. Frobisher still sounded doubtful.

'I do. And now I suggest we all go on board and find our cabins.'

After settling her belongings into her cabin, which she shared with Mrs. Frobisher, Joy walked around the main deck and found her way to the saloon. The opulence of the ship astounded her. The saloon was much larger than the one on the *Miranda* that had carried them over here. It was decorated with timber wall panelling and intricately carved figures, and, high above, ran a gallery with an ornate carved ceiling.

Grandfather had come to see them off, and he was now seated with Rufe, Kitty and David in the saloon. He rose from his seat as Joy approached, kissed her on both cheeks, and put his arms around her. After they hugged he stepped back, and smiled at her with sad eyes.

'My dear girl, I'm going to miss you terribly.'

Joy swallowed a lump in her throat. 'And I'll miss you too, Grandfather, very, very much. I wish we didn't live so far away.'

'Ah yes, the cruelty of distance. I only hope that you may be able to visit again one day.' He raised an eyebrow. 'Who knows? You may bring a horse to challenge for the Gold Cup.'

'Wouldn't that be something?' She grinned. 'An Australian horse challenging for the Cup.'

A half smile lifted a corner of his mouth. 'You might make it your goal.'

'I will, especially for you.'

'Then I shall make a point of staying alive to see it.'

'You'd better, or...'

Joy was cut off in mid-sentence as a seaman, clad in white uniform and cap, came through the saloon chanting, 'All ashore that's going ashore, all ashore that's going ashore.'

'Ah, time for me to go, I'm afraid.' Grandfather clasped his arms around her again. 'Take care, my darling girl,' he told her, as he stepped away from her.

'You too Grandfather,' she said, with a choke in her voice.

He walked back to the others and shook hands with Rufe and David, then he kissed Kitty on both cheeks before turning to head for the gangway.

David came over then and offered Joy his arm.

'Come on, shrimp, I'll escort you to the rail so you can wave goodbye to your grandpa.'

Joy was glad of his cheerfulness. It helped to dispel her sorrow at parting, and she blinked her eyes and slipped her arm through his.

'Yes, let's go and find a good spot.'

When they had a good vantage point, close to the gangway, they stood and watched as Grandfather reached the wharf, turned around, and stood waving.

David put his hand in his pocket and pulled out a large roll of red streamer paper. 'Here, I brought you a streamer,' he told Joy. He held it aloft and waved it, and Grandfather nodded, holding out his hands. David unwound a few feet of the ribbon and then, holding on to the end, he drew back his arm and threw the roll through the air. Grandfather caught it, and David passed the end to Joy.

'Here you are. Don't let it go, will you? I don't want to have to jump overboard for it.'

Other streamers went sailing through the air from all along the rail as passengers threw them to friends on the wharf below, and soon there were dozens of brightly coloured streamers reaching down from the ship's rail to those below who had come to see them off.

The gangway was raised with a rattling of chains. A minute later Joy jumped as the ship's funnel sounded an ear-splitting blast. The ship began to move slowly away from the wharf.

'Good bye,' she shouted, but she knew Grandfather couldn't hear her above the din of everyone shouting, and another blast from the funnel. She blew a kiss then and waved. He waved back, playing out the streamer as the ship moved away.

Streamers started to break, and others went sailing through the air to replace them, until there was a tangle of paper ribbons, some stretched out and some landing in the sea, in the ever-widening gap between wharf and ship. But Grandfather stood there holding onto his and waving, until theirs was one of the last streamers left.

The ship was moving quickly now and the streamer broke, leaving Joy holding a brightly coloured strip of paper hanging from her hand. She stayed by the rail, waving it, until the ship turned, with one final blast, to head down the river to the sea. And the wharf and everyone on it disappeared from sight.

The next morning Joy woke early and immediately thought about the horses. How were they? Were they adapting to life at sea? Her mind turned to the filly. And Gay Lass. How would they handle the crossing?

She hopped from her bed, careful not to make a sound to wake Mrs. Frobisher who snored gently in the next bunk. She pulled on her clothes and crept from the cabin. Where would the horses be? Well, not up here on the top decks reserved for the first class passengers. Making her way to the staircase leading down she descended to the next deck, which she knew was for the second class passengers, and then still further down.

She passed a couple of ship's staff, who looked at her curiously and touched their caps with a 'Good morning, ma'am', until she could go no further down. Uncertain of which way to turn, she stopped a boy carrying a tray who was headed for the companion way.

'I'm looking for the horse stables. Which way?' she asked him.

'Straight ahead, ma'am.' he told her, so she pressed on.

The neighing of a horse told her she was on the right track, and seconds later she came to an area divided into stalls, and there she saw the five horses, one to each stall.

She was not the first arrival, however, for David was already there talking to Josh Frazer, who was setting out feed.

David looked up with a startled look on his face.

'Joy, what are you doing down here, and so early?'

'I came to see how the horses are. They look as if they've settled in all right.'

'Yes, they seem to be all okay,' he told her, casting a critical eye along the row of stalls.

Joy went into the stall containing the mare, who had her head over the door waiting for breakfast, and her filly.

'Hello, my beauty,' she said, rubbing the filly's ears. 'How're you doing?' The horse stood still and snickered, turning her head slightly as if to encourage further massage. 'I have to think of a name for you. What shall it be?'

As she stood pondering, David came and stood next to her, stroking the filly's back.

'So, she's the first step of your dream, isn't she? Maybe you should call her Joy's Dream. How does that sound?'

Joy wondered if he was laughing at her. Turning her head quickly she saw his expression was serious.

'Joy's Dream?' She savoured the sound. 'Yes, I like that. You don't think it's a little egotistical, to call her after me?'

David shook his head. 'Not at all. I think it'll look good in the race card, and it has a nice ring to it. Joy's Dream. It sounds good to me.'

'In the race card? I never thought about that.'

'Of course. You do plan to race her, don't you?'

'Well, yes. Of course she must race. I guess I just hadn't thought that far ahead.'

'Then you'd better start thinking. With her breeding she should show a nice turn of speed, and winning is what will make her a valuable mare, able to produce the champion you want.'

'You're right, of course. I must give that more thought, even though she's just a baby yet.'

'It's never too soon to start planning.' He paused for a moment, as if turning something over in his mind, and when he spoke, he sounded serious. 'You know, Joy, we're both on the same path. We both want to breed a champion. Maybe we should think about sharing our ideas and knowledge. After all, you also have Gay Lass to consider, and I have my mare, Simon's Girl, so we'll both need to find a trainer. Do you think we should work together where we can.?'

The first thing Joy noticed was the he didn't call her shrimp, and the second was that it would be good to have someone with his extensive knowledge to discuss and decide things with.

'I think that's an excellent idea.'

David gave her a dazzling smile.

'Then that's settled. And here comes Josh with their feed.' Taking her by the arm, he guided her from the stall. 'Time for us to go up to breakfast, I think. Come on, partner, last one to sit down's a rotten egg.'

Partner, she thought. Well that was a darned sight better than shrimp. Could it mean he had accepted that she'd grown up since she left Australia?

It became the accepted thing for Joy and David to visit the horses together every day. He often fell into stride beside her as she walked around the deck, or appeared with a glass of lemonade as she sat in a deck chair.

His knowledge of horses and breeding amazed Joy, and they spent hours talking.

Together they stood watching the banks glide by as they sailed through the Suez Canal, and they played deck games or cards together to pass the time. When there was a concert on deck it was natural for him to choose the seat next to her.

As the days became weeks Joy found herself looking for him if he was not around. One day, when he didn't appear all day, she surprised herself by realising that his easy, undemanding companionship had become important to her, and that she no longer thought about Charles Quincy, or her grandmother, and their perfidy. In fact she was feeling quite her old self again.

When David appeared at dinner that night, light-hearted as usual, he offered no excuse for his absence all day. After dinner he headed for the door. 'I'm going on deck for a cigarette,' he told them.

Joy accompanied Rufe and Kitty for an after-dinner drink, but refused their invitation to join them and Mrs. Frobisher in the Games Lounge.

Instead she wandered out onto the deck, feeling unsettled. As she strolled along she saw the tip of a cigarette glowing in the dark. Changing direction, she walked toward it. It was probably David.

As Joy came closer a door opened, spilling out light, and she saw that it was David, but he wasn't alone. In the brief interval whilst the light shone out she saw David's dark head bent close to the fair head of a young woman. So deeply engrossed were they that they didn't look up at the sudden beam of light, but continued their conversation. The woman was Alice Preston.

Joy breathed in sharply as she felt a sudden, intense dart of anger and jealousy. Turning quickly, she hurried back in the opposite direction, stopping eventually to lean on the rail and stare out into the darkness. From inside she could hear the subdued tinkle of music and the muffled sound of voices, but out here she had only the sound of the sea and the moon and the stars above for company.

What was the matter with her? A voice inside her whispered, *Never trust a man.* But that was ridiculous. She had no claim on David. They were friends, nothing more. She wanted nothing more; she was totally focused on her ambition. So why did she feel like this?

As she stood there, for what seemed like forever, there was a footfall beside her.

'Ah, there you are. I wondered if you'd fallen overboard.' David leant on the rail alongside her. 'Do you feel like a turn around the deck?'

'No thank you,' she answered frostily.

'Oh. Okay.' He stood beside her, saying nothing. After a moment he pulled out his cigarette case, took out a cigarette and began tapping it on the rail.

In the dim light Joy couldn't see his face clearly, but she sensed he was frowning.

'Is something the matter?' he asked her.

'What would be the matter?'

'I don't know. That's why I'm asking you.'

'Nothing's the matter. Why are you asking?'

'It's not like you to hide yourself away in the dark like this for so long. I've been looking everywhere for you.'

'I thought you were too interested in Alice Preston to care about my whereabouts.'

There was silence for a few seconds, and Joy thought he was going to walk away, but he tossed the unlit cigarette over the side and turned to face her.

'I presume you saw me talking to Alice. Is that what this is about?'

'I don't know what you're talking about.'

'As it so happens, we were discussing Benjy and Lily. Nothing more.' He paused. 'Would you care if it had been something more personal?'

'I don't have any right to care what you do.'

He grabbed her arm and spun her around until they were facing.

'No, no right at all.' His voice was rough. 'Perhaps this will give you the right.'

With that his arms were around her, crushing her to him, and his mouth came down on hers.

Joy's heart skipped a beat, and then began a furious tattoo. David kissed her hungrily, as if he couldn't get enough of her, and his arms held her tightly against him, so that she could feel the strength of his body. Quivers started deep inside her as she kissed him back, loving the feel of him.

When he finally released her, suddenly, she clutched the rail to steady herself. She tried to read his face, but it was too dark to see him clearly.

'You kissed me once before,' she told him shakily. 'You said then it was to make me remember you. You called me a baby. Do you still think that about me?'

'No, far from it.' He touched her on the cheek, and then traced the outline of her face with a finger. 'You're all woman, and a very beautiful one. Woman enough to turn my world upside down. To make me feel lost when I'm not with you.'

Joy was conscious of a delicious tingling throughout her body, and she wished he would kiss her again, but first she needed to know his real feelings.

'What are you saying?' she whispered.

'I'm saying that I love you. But I didn't mean to rush you. I know you've been hurt, and I didn't intend to tell you yet. I wanted to give you time to heal. Time to see if you could get over Quincy, and feel the same way about me. Because I can wait.'

Even in the pale moonlight she could see the glitter in his eyes. She took a step closer so there were only inches between them, and smiled up at him.

'Perhaps if you kiss me again it will help me make up my mind.'

The next second she was in his arms again, responding eagerly to his ardent kisses.

When they finally drew apart, flushed and breathless, David held Joy at arm's length.

'So has that helped? Or do I have to offer a repeat performance?'

'I think once more would make me sure.'

'Well now, in the island of Tukulauie, if a couple kiss three times they must marry or be stoned to death. So you'd better think it over. If you let me kiss you again, will you be prepared to marry me?'

'I do want you to kiss me, and being stoned to death doesn't hold much appeal for me, so I suppose I'll have to say yes.'

She swayed toward him, her body eager to be pressed close to him once more, her lips already parting for the kiss. But he held her off.

'Wait. You have to say it. Tell me you promise to marry me.'

'I promise I'll marry you.' Once more she moved.

'Not so fast. I haven't heard a word about love yet. Why will you marry me?'

She laughed, dizzy with happiness. 'Because I love you.'

'Say it again. This time as if you're sure you mean it.'

Joy's heart lurched, and all at once she felt happy and excited and full of wonder at the miracle of this love that had crept up on her, under the guise of friendship. So strong was it that she had no doubt, no hesitation, as she glimpsed a future filled with passion and tenderness, excitement and contentment.

Her voice came, soft and low. 'I love you, David Cavanagh, and I want to be your wife.'

With a cry he scooped her into his arms, showering her face with kisses. 'Joy, darling, it'll take the rest of my life to show you how much I love you.'

Then his mouth was on hers again, and Joy lost herself in a sea of love and passion.

But even in the midst of it she spared a thought for the irony of coming across the world searching for excitement and happiness, when she could have found it in her own backyard.

275

Chapter Thirty Six

After freshening up and changing from their travel clothes, they assembled in the sitting room at Riverside, where Edward had champagne for them. He filled their glasses and then raised his own.

'I propose a toast to our newly engaged couple. May they have everlasting happiness. To Joy and David.'

'Joy and David,' they chorused.

'And now, a second toast.' Edward refilled the glasses. 'To the Barrons and the Cavanaghs. The marriage of these two young people will complete the union of two families who have the same goal in life, to breed champion racehorses. It's early days yet, but may we go forward, separate and yet together, sharing our trials and our triumphs, to great success.' He raised his glass. 'The Barrons and the Cavanaghs.'

Rufe and David rose and raised their glasses. 'The Barrons and the Cavanaghs.'

As Joy drank the toast, she felt as if she was witnessing a great beginning. Who knows, was it possible they would go on to create a dynasty? As Rufe said, who knows what the future holds?

They were disturbed by a commotion outside, as someone clattered up the steps and banged on the front door.

'Good Heavens, someone's in a hurry,' Edward said.

They listened as he opened the front door. There was the sound of hurried voices and the next moment Patrick burst into the room, looking exhausted and dishevelled.

The blood drained from Kitty's face. 'What is it? Is Mother? Or Jack?'

Rufe jumped to his feet. 'What's happened?'

'It's Redwoods,' Patrick gasped. 'I came as quick as I could. There's been a fire. Redwoods is burnt to the ground.'

Joy stared in horror at what she heard. 'Grandma and Grandpa? Are they hurt?'

'No. No one's hurt. They both got out safely, but Redwoods is gone. The house. The mill. Everything. Burnt to the ground.'

Joy's blood turned to ice at his words, and when Rufe spoke his voice seemed to come from a distance.

'Here, sit down, man.' He took Patrick by the arm and led him to a chair, pushing him down. 'You look all done in. Have you ridden all the way from Bulahdelah?'

'Yes. Jack sent me. He wanted you to know straight away.'

'How did it happen?'

'We don't know, but one of the men swears he saw someone running away as he ran toward the house.'

Kitty gasped. 'You mean someone started it deliberately?' Her voice was shocked.

'We don't know, but he's sure he saw someone. But it was dark, the middle of the night. I was woken up by Jack shouting. It's a miracle they woke up in time to get out of the house; it went up like a bonfire. We did what we could but we didn't have a hope. Then we saw fire coming from the mill, and we rushed over. Some of the men were there by then, but we didn't have a snowball's hope in Hell of saving it.'

Patrick looked as if he was about to burst into tears. 'We've lost it all, the house, the mill, the timber stacked in there, everything. All burnt to a cinder. As well as over half the land burnt out. There was just nothing we could do.' He ran his hands across his eyes. 'Jesus, I'm sorry.'

Rufe gripped his shoulder. 'Steady now, Patrick. Take it easy.' He looked across at Edward. 'Get him some brandy, will you?'

Edward nodded and crossed the room to where the glasses and decanters stood on a tray, and seconds later he handed a glass to Patrick.

'Here, drink this.'

Patrick tossed it down, and gave a shuddering cough.

Rufe patted him on the shoulder. 'Just rest a bit.'

Patrick nodded and leant back in the chair, letting his eyes close.

'If there were two separate fires, they must have been deliberately lit,' Rufe continued.

Every vestige of colour had drained from Kitty's face, and her knuckles were white from her hands gripping the arms of the chair.

'Who would do such a thing? Who would want to harm us like this? The only person I can think of is Craddock, and we know he's in England.'

'Yes, there's no way he could be here by now, so it wasn't Craddock.'

Dismay hung heavy in the room as they looked at each other in silence, none willing to voice the thought that was uppermost in their minds. Was this the end of Redwoods?

A kind of numbness spread through Joy's body. What of their plans? There would be no house to live in, no income from the mill, maybe no trees in the paddocks for the horses. She needed to go and see for herself.

Joy fought back tears as she reined in her horse at the entrance to Redwoods. Ahead the gaunt, blackened skeletons of once-proud trees rose from the scorched earth, their limbs raised in silent supplication to Heaven. A light breeze stirred the ash amid the blackened twigs littering the ground, which was all the greedy blaze had left of the once luxuriant undergrowth. Curled and shrivelled leaves drooped from the trees that fringed the track, testimony to the fierce heat from the flames. No bird-songs greeted them. No distant sound of axes ringing through the forest, only eerie stillness and desolation.

David drew a deep breath and reached across to touch her arm. 'Are you ready to go in?'

Joy nodded, swallowing past the tightness in her throat, and they moved forward.

Reaching what was left of the house they reined in their mounts and sat mutely surveying the remains.

Part of one wall still stood, charred and crumbling, standing sentinel over the great pile of cinders and debris of all that was left. The iron kitchen range, warped by the heat of the blaze, poked through the remains, its door hanging askew. The blackened remnants of a few household objects could still be identified – a kettle, a soup cauldron, a flat iron minus its wooden handle. Joy recognised her mother's brass bed, misshapen, its gleam gone forever, and the twisted iron frame that was all that was left of the piano that had always graced the sitting room. The acrid smell of burnt wood hung in the air, and a few lazy wisps of smoke still drifted upwards.

Joy's heart was heavy as she surveyed the ruin. This was the house she had grown up in, the paddocks and bush land where she had ridden Dancer to the sound of axes as the trees were felled. All gone.

Taking a deep breath she switched her gaze further, to where she could see a distant part of the forest that the fire had not reached.

There was still some unburnt land.

A surge of fierce determination filled Joy. This was not the end of Redwoods. Like the Phoenix of old it would rise again from the ashes. She wouldn't rest until it happened. But what would it mean for her and David?

****

Continue reading Kitty, Rufe, and Joy's stories in the third book of the Redwoods Trilogy *An Ambitious Woman*

****

About Kate

Kate grew up in a beach area in Adelaide, South Australia and after an absence of almost twenty five years, spent mostly in NSW, she has returned to her home town with husband Peter.

She has worked as a freelance travel writer, has had many short stories published and is the published author of four novels, including the Redwoods trilogy, which are stories of historical romance and family sagas and have received 4 and 5 star reviews.

Her books, *'Inheritance'* and *'Black Mountain'* are published by Escape Publishers and have received 5 star reviews. Kate now pursues her passions of writing, reading and listening to music, and is working on her next novel - *The Trophy Wife*.

Kate now writes Australian contemporary and historical fiction, and as long as you tell her, in reviews and emails, that you enjoy what she writes, Kate will continue doing so. Kate love chocolate, fine wines, dogs, music, and seeing new places.

Praise for A Liberated Woman

"Kate Loveday's writing is emotionally touching. The stories as they unfold on the different paths were done in a wonderful way while still tying the main threads together. I must say my emotions did become involved here for one of the story lines was heart rending for it is a portrait of life even in this day and age. The writer has a great way of telling her story in words. A historical romance that is not just Australia or London but a mixture of cultures and countries. This one is a good read for a long night where you wish good company. Only problem... It is somewhat of a cliffhanger!. " Anna Swedenmom

"Great reading. Loved the series... Looking forward to the last book in the series. Great stories and the all the people in them." Amazon

"Wonderful historical romance with a feel of Australia that makes me want to experience it even though I know it would be different today. This sequel to the awesome An Independent Woman reunites Kitty and Rufe while it focuses on their daughters." Alice L Kent

"A Liberated Woman is a romantic tale of women, young and old, coming to grips with the evolution of a new social order forming at the beginning of the twentieth century. Kate Loveday has penned a story that flows well. Readers of this book will get enjoyment out of seeing how the protagonists overcome the different situations they find themselves thrust into." Warren Thurston, Australian Author

***

An Ambitious Woman

The old ways are changing, but they can't change fast enough for Joy Barron...

She wants it all. Love. Marriage. Success. NOW.

Joy is determined Redwoods will become a successful thoroughbred stud, and dreams of breeding a champion racehorse. When David Cavanagh opposes her ideas she schemes to get her way, determined to make her dream a reality. She continues on her wilful way until tragedy strikes and fills her with remorse. Then Thunder, the big, black stallion enters their lives, and with him comes Josh Frazer.

David believes she is more concerned with Redwoods' success than with him and their marriage, and he goes to America with an open-end return date. Joy is broken hearted by what she sees as David's rejection. Josh is willing to take his place in her affections, but she is unresponsive to his advances. But when the children go missing Joy must turn to Josh for help and comfort, and her feelings change.

Against the heart-stopping background of the prestigious Gold Cup race week Joy must make the most difficult decision of her life.

Can a woman love two men? How can she choose between two loves?

Praise for An Ambitious Woman

"Aussie author Kate Loveday's stories about independent women are wonderful stories. She has many twists and turns and surprises, good and bad, in her stories that a reader doesn't expect. She writes so smoothly it is like the pen in her writing hand touches the pages and the words just flow out of her pen onto paper with such ease. Ms. Loveday's writing is smooth and intelligent. She blends everything together very nicely and tells a wonderful descriptive story of different types of people, some you'll love and cheer on and some you'll dislike immensely. This story was not just a romance novel, Kate has imbedded a wonderful cast of true to life characters and many circumstances they went through. It would make a wonderful movie." Alice L Kent

"More Please!

I enjoyed reading Ambitious Woman as the last in this trilogy. It concluded the story with an interesting and satisfactory ending and if there was more I would love to keep reading." Wendy...Amazon
****

The Trophy Wife

Full of courage and resolve, this is a story about reinventing yourself, and the intrigues of Fate. A story of love, friendship, disillusion and retribution as a woman strives to change her life.

It seemed as if it would be a fairy tale existence...

When young and lonely Erin McDonald leaves Newcastle for a job in Sydney shortly after her mother's death she meets high powered business mogul Giles Brightman. He sweeps her off her feet, and she is thrilled when he proposes. Madly in love she marries him, but she soon realises he wants nothing more from her than to look beautiful and be compliant – ready to accompany him whenever he wishes, charming to his business associates, and ready to accommodate him in bed whenever he feels so inclined.

Slowly Giles' violent side emerges, and after an attack that makes her fear for her life, Erin knows she must get away. With little money of her own, and a platinum Amex card, she develops an audacious plan to give her a second chance in life – at Giles' expense. But Giles won't let her go easily.

When she consults lawyer Aden Marlowe the last thing on her mind is a new relationship. She tries to ignore her attraction to Aden, and throws herself into her efforts to create a specialised high fashion boutique. Aden is captivated from the start, but he has a secret, and must hide his feelings.

Giles tries to sweet talk Erin into returning to him, but when his pleading fails he threatens her and demands the return of documents that he accuses her of stealing. Undaunted by his threats, Erin ignores him and continues with her plans, but her home is ransacked and her store vandalised. Aden suspects a sinister reason behind Giles' actions, and he and Erin work together to find the secret of the seemingly innocuous *Phoebus* share documents.

Can Erin overcome all the setbacks to find a new life...

and   a   new   love?

Praise for The Trophy Wife
"Second chance novel is too bland a term for The Trophy Wife.
I love women-of-strength novels and that is one on of the things Kate Loveday does so well. When young and lonely Erin McDonald leaves her home for a new job shortly after her mother's death, she is vulnerable to the practiced machinations of the urbane Giles Brightman and falls completely under his spell. Young, inexperienced, and loving does not equal weak, her love holds up under his growing busy-man routine but when he crosses a line, she walks. The tale of the rebuilding of her life, her soul, is the fascinating journey we travel with The Trophy Wife." *Jeanie W Jackson*

"Kate Loveday's stories of strong women are wonderful. Her writing is smooth and intelligent. She blends everything together very nicely and tells a wonderful descriptive story of different types of people, some you'll love and cheer on and some you'll dislike immensely. This story is not just a romance novel, Kate has imbedded a wonderful cast of true to life characters and the many circumstances they go through." *Alice L Kent*

Inheritance

An inheritance is usually a blessing . . . could it also be a curse?

An Australian rural romance about an unexpected inheritance that sends a city girl down deep into the country...

When Cassie Taylor inherits Yallandoo, a cattle station near Cairns in Far North Queensland, she is shocked.

What does she know about running cattle? But the property has been in her family for generations, and Cassie is not a quitter. She leaves behind her Sydney life and heads to the station, determined to make a go of it.

But a long drought and falling prices mean challenges Cassie doesn't expect. To save her heritage, she's going to have to come up with some new ideas — and fast.

Then the threatening letters start to arrive. Someone doesn't want Cassie to succeed, and they're willing to go to any lengths to stop her...

Praise for Inheritance

"INHERITANCE is a great romantic suspense story, but also a chronicle of Cassie's life as she grows into a woman. I really liked her characters. I also enjoyed how she incorporated the lore of the Aboriginal people of Australia in the story. Ms. Loveday has created a wonderful setting in Yallandoo. Her characters are wonderfully developed and come alive off the page. This is a great book!" Romance Junkies Reviewer: Lisa

"Overall I found Inheritance compelling. Kate Loveday has a wonderful talent for getting into each and every character's head and telling the story from their point of view. The different twists and turns in the story retain the reader's interest. A very believable story; one that draws the reader in and leaves them feeling as though they have not only met these people but have really managed to get to know them all, very well." RRAH reviewed by Kay James

"With her first novel 'Inheritance' ,Kate Loveday has created a fantastic read. I applaud her wonderful talent. Great work! Can't wait for her next book!" Sarah Cook , Author

Black Mountain

An adventure set in the Australian rainforest, where the race is on to discover a precious plant – and an even rarer kind of attraction.

Elly Cooper's friend Jackson has gone missing – along with a journal that contains her dead father's lifelong work and the recipe for a product he described as the 'fountain of youth', potentially worth millions.

The catch is that the main ingredient is a rare plant found only in the Daintree Rainforest in Queensland. And only her father knew where to find it.

Elly enlists the aid of ex–policeman Mitchell Beaumont to help her find Jackson, the journal and the plant. But someone else is on the trail of the precious plant, and it seems they'll stop at nothing – even murder – to get what they want.

It's a race against time in the tropical heat as Elly and Mitchell battle the perils of the rainforest – and the feelings growing between them.

Praise For Black Mountain

"First time reading this author and thoroughly enjoyed her description of the country, characters and story line. Will be checking out her other books." *Net Galley*

"This is a fantastic short read that is fast pace and exciting. I really enjoyed this story as it was something different and really captured my attention. Elly is in a race against time to find the flower that holds the secret to her father's fountain of youth oil. Only problem is she's not the only one looking for the undiscovered flower. Elly isn't out searching the rainforest by herself.

Spending so much time with Mitchell, Elly might find more than just the flower." *Lost in sweet words*

'I really enjoyed this book as it had a hint of romance and bit of intrigue. Plus I have always found Australia fascinating from afar and for that reason found this read fun, and exciting. There are many unexpected things that happen in the story that you will miss out on if you don't take a chance on this enthralling read. 'Black Mountain' is the place where adventure, romance, and mystery

abound; what more could one ask for? I would like to read more books by this author."
Lady P,Net galley
"Black Mountain is an exciting and complex adventure focusing on a race between greed and love." *Goodreads*
****

Connect with Kate Loveday

I really appreciate you reading my book!
The following are my Contacts:

Friend me on Facebook; https://www.facebook.com/kloveday
Follow me on Twitter: https://twitter.com/LovedayKate
Favourite my Smashwords author page:
https://www.smashwords.com/profile/view/PL
Subscribe to my blog: https://kateloveday.wordpress.com/
Visit my website: http://www.kateloveday.com/

*****